WARRIOR'S REWARD

Laughing One was a fledgling warrior, untried in the hardships and perils of hunting. But now his spear had tasted blood—the blood of the monstrously powerful saber-tooth tiger that he fought to save two young women.

Now these female strangers were his—and he was theirs as well. For the wounds he suffered put his life in their healing hands—and the feeling they stirred in him would make him challenge the authority of his tribal elders to have them as his wives. One was gentle and loving, willingly his for the taking. The other was as defiant as she was beautiful, and she was claimed by a shaman as feared as he was hated.

Laughing One was joined with these two very different women in the world of hunter and hunted, tribal tradition and the vast unknown ... where the darkness of the primal past in prehistoric America was yielding to the dawn of the dramatic time when the humans began to sense their power, wrestle with their passions, and claim dominion over an America of savage wilderness and stirring wonder.

Sisters
of the
Black Moon

by
F. J. Pesando

AN ONYX BOOK

ONYX
Published by the Penguin Group
Penguin books USA Inc., 375 Hudson Street,
New York, New York 10014, U.S.A.
Penguin Books Ltd, 27 Wrights Lane,
London W8 5TZ, England
Penguin Books Australia Ltd, Ringwood,
Victoria, Australia
Penguin Books Canada Ltd, 10 Alcorn Avenue,
Toronto, Ontario, Canada M4V 3B2
Penguin Books (N.Z.) Ltd, 182–190 Wairau Road,
Auckland 10, New Zealand

Penguin Books Ltd, Registered Offices:
Harmondsworth, Middlesex, England
First published by Onyx, an imprint of Dutton Signet,
a division of Penguin Books USA Inc.,

First Printing, February, 1994
10 9 8 7 6 5 4 3 2 1

Copyright © Frank Pesando, 1994
Cover painting by Jerry Lofaro
All rights reserved

 REGISTERED TRADEMARK—MARCA REGISTRADA

Printed in the United States of America

A Summoning

It was done without words and without chanting, for Passing Shadow had no wish to attract attention to himself. Darkness was a better shield than any hide coverings, and no nights were darker than these of the Black Moon. Now, while his magic was strongest, while his guardian spirit showed in the sky overhead, he would cast this one quick but all encompassing spell. He would summon the dream woman from out of her forest home.

The old man stood alone at the top of a grass-covered ridge. When he turned from the empty darkness of the savannah night he could see Black Snake's village far behind him. His own hearth fire burned as a small glow of color amid the deep shadows near the base of the ridge where he stood. The two wives who tended that fire would not worry about where he had gone. It would not trouble them if he were to wander away into the night and never come back. That was part of his bitterness.

When another glance around proved that he truly was alone, Passing Shadow stooped down beside a pile of wet leaves which rose as a black mound amid the tall grass. Searching, he found the thin stick he had hidden there. Holding the stick gently, he made light sweeping motions with his hands over the top of the leaf pile. Then he began to draw strange figure patterns along its edges.

Spell casting was the one thing among all others which he was most skilled at. Passing Shadow was a great shaman. Since he had first become a man, he had inhaled the fumes that made others go mad. When the smoke and powder drawn in through his nose had filled his lungs and made the world start spinning around him, he had never flinched. The ache of pounding temples and the weight of legs and arms that had suddenly become too heavy to move were necessary for this form of spirit summoning. Passing Shadow had soon learned to ignore them. He had chanted through whole nights while the blood had flowed from wounds on his arms and legs. Soon there had been no one

more adept than he at driving back the spirits of dead mothers
who hungered for their living children or forcing the ghost of a
murdered husband to release his hold on a young widow. There
were few spirits dwelling in the mountains and forests surrounding the Great Valley which he had not invoked to help him
with his killing or his curing. But this night things had to be different. This night there could be no breathing of magic fumes,
rubbing of sacred powder, or dropping of strange mixtures onto
hot coals. This time he was summoning a living woman, and
only the strongest kind of magic would do.

Many people among his tribe did not believe that the forest
woman truly lived. For them she was no more real than the
shadow of a summer cloud, something which would drift away
like fallen leaves on a quiet stream when someone tried to touch
her. It was said that she lived in the mountains where the sun
slept, and that her name could never be known to living men.
Even the thought of her made men mournful and humble. She
was the scent of hidden flowers, the warm breath of lovers late
at night, the bright shining eyes of a young woman courted by
her first man. She had been there forever, revealing herself and
then vanishing. Those men who ran after her found only mad-
ness. Those who saw her dance became unable to speak or
think. Her hair was very long and black and lay around her like
a great robe. Her body was slender and golden, now covered
and uncovered by her constantly flowing hair. A glimpse of her
eyes was as startling as the taste of frost on a summer afternoon, as unbelievable as a glowing moon in a sunlit sky.

Passing Shadow had heard this flow of stories all his life, but
he knew that the forest woman was more than simply something
dreamed of during a fever. She was out there amid all that darkness, waiting to be summoned. He had seen glimpses of her in
so many other young women; in the way a pretty girl had
leaned forward or laughed, in the way her hair had been faintly
shaken by the summer wind. And he had tried so many times to
keep that loveliness for himself. But all those young girls'
beauty had been no more than a stir of wind. With them, he had
been nothing more than a terrible old man to cry out at and run
away from. He was tired of having to whisper "Do not be
afraid" each time he took a new wife by the arm, only to hear
more weeping and shouting as she urged her family to come
and help her. There had been too many women who smelled of
fear and held themselves tight when his arms went around them,
who bit at his fingers and fought him or became limp when he

dragged them down onto his sleeping mat. Each marriage had begun full of pain and hurting and had grown more and more desperate until at last he had no longer felt anything for the woman except a deadened kind of hate. He had killed one wife and then another and two more after that. Even the two wives he had now only lived because he no longer had the will to get rid of them.

Passing Shadow believed in the forest woman because he needed to. There had been too many sunless days in his life already. He was old. His body sighed each time he moved, his bones creaked, his muscles ached. He was cold with all the waiting he had already done. Only the warmth of her breath could free him now. Only her touch could take away the bitter taste of a tormented life. But if he was ever to know her love, it had to be soon. The nights of countless winters had shrunk his body like an aging tree trunk. Soon his strength would be completely broken.

With quick and feverish movements, Passing Shadow began to take large handfuls of the rotting leaves and toss them aside. In the middle of the pile there were three small fish, still wriggling and gasping as they drowned in air. The shaman bit the head from each one and swallowed it, throwing the rest of the body out into the darkness. Each time he bit down onto the slithering cold flesh, he closed his eyes, thinking about the forest woman. The spell touched her now, like a wave of fingers softly brushing at her soul. It tugged and bit, pulling at her, moving her away from the life she had known. He had cut the bonds and set her drifting.

Now across the darkness he would send a spell that would bring them together. Looking at the stars, Passing Shadow took thistle leaves and rubbed them up and down his arms. The bristles were bunched tight in his right hand, and as he rubbed he imagined it was the gentleness of her touch that made his flesh tingle this way. There in the dark, staring at the shadows, he seemed to sense her. Breathing hard and fast, he threw the nettles aside and pulled some long black thorns from out of his medicine pouch. With these, he scratched his skin until the blood flowed. His teeth were clenched hard against the pain and he leaned forward with a terrible intenseness. When at last he picked up some of the rotted leaves to wipe the blood away, he whispered, "My blood has flowed. I have caused my blood to flow for you. Now you will know your way."

With an explosive sigh, Passing Shadow broke the moment of

immense strain. He forced himself to stand up. His eyes had been shut tight before. Now he did not look at the pile of bloodied leaves before him but only stared into the great cloudless depths of the star-shimmered sky.

The woman would come now. He was certain of it. The best magic was that which did not seem like magic at all. She would not be aware of the invisible spell which had shifted her life. The change would be like a shadow that moved just as the fire was lit, there and not there. For her each day would bring a strange new accident, an unexpected difference. She could not guess that every incident was like a wave, pushing her farther and farther toward some distant and as yet unseen shore. Without ever being aware of what compelled her, she would find her way to him.

The grass shifted quietly around Passing Shadow's legs as he paced hurriedly back and forth along the edge of the ridge. There was nothing else he needed to do, but he would not wait here in this village. He had waited much too long already. Instead, he would move north to Wanderer's village, and after that to one of the other two villages in the Great Valley. The woman would reach this valley soon, before the first frost came. When he saw her, he would know her, and suddenly all the things that had been lies in his life before would not be lies any longer.

CHAPTER ONE

The Tidelanders

Early morning in the coastal hills was neither as silent nor as peaceful as it seemed. The misty air of sunrise had simply softened the appearance of things, making the river look blue and empty in the drifting light. In the glistening tall grass, amid reeds turned bright by a still reddish sun, a cat let out a rumble from deep inside its belly.

Some turtles, which had settled near a shallow bank to catch the morning sun, jerked up their heads at the sound. An instant later they had scuttled off into deeper water. A squirrel shivered, then froze in place. Only a humming bumblebee seemed undisturbed as it blundered from flower to flower. Its insect senses failed to notice the cat stepping slowly forward from out of the deep grass.

Moving openly now, the cat walked without the twitching and hunched shiverings of an animal ready to strike at prey. Its blunted snout simply sniffed at the misty air as its eyes studied the sky with a more than casual interest. In size and color, it resembled a lion, but its bulk was greater. There was a bunching of muscles about its shoulders that had almost become a hump. More obvious still were the outsized canine teeth protruding downward from its upper jaw like misdirected tusks. These saber-shaped teeth, each as long as a hunter's dagger, were what gave the creature its sudden killing thrust.

The cat made a series of low, coughing grunts as it came down to the edge of the water; then added a softer, higher sound—an almost human moaning. One big paw spread wide across the shore mud. The other foreleg stayed curled back; its paw swinging uselessly above the ground. The intense brightness near the water had caused the cat's light sensitive pupils to narrow into small black slits, but it continued to glance upward every few moments. What it saw were the black shapes of vultures skimming through the air in wide circles above a not so distant kill. Lacking the ability to smell dead flesh from far away, the cat had learned to depend on the eyesight of the scavenger birds. It had been following these vultures since the sun had first shown on the eastern horizon.

For a moment, the cat gazed in hungry fascination at the circling birds. Then it growled and plunged down into the river. The swim to the other side was a hard one, done in a strong, jerking fashion. By the time the cat had hauled itself out again, it was shivering from the cold. The shivering became a wave of twitching as the cat flung the beads of icy water from its fur. With a final whine of distaste, the big animal hurried up along the riverbed, scattering crumbling bits of shore mud under its one good forepaw. The cat checked the position of the birds once more, wheeled about, and vanished as quickly as it had come.

Through the treetops overhead, the cat could see a group of small vultures swooping in low to check the ground around the carcass. High above them, a much larger bird moved on huge black wings. The great condor would continue to circle warily until the others had landed. Then, when it was certain of safety, it would come down like a black nightmare to battle for its bits of bone and flesh and rancid skin.

The cat shut its eyes, and the music of a purr rumbled through its chest. The food was close now.

On the open ground, the great cat's loping gait became more obvious. She was a female near the prime of life, but an injury had weakened her right foreleg, making the muscles twitch each time she moved it, and causing her to let out a low whimpering moan whenever some unexpected pressure sent a jolt of pain through her. One incautious swipe at a porcupine early in the summer had permanently maimed the leg and changed the entire life pattern of the cat. Now, as autumn approached, a mass of long quills remained wedged deep inside her lower leg, and festering sores marked where they had entered.

When the cat stopped to lift her head again, the birds were close enough to see her and draw back. She took a trembling breath, snuffing at the smell of rotting meat. Each time she sniffed, her lip whiskers twitched expectantly, but there was something which made her hesitate. The death scent came from the salty-sweet flesh of humans.

In the clearing, three dark headless bodies lay sprawled out on the grass. A bloody struggle had pulled them down, broken their strength, and left them there for the lice and flies to crawl over. Their hands hung empty of the weapons they had once held. Their legs were twisted; frozen in the last position of a failed struggle for life. At the moment of their death, two of the men had been running and had been hit from behind. The third had turned to face his enemies and had been killed in a different way.

The cat lowered her head and let out a deep, guttural growl. This was not the meal she had hoped for. Humans were strange and dangerous things. Being close even to dead ones made her restless.

In earlier times, she would have fled the place, but the porcupine quills had left her half starved and in poor condition. Hunger was more terrible than fear. She stayed near the edge of the clearing, still wary, while the vultures moved in. With a sad crying, the dark birds spiraled down from overhead, flopping about in awkward hops before approaching the dead men. Their fluttering gray shapes soon hid the corpses in a whirl of wings. As the cat watched them feed, her fear lessened.

Finally the great condor itself skimmed down. Huge wings flapped heavily against the air. The caution that had made the giant bird hesitate was gone, and so was the nervousness of the cat. She moved forward to challenge the other scavengers.

Unwittingly, the saber-toothed tiger was again changing her life pattern. After this meal, the fear of humans which had kept her safe from their spears and knives would be greatly lessened. Unable to catch game on her own, she would seek out humans again the next time hunger urged.

Some distance away, in a different valley of the same river, the tribe to which the three dead men had once belonged was attempting to build a makeshift village. The night had been cold, and even before daybreak humans had begun to move about, stirring up what was left of the campfires. Gradually small spurts of flame began to appear among the ashes. Their flickering light reflected on the naked chests and arms of the women who tended them. In the first light of morning, these wisps of flame and smoke were the surest signs of human presence. Only a few of the village huts had been completed, and even these did not stand out. Their low, domed shapes, covered in leaves and grass, blended so well with surrounding plants that a person walking upwind might have passed within sight of the village and not noticed it among the shadows.

There was a defeated quiet about the camp, caused by more than simple drowsiness. No laughs or raised voices followed the

activity around the fires. Young men did not joke with one another. Women did not quarrel among themselves the way they
usually did when on trek. There were no sly smiles between
lovers or exasperated sighs from the mothers of young children.
Things had soured for these people. Nearly half their number
had not survived this one terrible summer. Last spring they had
roamed freely across the tideland flats which bordered the great
western ocean. Now they huddled together amid unfamiliar, forested hills. Their stomachs longed for the shellfish and surf fish
which the waves had provided. Instead, they fed on cold berries
and dried meat. The nearness of the river offered some comfort,
for the Tidelanders loved all waters, but none so well as the salt
extensions of the ocean itself. They were gatherers more than
hunters, a wandering people who, until recently, had never had
to fight for territory or survival.

Once there had been twelve villages of Tidelanders, and all
the coastlands had seemed to be theirs, but that was before
strangers had moved in from the north. No one was sure when
the stories about the strangers had first started being told. Some
said it had been in their fathers' time. Others insisted that even
their grandfathers had known about the strange warriors who
tipped their spears with cut stone. At first the strangers had simply ambushed any groups of Tidelanders who had wandered too
far north. The victims had been killed quickly, and the goods
they had been carrying had been stolen. Gradually though, like
a child testing its strength, the tribe of strangers had grown
bolder. Soon they had begun surrounding Tideland villages in
the dark and attacking as soon as dawn had given enough light
for their spears. When the strangers had attacked, they had
charged straight at their enemies, knocking aside the defenders'
clubs and snatching whatever goods they could find. In those
early days, the strangers had killed everyone, taking no captives. Later, when they had learned the value of Tideland
women, their tactics had changed. Now their raids were made
with the special intention of taking women. Tideland men were
still killed as before, but captive women and children were kept
and cared for. Still, if a woman struggled too much, she would
be clubbed to death immediately. The strangers had no patience
with stubbornness.

Big Tree's band had learned all of this abruptly, firsthand,
less than two seasons ago. Since then their lives had been
marked by a series of retreats before ever more persistent enemies. As the strangers' numbers had grown, the strength of this

last Tideland band had lessened. Now there was only Big Tree, two other old men, three boys who had just passed their manhood rites, and five hunters of proper fighting age. Even in this dwindled group, the surviving women greatly outnumbered the men.

Most of the remaining women were also older than the men. Several, like Sacred Dance, had been widowed twice and were well past childbearing age. Many others were too laden down with young children to be desired by the men of the stranger tribe. But among these women there were also four girls who would have been considered beautiful. Two of these were sisters and slept side by side next to Sacred Dance, their widowed mother. Morning Land, the elder daughter, had already been captured once. Stories of her escape and her clever ways of evading her captors had been told and retold throughout the camp. White Bird, the younger daughter, was a firm believer in her sister's cleverness. Even as a child, White Bird had adored Morning Land. Now, with her skin still pale from the seclusion of puberty, White Bird was eager to imitate the most valued woman left in the Tideland band.

On this day, Morning Land and White Bird were as sullen as the rest of the village. White Bird was sprawled out awkwardly in a posture which was meant to indicate lazy indifference, but which was so uncharacteristic of her that it conveyed just the opposite. Her large, dark brown eyes seemed empty and idle, as if nothing here could match the interest of her own dreamy thoughts. In fact, she was simply exhausted, for neither she nor her sister had slept much the night before.

Beside her, Morning Land was working on a pile of dried milkweed stalks, gradually transforming them from weeds into usable ropes. After holding a stalk in her mouth and chewing it until the bark started to break into strands, she set the chewed piece down onto a flat stone and tapped it gently with a small rock. Restraint was needed, for too hard a pounding would ruin the fiber. When the splinters of inner bark felt workable under her fingers, she twisted them into strands and then later twisted the strands into cords. It was a tiresome chore, but it gave her something to concentrate on.

Morning Land was hunched over her work, with her knees up and her back bent against the surrounding forest. She wore a fur robe over her shoulders, as if trying to hide herself as much as possible. The strain of being hunted showed both in her tangled black hair and in the streaks of soot across her face. Her hands, lacking their usual grace, hurriedly pulled and jerked at the weeds.

Despite the tiredness and worry of constant running, there was still an uncomfortable beauty about Morning Land. Her young woman's body was rounded and arched in a smooth, firm way that seemed more perfect than those of the other Tideland girls. More than the fineness of her features or the glowing warmth of her hazel skin, it was Morning Land's shining dark eyes that made her so unsettling to look upon. There was something subtly dangerous about those eyes, especially when she was startled and did not have time to conceal her thoughts.

A short distance away, Sacred Dance tended the cookfire and kept watch over her daughters. She worried about them both, deeply, but Sacred Dance worried about so many things that this was just one more shadow in a long series of troubles. Since the band's arrival in these hills, joys had been short-lived. As the stinging fumes from the cookfire rose up into her face, Sacred Dance winced and began cursing softly to herself. White Bird, whose hearing was keener than most, noticed immediately.

"What makes you so angry, Mother?" she asked.

To hide her worry over her daughters, Sacred Dance complained about other things. "The cold inside my bones feels like it is killing me," she grumbled. "I feel like I have just spent the night sleeping in the bush. If I spend another night this way, it will make me sick inside. I am an old woman, not a young hunter. When the cold comes to my bones, it hurts."

"Last night I moved all over the place," White Bird agreed. "It was so cold, no one could sleep well."

"I slept sitting by the fire, like this," Morning Land added. She assumed a hunched over position, with her arms resting on her drawn-up knees and her head sunk forward into them.

Sacred Dance frowned at her daughters. "Ehnn, lazy ones. You are without sense. You will sit here until the rain comes and water drips from your nose. We have different ways, my daughters and I. Even this fire was made by me. We have no hut to shelter us because my daughters choose to sit while others work. Why are you such lazy ones? Does a baby grow inside you, making you have so many foolish thoughts?"

White Bird was confused by the outburst. "Mother, the light is still growing. The grass will be too wet to gather."

"Who listens to an old woman?" Sacred Dance complained. "Not her daughters. You do not dig holes in the earth after the sun has made it hard. Set the bones of the hut now, when the ground is wet."

"Do not be so angry, Mother," Morning Land said quietly. "You will sleep inside your own hut before night comes again."

"Shaaa!" Sacred Dance snorted. "This is not a clean place. The forests are cold. Mist rises from this river each night, and not even our furs can keep the water out. We must be clever now, or sickness will enter our blood."

"We were hungry, Mother," Morning Land reminded her. "While the others built huts, we went to gather berries. Then wood was needed for this fire of yours, and we were the ones who carried it. The dark came too soon for us to build your hut."

"There is no darkness now," Sacred Dance grumbled.

The huts which Sacred Dance's daughters had seemed so loath to build would form part of a larger village circle. Even in these strained times, the Tideland band could not forgo their need for order. Whether they dwelt on tideland flats or in forested hill country, their villages were always shaped in a circle. The entire thing was conceived without conscious planning or cooperation. To each villager, the frame of it was obvious. They knew whose family their hut should face and which way their entrances should lean. The shape of their village reflected the character of the Tidelanders themselves, a people who seemed to be forever overlapping onto one another's doorways.

By midmorning, the sisters had most of the materials they needed for hut building. Piles of willow saplings lay neatly to one side, chopped down earlier by the vigorous efforts of White Bird. Each sapling trunk would help to form part of the hut's outer frame, while the flexible smaller branches could serve to keep the poles in place. White Bird was already gathering bundles of tall grass from a neighboring slope. It was left for Morning Land to design the hut frames.

She began by using her digging stick to trace two wide circles in the dirt. These marked the base areas of the two huts. One circle was larger than the other, since Sacred Dance's single dwelling did not need to be as big as the hut occupied by her two daughters. Next, Morning Land marked where the holes would be along the circumference of each circle, spacing the holes half an arm's length apart and leaving an unmarked area for the hut entrance. The twin frames would be quite close together, and their entrances were designed to face each other as well as the center of the camp. This way the daughters could keep close watch over their mother. They would almost be living in her doorway.

Using her digging stick to break through the soil, and pulling out the loose dirt with her fingertips, Morning Land dug a hole in each of the places she had marked. After all of the base holes had been dug, she began fitting in the upright poles. The thicker end of each sapling was twisted and wedged into a hole in such a way that it naturally curved inward toward the center of the hut circle. To make the fit tight, Morning Land pounded dirt in around the buried ends with her feet. Eventually she had two rings of upright poles.

It was time to begin the lashings. Picking up a smaller sapling, Morning Land tied it crossways over three of the upright poles. As she added more and more of these braces, they looped around the outside of each hut like a series of circular hoops. Only the lower parts of the upright poles were joined in this way. The upper ends of the saplings remained free.

Morning Land needed help for the next stage, so she waited until White Bird arrived with another bundle of grass. The younger sister looked at the developing hut frames appreciatively for a moment, then turned to leave.

"Stay here," Morning Land called. "The poles are ready to be lashed."

White Bird was grateful for the interruption. Now that she was fully awake, she seemed more like a young girl than a newly matured woman of the tribe. "I have been walking a long time," she said.

Morning Land knew that this was only partly true. White Bird had been leaping about through meadows and pushing herself in among tall reeds into places where the earth had the coolness of moss. She had been giddily cutting a path through those fields with her stone blade and pulling up grass with her hands until it went flying out behind her. White Bird ran at work, taking pleasure in the sheer jumping movement of it all. She rarely ever simply walked.

"A little while and the sun's heat will be on us," Morning Land said. "Help me lash this."

The two sisters stepped inside the larger circle of upright poles to begin work. Morning Land grabbed a long willow sapling and slowly bent it downward toward the center of the circle. White Bird did the same with a pole on the opposite side. When the tops of the two saplings came together, White Bird held them while Morning Land used strips of bark and smaller branches as lashings to fasten the poles in place. As soon as the first pair of poles was securely bound, the girls grabbed two more saplings and repeated the process. In this manner, they worked their way around the circle until every pole had been joined to another. The roof formed quickly, for both girls were well used to this kind of building.

When the poles of the smaller hut had also been joined at the center, Morning Land stepped back to admire their work. Despite the fragile look of the frameworks, Morning Land knew that they would be strong enough to last against any sudden storms or gusts of wind. A second layer of dirt wedged around the base poles would ensure stability. Since Tideland girls swept the earth floors of their homes each day, the soil would eventually wear away until the floor level of the hut became lower than the surrounding ground. This would also help to strengthen the frames.

After a long moment, Morning Land noticed that White Bird was still standing beside her. She turned to her sister impatiently.

"You will have to carry more grass on your shoulders before these huts will be finished," Morning Land said, giving her voice a cool tone of insistence.

White Bird was reluctant to leave. "There are other branches which need lashing," she pointed out.

Morning Land grunted. "And there is still grass on the hillside that will not gather itself," she grumbled. "Follow your own tracks, lazy one." Yet, even as she said this, Morning Land knew that it was neither tiredness nor laziness which made White Bird hesitate.

"I was still in the tall grass when I heard something moving behind me," White Bird said. "It frightened me. It made me think of all the things that could hurt or kill me."

Morning Land nodded. "All of us hear noises," she admitted. "Every night and every dawn there are those who stir up the fires and wake their friends. 'I have heard things in the forest,' they say. Each time a bird calls, we think the strangers are signaling to one another. Every day we wait for them to attack us again, but you are safe from those men now."

White Bird stared at her sister. "Why should we be safe here?" she demanded.

"Our men have gone hunting," Morning Land explained. "There is no one left for the strangers to trick. They do not need to sit and wait. If they wanted to steal women, they would. If they had been out there behind you, you would already have been taken."

White Bird stared back toward the meadows. "Only an animal," she whispered, still trying to convince herself. She was reluctant, but when she saw Morning Land watching her expectantly, White Bird turned and started to walk away across the slope.

Morning Land continued to watch White Bird until the girl vanished over the ridge. Sometimes it was more than just her sister's moods that puzzled Morning Land. White Bird had changed greatly in what seemed like only a little time. White Bird's legs were no longer thin and she did not scamper about with just a string of beads around her waist as she had a summer before. Now an apron of short leather strips covered the front of White Bird's thighs, and a second, wider apron spread across her roundly fleshed buttocks. On White Bird, whose hips were large, this woman's dress looked very womanly. Every Tidelander youth she passed knew that White Bird was ready to marry.

Morning Land returned to the business of hut building. Using the clumps of grass which White Bird had cut, Morning Land began covering the hut frames with overlapping rows of bundled leaves and straw. She worked steadily, barely noticing the comings and goings of her sister. It was not until she had finished trimming the fringe of grass over the entrance of the second hut that she realized White Bird had been watching her.

For White Bird, there was always something magical about the way her sister worked. Morning Land let her hands play over the lashings, never knotting any of them; only twisting them into intricate loops which held more firmly than any knot ever could have. Under her guidance the grass bundles swirled together and joined without seeming to. They never fell apart as they so often did when White Bird tried to fasten them. White Bird began each task with freshness and eagerness and poured into it all the energy she had, but her touch was never as soft as Morning Land's. As often as not, White Bird ended up frustrated and staring down angrily at her own clumsy fingers.

Yet, to White Bird's thinking, Morning Land had grown old sooner than she should have. Morning Land was sure of herself and willful the way old people usually got, but for all her beauty, she still sat alone at a bachelor fire. That lacked all sense to White Bird. Men had always wanted Morning Land.

Long before Morning Land had ended her confinement and received the woman's apron, men had begun showing interest in her. By the time she had become a full woman, Morning Land had become the leader of a whole group of young girls. Gray Deer had been there, with her shimmering golden skin, and the slender but dull-witted River Flower had tried to keep pace as well. Even Red Blossom, Big Tree's only daughter, had chosen Morning Land as her best friend. Together these four had wandered the inlets and coves of their homeland, spending more time adorning themselves than gathering food. They had made flower ornaments for their hair and had decorated their aprons with clinking bead shells which made a musical sound whenever they walked. Ground mint leaves had been rubbed along their legs and arms to give their skin a sweet forest smell.

As younger sister, White Bird had followed after this vain foursome, fetching them mint plants from the bush and searching the shoreline for pretty shells that they might like. It had only seemed natural to White Bird that everyone should wait upon these women of the apron. After all, even the proud young hunters of the tribe had cut grass for the girls and helped to gather their food. The more they had been served by the men, the more the four had giggled and laughed at the hunters. White Bird still remembered how empty and defeated the high laughter of Morning Land had made her feel. She had stared at her own small breasts and wondered if they would ever become firm and upthrusting like her sister's. She had tried to decorate her own hair with flowers and to match the easy, swinging stride of the others, but she had always seemed too short and too awkward. Her ornaments had only amused the other four.

Beautiful to watch, the four girls had become increasingly pleased with themselves. They had shrieked and giggled while older women talked. They had teased both boys and men so openly that they had rarely been able to walk through a field without some young hunter following behind. The more they had refused these men, the more they had been pursued. Eventually Gray Deer and River Flower had grown tired of the game and chosen husbands, but for Morning Land there had seemed to be no end to it. Each season, instead of growing plump with child, Morning Land had remained flat-bellied and beautiful enough to make men desperate.

Finally her parents had had enough. Fearing that Morning Land was attracting too much attention, they had agreed to give her to one of the band's older hunters. They had momentarily forgotten Morning Land's stubbornness.

On her wedding day, Morning Land had dumped ashes over her head. When Sacred Dance had brushed them away, Morning Land had dirtied herself again. It had been a bad sign. Though her new husband had done all he could to please her, Morning Land had remained passive and reluctant. As soon as the hunter had fallen asleep, she had crept past him in the night and returned to her own hut. This had happened every night for more than a full season. During all that time, Morning Land had refused the man, never letting him touch her. Finally he had grown tired and left.

Morning Land's next husband had come from a different Tideland band, and had lived far away across the salt marshes. Though this husband had been young and attractive, it had seemed to make no difference to Morning Land. She had not struggled on the day he had come to fetch her, but two days later she had arrived home again, having crossed the marshes during the night to get there. The hunter had come for her again, and she had fled from him again. Despite the ridicule from the other members of his band, the young husband had persisted. Morning Land had shown little patience with his loyalty. She had continued to take every chance she could to flee from his hut. Perhaps she might have relented eventually, but after one of her long flights through the marshes her husband had not returned to fetch her. Soon Morning Land had learned that he would never come after her again. He and his entire band had been killed by the strangers.

Overly willful and overly proud, Morning Land was now thought to be unlucky. The few remaining young hunters in their band now spent their time with other, less difficult girls. Only White Bird remained faithful, and even she often doubted the wisdom of what her sister had done.

White Bird's musings were interrupted by an impatient grunt from Morning Land. "Ehnn," Morning Land grumbled. "If you are not walking anywhere, come and help me with this."

"You are almost finished," White Bird replied. "There is nothing left for this woman to do."

Morning Land shook her head, then stepped back once more to look at the newly covered huts. Side by side, the two dwellings looked like the nest of some great bird. "I think even our mother will start to like this home," she said.

White Bird disagreed. "Mother is not going to cry out, 'Oh my children, my wonderful children!' when she sees that the huts are built," White Bird insisted. "All she will do is lie down in her hut and say, 'Where a woman sits, that is where she stays.' Then she will fall asleep, and we will be left to make the fire."

Morning Land looked startled, for White Bird's voice and manner had perfectly mimicked their mother's. *"Atoshe!"* Morning Land exclaimed. "What has happened? What makes your voice sound like that?"

Pleased by Morning Land's reaction, White Bird imitated the high, fluting laughter of their mother, and followed it with a shuffling mimicry of Sacred Dance's walk. White Bird stomped and stumbled about so much that it looked as if she might tumble into the river at any moment. When she saw that Morning Land was laughing, White Bird assumed a stern expression and shook her finger at her older sister.

"So lazy," White Bird scolded, again using her mother's voice. "Something is always touching your stomach. You are always hungry. Other girls work, but you do not. *Shaa!* What did I give birth to?"

"You are full of bad talk!" Morning Land exclaimed, but the laughter in her voice showed that she was not offended.

"Be glad that you have a mother to help you," White Bird continued, again assuming her mother's tone. "I do not know why you are still living alone. You should be looking for a wife's place beside some hunter."

Both sisters were laughing now, but when Morning Land looked around guiltily and saw some of the villagers watching them, she placed her hand across White Bird's mouth. This and a cautioning nod were enough to make White Bird quieter, yet the sisters continued to look at each other and giggle for some time afterward.

The next morning, Sacred Dance and her family left the village at daybreak. Few of their fellow villagers noticed them going, for the men had killed a tapir the day before, and most had spent the night feasting. While the hunters snored near the entrances of their huts, the widow and her two daughters stepped past them cautiously, following the edge of the river.

There was no happy shouting or carefree bantering among the three as they moved. With nothing but their knife-shaped digging sticks to protect them, they stepped silently, stopping to gather newly ripened berries, and fixing the location of any dried wood in their minds so that they could pick it up on their return journey. Once a great shadow moved across them and they looked up to see a huge, black-winged condor soaring low just over their heads. Riding the drafts of air that stirred about the river, the powerful bird swept close enough for White Bird to see its cold-looking eyes staring down at her. Another flick of its wings, and it was moving again. In a moment, it had vanished behind the treetops.

As she always did on such journeys, Sacred Dance took pains to teach her daughters while they walked. She pointed out the good berry bushes and showed them where some grapevines had shriveled and dried from poor light. She prodded at roots with her digging stick. Once all three women stopped to pull out a large, edible root, but these pauses rarely slowed them, for Sacred Dance never lingered in any one place. Assuming that her daughters would understand her gestures, this plump, brownish woman prodded, pointed and beckoned by turns without ever varying her walking gait. Her daughters had little trouble keeping pace, for they were well used to their mother's ways.

It was still early morning when they reached a place where the river widened and shallowed. The noise of the flowing water grew less as the current became gentler, and in the great warm calm of this spot plants shimmered all around. The riverbank was shaded on one side by a grove of fully matured oak trees. The mud flats along the opposite shore were heavily overgrown with tall stands of cattails and tule.

The three women stopped and blinked, almost holding their breath as they began to recognize the value of their discovery. The rootstalks of the cattails and tule were full of starch during this season. Pulling them out of the wet muck would be quick work. The cattails were more abundant, but the rootstalks of the tule had a faintly sweet taste which the two daughters loved. Farther out in the river, the familiar pointed leaves of arrowheads rose above the water's surface. The roots of these plants grew into rounded tubers deep in the oozy mud of the river bottom. Collecting them would be more difficult than gathering cattails, but the young women were skilled at wading into waist-deep water and feeling out hidden objects with their feet. They might not even have to do this much. The cattail reeds sheltered muskrats, and muskrats loved arrowhead tubers as much as people did. If the girls could find where these small animals had hidden their stores of tuber, it would save them having to wade out into the cold river.

Stunned and joyous at the same time, Sacred Dance walked back and forth, standing quietly in one place or stepping quickly down to the water's edge in another. While she stared at the wavelike motions of the reeds, Morning Land and White Bird separated and searched the edge of the mud flats. White Bird crawled straight in among the reeds, dragging her basket and digging stick after her. She glided down easily amid the coolness of shining green stems. Ignoring the tickling edges of the leaves, she delicately picked out the thickest and most promising-looking roots for her basket. Her hands pulled up some of them easily, but others had hidden links and were firmly fixed in the soft ground. These White Bird grasped with both hands, arching her back and tugging with teeth-clenching effort until the roots' links suddenly gave way. Once loose, the reeds were quickly broken, and the upper stems discarded. Soon White Bird's basket was piled high with glistening roots. Content that she had enough, White Bird wiped the sweat from her forehead and began to explore the reed wilderness around her.

On the shore, Sacred Dance noticed the sudden lack of movement and grew worried.

"*Atoshe!*" she called, staring into the reeds. "White Bird! Where are you?"

There was silence. The reeds shimmered quietly in the sunlight.

"White Bird!" Sacred Dance called again, making her voice louder than before. "Have you been bitten? Are you hurt?"

There was a loud splash, and a cluster of reeds shuddered against the sky. White Bird's head appeared abruptly above the shivering tule. "Why are you calling me, Mother?" she asked in a worried voice. "Did you see something?"

"I did not see you," Sacred Dance replied.

"I sat down inside these reeds to rest," White Bird explained.

"This river is cold," Sacred Dance warned. "If you stay in the reeds, you will start to tremble. Then the sickness will grab at you. Come out into the sun."

"I need to find more things for us to eat," White Bird insisted. Then, relenting, she added, "When I am finished, I will sit out there in the sun and talk with you."

White Bird ducked back amid the reeds before her mother could protest further. In a moment, the tule swayed as evenly as before.

Sacred Dance shook her head. The uneasy feeling had not left her. Unseen dangers were common in these forested hills, and

Sacred Dance had a fear of dark woods. Clear shorelines rimmed with beaches were the places which made her people feel comfortable, never tree-covered slopes. Since the tribe's retreat into these hills, Sacred Dance had gradually learned to overcome her dread of them, but on this day the old fears returned. Rich in food though it was, there was something about this place which frightened her.

Morning Land heard the voices of her mother and sister, but paid little attention to them. She was studying the tracks and spoor scattered across the edge of the mud flats. She easily recognized the hoof print of deer and tapir, and the paw tracks of raccoons and bear. Coming down from the woods was the trail of another large animal. Though the prints were as big as those of a bear, the spread of the toes and absence of claw marks showed that this was the spoor of a large cat.

Morning Land edged nearer. As she bent over the tracks, she noticed traces of hair marks between the animal's toe prints. The print of one of the cat's front feet was more swollen than that of the other, and there was an unevenness to the trail, as if the animal were limping as it walked. From the freshness of the spoor, Morning Land guessed that the cat might still be close by. It could even have watched her as she passed or sniffed her scent from somewhere out of sight. The thought made Morning Land shiver.

Alerted, but not truly frightened, Morning Land scanned the ground for further signs. Big cats, like bears, were a reality her people had learned to deal with. Fierce and powerful though these animals were, most proved more shy than threatening. Women following foot paths were alert for any cat spoor which might cross their trail. When these signs were present, it was wise to stay away from tall grass or thick brush, but a woman with a family to feed could not simply stop walking about because large cats were nearby. Sometimes a test of wills would ensue out on the open ground, with women and cats studying each other. The women would speak softly and approach slowly, and usually the great cats would give ground. Still, a woman must be courteous and respectful, never crowding too near the big animals, for the punishment for carelessness came quickly.

After a few moments, Morning Land decided that the cat's trail was not as fresh as she had imagined. The animal might have come down to drink from the river at dawn or perhaps even at dusk the night before. By now, it could be far away over the hills. Relaxing, Morning Land started to turn back toward her family. Then, for the second time, she hesitated. There was something else marking the ground behind the cat's trail. Just the sight of it sent a cold rush of fear into Morning Land's belly.

She knew what she would find even before she stepped up from the shore. Barely visible in the hard ground were the footprints of eight men. Rain had partly obscured the old trail, sweeping it completely clean in places, but for Morning Land it was enough. She had seen these same types of prints beside a rocky shoreline less than two moons before. Then she had been fleeing for her life. The tracks had been made by the odd-looking, long-toed, moccasined feet of the strangers. Her enemy had come this close to the new village.

Morning Land wheeled around and glanced anxiously at the woods. There was no change. The sun still shone down over the river. A slight breeze still ruffled through the fall leaves. A short distance away, White Bird and Sacred Dance continued to gather tule and cattail roots. It was all shining reeds and bright trees. Nothing to suggest danger. Yet the warriors who had killed half her tribe had been in these woods, and she and her mother and sister were alone, with nothing to defend them but pointed digging sticks.

"*Atoshe!*" she called. "Mother. They have been here. Do you see it? We must hurry."

Several days passed before anyone came near that section of the river again. During those days, the women gathered acorns from a grove of oak trees growing along the southern slope of a nearby hill, and collected berries and pine nuts from other places along the river. It was not until these foods had been used up that the women let Sacred Dance guide them to the place of reeds. By then, the warning whispers of Morning Land had nearly been forgotten. A rainstorm had washed away all trace of the trail she had seen, and most of the village men were convinced that it might never have been a real trackway at all.

In fact, there seemed to be nothing threatening or unusual about that section of the river on the morning when the tribe finally arrived. The glistening, golden green stands of cattails and tule still shivered in the autumn wind, waiting to be plucked and stripped. A flock of robins were hopping about in the sunlight under the oak grove, pecking vigorously at the grubs hidden in the fallen acorns. Other birds had alighted around the big trees as well. It was a day that encouraged laughter, filled with the wet leaf scents of fall and the hum of insects which were still loudly alive in the sunshine. On other such days, the women's voices would have sung out into the clear morning air in a melody of chattering, laughter, and singing. Now, though, they had grown more cautious. The talk among the older women was brief, and spoken in flat, unemotional tones. With rustling bark skirts and infants carried in slings across their backs, these women scavenged the open areas of grass. Berry bushes were stripped of fruit, grass bulbs were pulled up, and even logs and rocks were overturned for the grubs that lay beneath. The women's hands grabbed at whatever food was available, barely pausing to shake off dirt or wetness before stuffing their prizes deep into the collecting baskets.

The task of uprooting cattails at the river's edge was left to the younger women, who had the strength to pull the long rootstalks from the muck. Able to follow even deer trails with ease, these girls walked with a high, vivacious step as they moved into the deep, shivering calm of the reeds. Only Morning Land and her sister actually went into the river itself. They were after arrowhead tubers, and their quiet wading seemed a sharp contrast to the frantic efforts of those on shore.

The few men who had come with the women were much slower and more deliberate in their actions. They did not talk or laugh. The spears they held remained clutched in their hands, and with glinting eyes they searched every shadowy place along the river. Their fear of the strangers had become so great that even the sight of the young women bending up and down amid the reeds could not lull them into cheerfulness.

Morning Land had little trust in the young men who stood watching their group. Despite the fierce appearance of their wooden spears and stone axes, the ashen looks on these men's faces suggested that they would be more likely to jump and run than attack. Even now, any half-seen movement was enough to make them whirl around anxiously and clutch their spears. So far, the only people these hunters had managed to frighten were the women, who, because they did not call out and walked on the pads of their feet, were much quieter than usual.

Sacred Dance shared her daughter's distrust of the hunters. She knew from experience how Tideland men acted under stress. The old woman guessed that if an attack ever did come, it would end in another frantic scramble for the village.

Unlike Morning Land and the others, Sacred Dance was the only woman who did not seem intent on food gathering. She stood on a small rise near the far side of the oak grove and stared out across the river in dismay. This was the area she had discovered, and food which could have lasted her daughters through half the winter was being cropped in a single morning. There would not be any need to come to this place again. Her fellow tribeswomen were seeing to that. Sacred Dance crossed her arms in front of her and clicked her tongue in disgust.

The old woman stared across the shining river to where her daughters slowly waded through the water, making idle, rhythmic kicks in their search for tubers. At that moment, the two girls seemed very innocent and beautiful, and for no particular reason Sacred Dance's eyes clouded with tears as she watched them. The apprehension she felt she dismissed as tiredness, but she could not make her eyes stay clear. The light reflections and the sound of the water had a numbing effect on her overwrought mind. Dazed, she stared emptily at the silver sunlight spreading into the shallows, swirling through the reeds, and flashing brilliantly from the more open reaches of the river.

Finally, impatient with herself, Sacred Dance began to gather acorns off the ground. Yet even as she grabbed up handfuls of the fallen nuts and plunged them into her basket, she continued to feel strange. It was as if something were waiting for her to grow careless. She threw her head back and looked around. A distant snapping came from somewhere above her as a squirrel leapt branches in its search for acorns. The other women still clustered in groups near the river, avoiding even the shadows of the forest. Nothing unusual. She was working very close to the woods, though, and decided to hurry. With her heart beating louder than before, Sacred Dance bent down to her gathering again.

Several strides away, under cover of a thick growth of poplar branches, a warrior was waiting. He and his fellows had been there since the Tidelanders had arrived. Immensely patient, they had watched the frantic actions of the gatherers and had noticed how the women stayed a safe distance from the woods. The warriors had stalked the group silently; had crept on hands and knees so softly that no scuttering of dried leaves or wavering branch had given away their position. The last remnant of Big Tree's band had been surrounded and cut off without ever seeing or hearing any sign of their enemy.

The warriors were ready now. With imperceptible slowness, their hunched bodies shifted into position. Too clever to show themselves until the last possible moment, the warriors squatted down and kept their spears poised. At the instant of attack, they would stand and throw. Those men who did not fall to their spears would be finished with war clubs and knives. The women would be taken easily.

Sacred Dance could not concentrate. Something was worrying the edge of her brain, almost like an itch in some unscratchable place. Her hands grabbed hurriedly at the acorns, jerking them up out of the warm grass with such haste that dirt stained her fingers. Clutched too tightly, one handful of acorns spurted out onto the grass again, and Sacred Dance had to gather them a second time. She did not understand this sudden nervousness. Her heart felt much too loud in her chest, and she was cold, despite the heat of the sun.

Sacred Dance stood up. She stared at the woods as if she were seeing it for the first time. She looked for a shadow moving among the other shadows, but found nothing. She turned toward the river and saw that no one there had shouted or changed position. Still she sensed some secret danger which could destroy her.

Slowly breathing in and out, Sacred Dance forced herself to stand calmly. To run screaming down the slope toward the river would only panic the others and perhaps drive them straight to whatever was waiting here.

Slowly, rigidly, Sacred Dance took a backward step down the slope. The half-filled collecting basket stayed tightly clutched in her hands. The old woman's self-willed calm lasted for one more step and then the poplar branches in front of her suddenly shuddered as a huge hand pushed them aside. The black-painted man who emerged before her moved with a great silence.

In her mind, Sacred Dance screamed. Her legs responded, spinning her around and straining to push her free. She was still jumping forward when the warrior hurled his spear.

It struck her on the back and sank its blade deep into her, hurtling her forward even faster with the force of its impact. Sacred Dance toppled onto the ground with a crunching thud.

She was badly hurt. Blood and froth hissed from the wound in her chest as she lifted herself to her knees and started to stand. Then the dark shadow of a man ran at her from behind. The fingers of one callused hand clutched at her hair, pulling until her head was twisted back. The other hand swung down at her. Its fist clutched a heavily rounded war club. The club struck with skull-crushing force, breaking the bone of her forehead into two pieces. Sacred Dance tried once more to stand, but the muscles controlling her body were no longer hers. She twisted and thrashed about in the grass as the furious warrior struggled to keep his grip on her hair and club her at the same time. The only power Sacred Dance had left was the power to scream. She did not feel much pain. There was a swirling rush in her head, and her sight became blurred. In her last moment she wondered what would happen to her daughters.

Out in the river, White Bird had been looking in her mother's direction when the attack had begun. She had stared unbelievingly as the old woman had fallen forward down the slope with a spear shaft sticking from her back. The whir of movement had sped so quickly that White Bird had not known which woman had fallen until she had heard Sacred Dance's death scream.

As Sacred Dance crumpled under the blows of the warrior's club, her younger daughter struggled to reach her. It was the waist-deep water which saved White Bird's life at that moment, for its pull prevented her thrashing legs from gaining any speed. She could only stumble forward over the mucky bottom sludge, screaming as she went but unaware of it. When she tried to go faster, White Bird fell to her knees and splashed facedown into the river. It took only an instant to lift her head again. Then, crouched on her hands and knees in the shallow water, White Bird saw something she would always remember. She watched her mother die.

Morning Land had been reaching down to grab at a tuber when she had first heard her sister's screaming. She stood up quickly, pulling the tuber with her, and looked around in confusion. Some Tideland hunters were running wildly along the shore. Their spears were in their hands but they were obviously not hurrying to attack. Other, larger spears were being hurled from the bushes. One slashed through a Tidelander's neck and he fell, kicking, onto the ground. No one stopped to help him. Deserted by their men, women rushed about hysterically along the bank, some stumbling in and out of the water in their panic. What was happening? The entire oak grove seemed to be alive with thudding spears and swaying branches and screaming women. Morning Land could not see anything but blurred shapes. With White Bird screaming so loudly, it was impossible to hear anything either. Morning Land's sister had already gone some distance from her, and seemed to be struggling against the current in a frantic effort to reach land.

Morning Land's mind cleared slowly. She watched White Bird fall to her knees in the water. She heard her sister call out

"Mother!" and saw the girl struggling to get up again. Still it did not make sense. Her mind would not accept what should have been obvious.

Across the river, the strangers had succeeded in separating the Tideland women from their husbands. As the warriors moved toward the women, their raised clubs showed their readiness to strike down anyone who resisted. As yet, the Tideland men had not thrown a single spear at their attackers. All the frightened men could do was call out to their women and urge them to "run away." Certainly the Tideland men were doing their best to run away themselves. So little did the strangers value the Tidelanders' courage that only a few warriors were sent after the fleeing men. The rest stayed with their newly captured women. Some warriors were already stooping down to pick up fallen spears. It was while she was watching them that Morning Land saw the dead body of her mother.

Sacred Dance lay near the edge of the river, her face bloodied, her eyes wide and empty, her mouth still open from its last scream. Morning Land gagged at the sight.

There was no time for shivering and moaning to herself. She stood in the middle of a river, with shouting warriors and terrified women on the nearest shore. Death was very close.

Choking back her own screams, Morning Land spun round and splashed forward to White Bird's side.

White Bird was still in knee-deep water, shouting and sobbing by turns. When Morning Land grabbed her arm and tried to pull her out into deeper water, she shivered free. Undeterred, Morning Land threw herself forward and knocked White Bird belly down into the river. As White Bird sprung up again, sputtering in protest, Morning Land clasped her right hand firmly across the girl's mouth.

"Do not scream!" Morning Land hissed. "If you yell out, they will kill you!"

For an instant longer, White Bird fought to retain her balance. Then she gave in and allowed Morning Land to pull her backward toward the middle of the river. Having nearly choked, she could do little more than whimper in Morning Land's arms.

"What were you doing?" Morning Land whispered as the two floated farther away from the shore. "Our mother is already dead, and you cannot fight with these men. We must get away and hide before they see us."

White Bird nodded and began to swim, but it was too late to remain unnoticed. Up on the grass, some warriors had seen the girls in the water and were starting to follow them. The men did not try to wade in after their quarry. Instead, the strangers began running along the bank, certain that the river would soon narrow as they went upstream. Though Morning Land and White Bird were swimming strongly, the current was against them. In the unequal race, the warriors seemed certain to win.

Chance, which had worked so much harm on the Tideland tribe, now turned in the sisters' favor. As the girls sped forward through the water, they passed a place where several big rocks overshadowed the river. Here the five remaining Tideland hunters had made a vain attempt to cross the current ahead of the warriors. Surrounded, the hunters had finally rallied and were shooting spears at their enemies. Those warriors who had been chasing the sisters now found themselves caught up in this final combat. Outnumbered by men of superior skill, the last five Tideland hunters would soon be killed, but in their struggle they gained time for the girls in the water. Morning Land and White Bird were able to reach a place beyond the sight of the strangers and climb out through the reeds of the opposite shore.

Wading among the reeds, White Bird gagged and spat. Her feet stumbled and splashed heavily through the spinning swirl of muddy water. Several times she nearly tripped on the cattail rootstalks. She was gasping, and her chest felt very tight. Left to herself, she would have crouched down amid the reeds and rested, but Morning Land kept tugging at her right hand. At any moment, Morning Land expected to see the warriors charging across the river after them.

"*Atoshe!* You are drowning me!" White Bird panted.

Morning Land eased her hold only slightly. "They will kill us," she warned. "Hurry. Even from here their spears can knock you to the ground. They will not go away until they have taken all the women."

"Shaa!" White Bird staggered up onto the shore and squatted down on the dried mud. "Where will we go?"

Over the noises of the river, Morning Land could still hear the sound of men fighting. "Get up!" she ordered. "Sit here and you will be caught. We are going up into the hills, where the white snows are. If we climb far enough, the strangers will not come after us. They will stay with the other women."

"How can we run so far?" White Bird sobbed.

"Run," Morning Land urged. "If you do not move quickly, they will hit you. Warriors know how to run well after women."

With no time for arguing, Morning Land pointed toward the

forest and started up the stony slope. White Bird stared at her for a moment, gave one more bleating sob, and hurried after. What began as a quick walk soon became a full run. The grace of the two young women was obvious as they dashed forward across the leaf-caked floor of the woods. Like the swift prey their hunters often chased, the sisters leapt and bounded around forest obstacles; springing high over earthen mounds and landing lightly enough to continue their run without a stop. The dapple pattern of sunlight through leaves showed against the agile sleekness of tanned legs as the girls hurried on toward the eastern hills.

After a while the slope of the ground became too steep for running, and the girls' pace slowed. By this time, both sisters were sweating heavily, but they continued to walk even though all the muscles in their legs hurt. They were nearing the top of a small mountain, and above them the trees gave way to bare rocks. Already the air was colder.

"We cannot live here," White Bird complained. "Night is close. We have no fire to sit by, no food to eat, no hides to wrap around us. The cold will kill us."

Morning Land acknowledged the truth of this. Both girls were naked except for their aprons. All of their collecting baskets, digging sticks, and slings had been left at the river.

"This is the only way," Morning Land insisted. "If we go back down this hill, we will be killed or caught."

While White Bird waited in among the trees, Morning Land climbed farther up the slope until she had crawled out onto one of the exposed rocks. Edging her way up the side of the stone as silently as she had crossed through the forest, Morning Land did not look down until she was near the top. The rock had been baked in sunlight all day and still felt warm under her hands, but there was a cold wind on her back that made her shiver. When Morning Land finally did look down, her trembling increased. All around her she saw great forested mountains, beautiful in the oranges and yellows of fall. From this height, the river seemed very small and far away. Mist had drifted in above it, filtering the light. Morning Land thought she could see the village huts, but they were too distant for her to notice any signs of movement around them. Everything seemed lifeless. To the west, a solitary wisp of smoke indicated where the strangers had made their own camp.

The golden light of the setting sun added a rich beauty to the scene, but there were no eyes to see it other than Morning

Land's. She gazed at the forests, the hills, and the few reddened clouds and felt only emptiness. Soon it would turn dark and grow colder still. Already the icy wind stung her face. She could not linger there, and she had no wish to. The world she had known had already grown distant. White Bird was all that remained of it.

"Above us there were only rocks," Morning Land told White Bird as soon as she was back among the trees again. "The night here will be cold. We must climb down to where it is warmer."

"This is a place to suffer in," White Bird agreed.

The sisters continued walking until the top of the mountain lay between them and the wind. Then they made a high pile of fallen leaves and burrowed into it. The two sisters spent the night clinging to each other like lovers in a place sheltered from the worst of the night's cold. The darkness was very quiet on the mountainside. Once, White Bird woke in the night and heard a big cat coughing far away, its growling no more than a distant echo. White Bird poked her head through the leaves, but there was nothing to see in the black forest, so she soon buried herself beside her sister once more.

"We roll ourselves up like wolf cubs," she murmured, "and still we shiver and shiver."

In the morning, the girls were awake before dawn. As the sun rose, they were already walking. With the growing brightness, a warm flow of air began to blow in and out among the trees. To White Bird, it barely seemed possible that they were still alive. She had been almost certain the night would kill them. Despite the bruises on her body and the aching in her muscles, White Bird felt hopeful. Her faith in her older sister had grown more unshakable than ever before.

Chance favored Morning Land's plan for traveling through the mountains. The winter cold and sudden snows of fall held off long enough for the sisters to hurry across high passes which would soon become blocked. In her determination to be rid of the strangers, Morning Land had finally succeeded in putting a barrier between herself and her enemies that even the bravest of their warriors feared to cross. The strangers never did follow after the sisters' trail, but the crippled saber-toothed tiger, which had already been foraging high up in the hills, found the women all too readily.

CHAPTER TWO

Moon Of The Hunter

The afternoon sun shone down through hazy autumn air onto a section of river shoreline that seemed more brown than green. Tan clumps of dried grass reached almost to the water's edge, and behind the grass, stands of aspen, hickory, and birch trees had turned golden with the frost. Their leaves quivered and trembled in glinting shivers of color when brushed even slightly by the afternoon breeze. Some leaves, which had fallen off early, now floated like crisp golden specks on the water's surface. Even the river looked brown, for its shaded surface reflected the colors of the forest rather than the far more distant sky.

There was a faint shuffling on the ground beneath the aspens, then silence. A few moments later the sound was repeated, this time from behind a section of birch trees. The soft rustling of dried leaves was immediately followed by a low moaning. For a while, this was the only sign of the big cat. Then, with a quick swish of padded feet through the leaves, the cat moved out into the open grass along the riverbank. Huge and bright in the autumn sunlight, with her fur only slightly darker gold than the leaves behind her, the cat paused at the edge of the river. She raised her head to look across the water.

There was something on the other side of the river, so far upstream that it was just within view. Panting, the cat squinted until her greenish yellow eyes had focused on the shape of a solitary bull mastodon. The mastodon's dark, tangled hair showed clearly against the yellow of the autumn grass and the brilliant, shifting color patterns of the trees behind it.

Old and nervous, the mastodon seemed to feel the nearness of the cat. It raised its trunk into the wind, smelling the dust scent on leaves, the tartness of ripe grapes, the dry odor of ragweed and fall clover. Then the breeze shifted, and with those other smells came the first trace odor of the cat's warm pelt. The cat scent stirred memories of the elephant beast, making it distrustful of its nearly blind eyes. A moment later, the mastodon's harsh warning trumpet bellowed along the riverbed.

The cat was unimpressed. She looked straight at the mastodon with seeming indifference, secure in the width of the flowing water which lay between them. Soon, though it was huge enough to have crushed the cat easily under its enormous feet, the mastodon became worried. With an ungainly shuffling, it smashed its way back into the sheltering trees.

Satisfied, the saber-toothed tiger lowered her head to lap at the water. Her tan-colored fur blended well with the grass, and when she stayed motionless like this, she was almost invisible. But the cat rarely remained still for long. As soon as she had finished drinking, she raised her dripping muzzle from the river and began to worry at her crippled foot. The licking and chewing and growling did little good. Most of the hair on the inner side of the injured leg had already been chewed off by the cat in her efforts to get at the festering quills. No matter how hard she tried, the cat could do nothing to ease the pain of her wounds, for every time her leg muscles flexed, the barbed points of the quills became wedged more deeply beneath her flesh.

Eventually the cat quit her efforts and gave voice to a series of coughlike grunts. Hunger forced her to move again. Below her stretched an enormous valley, and along its distant grassy plains there would be food.

Not far ahead of her, two other travelers were also moving down through the hills toward the valley floor. Like the saber-toothed tiger, the Tideland sisters had left the area of the first river and had found this second one which drained into the great central valley. Weary of the green pine forests and steep slopes of the coastal mountains, the young women welcomed the sight of open land. Already the new river had led them out of the high hills and into an area where the ground sloped only gently. Instead of rock outcroppings, golden fields of grass stretched between groves of oak trees.

The sisters walked cautiously along the stony slope of a ridge, stopping beside an elderberry bush to pluck at its dark clusters of fruit, but otherwise staying in the open places where there was less chance of being stalked by predators. The two formed a working team, with White Bird carefully stepping into the same spots where Morning Land's feet had been. Their strides were long and deliberate, and their weather-toughened feet came down almost noiselessly onto the dry gravel.

The sisters were better equipped than they had been on the day they had fled from the strangers. Each girl had woven herself a carrying basket, formed a stone chopper by breaking flakes off a hand-held rock, and used that chopper to fashion a spearlike digging stick. Capes made from strips of willow bark protected their backs and shoulders from the sun. A few days earlier, Morning Land had carved the twirling sticks she needed for making fire, and since then their nights had been warmer. Instead of lying naked on frost-cold ground, they had kept their stomachs toward the fire's head and covered their backs with bark capes.

These small comforts had not lessened the girls' fears. The mountains they had crossed had seemed hard enough in the morning sunshine, but it had been the nights that had brought out the strangeness of those lonely hills. The light from their fires could not make the surrounding darkness vanish. Brightening a blaze by adding sticks did not prevent them from seeing things in the flickering shadows. It was more than wind or wolf howls or unexplained rustlings that chased away their sleep. A dread seemed to come upon them, a dread which only partially slid away as the morning light flowed in from the east.

Most frightening of all had been the noises of the big cat. It had been with them all through their journey—at first only as a faraway coughing, but gradually growing nearer. Each night the sisters had listened for it. Sometimes the cat moaned like a woman in pain, and sometimes it only made low growls, but its voice was always unlike any other night creature's.

Their last night in the mountains had been the worst. A wind as cold as an ice cave had hissed through the pines high above them. Stirred by it, the wolves had begun a chorus of barks and yips, their plaintive, far-carrying voices only slightly mellowed by distance. Then, just as the sisters had begun to drift between sleep and wakefulness, the cat had come. Though they had heard it for so many nights, the animal had always remained unseen before. This time it had come very close. White Bird had smelled its musk scent in the wind and heard the soft padding of its feet circling their camp. The cat's growling had rumbled out of the shadows for most of the night. At dawn, they had seen the footprints it had left as it had walked around them. Only their fire had kept it away.

Even now, as they walked the ridge, White Bird wondered if the cat was following them. A fire had saved their lives the night before, but fire was not always enough. When hunger drove the cat to desperation, it would risk a singeing to take what it wanted.

On the other side of the ridge, a wild plain of yellow grass stretched out before the sisters, reaching as far as the distant horizon and high up the sides of the enclosing mountains. Lines of bushes and islandlike clusters of trees broke above the surface of this grass, softening its yellow glare with tones of green, red, and orange. Animals moved everywhere on that great vast plain. There were herds of quagga horses which made curious yapping noises. Low humped camels moved in smaller groups, puffing and snorting as they grazed. Pronghorns let out fitful, sneezing sounds as they cantered about in the whistling grass. Only the more distant herd of long-horned bison seemed strangely silent. Morning Land searched the horizon for traces of campfire smoke, but there was none. She had been looking for signs of humans since they had begun walking down from the mountains and had found nothing so far.

Most of the trees and bushes the girls saw were low to the ground and seemed almost stunted after the tall pines of the mountain forests, but there was one giant solitary oak tree that towered above the grassland. Its rounded crown cast a wide circle of shade below it, and its heavy, outstretched branches cupped upward into the cloud-filled sky. Without knowing exactly why, the sisters were drawn toward that old oak. Instinctively, they moved down the side of the ridge in its direction.

While White Bird enjoyed the sensation of walking on level ground again after so many days of climbing up and down hillsides, Morning Land searched for trail markings. Whenever the grass in front of them looked as if some large animals had crossed through it, she immediately slowed her pace and kept her eyes focused on the ground. Rounded hoof marks, great shapeless pads of manure, and partially chewed weeds—these were all promising signs for a hunter to follow, but they were not what Morning Land wanted to find. She was looking for humans. Though she did her best to hide her worries from White Bird, Morning Land had little hope that the two of them could survive much longer on their own. The cat which followed after them now was only one of the dangers they faced.

Impatient with her sister's slowness, White Bird grunted and pointed toward the western horizon. "The sun is already getting close to the mountains," she complained.

"We will sit in the shade of that big tree," Morning Land

said, without looking back. "There must be water close to it, and grass and branches for a hut."

"I will not help you make any more huts," White Bird grumbled. "Huts are no good here. A cat could bite you on your leg and drag you out while you were sleeping. It would wait until the fire became embers, and then it would come."

Morning Land turned and looked back at her sister wearily. "What will you do then, unhappy one?" she demanded. "Are you going to lie out on the open ground?"

"We have lived like the animals live," White Bird replied. "Now I am beginning to think like one. They do not sleep on the ground when the big cat prowls. They sleep high in the trees. We have found the tallest tree of all. Now we should climb up into it."

"Shaa!" Morning Land exclaimed. "You are truly senseless. Even if you are going to climb about like a squirrel, you cannot sleep like one. When you grow tired, you will slip and fall. Then the cat will find you dead at the bottom of your tree."

White Bird clung to her idea. "A woman can sleep happily even in a tree if her sister is beside her, watching. One of us will sleep while the other looks on. If the one who sleeps starts to roll or fall, her sister will catch onto her and hold her."

Morning Land shook her head. "You cannot hold what you cannot see," she insisted. "In the darkness, you would fall right through my outstretched arms. It is very black up in a tree at night."

"We could build a fire on the ground below us," White Bird persisted. "Then we could see as well as if we were sleeping inside a hut."

"A fire just dies when there is no one to feed it," Morning Land said. "It would not last in the darkness. Then we would be blind."

"If we held close to each other, we would not need to see."

Morning Land gestured impatiently. "Young sisters should listen to older ones," she grumbled. "If you fall from that tree, you will not live long enough to worry about the cat."

"Neither of us will live if the cat comes for us," White Bird retorted. "I will not sleep on the ground another night."

Morning Land looked annoyed and muttered, *"Shaa henaki,"* under her breath. Then, because she could not think of anything to say, she stopped speaking altogether. The sisters continued walking in silence.

The lone oak tree had been hazy with distance when they had

first seen it, but as they grew nearer it began to tower above them. They felt trembling leaf shadows on their backs once they had crossed into the great circle of its shade. Out in the sunlight beyond, the grassland was shimmering with afternoon heat, but under the bulk of that tree there was a cavelike coolness. The girls had to walk carefully to keep from stumbling on fallen acorns which seemed to be spread out across an entire field. The oak's trunk was wider than two village huts, and like all giant trees, it sheltered many creatures. The bark along its trunk was marked with the acorn-studded holes of woodpeckers. Towhees, sparrows, and robins had all found nesting places in the forks and crisscrosses of its higher branches. Near its pinnacle, two great hawks had settled as well, their nest looking gigantic amid all the rest. Morning Land decided that she liked this old oak. It was the type of tree her people most admired; one with sweet acorns and bark which bled when cut. Such trees were like mothers to the entire forest. Perhaps this one could shelter two Tideland girls among its family.

White Bird was simply glad that they had stopped walking. Having been awake all night listening to growling cats and yapping wolves, she began to sleep as soon as she closed her eyes.

The sight of White Bird curled up trustingly on the ground beside her made Morning Land all the more determined to keep them both safe. She envied White Bird's easy way of relaxing completely, right down to her fingers and toes. The young girl never needed urging. When it was time to rest, she simply did so. Morning Land sighed. Things were much harder once a woman grew older.

Morning Land shook her head, sat down on some rocks near the base of the great tree, and tried to plan what she should do. The tree was even more impressive now that she was directly under it. Its massive, furrowed trunk led up through branches and layers of leaves which seemed to reach forever. There were plenty of acorns still in the tree, all with the long, conical shape her tribe loved so much. They could stay in this place for days if necessary, feeding on the acorns alone. It was a good choice.

When White Bird awoke a while later, Morning Land had already built a fire and was pounding acorn mash with her stone chopper. This, along with the berries and roots they had gathered on the way, would form their meal. Hungry though she was, White Bird felt too guilty to ask for food. Unlike herself, Morning Land had been strong enough to stay awake and work.

"I had a dream," White Bird told her sister. "I dreamed I was back in the village where our mother and father used to live. So many other people were there as well. I saw young women like ourselves, and their husbands were all still alive. Everyone talked about little things and there was meat to share. No one was alone."

"The *Ahiri* have been troubling you," Morning Land said, referring to the small demons which haunted people's dreams. "What good can a dream like this do for us now? We are in a strange country. There is no longer anything in our old village which could help us. The strangers have killed all that."

White Bird swallowed painfully, for her throat burned with thirst. She had been sweating when she had lain down, but now she felt cold.

"There is a river," Morning Land said, pointing toward some nearby willow saplings.

White Bird nodded and stood up. For a moment she stretched and rubbed at the red marks which the grass had left on her body. Then she walked cautiously in the direction Morning Land had pointed to.

White Bird's caution increased as she neared the edge of the stream. Ever since the death of her mother, she had not been able to come close to a river without feeling a sudden rush of panic. She found herself watching for something in every dark stretch of woods.

Thoroughly alert now, White Bird crouched down on the riverbank and began cupping water in her hands. Her eyes followed every insect as it darted past. She had intended on one quick drink, but the cold wetness made her mouth seem all the more dry. As she looked at her cupped hands, White Bird frowned. Tideland women did not drink this way. On impulse, White Bird waded forward into the stream. She kept on moving until she was up to her waist in tingling cold water. Before she stepped back onto the shore again, even her hair was dripping wet.

Morning Land noticed the change in her sister as soon as White Bird returned. She watched the young girl for a moment as White Bird bent to warm herself by the fire. Then she said, "We are still without a hut."

White Bird frowned. "I do not want to live in a hut anymore. If you sleep on the ground, you will sleep by yourself."

"If that happens, it will happen," Morning Land said, trying to hide her hurt feelings. "Get up and sit in your tree. I will keep this fire."

Challenged, White Bird had no choice but to begin climbing. She sprang up onto the massive trunk, her groping hands and feet searching for bulges and holds in its furrowed bark. She had scrambled nearly halfway up to the first branch when she paused and looked down. Morning Land seemed to have grown much smaller. White Bird did not want to leave her sister behind on the ground with the night coming near, but she could think of no way of persuading her. With a hard breath, she went on climbing. In a few moments she had reached the first main branch. Twisting and grabbing, she managed to pull herself up onto it.

The branch was enormous—far thicker than White Bird had expected. At first, she stayed on her hands and knees, but when she saw how wide it was she decided to sit instead. The branch was too thick to be straddled comfortably, so she changed to a squatting position.

"Atoshe!" White Bird called out triumphantly. "I can walk about up here. It is like standing on the ground. Climb up with me, sister. You will see with your own eyes."

Morning Land, who had been watching White Bird carefully, now followed her younger sister. Soon both women were perched on the huge branch.

"Stay up here with me," White Bird urged. "We will spend the night in our tree. No cat could reach us here."

Morning Land began to tell stories of people who had fallen from trees and died, but White Bird was unconvinced, and Morning Land was too tired to argue. So it became accepted that the old oak tree would be their shelter.

The sisters returned to the ground long enough for a hurried meal. By the time they had finished, it was too dark to go down to the river again, so White Bird led the way back up into the tree.

Once they were on the branch again, the girls grew silent. This was the hardest time of the day for them. Now that the need for work was over, the thoughts which they had kept shoved away throughout the afternoon came flooding back. Looking out at the reddening sunset, both girls could remember countless nights spent in the company of their tribe. They missed the voices and the laughter. Below them, their own slowly burning fire seemed a pitiful reminder of the circle of hearths that had formed their village. It was all gone now.

Morning Land hugged her arms close against her chest, less as protection from the physical cold than from the chill bleak-

ness of her own thoughts. Sometime just before the darkness
became complete, she noticed that White Bird was crying. It
was a noiseless grief, with tears sliding easily down the young
woman's cheeks. Not knowing what else to do, Morning Land
reached out and pressed her sister close against her. White Bird
remained stiff and unyielding in her arms.

"Shaa henaki," White Bird whispered. "Why are we living
like this? Why are we left with nothing?"

Morning Land did not speak, because there could be no answer. Looking down across the enormous valley as the last of
the sunlight drew back from the mountains, she could not say
whether they would ever feel happy again. All she could do was
settle close to her sister. With their shoulders covered by their
bark capes, they would have to sit out the night this way.

Morning Land stretched out her legs in front of her. "Ehnn."
She sighed. "This branch does not even move under me. It is
like the ground."

White Bird would not be distracted from her brooding
thoughts. "Our mother has died," she muttered. "Could this be
her spirit which follows after us? Is that what death is like? Perhaps mother's ghost is still here and will not leave us."

Morning Land did not want to consider this. She already had
an uneasy feeling as she looked out across the shadowed landscape. A wolf howled, and others answered, for a pack was
gathering. Morning Land sensed other dangers there, somewhere just behind the hills. This was no time to talk of spirits.

"Our mother left us many days ago," she said. "Things are
finished with her. It is only a cat which follows."

The ululating cries of the wolves started up again, accompanied by growls and panting noises. The pack was no longer
searching. Footsteps shuffled quickly through dried grass.
White Bird heard the wolves move away from her tree. Their
sounds were all coming from one direction now. A frightened
bellow echoed back across the veldt, and the wolf noises increased. There were snapping sounds, growls muffled in fur,
quivering snarls, and the sound of one beast worrying another.
A last plaintive squeak faded into an agonized moan. Then silence. The wolf pack had killed some unwary calf.

White Bird wiped at the tears on her face. "We are going to
die," she decided. "It will not be finished with us until we are
dead like the others."

"Why are you so miserable?" Morning Land asked. "The others are not all dead, and death will not take you this night either."

"What will happen to those women who were not killed?" White Bird asked.

"The strangers have their own women and ours besides," Morning Land replied. "The wives of the strangers will not be happy to see our women in their village. They will shout and beat the captive girls, and perhaps shout at their husbands, too."

White Bird shivered. She knew that Morning Land had been a captive and understood about these things. "You never waited until you had reached their village," she said.

"No," Morning Land whispered. "I was only with them for two days. By that second night, most of the women were scratched and dirty, so the men allowed us to bathe. Then they took out red earth which they had hidden away, and they began to paint us. Some of our women did not want the paint on their bodies and tried to push the men's hands away. They were beaten and threatened. I let those men paint me.

"We were all so tired that we were ready to fall down." Morning Land added. "All we wanted to do was sleep, but now the men wanted us. The man who had walked behind me on the trail poked at my flesh and laughed. Soon he was pulling himself onto me. It hurt. It felt like he was pulling me apart. I twisted, but he just grabbed my arms tighter until they felt like they would break. After him, there were others. These men wanted to sleep with a woman, not to marry her. They did what they wanted and left. I lay there, hurt and sore. Then I crawled into a dark place away from the fires.

"Another woman was sobbing there in the darkness. It was my friend, Gray Deer, and she said, 'We must run away. No one watches us now.'

"I was sore and tired, but I knew she was right. We ran away together in the dark. Perhaps we would have escaped together, but Gray Deer's leg had been hurt and soon she could not run anymore. She just slumped down beside a tree to wait for the warriors. I tried to make her go on, but when she would not move, I just left."

Morning Land paused, and both girls listened for a moment. Out on the veldt, the feeding wolves continued to gulp and yap over their meal, but the wider silence which had followed the kill was now replaced by ringing insect calls. In the high grass, countless crickets and katydids yielded to an overwhelming need for noise. Small in themselves, the combined voices swelled under the clouds until all the land resounded with chirping.

"How can we keep living out here, in all this?" White Bird asked.

"I have done it before," Morning Land reminded her. "When I fled from the strangers, I walked and walked, stepping on stones and where the ground was too hard to make a print. I left no tracks for the warriors to look at. When I finally stopped doing this, I was truly lost. I came to the top of a small hill and looked, but everything in the distance seemed gray and misty, the way it is when there is a great fire. All around me was strange forest. I saw a large animal running far away from me down the side of a hill slope, but I could not tell what it was. The land was very big, and all of it just trees. Our village seemed as far away as the night stars. I was very lonely.

"After three days, I reached a large river, and I followed it for a while, hoping it would lead toward the sea. That night, it rained. Everything around me dripped all night. If I touched a branch or brushed a leaf, water poured down onto me. By morning all the woods near the river were covered in a white mist. I could not see where to walk, so I stayed there until the sun was high and the mist disappeared. Then I went on walking.

"I walked on for many days. Each night I slept in a different place, but I listened to the same noises from the river. After dark the frogs would begin to sing—*aka, aka, aka*—like that. Each morning, I would wake to find new tracks around me in the shore mud. I saw many bear tracks, and once I found the footprints of a big cat that had walked all around me in the darkness. Every day I looked for the smoke from our people's fires, but I never did see any. Though I was afraid and thirsty and hungry most of the time, I just kept walking. That is what we must do now."

"You had a place to walk to," White Bird protested. "You knew that our village was still out there somewhere. All you had to do was find it. What can we find here?"

"Listen to me, then," Morning Land said. "I had given up all hope just as you have now, but then one morning I found the footprints of a man, a hunter, and I followed them. I knew from the way he walked that this hunter must be one of our people. The hunter was Hugging Bear, and he had been without luck all day. That was why he had gone so far from our village. I just stayed behind his tracks. Ehnnn, that is what I did. By nightfall I was home."

"We will not find Hugging Bear's tracks here," White Bird said bitterly.

"No," Morning Land admitted, "but there may be other people here. That is why I look for their tracks each day, and that is why you should not be so full of tears."

"*Siyemou,*" White Bird whispered, not trusting the sound of her own voice. "You are the one who makes me feel strong."

These words, spoken so gently, were like a smile in the dark to Morning Land. For a moment they drowned out the ghostly sounds of feeding wolves and the thought of cat eyes searching the veldt. Only gradually did Morning Land's sense of danger return.

A twig cracked somewhere on the ground below. Instantly Morning Land's body became very straight and rigid. She stared down at the flickering glow of their fire, wishing she could trace things with her eyes in the dark as easily as a cat. The snapping came again and this time, knowing it was only wood breaking in the flames, Morning Land relaxed.

There were other sounds now. A rustle, like something being dragged through brush, came from the intense darkness that lay just beyond the red circle of firelight. Something else scurried past near the bottom of the tree. Then, quite distinctly, there was a low moaning. Before Morning Land could do more than hold her breath, she felt something grab at her hand.

In her shock, it took a moment for Morning Land to realize that the thing clutching at her was White Bird. Impatiently, she shook off her sister's grip.

"Have you no sense?" she whispered irritably.

White Bird's voice shivered. "I heard the cat."

"Listen," Morning Land hissed.

The moaning sound repeated, a wavering, wailing call that floated out from the blackness. This time it was followed by a snorting bark and a querulous crying.

"Uca (porcupine)," was all Morning Land said.

White Bird sighed as the tension passed from her. She felt very stupid. "It makes a lot of noise," she whispered.

"Uca's voice is truly terrible," Morning Land agreed. "*Eeeee weeeee, eeeeee weeeee, eeeeee weeeee*—on and on. It calls as if something were killing it."

"Everything I hear makes me want to cry," White Bird admitted.

"You have always hated Uca's noise," Morning Land said. "Every fall, when we went on the long walks across the tide-

lands, that was the one sound which frightened you. We went
deep into the hills in those days, and everyone grew tired. Walking was difficult with the sand forever crunching under our feet.
You always began each day in a great hurry. No one walked fast
enough to keep you happy. You ran all over, picking up roots
and pieces of wood, until you suddenly grew tired. Ehnn. That
was when you stopped having thoughts about food and began
begging for someone to carry you."

"I remember," White Bird said softly. "The other children
would ride on their brothers' shoulders, but when I was truly
tired, I would run back to you. I knew I could get rest then. You
would always say, 'Poor little White Bird,' and pick me up."

"Siyemou . . ." Morning Land let her voice drop, because
now there were other noises. She wanted to think it was still
just *uca* or maybe a hissing of burning wood, but this felt different from everything else. The sound came from the direction
of the ridge they had walked across. It began as a low growling
and rose into a long moaning wail that ended in a quick series
of coughs. When it was over, the darkness seemed even more
threatening.

White Bird clung to her sister's arm again, and this time
Morning Land did not shake away the hold. White Bird wanted
to be told that this call which had filled her with such panic had
been made by a wolf or some other animal. But the wolves had
quit their feeding, and the porcupine had stopped its noise as
soon as it had heard the cat.

The sisters stayed motionless, waiting. They knew that each
time the roar came, it would be closer, for the cat was searching
along their trail.

After a while, the cat's voice could be heard from the other
side of the stream. Between roars and grunts, the noises it made
changed to a painful crying. Judging from sound alone, there
might have been a suffering woman out there in the darkness.
The girls waited for the call to be repeated. When it was not,
they knew that the cat was coming still nearer.

White Bird let go of her sister and picked up one of the
wooden digging sticks. Morning Land felt along the branch until she had found her digging stick as well. The hard feel of the
pointed wood under her hand was comforting.

Peering down through the leaves, Morning Land was surprised how peaceful everything looked. Light from their
dwindling fire flickered along one side of the tree, making the
furrows in the bark cast moving black shadows.

Somewhere just beyond the firelight a rock shifted slightly. The noise was followed by the clatter of a small pebble rolling downhill. As the sound faded over the empty grass, the pulse beat of the two girls quickened. It had been very close.

The sisters listened to the crickets and the far-off sounds of the autumn night. Then came the shush of padded feet on dried leaves. Something heavy and soft-footed was walking toward the trunk of the tree. Morning Land's eyes searched the ground, but though the soft steps came closer, the dark cat-shape never appeared.

There was a sudden shudder as the heavy body of the saber-toothed tiger leapt up against the side of the trunk. Its claws scratched at the bark somewhere behind the girls. White Bird spun around, nearly knocking Morning Land in the face with her digging stick as she did so. It had not occurred to either sister that the cat would approach from the dark side of the tree.

The part of the oak tree which was away from the firelight was completely black, for even the starlight could not shine through its depth of leaves. There was nothing for the girls to see. All they could do was listen to the thud and scratch of heavy paws striking against the bark again and again. White Bird half imagined the widespread claws reaching for her, but each time it leaped, the cat was flung back. It hissed in frustration. The women were too high off the ground for the cat to reach them, and its swollen front paw prevented it from climbing up after them.

Abruptly the snarls and the shaking stopped. The night seemed empty again. For a hopeful moment, White Bird imagined that the cat had gone away, but then she realized she had not heard the sounds of it moving off. It still waited, black and huge, somewhere below her.

White Bird was surprised by the shivers which trembled along her back and neck. Each time she breathed, she could smell the heavy sweat of her own body. She did not remember ever having been this frightened before.

For Morning Land, too, this was the moment when courage failed her. She hated not being able to see the cat. Even though the tremors had stopped, she remained lying belly down on the branch, staring blankly at the wooden digging stick in her hand. What good was this little stick with its sharpened point when she did not even have the courage to move?

A hard thud shook the tree again, almost knocking the

wooden stick from her grip. Morning Land screamed and
grabbed at the branch, terrified that she was going to fall.

"There!" White Bird shouted. "There at the bottom of the
tree!"

Morning Land could still see nothing in the darkness, but she
could feel the branch shivering beneath her and her own heart's
terrified pounding in her chest. There was a crash as a heavy
body fell back against hidden branches, then more angry snarling. The cat plunged at the tree one more time before stopping.
At last, with a low rumble, it padded off into the night.

Neither girl moved. Both were lying stomach down on the
branch, certain that they would have fallen off if they had been
sitting up during the last attack. Morning Land's fingers ached
from where she was gripping the bark, but she did not loosen
her hold. Beside her, White Bird sobbed quietly.

The cat had not gone far away. It circled the tree several
times, passing just beyond the edge of the firelight. Finally it
walked slowly over and stood right beneath the two sisters. It
stood there for a long while, looking bigger in the firelight than
anything they had imagined. Its head was held low at first, as if
it were searching for a scent. Then it let its eyes drift upward.
Its gaze moved along the branch until it seemed to be looking
straight into White Bird's face.

As she stared back down into those cold, pale cat eyes, White
Bird felt numbed by unreasoning fear. Though she wanted to
pull away, she was having trouble moving at all. Her body lay
on the branch like a lifeless thing.

The cat's first motion was to lunge upward with terrifying
speed. It covered the space between the ground and the branch
in an instant. White Bird saw the claws of its good forepaw
swing up toward her face and then slip back to dig against the
heavy bark. Her eyes jerked and she trembled all over, but she
did not have the strength to lift her head away.

Morning Land did it for her. Before the cat could recover its
balance for another leap, Morning Land seized White Bird by
the shoulder and yanked her violently upward until they were
both well away from the edge of the branch. Neither sister saw
the cat's next jump, but the branch pulsed with the impact.
Strangely, the trembling vibrations in the wood no longer terrified White Bird. A calm had begun to fill her mind.

The two sisters were once again belly down on the branch,
trying to keep their balance when every lunge of the cat threatened to shift them closer to the edge. The cat could not reach

them where they were, but if one of them grew tired or careless she could be jarred loose in an instant. Then no amount of yelling or clawing would keep her from spilling down through the darkness toward the hungry beast on the grass below.

Something had to be done to discourage the cat from leaping at the tree.

White Bird remembered the digging stick she still clutched in her right hand. It was longer than Morning Land's—almost like a small spear. One hard downward thrust might be enough. White Bird was strong. All her life she had pounded acorns to mush and hacked at baked soil with her digging sticks. If she could use both hands to push out with her full weight when the cat jumped upward, there might be a new bleeding wound along its furred back.

White Bird moved quickly to the edge of the branch, anxious to try this plan before she became frightened again. Breathing with determined slowness, she forced herself to a crouching position and gripped the wooden stick with both hands. She could lose her balance easily now, but she refused to think of that.

White Bird barely had time to raise her digging stick before the cat leapt at her. It sprang straight up, ready to strike at her with its outstretched claws.

Horrified, White Bird screamed and stabbed down with all her strength. Pointed stick and cat slammed against one another and the point dug in, driven as much by the force of the cat's own leap as by White Bird's arms. The wooden point sank through the muscular shoulder hump until its tip struck bone. Then it splintered into two pieces. White Bird felt the stick being pulled from her hands and let go at once. Had she hesitated, she would have been dragged down with the cat.

The saber-toothed tiger twisted in midair, shrieking as it flailed through space. The wounded beast dropped back to earth without even scraping against the tree.

White Bird had no time for triumph. In striking at the cat with all her strength she had overbalanced herself, and she nearly toppled headfirst into the darkness. Only Morning Land's arms about her waist held her back. When she realized how close she had come to falling, White Bird's fear returned to her in a great surge of panic. She clung to the bark with desperate strength, suddenly unable to move.

On the ground below, the cat was clawing and snarling in an insane fury. It tried to twist itself in half, to grab the digging stick in its teeth and crush it to splinters. Leaves and grass exploded around the cat as it lashed out at everything within reach. Then, with a crackling sound, the long end of the stick was wrenched free, though the hard point remained wedged inside the cat's shoulders.

The wailing and snarling and moaning continued for what seemed like a long time. At last, exhausted but still spitting mad, the cat lurched to its feet again. Blood was pulsing out of the wound in its shoulder, and its eyes glared with a wild hatred as it looked up at the women once more.

Determined to pull these women down to where it could claw them and stab its teeth into their soft flesh, the cat began leaping again. White Bird was barely able to yank herself back before a huge paw appeared at the edge of the branch where she had been lying. The paw was there only an instant, for the cat could not keep hold of the bark, but this was enough to completely unnerve the young girl.

The whirling fury of the cat continued as it flung itself upward again and again, tearing at bark instead of prey. Breathing harshly and sobbingly, White Bird withdrew further and further into herself. She did not know how long she lay there clinging to the tree, and she did not recognize the whimpering sounds that were coming from her own throat. She barely felt the branch grow calm again. It was not until Morning Land had lifted her to a sitting position and hugged her close that White Bird realized the attack was over. Even then, she continued to cringe and sob, keeping her eyes tightly shut. Nothing would make her look down at the ground.

Morning Land kept her arms around White Bird, pressing her sister's face against her chest. She could feel the young girl crying softly, achingly, against her skin. Morning Land's own mind was still muddled. It was hard to believe that the cat's strength had finally given out. Even though she had listened to it padding down toward the river, making terrible snarling growls as it went, Morning Land did not trust the silence which had settled around the tree once more. The cat would stay close by.

That was what frightened Morning Land the most. She and her sister could not remain in the tree. Without food or warmth, they would be driven down from the sheltering branches, down to the open grass where the cat was faster and stronger than they were.

Morning Land almost hoped that White Bird would remain crouched and dazed like this. It was better than waking to the full terror of what they faced. To live, they needed help. Someone must help them. But nobody would. There was no one out there, no one at all. Just bushes and grassland, all of it as hard and unfeeling as the tree they crouched in.

CHAPTER THREE

Laughing One

A chill night had left the valley under a thick layer of fog. By the river this fog blanketed everything, but up in the hills it was already thinning under the heat of the morning sun. Mist weaved in and out around the higher stands of trees, making them seem like isolated islands in a strange vapor sea.

At the crest of one of these hills, a young hunter stood on a rock overlooking the great valley. He knew the country and was happy to be back in a place with familiar landmarks, but on this day he found the view less beautiful than discouraging. The night before, he had noticed a light coming from the direction of the great oak tree, and he had risen early in the hope of discovering its source. But with everything covered over in fog, there was little chance of finding any camp.

Laughing One, third and youngest son of Wanderer the chief, was disappointed. He had grown tired of his manhood journey, and the mysterious fire was the most promising diversion he had discovered thus far. He knew that no one lived in this northern end of the great valley. Even the hunters rarely wandered through here. This was supposed to be a place of spirits.

The young man sighed. His wish was to be home in his village, not in some haunted place. Like every male child born to the valley people, Laughing One had to undergo a series of trials to prove himself worthy of becoming a hunter. This journey was the greatest part of that test, and he had delayed it as long as possible. Already there were grumblings about him among the village elders. The old men understood that young boys were not always eager to take their place as adults. It was far easier to play the hunter near home than to venture alone into the hills and survive there. Yet no other boy in memory had waited as many summers before going as Laughing One had. Wanderer's youngest son had become an embarrassment to the chief.

A pleasant, likable boy, Laughing One appeared content to sit quietly near the men and listen to other hunters' stories. While he often joked with the girls his age, he seemed to feel no need to marry any of them. His mother, Summer Wind, would click her tongue and say that she had never heard of a boy who would not marry, all the while trying hard to hide how pleased she was that her favorite son still stayed near her lodge. Wanderer was gruff, sometimes walking past Laughing One without apparently noticing his son. Yet the chief could rarely keep this up for long. More often he would be seen telling the boy stories about the great hunters he had known. Even the two older brothers were concerned enough to bring Laughing One with them on their hunts. No one else in the village truly minded the boy's slowness to mature. Some women joked about him, but theirs was a friendly kind of laughter.

It was the elders from other villages who had begun to cause trouble over Laughing One. Quietly, but with persistence, they had reminded Wanderer that a chief's son could not be allowed to ignore the ways of his tribe. Wanderer had listened intently, as he always listened when other important people spoke, and soon he had been persuaded. Many days earlier, Laughing One had agreed to make the journey.

Since starting on his own, the young hunter's confidence had grown a great deal. Laughing One had been trained well. His movements attracted little attention, he could throw a spear with deadly accuracy, and he had not gone through a single day without finding food. He was also cautious; never failing to watch where he stepped, and never growing too tired to search for hoof marks or spoor in the cracked soil. His days had been lonely, but without accidents. During this one Moon of the Hunter, he had camped in the depths of nearly silent forests, walked in the shadows of mountains, and wandered alone across their upper slopes, with glacial ice gleaming in the sun overhead. Despite all he had seen, nothing had lured him from his fixed path until now. This simple glimpse of a small camp-fire was somehow more compelling than all the great boulder slides, meltwater rivers, and spiraling slopes.

At this moment, the vapor-covered valley truly looked like a region of the spirit world. Almost anything could be hidden behind those mists. After what had happened the night before, Laughing One was no longer sure what he would find down there. He had heard growling, moaning, shrieks, and something that had sounded like a woman screaming. He was tempted not

to enter this place at all, but the fire he had seen had goaded his
curiosity. What form of spirit needed a hearth to warm itself?

There was only one way to be certain. Holding his spear in
his right hand, Laughing One stepped from the rock and began
to follow a narrow game trail which led downward into the
great valley.

Though the sunlight was already beginning to color the tops
of the taller trees, the lowland areas remained shrouded in damp
ground fog. The leaves alongside the trail Laughing One followed hung limp and dripping in the autumn stillness. As
Laughing One passed through the fog, his eyes became less use-
ful than his other senses. He could hear the calls of orioles,
woodpeckers, and other birds coming like disembodied voices
through the mist. His owns footsteps were nearly silent against
the water-softened ground.

While he walked, Laughing One studied as much as he could
see of the trail ahead, as well as the ground to either side of the
path. He had been with his brothers often enough to understand
the need for caution, especially when traveling alone. Though
Laughing One was well armed by his people's standards, he still
had good reason to avoid the prowling beasts which might be
lurking behind this shadowless fog. The knife that hung around
his neck beside an empty amulet pouch was designed for butchering rather than killing. It was only his stone-tipped spear
which gave him strength. Armed with such a weapon, Laughing
One's brothers could fatally wound a bison while staying a safe
distance away. Even Laughing One, who was still untried at
such things, could hurl his spear across the center of the village
and into the roof of an empty lodge on the opposite side without
trouble.

Though he had not seen anything more threatening than the
droppings and tracks of a porcupine, Laughing One still sensed
danger as he moved through the thick, clinging air. Now that he
was in the more open section of the great valley, with wide
stretches of grass separating the various clumps of trees, he had
expected to feel safer. Instead, he was more blind than before.
The fog kept getting thicker as he continued to move downhill.
It had washed the color from the land, making everything pale
or white. Laughing One did not trust this featureless world.

Laughing One walked through the open grass, hearing the
soft whispering noises it made as the tops of its blades brushed
against his legs, but listening for other sounds. There were no
landmarks to show him direction. Only what he heard and what

he saw on the ground below his feet had meaning. After a while, he came to a place where the grass had been trampled down under the giant, rounded feet of a mastodon. Wrinkles in the huge beast's footpads had left sandlike ridges in its prints. There was only one set of pad marks, for the great beast was walking by itself, but interspersed with the prints were large mounds of dung. Moving closer to one such pile, Laughing One held his left hand out in front of him, his downpointed fingers checking for traces of heat. Though it did not steam in the gray mist, the dung had not cooled completely. Somewhere behind Laughing One, the mastodon still browsed on shrubs and grass. Only the thickness of the fog hid it from view.

Padding swiftly on through shining wet grass, Laughing One soon stumbled upon another hidden creature. The white fog had thickened the air so much that Laughing One was already dangerously close before he noticed a black animal silhouette standing beside a large pine tree. This time the immense head of a long-horned bison emerged from the mist. Laughing One grew quiet at once and stopped moving, but the bison continued rubbing its head and horns against the rough pine bark. Its scraping had already left a light-colored ring around the trunk of the tree.

From the unconcerned indifference of the great animal, Laughing One guessed that it had not discovered him. Its eyesight was poor even on clear days, and the faint morning breeze was blowing Laughing One's scent away from it. Unwilling to risk startling the bison, Laughing One stood motionless for a long while and simply looked at it. Despite the fog, he could see the bison's black head quite clearly, as well as the crinkly brown tufts of hair along its shoulder hump.

After what seemed a long time, the wind shifted slightly, and the bison's mood suddenly changed. It grunted and began to take great whiffs of the damp air into its lungs. The more it sniffed, the louder its grunts became. The bison began to step forward, stiffly and menacingly. It thrust down one foreleg with a driving blow against the ground. Feeling its way forward in the fog like a great blind thing, the bison kept its head low and continued to strike the earth with its front hooves. Laughing One held his breath in an effort to remain motionless, but the agitated snorts of the bison continued getting closer.

In a sudden flash of movement, the bison's tail lifted. A bellowing roar came from its throat. Then it charged.

Laughing One's spear was poised to strike, but the bison was not running at him. Instead, it pivoted around and charged in the opposite direction, smashing its way through a thicket of willow saplings. As the bison crashed off into the fog, Laughing One heard a different sound—one that he recognized instantly. It was the enraged snarl of a saber-toothed tiger.

Laughing One backed away from the noise, trying to understand what had happened. Since the bison had smelled the cat instead of Laughing One, the cat must have been lying in wait inside the willow thicket behind them both. Had the bison not moved first, Laughing One might have stumbled into the cat's ambush.

Sweating despite the chill air, Laughing One stood very still and listened. He could hear the soft padding of the cat's feet as it moved away to his left. The cat was grunting and moaning as it walked, and did not go far before lying down again. Laughing One realized that the animal must be injured.

Once again there was only fog and silence, but Laughing One was far from calm. The cat sounds had left him feeling vulnerable. Few creatures relied on sight more than a human hunter. Only chance and the wind had been in his favor. If he did not move away quickly, the cat might still sense his presence and circle around.

There was one thing which puzzled Laughing One. Had the cat been stalking either the bison or himself, it would not have been lying upwind of them. There had to be some other prey which the saber-toothed tiger had been waiting for. But what prey was weak enough to be hunted by a wounded cat?

Remembering the fire and the woman's scream, Laughing One continued searching the ground for clues.

Since the cat had gone off on his left toward the river, Laughing One backtracked along its trail in the hope of finding some trace of what it had been stalking. He did not take long. On that chilled morning, when every leaf was still wet with mist, the ground remained damp and motionless enough to hold imprints from the day before. Laughing One found a human footprint pressed down among the leafmold. Too big for a child's and too small for a man's, the track could have been made only by a woman.

A moment later, Laughing One realized that he was actually following the trail of two different women. One was taller and lighter than the other, but both moved easily over this soft ground. Judging from the length of their strides, Laughing One guessed that they were young women, unencumbered by heavy loads or the weight of children. The footprints led toward the east. As Laughing One looked in that direction, he saw the blurred shape of the great oak tree gradually becoming more visible through the fading mist. He started walking toward it.

The women he was following had not been clumsy. Their footprints indicated an easy, loping stride, and the short woman's footprints overlapped those of the taller leader. Laughing One was beginning to guess at the women's appearance when a third set of footprints suddenly emerged from the undergrowth and ran alongside those of the humans. They were the pug marks of a great cat; probably the very one that he had heard in the underbrush only a few moments before.

Laughing One was familiar with the saber-toothed tiger's kind. Known for their good eyesight and hearing, these fierce cats were best at ambushing their prey, and could be very dangerous in forested areas near overgrown river shorelines or alongside shallow lakes. While most big cats did not bother human hunters unless provoked, this particular cat was too stupid to be predictable. One of these cats had killed a boy and badly mauled three women from a nearby village. Another had chased a girl from the edge of the river back to the corner of her village before seizing her by the neck and killing her. Aside from these stories, there were many others in which the saber-toothed tiger became the victim. Though the cat's great strength could make it very dangerous if it were stumbled upon by accident, most hunters felt slightly contemptuous of it. The dagger-fanged animals were easily confused by loud noises or unexpected movements. Once startled, they seemed unable to continue their attacks.

As Laughing One moved still closer to the old oak, the cat and human trails merged into one. He had already guessed that the great cat had been stalking the two women. But when he saw its pug marks pressed down over the human footprints, the breath began to come more quickly in his throat. Had he not been certain that the animal was lying up near the river, Laughing One might have turned away. As it was, he stared wonderingly at the huge tree ahead of him.

Something was crouching in one of the lower branches of the old oak.

Moving very slowly, Laughing One approached. He saw the two women as black silhouettes hunched together on the branch. They seemed to be sitting motionless and waiting for the fog to lift. Since their backs were toward him and they were staring off in the direction where the cat still lay hidden, he assumed that they must have heard it snarling as well.

Laughing One was passing under the shadow of the tree's outer branches now, and he paused to study the ground ahead. There were bare places where the grass had been torn up and dirt had been scattered all around.

A high-pitched shout from overhead made him look up. One of the women had seen him. She was gesturing frantically to her companion. The next instant, two dirt-smeared faces stared down at him from the great branch, their eyes wide with excitement.

Laughing One did not move. He stood in the open where the crouching women could see everything he did. Speaking for the first time in many days, he called, "Who are you? Where is your village?"

With the rich tan color of their bodies nearly lost amid the green and brown of autumn leaves, the actions of the women were difficult to follow. Both were trying to talk now, but their words came out as a garble of noises. Though Laughing One listened intently to the light, rolling sound of their voices, the words meant nothing to him. Their talk sounded like the pulse of a repeating chant—"*Ahiyahi yiahyiah ahe ah ah*"—repeated over and over again. Still, the two appeared so obviously glad to see him that the young hunter felt flattered. Stirred by their eagerness, he smiled up into their worried faces. Then he tried to reassure them that the cat was no longer close by.

To Morning Land and White Bird, Laughing One's speech was also puzzling. Shocked to see anyone in this wild place, they had not thought of any plan to make themselves understood.

From the movements of their hands, Laughing One guessed that the two women were trying to warn him about the cat. They seemed anxious to have him join them on the branch. Rather than stay alone under that dark tree, Laughing One obliged. He slipped his spear under the strap that supported his weapons' pouch and scrambled up the trunk much as White Bird had done the day before. In a few moments he was perched on a nearby branch, studying the two girls.

It was not an easy moment for the Tideland sisters. The effects of their ordeal showed. Morning Land's face was streaked with layers of tears, dirt, and sweat that partially disguised the delicacy of her features. Her eyes seemed unnaturally large and strained as they looked up at the hunter, and the skin was red around them. The black hair clinging to her head and neck in a matted tangle added to the impression of wretchedness. She looked tired, and at this moment she seemed much older to Laughing One than she really was. White Bird's face was nearly hidden completely under her dangling hair, and she was happy to keep it that way. She knew she must look even worse than her sister. She was also aware that they both smelled heavily of sweat and urine. It shamed her.

Hiding her own fears, Morning Land crept along the branch in the direction of the stranger. She came forward smiling and nodding her head, not bothering to talk for the moment. The only sound Laughing One heard was the soft rustle of the small leather apron around her waist. Laughing One drew back a little as Morning Land came near, and this seemed to convince her that he was harmless, for she crouched down so close to him that he could have grabbed her if he had wished.

For a long moment the two simply stared at each other. Then Morning Land smiled, placed her finger against her chest; and said her name. To Laughing One, it sounded as if she were saying, *"Ir-yah-i-yah-ee."* She had to repeat it many times before he was able to pronounce the sound himself, and while he understood that it was her name, he was not at all sure he would be able to remember it.

"Laughing One," he said, touching his own chest.

Morning Land repeated what she had heard. *"Tua-arikii."*

When she felt she had it right, Morning Land smiled politely and lowered her head a little. Though she did not appear to be staring at him, Laughing One sensed that she was studying him very carefully. After another pause, Morning Land pointed to her sister and said, "White Bird," which, to Laughing One, sounded like *"Yi-quay-is."*

Frustrated, Laughing One continued to ask questions. "Where are your people? Have you been here alone for very long? Why do you sit up here instead of down by your fire?"

Morning Land cocked her head attentively while he spoke, trying to make sense out of his words. Then she smiled at him and shrugged. As Laughing One watched, she turned to her companion and began a hurried conversation. Though he still could not understand anything which they said, Laughing One found the sweet, high sound of the women's voices pleasant to listen to. He did not know whether it was the musical tones of their language that lulled him or simply the fact that he was

with people again, but for the first time in many days he felt
happy.

"Ehnn. What is this man? Is this someone who will help us?
Why does he refuse to talk? He is only grunting."

The complaining tone had come back into White Bird's voice
again. Her excitement at seeing Laughing One was beginning to
fade now that she realized he was not part of a hunting party.
She also hated having him stare at her. It reminded her of how
dirty and ugly she felt. Her hair itched terribly, her eyes were
almost swollen shut from crying, and her legs felt as if all the
muscles in her thighs had cramps. Worst of all was the thirst she
had.

Morning Land had already tried unsuccessfully to comfort
her sister. Now all she could do was be patient, and even that
was becoming a strain.

"*Shaa henaki,* senseless one. We talk in our voice and he
talks in his. They are not the same."

"What can we say that he will hear?" White Bird pouted. "I
do not want to sit in this tree any longer. We should go back to
his village. He is too young to have a wife already. Perhaps he
will want to put us inside his hut."

Morning Land spoke softly, but with a sureness that had always given her authority over her sister. "If he is young, there
are others who will tell him what to do," she said. "If we go to
his village, other men will take us. This boy cannot help. We
mean nothing to him."

"How can you sit in this tree and refuse?" White Bird asked
incredulously. "The pain we feel now is only going to grow
worse. We need hunters to protect us. You must talk to him
again."

Morning Land looked doubtful, but she nodded and turned
back to face Laughing One.

Leaning forward, Morning Land began pointing to the various
things around her—branches, leaves, grass—and giving the Tideland name for each. Laughing One pronounced every new word
until she was content he had it right, then gave his own people's
name for the same object. Morning Land did her best to mimic the
young hunter's words, but found the clipped, guttural sound of
them difficult. Her people spoke in a smooth, rolling manner, with
the words tending to slide into one another. Laughing One's tribe
was more abrupt. Their words often ended unexpectedly in sudden
silences. While all of this would help eventually, for the moment

it left the girls little better off than they had been before. At last
Morning Land shrugged her shoulders in despair and turned to
White Bird.

"Shiiwe!" Morning Land sighed. "It is nothing. He is trying
to learn our talk, but something refuses to work. I am too tired
to go on."

Frustrated, White Bird turned her anger against the young
hunter. "I do not like the way he is just sitting," she grumbled.
"He is rude to stare at us. Does he refuse to help?"

Realizing that they could not afford to offend the stranger
with a show of bad temper, Morning Land tried to calm her sister. "He refuses nothing," she said softly. "I do not know how
to ask him. If we had food, I would take some and give it to
him, but we have nothing. Perhaps he thinks we are the rude
ones."

There was a pause, during which all three people in the tree
just stared at one another. Then Laughing One developed a
plan. No longer speaking, he lifted his right hand and pointed to
himself. Then, clenching the hand into a fist, he held it in front
of his chest and slowly moved it downward. Lastly he flattened
out the hand and made a waving motion.

"Why are his hands moving without stopping?" White Bird
asked irritably.

But Morning Land understood. Ignoring her sister, she leaned
forward once more and repeated the signal, her arm trembling
with excitement. The hunter responded with further gestures.

White Bird clutched at her sister's leg. "Have you started to
talk?" she asked eagerly. "What has he told you?"

"I understand a little," Morning Land replied. "His people do
not live near this place."

"This waiting is ruining me!" White Bird moaned. "Where
are his people? What have you been talking about?"

"Atoshe!" Morning Land snapped. "In the name of our
mother, be quiet now. I must learn what I can."

More carefully made hand gestures and movements followed
as Morning Land and Laughing One tried to understand each
other. There was some stumbling and uncertainty, for the signs
their people used were not entirely alike, but the basic meanings
gradually became clear.

Unable to read sign language and afraid to interrupt her sister
again, White Bird spent the time studying the young hunter. He
seemed nearly as tall as Morning Land, but his shoulders were
not as broad as those of the men she was used to and his arms

appeared too thin to have much strength in them. Strangest of all was his shoulder-length hair. No Tideland hunter would ever have let his hair grow so long. The young man's features seemed normal enough, and there was a kindness in his dark eyes which White Bird liked, even though his speech was frightening to her. She remembered how pleasant his smile had seemed when he had first looked up at them. Suddenly she felt a need to have him smile at her again.

At last Morning Land nodded at the stranger and turned to White Bird again. "He has not seen his village for many days," she said quietly. "His people are far away from here."

White Bird was bewildered. She stared at her sister blankly while the tears began to build around her eyes again. "The cat is going to kill us," she decided. "It will still be here when this hunter has gone away to his people. What can we do against it ourselves?"

"We will have nothing," Morning Land agreed.

This admission on the part of her sister had a strangely calming effect on White Bird. It was over, then. Help was not coming after all. Once she admitted it to herself, she found she could bear the idea. They were no worse off than they had been before. In a hushed voice she asked, "Why does this person walk by himself? What was he doing under this tree?"

"He left his parents' village for a reason I do not understand," Morning Land answered. "He will go back when this moon is finished with. We could follow him there."

White Bird studied her sister's face. "You are afraid to go to this stranger's village," she decided.

Morning Land shrugged. "He is the only man left to us," she said quietly. "If we go to his people, we will have food to eat and skins to wear."

"How can we possibly follow him?" White Bird asked. "The cat will come before another night is over. It will strike us here." White Bird touched the back of her neck. "It will kill all of us."

"Shaa henaki," Morning Land grunted. "He is a hunter and he has a spear. He saw the cat's trail and heard it moving, a long way from this place. He knows its ways."

"What can he do by himself against that cat?" White Bird demanded.

"We will help him."

As Morning Land began to make the hand signals again,

White Bird watched her carefully, trying to understand what was being said.

Laughing One was becoming impatient. It was uncomfortable enough sitting on the branch and trying to make hand signals at the same time, but the women made it worse by stopping in the middle of things and talking between themselves. There was something else that upset him as well. The longer he watched the two girls, the more he sensed their helplessness. He already guessed that they had been abandoned by their people, and from the way they crouched close together like two frightened fox cubs it was obvious they were unused to being alone. He would have to help them now, which meant that their weaknesses became his. By himself, Laughing One felt confident that he could outwit any wounded saber-toothed tiger, but with two badly frightened women to care for, his chances were lessened.

The older woman was signaling him again, and the younger one craned her neck to watch. Laughing One could wait no longer. Gesturing for the women to follow him, he climbed back out of the tree.

Laughing One was already squatting beside the smoldering ashes of the girls' hearth when he realized that the two had not moved. Glancing up, he saw both women still crouched on the branch overhead, staring down at him just as they had done when he had first arrived. Laughing One repeated his hand signal, making it clear that they were to climb down and join him. The older woman shook her head.

"Kai! (Come down)" Laughing One ordered, pointing to the ground.

Still the woman shook her head. Laughing One felt like shouting at her, but instead he simply shrugged and turned his back on the girls. He had more important things to do. The hearth had almost burned out, and unless the coals could be fanned quickly there would be no flame left. Laughing One had the tools for making fire, but it was always easier to stir up one which had already been lit. Ignoring the excited jabbering of the women behind him, he started to gather tinder and dried wood.

By the time Laughing One had the hearth burning again, Morning Land had made up her mind to climb down. She moved very cautiously, for she felt stiff and was worried that her legs might suddenly cramp. When she at last dropped to the ground, her legs did double up under her, making her fall awkwardly onto her buttocks. She got up hurriedly, breathing fast

and almost crinking her neck as she glanced around. Laughing
One turned when he heard her fall and watched her. While
Morning Land moved her feet to ease the tingling in her legs,
she tried to return Laughing One's stare. It did not work. For
some reason, the young hunter's eyes made her nervous. She
quickly turned away and began talking to White Bird.

White Bird flinched at the thought of going out onto the open
grass again. Despite Morning Land's attempts to calm her, she
refused to move. She remained on the branch, with her hands
and voice trembling, looking very small and very lost. Morning
Land felt pity for her young sister. It was rare when White Bird
gave in to her fear like this.

Unwilling to waste more time arguing, Morning Land asked
White Bird to throw down their digging sticks and stone choppers. A moment later, these tools thumped down heavily at
Morning Land's feet. As she picked them up and turned to walk
toward the river, Morning Land sensed that Laughing One was
still watching her.

The young hunter had been startled when he had seen Morning Land standing erect for the first time. He had not realized
until then how beautifully formed she was. As she walked past
him with her quiet, easy stride, Laughing One suddenly understood that this was not an ordinary woman. Despite the dirt and
sweat, she moved with a suppleness that would have made his
brother's wife, Beautiful Star, clench-toothed with jealousy. For
the first time, Laughing One began to think about what would
happen if he were to bring such a woman back to his village.
She was someone the men would fight over. With an instinctive
understanding of his people's ways, Laughing One knew that he
would never be allowed to keep such a woman. Half wild and
unable to speak their language, this girl would still end up as
the bride of some important person. He could have no part in
her future.

As Morning Land disappeared from view behind a willow
thicket, Laughing One again became aware of just how far from
his village they still were. The veldt suddenly seemed more
lonely than it had during all the other days of his solitary journey. These shy, quiet-voiced women depended on him for protection from the saber-toothed tiger, and—not for the first
time—Laughing One doubted his ability to do what was
needed. He missed the companionship and advice of his brothers. Fighting Eagle would have known what to do. Laughing
One's eldest brother had once fought with a plains lion and

lived. Fighting Eagle had killed a quagga horse, and the lion had followed after him, lured by the smell of meat. When Fighting Eagle had stooped to butcher the quagga horse, the lion had attacked. Their battle had been short and vicious. After wounding the lion with his spear, Fighting Eagle had been forced to finish the fight with his stone knife. Fighting Eagle had lost his left thumb to the lion's jaws, and there were long claw scars all across his shoulders and back, but he was the only man in all their tribe who had ever faced down a great cat and lived. Now it seemed that Laughing One would be forced to do the same.

Laughing One decided to take a closer look at the marks around the trunk of the oak tree. He knew the other woman was watching him. He could hear the branch creaking under her weight as she changed position when he came near. Briefly, he glanced up into her worried face.

"*Anata* [shy one]," he said, and smiled. Then he remembered her name. "*Yi-quay-is,*" he added, and pointed to the ground. The girl did not respond.

After that, he ignored her. The marks on the tree held his complete attention. Laughing One noticed a torn piece of rough bark, touched it gently with his fingers, and felt it break away under the pressure. The cat's claws had gouged the wood in many places, and their marks showed how close the cat had come to reaching the girls. Laughing One then studied the cat's pug marks on the ground beneath the tree. They indicated where the animal had crouched before each spring, and where it had fallen back to earth again after jumping at the branch.

The young hunter tried to remember more of what he had been told about these dagger-toothed cats. Two summers before, his other brother, Trusted Friend, had witnessed a struggle between a saber-toothed tiger and a ground sloth. The cat had been young, more stupid than most. No other creature, not even the giant bear, would have been foolish enough to face the huge claws of a grown sloth. The sloth had been three times as large as the saber-toothed tiger and had shown no fear when the cat had come snarling out of the bushes. It had simply sat on its great stub tail and opened its enormous arms.

For a while the cat had circled, trying to catch the sloth off guard, but the sloth had only turned with it. At last the frustrated cat had simply attacked.

From his place in a nearby tree, Trusted Friend had not seen the actual lunge. To him it had seemed as if the two bodies had simply joined in a dreadful embrace. While the cat had driven its long teeth into the sloth's throat, the claws of the sloth had ripped down onto the saber-toothed tiger's back. In a few moments, both animals had died.

A creature this determined would not be frightened away by fire or a barricade of branches. Nor did it seem likely that the women could travel fast enough to outdistance it. Laughing One knew he would have to kill the cat. During the many nights when he had sat around campfires listening to hunting stories, Laughing One had learned a great deal, but most of the talk had been about ways of avoiding the big cats. Laughing One had been trained to be alert for cat signs and had been told what to do if he met one by accident. None of his fellow villagers had expected him to actively seek out and kill a saber-toothed tiger.

Fighting Eagle had once said that a cat could be bluffed or distracted by sudden unexpected sounds. Objects thrown into nearby bushes or meat dropped in front of a cat unexpectedly could make the animal pause long enough for a hunter to hurl his spear. The spear, Fighting Eagle had insisted, was the only good weapon for fighting with a cat when it was on open ground. If the animal got close enough to pit its muscles against those of a man, the human hunter would soon be torn apart.

Laughing One did not have time to hunt down a deer or quagga horse to serve as bait. The best he could do would be to fashion himself another spear. There were spare spear blades in the weapons' pouch he carried across his back, but he would have to find and trim a sapling to make the spear shaft. This would be difficult, since chopping down saplings took time, and he had only his knife to work with. Somewhat reluctantly, Laughing One approached a nearby bush and began tentatively slicing at the wood with his blade. It was slow work. The fine-edged knife had been designed for stripping carcasses and skinning hides, not hacking wood. If Laughing One struck too hard with it, the blade would snap.

White Bird was guilt-stricken. After watching Morning Land walk boldly down to the river and after seeing this stranger carefully examining the cat's pug marks in the ground, White Bird realized how cowardly she must appear. The longer she watched the young man's ineffectual attempts to hack down a sapling, the more she realized that her help was needed.

Without bothering to decide further, White Bird began coming down from the branch. Compared with the way she had climbed into the tree the day before, White Bird's movements now were painfully awkward. Her legs were cramped, and even her hands were slow to respond. Halfway down the trunk she lost her grip and flopped down heavily onto the ground.

Fortunately, the jolt was painful but not damaging, and there was no one watching. Laughing One glanced up when he heard the noise of her fall, but quickly turned back to his work. Morning Land was still away in the river, somewhere out of sight. Unobserved, White Bird stretched her arms and legs for a moment, marveling at how good it felt. She had an urge to run to the river and splash in it until all the sweat and dirt had been swept from her skin. Instead, she walked over quietly to where Laughing One was still making a valiant attempt to hack apart a bush.

It was not until White Bird was standing in his light that Laughing One looked up at her. He was slightly surprised to find she had come down from the tree after all. When she pointed to the stone chopper which she held in her hand, Laughing One frowned. Curious, he stood back and watched while White Bird began cutting. She worked with the deftness of someone who had spent a lifetime preparing hut frames, and her skill was appreciated. In a short while, she had cut and stripped three shaft-sized poles. Laughing One smiled at her as she gave them to him, and White Bird felt a glow of pleasure.

But now other things needed doing. While Laughing One brought the wooden shafts back to the fire, White Bird slipped unobtrusively behind the willow bushes and headed for the river.

The three shafts White Bird had given Laughing One had been cut from the stems of young aspen trees, and were straight enough to be made into workable spears. Laughing One hefted each of them, testing to see which was straightest and which was the most evenly balanced. The feel of the wooden shafts under his fingers helped to reassure him. Two could be made into good weapons.

Sitting near the fire, Laughing One began to strip the poles and get them ready for hafting. He used his knife to chop and hack the ends of the shafts into the rough shapes of good spears. When his knife became clogged with wet sap or bits of wood, he cleaned the blade by brushing it against the callus-hardened heel of his right foot. With much squinting and cocking of his head, he whittled down the front of each shaft, shaving it smooth and cutting out a deep notch in which he would eventually wedge the stone spear point. When he grew tired, Laughing One paused long enough to pull several lumps of pine resin out of his weapons' pouch and place them on top of the warm hearth stones. The heat-softened resin would become gluelike once it hardened again and would help keep the stone points firmly wedged onto the shafts.

As he worked, Laughing One listened uneasily. Though the grove was silent, he could hear splashing off to his left. The sounds were mixed with the soft murmur of female voices.

For a moment, Laughing One's knife fumbled as it moved over the wood. The thought of the women down at the river unnerved him. He did not understand why they had suddenly changed from being afraid to even leave the tree to have no caution at all. Had he been able to speak their language, he would have called to them. As it was, he could only grumble and shake his head.

White Bird returned just as Laughing One was preparing to fasten on the stone spear points. With her long hair dripping from a plunge in the river and her collecting basket piled high with cattail rootstalks, she walked comfortably, her hips gently swaying back and forth. The young girl sighed as she felt the cool breeze on her drying skin. Laughing One could not know that it was his own apparent sureness which had given her such confidence. As she approached the oak tree, White Bird glanced around eagerly for the young hunter who had made her sleeping place safe. When she saw the dark red stone points spill out of Laughing One's weapons' pouch, she held her breath in wonder. Carefully, not wanting to disturb his work, White Bird approached the fire and squatted down.

Laughing One glanced up as she knelt beside him with her basket, but he said nothing. White Bird felt giddy and self-conscious in front of this serious boy. For something to do, she began to pluck the cattail roots out of her basket, pretending to study each one of them before dropping it onto the grass beside her. She was really watching the stone spear blades as Laughing One fingered them casually in his hands. Taking one of the softened resin blocks, Laughing One squeezed its paste along the front of a spear shaft, using a stiff blade of grass to spread the resin evenly around the hafting notch. After the front of the shaft had been coated, he picked up one of the red stone points and smeared sticky resin along its base as well. The point fitted exactly into the wooden notch. Laughing One bound it in position with a bit of coiled sinew, which had also been kept in his weapons' pouch. Since the sinew had dried, he was forced to lick it until it softened again. When the sinew was manageable, he wound it around the blunt end of the spear blade and the wooden splice, pulling the sinew in quick jerks until it was tied tightly. Finally he began to rotate the spear in his hands. As he did so, he sighted along its length to check for straightness.

White Bird stared at all of this as if she thought the hunter might vanish were she to even blink. None of the men in her own tribe could have made such a weapon, yet Laughing One did it easily, almost casually. White Bird wanted to touch the magical spear, but was afraid this might anger the young man. Instead, she let her hands twitch in her lap and tried to pronounce his name.

"Tua-arikii."

Laughing One smiled at her. With a series of gestures, he tried to explain what he was doing. White Bird did not understand any of it, but she nodded and smiled anyway.

As he worked on the second spear, Laughing One watched the young girl in front of him. He looked at her hands and her breasts and the rounded curve of her hips; decided she was not so beautiful as her companion and was glad of it. A woman who was not too beautiful might get a young husband instead of being married to some village elder. Laughing One might even be able to claim her for himself.

The idea was somehow appealing. He liked the dark warmness in White Bird's eyes, the way her black hair kept shifting in the autumn wind, the small beads of water that dripped down onto her softly moving breasts. Most of all he liked the eagerness with which she watched him. Her body did not move with the undulations and provoking twitches of Beautiful Star, but though this girl did not try to arouse, she did.

When Morning Land returned with a second basket of cattail roots, she saw her sister sitting attentively across from the stranger. She did not understand why, but the sight angered her. With a sharp, commanding tone, she told White Bird to begin pounding her roots.

The expression on Morning Land's face startled White Bird and made her blush. With a shrug, she hurried over.

Laughing One frowned as he watched White Bird scrambling to join her sister. He did not like the harsh sound in Morning Land's voice, and he disapproved of the way White Bird jumped to obey. For a moment, he glared at Morning Land, but she returned his stare with a cool, evaluating glance of her own.

Grumbling, Laughing One went back to fastening his spear points.

Oblivious of the tension between her two companions, White Bird quickly began pounding the cattail roots into an edible mush. This was cooked without ceremony, scooped into some empty clam shells the girls had found, and given out. White Bird saved the largest portion for Laughing One, who nodded appreciatively and smiled at her once more. Without understanding the reason, White Bird felt happier than she had in days.

As he ate the nearly flavorless paste, Laughing One listened to the hurried and still incomprehensible talk between the two women. They were much less shy with him now, and already he could see a difference in their personalities. The younger sister, the one he called *Yi-quay-is,* was more emotional and chattered excitedly in a high voice that seemed very pleasant. From the food she had offered him and the gentle way she said his name, he sensed a friendship building between them. The other woman was much colder. Her words rolled out as evenly as her sister's, but whenever he looked over at her there was a sudden silence. She watched him warily, her face showing distrust.

Laughing One's interest in the two women kept him from noticing the changing light and coolness in the grove around them until the meal was finished. The breeze was now strong enough to cause a rustling in the leaves overhead, and the midday heat had already gone. For a moment, Laughing One enjoyed the wind, feeling it send a tingling coolness over his skin. Then he remembered that if it were cooler here, it would also be cooler in the brush where the cat was lying. Laughing One had expected the cat to stay in one place through the hottest part of the day. Now that the air was cooler, the animal would begin to move again.

The women were still talking when Laughing One heard a soft scratching sound, not unlike the scuffling of a squirrel hurrying over dried leaves. Laughing One felt himself stiffen at the noise. It came from the bushes behind him. Though he continued to hold the clam shell and swirl the paste with his fingers, his mind was now intent on listening.

Then a branch snapped in a different place, and Laughing One thought he heard animal breathing. The girls' talk covered most other sounds.

Laughing One turned his head slowly and stared at the thicket, trying to sense what was hidden behind those shivering leaves. He set the half-empty clam shell and reached for his favorite spear.

When she saw him move, White Bird stopped talking. One look at Laughing One's tensely poised figure was enough to make her grab at Morning Land's right arm. The two women sat rigid, unsure of what to do next.

Without turning his head to see if they understood, Laughing One slowly lifted his free hand and pointed back toward the tree.

Morning Land was the first to react. Taking hold of White Bird's left hand, she hurried her sister toward the trunk of the oak tree. White Bird was still confused, but felt a familiar surge of panic rising in her as she stumbled after Morning Land. Her legs, arms, and body all knew what to do even without her thinking about it. As soon as they were near the trunk, White Bird leapt up and grabbed the rough bark with both hands. Her legs found a foothold and began pushing her higher and higher, faster and faster, until she was scurrying like a squirrel up into the sheltering leaves, Morning Land grabbed one of her stone choppers, held it in her mouth, and followed her sister.

Trying to seem calm, Laughing One gathered up the two newly finished spears in his left hand. His most trusted weapon remained poised for throwing. When he had all three wooden shafts in his grip, he began to back toward the trunk of the oak tree. Beside him, the hearth fire continued to crackle in the afternoon wind. A lot of his tools were still on the ground, including the coils of sinew, the lumps of resin, the unfinished shaft, and the two stone spear blades. Laughing One would have to leave them.

Laughing One doubted that he would be able to reach the branch before the cat attacked. His feet felt clumsy and slow on the grass, though the rest of his body was keenly alert. The sweaty feel of his hands as they clutched the wooden shafts, the smell of pine smoke from the fire, and even the twitching of individual leaves on the bush he was staring at were all vividly imprinted in his mind.

When at last he stood with his back to the trunk of the tree, he hesitated. Laughing One did not want to turn away from the bush, but he had to do so in order to climb the tree.

A noise from above made him glance up. Morning Land was leaning far over the edge of the branch and reaching down with both arms. She was calling to him, but he had no way of knowing what she wanted. Instead, he handed her the two new spears, one at a time. Morning Land took these weapons readily enough, but she continued calling and pointing to some object on the ground. It was White Bird's stone chopper. Laughing One crouched down, grabbed it, and tossed it up to her. He was surprised at how easily Morning Land caught the flying stone blade. Finally, still hesitant, he handed her his best and last spear.

At this instant, when he was unarmed, fear took over. Laughing One scrambled up the side of the tree, scrabbling and ripping at the bark with his fingers. He heard a hollow thudding in the grove behind him and moved still faster, half expecting to feel the cat claws digging at his legs and pulling him earthward again.

In a moment he was up on the branch and safe. He slumped, gasping, against the trunk, the huff, huff, huff of his own breathing blocking out everything else. When he could listen again, he realized that the creature in the grove below was moving the other way. Its feet made a heavy shuffling noise very different from the soft padding of a cat. It was a porcupine, not the saber-toothed tiger, which had been hidden by the bushes.

As the realization came, Laughing One's chest shook with a soundless, humorless laughter. There had been no cat there at all! Nothing dangerous stalking them. Nothing running after him. There was no cat under the tree. He had frightened these women for nothing.

Ashamed to look at the two sisters, Laughing One stayed at the thickest part of the branch and squatted there with his shoulders hunched over. His weapons' pouch had opened during his frantic climb, spilling all that was left of his tools onto the ground. His precious spear thrower was somewhere below on the grass, but he was not ready to climb down and look for it. At least his spears were safe.

Laughing One would not look at the women, but after a few moments he felt a gentle touch on his right shoulder. It was White Bird. The sympathy in her eyes showed that his fear had reminded her of her own. It made him vulnerable and human like herself and she liked him better because of it. Morning Land's thinking had gone slightly further. She recognized Laughing One's fear, but she had also seen the way he had tried to guard the women's retreat into the tree. No Tideland man would have done as much for strangers. Morning Land found herself beginning to like this awkward young hunter. As he looked over at her, she smiled. Only much later would Laughing One realize how rare that expression was for her.

The three young people continued to sit quietly, taking great comfort in each other's closeness. Each of the sisters held one of Laughing One's makeshift spears. He had intended to bring some stones for throwing, but had forgotten everything in his sudden panic. Now he noticed the girls' stone choppers. With halting hand gestures, he indicated that they should throw these into nearby bushes when the cat approached. The unexpected noise might be enough to confuse the animal. Finally, with his own prized weapon firmly gripped in his right hand, the hunter took up a watching position at the thick end of the branch.

The wind which had worried him so much before now caused a shivering sensation along his back. Just as Laughing One was wishing for a fur to wrap around his shoulders, White Bird rubbed up against him. Morning Land joined her a moment later, for the three had only body warmth to protect them against the growing chill of the fall night. Soothed by the closeness of the two women beside him and by the musical hum of their voices as they talked quietly between themselves, Laughing One began to drowse.

CHAPTER FOUR

Face In The Shadows

As twilight settled in around them, Laughing One found it more and more difficult to stay alert. Whenever he caught himself starting to doze, he would straighten his back, flex the muscles of his spear arm, and search the ground below. As a way of keeping awake, he listened to the murmuring talk of the two women, but their language seemed like random babbling, and in his tiredness their words blurred together. After a few moments, he would begin to drift again. The warmth of White Bird's side and leg next to his reminded him of the campfires he had huddled around at home, and her musical voice was not unlike his mother's singing.

He was only jolted into wakefulness when White Bird suddenly shifted position beside him. As she moved away, a chill gust of air swept along his thigh, making his whole body shiver.

The girl had heard something. Laughing One saw her hunch close against her sister, her eyes staring off at some hidden point in the shadows. When Laughing One tried to follow her gaze, he suddenly realized how dark it had become. Out on the grasslands, the last faint colors of sunset were vanishing behind the mountains. Laughing One jerked his head around. Even with the fire down below, he could not see much beyond the edge of the tree's outer branches. He could not hear much either, for the wind rushed through the tree with a trembling force that ruffled the hair along his neck and caused the oak leaves to slap back against the branches in a steady rustling. With the wind deadening his ears as much as the darkness dimmed his eyesight, it would be easy for the cat to approach unnoticed.

Though he doubted that the girls had heard the cat, Laughing One slowly got back into a crouching posture. His neck felt stiff, and his arms tingled from having been too long in one position. Laughing One started to move them back and forth, hunching and shrugging until the muscles began to flex easily once more.

The world beneath the tree was one of bushes and shadows. With the rising wind twisting branches, tree shadows swung back and forth across the open grass. The same wind had nearly quelled their fire, which was already little more than flaming embers. Even the white smoke trails that rose up from it were scattered by sudden gusts.

A black shape moved among the shadows, slipping by silently at the very edge of the ring of firelight. It seemed deliberate in its slowness, moving with a willed calm. A moment later it appeared again—on Laughing One's right this time. The animal submerged back into the blackness almost at once, but not before Laughing One had guessed what it was. He knew the saber-toothed tiger was circling around to the dark side of the tree.

The two women had seen the hulking shape as well. Like Laughing One, they peered down cautiously, listening for the soft padding of approaching footsteps but hearing only the wind. Rigidly, with the spears clutched in their hands, the sisters forced themselves to wait.

Laughing One was the first to notice the scraping sound of sharp claws scratching against bark. It was followed by a low snarl which seemed to come from somewhere directly below. Unable to see anything, Laughing One tried to imagine what the cat might be doing. His questions were answered a moment later when he felt the solid thud of something heavy bounding against the tree. The cat was attempting to leap for the branch once more.

With the first jolting impact, White Bird shrieked and dropped the spear Laughing One had given her. The weapon rattled against the branch for an instant, then fell into the darkness. Morning Land held onto her spear, but she had slumped forward onto the branch with a muffled sob.

The cat circled around the front of the tree and sprang again, its claws grappling for a hold on the splintering bark. The second jump it made was better than the first, and brought the cat to within a hand's stretch of the branch. As she felt the branch shake beneath her, White Bird covered her face with her hands and screamed. Laughing One recognized the sound as the spirit voice he had heard the night before.

In the moonless dark, the leaping animal seemed ghostlike, disappearing into the shadows the instant each jump was done. Huge and black though it might be, Laughing One had little hope of hitting such a target. Instead, he found himself listening

for the cat. From the heavy thud of its impacts, he tried to guess
how high the animal had gotten. After a while he realized that,
despite its determination, the beast was losing ground. Though
its paws banged against the tree bark, the branch the humans
crouched on had not been harmed.

Abruptly the cat broke off—growling and panting—snapping
its long teeth angrily. The branch stopped moving and the wind
suddenly became the loudest sound again. The firelight had
grown so faint that Laughing One could not tell whether the
beast had stayed in place below them or had moved back into
the surrounding brush. He only knew that there was a pause.

The young hunter looked to see what had happened to the
two women. White Bird was sobbing and shaking, with her face
still hidden. He could expect nothing from her. He cursed himself for having given her one of his spears. Now it was lying
useless down in the grass.

Morning Land was hunched protectively over White Bird.
While her left hand held the spear, her right arm was wrapped
across her sister's shuddering back. After a moment she felt
Laughing One touch her and turned to face him. Frightened and
vulnerable though she was, she yet had sense enough to offer
Laughing One the spear she held. He motioned her hand away,
indicating that it was something else he wanted. Slowly she remembered how he had asked them to throw their stone choppers
at the cat. She gave him the one she had fastened to her waist
skirt.

For what seemed a long while, the two strangers stared at
each other. Apart from the wind, the only sounds in the tree
were White Bird's broken whimpers. Then a thick, muffled
growling announced that the cat was approaching once more.

The beast was so occupied with its elusive prey that it did not
seem to mind or notice the nearness of the crackling hearth.
Laughing One watched in wonder as the black form slowly
stalked out into the firelight. It was the first time he had really
seen the creature and he was impressed by its size. The cat
walked unconcernedly past hot coals that would have frightened
off bears or wolves or almost any other animal. The low growl
continued to rise up steadily from its chest as its wide paws
padded quietly over the grass. It made no effort to conceal itself
now. Supremely confident in its strength, it had simply come to
kill the two women and the boy who was with them.

Even in the dim half light of the fire, Laughing One noticed the limping right leg and the stump of a wooden digging stick wedged deep into the hump of the cat's muscular shoulders.

After a moment the cat leaped at them.

Laughing One watched it coming; saw the great yellowed fangs flaring beneath its wet muzzle. When its face was so close that he could stare straight into its eyes, he jabbed down hard with his spear.

The stone blade sliced across the cat's face. It missed the eye Laughing One had aimed for by less than a finger length and ripped open the skin on the one side of the animal's jaw.

The cat shuddered with the sudden jolt of pain, then toppled back toward the ground, spitting fury. Blood streamed from the new wound in its face, making its muzzle look mangled. Angry grunts and snarls filled the darkness.

As the cat hissed and wailed its fury down below him, Laughing One reached for the stone chopper. It was hard and heavy in his grip. With a yell, he pulled back his left arm and hurled the stone blade out into the night. It crashed its way down through the leaves and landed at the edge of a nearby bush.

The cat staggered back at the unexpected sound. It let out a surprised huff and turned its head to search for the intruder. At that moment, the light of the dying fire was reflected back as a red glow in the saber-toothed tiger's eyes.

Laughing One threw his spear.

Aimed by instinct as much as sight, the spear darted through the darkness so quickly that the cat had no warning of it until the instant before it struck. The sudden flicker of movement at the corner of the cat's eye was enough to make it start to turn, but there was no time for crouching down or leaping aside. The stone blade entered the soft flesh at the base of the cat's neck and sliced into the vulnerable organs of its chest. The animal crumpled under the shock of this deep wound, spinning about and whipping at air with its claws. It hissed, rolled, and thrashed, pressing its back against the grass, screaming and shrieking against the thing that had come so dangerously close to its heart.

From his place on the branch, Laughing One stared at the cat and willed it to die. He knew his strike had been good. The beast could not live with such a wound. It could not.

Yet, down below, the cat kept moving.

The cat spat, clawed, and snarled. It wrestled with the spear, trying to force away the deadly blade. While its jaws snapped and chewed at the wooden shaft, a choking bubbling came from its throat. The cat did not sound like an animal anymore. Its moans were human, womanlike—a tormented crying far worse than anything Laughing One had imagined.

Suddenly it was over. The cat's shuddering fury ended with the spear shaft snapping in half. Having shed the outer part of the weapon, the saber-toothed tiger staggered up onto its feet and began to limp off. Laughing One had a final glimpse of the animal moving away weakly into the darkness as if it had been kicked by something far heavier than itself. For another moment he could hear the animal's footsteps shuffling through the long grass. Then the wind covered that sound as well.

The young hunter sat back, panting. His stomach felt sick and his arms ached, but he and the sisters were safe. The cat would be dead by morning. Then he could take the two women and leave this place. Laughing One turned to look at the sisters. They were still huddled together, but the sobbing and crying had stopped. Instead, both were staring back at him. He wished he could tell them that there was no longer any reason to be afraid, but it was too dark for hand gestures and his words meant nothing to them. For a while he continued to sit apart.

The night was restless. Above the wind, wolves could be heard on the other side of the river. The squalling of some frightened animal accompanied their yelps. Then both moved away. Farther off, the bellow of a much larger creature disrupted the silence again. Laughing One's battle with the saber-toothed tiger had been only a small intrusion in this nighttime world of the savannah.

The full moon was finally beginning to show in the east; its light sparkling across the tops of shivering branches. The well-spaced trees and the open grassland beyond them were suddenly visible in the pale light. It was a cold moon, surrounded by wind-chased clouds. The same cold wind swept across Laughing One's back. He could not stay there by himself. He needed the women's warmth if he were to survive the chill of the night without a fire.

Laughing One hugged his arms against his chest and pantomimed a man suffering from cold. His shivers were only half acted, but the message was clear. Then he pointed to the two women and gestured for them to come close. To his surprise and relief, they responded.

Morning Land released her hold on White Bird and crawled toward the hunter. It was obvious from the way she kept both knees on the branch and felt her way forward with her hands that she expected to be jolted at any moment. Nevertheless, she did not stop until she was at the hunter's side. Somewhat hesitantly, she handed him the one remaining spear. As Laughing One took it from her, Morning Land moved into place beside him, shivering slightly as the cold of his skin brushed against hers. Laughing One felt grateful for the warmth from Morning Land's body.

White Bird followed her sister, and soon all three were crouched close to one another. With none of her sister's inhibitions, the younger woman snuggled up affectionately against the hunter. Laughing One felt the coolness of her smooth thighs press next to his, and smelt the scent of cedar leaves in her hair. As he wrapped his free arm across her back in response, he felt a warm satisfaction. It was the first time that anyone had admired him in this way, and the feeling aroused a sense of pride and worth that had so long been dormant in the boy. Without understanding the reason for the change, Laughing One would never again permit himself to be idly mocked by other men.

Morning Land was surprised and slightly abashed when she saw how openly affectionate White Bird was being toward the stranger. Her younger sister was rubbing her face against his ear and cheek in the nuzzling gesture Tideland girls normally used when greeting old friends or lovers. Still, the night was cold and they had no other way of expressing gratitude. Once the greeting had been started, Morning Land could scarcely keep aloof from it. With a gentle smile, she pressed closer herself, touching her knees against those of the hunter. Though she placed one of her hands on Laughing One's leg, it was nothing like the vigorous hugs White Bird was giving. Laughing One did not really notice Morning Land's hesitancy. He was too preoccupied with her sister.

Seemingly quite far away, the hearth fire flared up for a moment, lighting one side of the great tree from below. It showed Laughing One, sitting with his knees pulled up against his chest, surrounded and embraced by two women who hugged him without speaking. The three looked very small against the high tree. but at that moment not even the wilderness could lessen the sense of importance in Laughing One's heart. Soon he was sleeping quietly.

The night was fitful. It was so cold that, even settled close to one another, side by side, they could not sleep for long. Their body warmth prevented the worst of the chill, but Laughing One would never again want to spend a fall night without the comfort of a fire. By morning the nearness of the two women had become a necessity. Even with their bodies pressed next to his, his feet and back were painfully chilled. It was this discomfort which roused him early, when the first gray of morning showed over the horizon.

Moving away from the women, Laughing One dropped his legs over the edge of the branch, swinging them back and forth to relieve the tingling. His neck was cramped, and as he rubbed at the muscles with the base of his hand, he glanced out into the new day. The icy wind had finally stopped, leaving a layer of fog over the valley once more. This time the fog was not as thick as it had been the day before, but with the sky overcast in gray, the sun still seemed very distant.

Remembering the cat, Laughing One looked down at the ground beneath the tree. In the cold sunrise, splattered blood showed as dark patches on the grass. There were bald spots along the oak's trunk where the cat had torn off clumps of bark, and at the place where the cat had struggled against its wound, pug marks mingled with scattered tufts of hair. The spear White Bird had dropped in her panic lay a stone's throw away, untouched.

But the cat had not died in the open. A good hunter could follow game even where the ground was hard. On this water-softened earth, the tracks were quite visible to Laughing One's trained eyes. The cat's trail led off into a nearby stand of scrub. It had probably not gone far.

Was it still alive? Laughing One stared gloomily at the rough-edged vegetation that had suddenly become sinister again; trying to measure the distance from tree to bushes in terms of running strides. Like all of his tribe, he was used to running long distances, but he had no illusions about his speed.

Once Laughing One was beyond the range of the tree's branches, there was little chance of his climbing back up. And if the beast charged—if he were brought down and ripped apart by the saber-toothed tiger—what would happen to the women?

Laughing One was so preoccupied with his thoughts that he did not notice the sisters moving about until White Bird came to sit beside him on the branch. She knelt down next to him and smiled with a shyness that seemed out of place in view of their closeness the night before. Her hair was disheveled and there were dirty tear streaks over much of her face, but Laughing One was glad of her company. He smiled back a little wanly. His growing fear must have shown in his face, for her expression changed slightly as she looked at him. Then she turned away and took several deep breaths of the mist-heavy air.

Laughing One stared at her, wondering who she was and what had brought her into the valley. He was convinced that her tribe did not live there. If they had, his own people would have discovered them long before this. There was also the strangeness of her language. None of the people who lived in the great valley talked the way these two sisters did. Laughing One felt a strong need to speak with her. He tapped her on the shoulder to get her attention. As she turned to look, he smiled.

"*Yi-quay-is* (White Bird)," he said slowly.

White Bird smiled, pressed her hand to her chest as she had seen her sister do the day before, and repeated her name. Then she pointed to the young hunter's chest and added, "*Tua-arikii* (Laughing One)." She twisted her mouth into an ugly shape as she attempted to mimic the harsh syllables and the result was barely comprehensible, but she took such obvious pride in her accomplishment that Laughing One's smile widened.

White Bird lowered her head graciously.

Laughing One nudged her again, pointing this time to both her and Morning Land, "*Toku mae aunan*? (Are you sisters)?" he asked.

At first the young girl simply smiled at the same sounds, but when Laughing One repeated his question, she strained to hear better. Quietly putting her hand on her right breast and pointing also to the bared breasts of her sister, she said, "Aika manabea (We are women)."

Laughing One stared at White Bird. The sound of her voice was so light that it reminded him of bubbling water.

Seeing herself pointed to, Morning Land crawled over to join the others. With a series of repeated words and hand gestures, hunter and Tidelanders struggled to speak to one another. Laughing One finally learned that the sisters had come from beyond the western mountains, at a place of "great waters." When he asked about the rest of their people, the sadness of the women's expressions told him more than their words could. He understood that the sisters were the last of their tribe.

As they were talking, Laughing One noticed a stone chopper strapped to White Bird's waist skirt. He had felt its hard, lumpy shape when she had pressed against him the night before. Now he sensed a use for it. With hand signals he asked the girl to give the chopper to him. Confused but obliging, White Bird un-strapped the stone wedge and held it out for Laughing One.

His face grim with concentration, the young hunter hefted the stone chopper carefully, getting a sense of its shape and weight. Then he made a long throw. The stone implement whizzed out in a smooth arc that sent it crashing down amid the bushes. There was a rustling and a rattling clatter as the chopper rico-cheted off hidden branches. Then it landed with a soft thump, as if it had plummeted onto a mound of loose earth. The impact brought an angry snarl from the cat. The sound rumbled up om-inously from beneath the leaves.

White Bird turned her head and stared wide-eyed at Laughing One. The young hunter's face revealed heightened alertness but not panic. The snarl had told him all he needed to know.

As his heartbeat came faster, Laughing One began to get ready. His knife still hung like a talisman from the thong around his neck. He picked up the makeshift spear, looked over its fastenings, and hefted it in his hand. Though it did not have the balance of his other weapon, the shaft seemed strong and the stone point had been struck by Spear Maker. He slipped the spear under the strap that held his empty weapons' pouch and prepared to climb down.

When White Bird guessed what he was doing, she reached out and grabbed his arm to stop him. Laughing One turned, sur-prised by the strength of the grip, and stared into her face. The girl's eyes showed something he had not expected, what he had seen in his mother's face on the day he had left for this hunter's journey. In a strange way, Laughing One felt pleased.

"*Yi-quay-is* (White Bird)," he said. "*Ana ka to* (I will climb down)." Then he shook his head and gently removed her hand.

The girl made no further protest, but she slumped visibly. The other sister was looking at him as well. There was a soft-ness in her expression he had not noticed before. What was it? Pity? Friendship? Something that made him want to stay all the more badly. Not trusting himself further, he turned his back on the women and began to climb along the branch.

Laughing One dropped to the ground a moment later. The soles of his rawhide moccasins squeaked against the wet grass, and for a panicky instant he thought he was going to fall. Then he righted himself, pulled out his spear, and stood waiting. His attention was focused on the bush where he knew the cat was hiding, but he took in other details. The fire was barely smol-dering in the dank air, nearly shrouded over with mist. It would have to wait. He knew that the rest of his tools, including his spear thrower, were scattered about somewhere amid the grass, but they would have to wait as well.

Laughing One was frightened, and his senses were heightened by fear. He could almost taste the earthy scent of the wet grass beneath him. Around him, the morning birds were singing in a ceaseless, chirping babble that was unaffected by the tension on the ground below. He listened for the crack of branches, and heard only the shimmery voices of preening birds.

Laughing One did not know what he had expected to happen once he had reached the ground, but everything seemed the same. He could see no movement in the bush where the cat was hiding. If he had not heard it snarling, he might have convinced himself the animal was dead.

Carefully and quietly, without quick movements, Laughing One started to cross the open stretch of grass between the tree and the bush where the cat lay hidden. Overhead, he could hear the giant oak branch creaking as the women moved about on it, but he ignored the sounds. It did not matter if the women were watching him. Nothing mattered now except the cat.

Though Laughing One was unaware of it, the two sisters were no longer on the branch. Morning Land was already climbing out of the tree. She had seen the unused spear that White Bird had dropped the night before and was coming down to get it.

Morning Land's bare feet thumped lightly onto the cool grass. She hurried over to where the spear was lying, not daring to look up until she had the weapon in her hands. When she did look up, she realized that White Bird was still beside her. The younger sister held a splintered digging stick which they had carried with them over the mountains.

Neither sister was sure what to do next. Together, away from the tree, they glanced quickly around. The grove was quiet except for the solitary form of the young hunter.

Stepping forward slowly, waiting, listening, and then stepping again, Laughing One moved between the safety of the tree and the hiding place of the cat. Behind him, the women and the oak had faded into things he could never turn back to. This time he could not climb out of reach or stay poised in a place where he could fling his weapons down upon an enemy which had twice his strength. Now it was only this one spear and a stone knife.

The trembling of a leaf in front of him made him flinch to a stop. There had been no wind to stir that branch.

Slowly, while Laughing One stood there, the cat emerged from its watching place. He could see the great head, the long, yellowed teeth, the blood caked in clumps around its muzzle. Next the wide, swelling shoulders appeared and, finally, the beast's horribly wounded chest. The gash his spear had left was surrounded by rays of splattered blood and matted fur. A reddish fluid dripped down each time the cat moved its legs, and Laughing One wondered again why the animal had not died before this. The animal walked as if each step brought new pulses of pain; it was not staggering, but looked straight at him, smelling his fright.

The cat was fully exposed, a perfect target. If he could fling his spear now, before it summoned its strength to strike, he might still kill it. Laughing One raised his spear arm and prepared to throw.

In that same instant, the cat lunged forward.

Laughing One flung his spear, but the cat was suddenly huge and monstrous before him. He saw its enormous spreading paws and its eyes receding into blackened slits behind the gaping mouth. He barely had time to raise his left arm across his face before it was on top of him.

Laughing One's spear had struck the cat's throat and had left another deep wound near the first, but it did not stop the thud of impact or keep the flared claws from cutting down into the hunter's skin. Pinned on his back, Laughing One tried to reach for his knife, tried to push himself away. The cat's strength was far greater. He was too close to fend off its claws. The cat's body felt hard, while every part of his seemed soft and vulnerable. Ripping claws cut at his arms, seared into his thighs, and he knew he would be torn apart.

When she saw the young hunter go down beneath the cat, Morning Land let out a shriek of hatred. Without thinking, she ran forward, spear in hand. She was not stopped by the snarling fury of the cat. She simply closed in and jabbed with her spear. The first strike merely grazed the animal's neck, but it saved Laughing One's life. The cat was distracted at a critical moment, forced to use the last of its failing strength to ward off this second intruder. Still hunched over the struggling hunter, the animal spun around and spat at the woman.

Morning Land was suddenly terrible in her fury. Wild impulse seized her. She screamed and stabbed, again and again. The cat swatted out viciously with its good paw in a last effort to defend itself, but Laughing One's second spear had already been embedded dangerously close to its heart. This final burst of struggle was enough to wedge the point deeper. As the great cat staggered off Laughing One's body in a feeble attempt to spring at the shrieking woman, its strength gave out and it collapsed on its side. Morning Land's jabbing spear cut through the cat's eye into its brain, but the blow came too late to have effect. The saber-toothed tiger was already trembling with death.

The death of her enemy did not stop the woman's rage. She circled around the beast's body in a way that resembled some insane dance, repeatedly plunging in her spear and pulling it out. Blood sputtered forth with each new gash made by the stone point. As the gold color of the animal's fur changed to matted brown, Morning Land screamed in a wild howling that was more like agony than triumph. Never far behind her sister, White Bird joined in, pounding the cat's head with her wooden stake until the skull split. No longer shy or cautious, both sisters continued to bludgeon and stab the motionless cat. The carcass was soon nothing but a frame of splintered bones, beaten flesh, and blood-soaked fur, huge and shapeless in the growing sunlight. There would be no hide left to mark this victory.

Amid the noise and fury of the two women, Laughing One tried to get up. The cat had been on top of him for only a few moments, but his right arm and thigh were covered with rips and gashes. Dizziness came as the young hunter got to his knees. The sudden giddiness threatened to overwhelm him. His head pounded with the effort of moving, and with the strained screaming of the two sisters. Surrounded by a hysteria of high-voiced shrieks, he remained in a half crouch, the pain of having been mangled adding to his confusion.

Unnoticed by the sisters, Laughing One gradually overcame the spinning in his head and stood. He felt weak but knew that his only chance of living depended on cleaning his wounds. While the women went on with their one-sided struggle against the dead cat, he limped down to the river and waded in. The cold water stung and cooled at the same time. Laughing One stayed there, waist deep, until the pain in his leg numbed. Though he tried to stoop down and drink, the rush of dizziness returned as he bent over and he quickly straightened. It was his fear of collapsing in the water that made him come out again. Shivering badly, he stumbled back up the trail. Loss of blood was already taking away his strength. His hand came away smeared bright red each time he touched his thigh. He saw himself falling and dying alone in this unfriendly part of the great valley. In his village, he would have had hope of getting help for his wounds. Here he had none.

The sisters' fury had quieted while Laughing One was at the river. When he came back, they were both hunched near the hearth. Morning Land had managed to stir up enough hot ashes to get a flame burning, and White Bird was feeding it with small sticks. Their domestic appearance was shattered by the fact that they were still splattered with blood. White Bird was sobbing silently, but Morning Land's gaze was cold and emotionless.

The women looked up as Laughing One came near. One glimpse of his ripped body was enough to bring both of them to their feet. Before he could speak, the sisters rushed toward him.

From the flurry of words that passed between them, Laughing One understood that his companions meant to help, but he could no longer see the expressions on their faces. The world was growing pale and blurring over. His face felt very cold.

"Yi-quay-is," he whispered.

But White Bird never knew what Laughing One intended. In that instant he passed out and collapsed in front of her.

CHAPTER FIVE

The Forest Women

White Bird shrieked when she saw the young hunter fall.

"*Atoshe!* The cat has killed him!" she wailed.

Morning Land gently turned the hunter over and lay him on his side. Lacking anything else, she pulled off her waist skirt and pressed it down hard over the place where the bleeding was greatest. "*Shaa henaki*, little fool. I know when one is dead. This man still lives among us. Learn what a woman should do. I want you to take all of the things that have fallen onto the grass and bring them here to me."

White Bird hesitated, showing her reluctance to leave the wounded hunter.

"Ehnn, do not wait," Morning Land ordered. "If the sickness enters his chest, it will truly kill him."

As White Bird walked away across the grass, Morning Land pressed her waist skirt against the hunter's wounds. The gashes on his arm did not look dangerous, but the blood seeping out from the terrible rips in his thigh was another matter. Morning Land knew of the sickness that came from animal clawings and bites. The cures she had learned were not difficult to follow, but the sisters had nothing to work with. Morning Land needed long thorns to pin together the hanging flesh and a poultice of ground herbs to stop the poison.

A series of clattering thumps broke her concentration. White Bird was hurrying over the grass, throwing everything she found into a small pile. Suddenly she let out a howl of dismay. Her waist skirt had snapped under the weight of the stone chopper she had fastened to it, and now she was standing completely naked.

Morning Land, already naked herself, was not sympathetic. "Ehnn, sister. This man feels pain. He may soon die of that pain. Bring your waist skirt, and the other things you have found."

Grumbling, White Bird gathered up the items against her

chest, placing her ripped waist skirt on top, and stumbled toward the hearth. After dropping them at her sister's feet, she hunched over self-consciously.

Morning Land placed White Bird's waist skirt over her own. Both were soon soaked with the young hunter's blood, but the pressure was slowing down his bleeding. As she kept the waist skirts in place, Morning Land looked at the tools White Bird had brought. There was little they could use other than the emptied clam shells. Finally Morning Land noticed the hunched-over posture of her sister.

"No one watches you, shy one," she advised.

The truth of what Morning Land said was too obvious to deny. White Bird thought about it for a moment, then leaned over the body of the young hunter.

"Will he live?" she asked.

"Not if we continue to sit together," Morning Land replied. "His skin is hot. Go to the river. Get sweet-smelling pond lily—white or yellow flower. Bring the leaves and roots."

"Pond lily," White Bird muttered. "Uhnn, where?"

Morning Land silenced her with a look. "Go and search for them. Get strips of willow bark. Pick thorns and nettles—both leaves and roots. When you grab the nettle, press its hairs to the stem. You will not hurt your hands. Go and get these things."

White Bird stood in the soft grass, quietly plucking the barbed seeds from a grass flower as she tried to remember all that Morning Land had asked for.

Impatiently, Morning Land pointed in the direction of the river. "Go look over there. It is better than searching in the bush. When you come back, tear the bark from a pine tree—the inner bark, where the sap is wet."

"What are you saying?" White Bird demanded. "I will walk and walk before I find all these things."

"I am not one to lie down by the fire while you work," Morning Land retorted. "Find what you can."

Carrying the old digging stick as if it were a giant knife, White Bird hurried down toward the river. Morning Land watched her go, then glanced down at Laughing One. The waist skirts were clotted with blood, and Laughing One's bleeding seemed to have slowed under the pressure from her hands, but the hunter's wounds could not wait until White Bird returned.

Morning Land's eyes scanned the edge of the grove, and stopped when she noticed a small pine tree, barely visible behind a screen of willows. Fear made her very efficient. Leaving the hunter as he was, she grabbed up the remaining stone chopper and hurried over to the tree. Keeping the base of the chopper firmly braced against the heel of her hand, she hacked at the pine until she had slashed free enough strips of inner bark to serve as bandages. These she twisted around Laughing One's mangled thigh, using them to bind the waist skirts over the wounds. Only then did she pause to think further.

The fibrous bark of the pine would help clot the flowing blood, but was not enough. Two other healing substances were close at hand; charcoal from the hearth fire and pieces of white oak bark torn free by the cat. Morning Land searched the edge of the grove until she had collected two stones—a round one and a flat one—to be used for grinding. Then she pounded the charcoal and clumps of oak bark into a thick powder.

Laughing One had not moved since she had lain him on his side. His breathing was heavy, almost rasping, and his face seemed very pale. When Morning Land bent over him to brush away some of the hair that was sticking against his forehead, she knew his spirit was drifting. Carefully she removed the bark strips and lifted off the blood-soaked waist skirts to expose his wounds. She saw again how deep the cat's claws had cut. The bleeding had almost stopped, but the claw slashes were deep enough for poison to have entered. River water, collected in emptied clam shells, was only a trickle that did not wash them clear. Morning Land's best hope was the powder she had ground. This she dabbed in a thick layer over the cuts. Finally the pine strips were rewrapped around Laughing One's thigh to cover the wounds.

The Tideland woman stood up and stretched her back muscles. She was worried about the unconscious hunter. They had so little to help him with; no hides to keep him from shuddering in the cold, no scrapers to clean dry the bark they had stripped, no sealed reed baskets to carry water up from the river in. This was the hardest time of all for the wounded man, but she could not stay with him throughout the day. There was food to be gathered, a hut to be built, and firewood to be collected before the heat of this day cooled into night. White Bird could not do all of it alone. Gathering up the blood-stained aprons, Morning Land hurried down toward the river. Behind her, Laughing One lay alone beside the hearth fire, with his eyes closed and his unconscious face turned up toward the morning sky.

There was no sign of White Bird down by the river. Either the girl had not come this way or else she had quickly gotten discouraged and moved elsewhere. Morning Land clicked her tongue in mild annoyance as she set down the waist skirts and began to wade into the water.

The river was cold enough to make her skin bristle, but as it grew deeper around her, Morning Land's worry over the hunter dissolved into a quiet contentment. It had been so long since she had been able to bathe in this way, without having to watch the shoreline for signs of an enemy. In a rush of satisfaction, she realized how free she was at that moment. She felt her skin growing clean again as the current washed off the gore and blood of the dead cat. Giving in to an impulse, Morning Land dove straight under and came up sputtering like a seal. Her long hair swirled in a spray about her head as she used her hands to rub free the last traces of filth. Then, shivering but happy, she returned to the shore.

She paused when she reached the place where she had left the waist skirts, and stood staring down at them. They were both too filthy with blood to ever be cleaned. The thought of putting them on again repulsed her. After a moment, she picked them up and tossed them out into the river.

Then she walked back to their hearth and sat beside the injured hunter. He still looked pale, and his skin felt cool. The scratch marks on his arm were dirty. Not wanting to let them heal like that, Morning Land used water in a clam shell to wet one of the pine-bark strips. This in turn was used to rub clean the hunter's arm. The action caused the cuts to bleed again. Wetting the bark strip a second time, Morning Land rinsed the scratches once more before putting on what was left of the charcoal and bark powder. Then she bandaged the cuts. Having gotten this close to the hunter, she noticed that he smelled strongly of sweat and blood. One more wetted strip of bark wiped clean the rest of his body. In order to do this, Morning Land had to unfasten Laughing One's empty weapons' pouch and lay it aside.

The hunter stirred when he felt the strap being lifted from his shoulder. He muttered something Morning Land could not understand, and for an instant his eyes opened. They moved about without seeming to focus on anything, then closed again. Morning Land waited to see if he would wake entirely, but he did not. Soon his breathing was regular once more. She went on with her work.

When everything was in order, she left the hearth and approached the body of the saber-toothed tiger. She had been avoiding this as long as possible, for now that her frenzy was over, she felt queasy every time she looked at the dead cat. Even broken and mutilated, there was something sinister about the animal. Blood was splattered on all of the nearby grass, and the death smell of the thing had already lured swarms of autumn flies. They buzzed noisily for position on the corpse, crawling around its ears and over its nostrils. When Morning Land approached, some flew off to buzz around her head. Repulsed, she swatted at them before stepping back. With her arms folded protectively across her chest, she stared down at what was left of the cat.

She would have to drag the body away from their camp before it started attracting other things besides flies. The idea of touching it again nauseated her, but she knew it was cowardice that made her hesitate. The thing was hostile even in death, and not only because of the predators its smell would bring. The spirits of all those it had slain might continue to linger in the region of its corpse. She had to be rid of it now and forever.

Taking a heavy breath, Morning Land quickly stepped forward and grabbed the animal's two hind feet. With the first jolt of movement, the flies took to the air. They formed a swirling cloud around both woman and cat; their shiny blue-green bodies glistening in the sunlight as they dove and swirled in front of Morning Land's eyes. After a short while they began to make tentative landings on her face, her hair, her neck, and a dozen other places. Morning Land's skin twitched against the feel of them, but she pulled all the more vigorously. Each breath she took filled her lungs with the stench of dead meat. Her feet banged against rocks and hidden sticks, and she nearly stumbled several times. Morning Land bared her teeth at the flies—silently cursing both them and the smashed body of the cat—and kept on dragging.

When it was over, Morning Land walked back alone through the oak grove. She had wiped her hands clean on the grass several times, but they still felt sticky. Her skin seemed to itch in each place where a fly had landed. Morning Land's pace slowed as she neared the fire and the sleeping form of the hunter. Then, abruptly, she turned away and ran down toward the shore. Only a second plunge in the river would free her from the stench.

By the time Morning Land returned to the hearth fire, White Bird was back. The younger girl had laid the items she had collected on the ground next to the hunter and was gathering firewood from the edge of the grove. As she worked, White Bird hummed a soft Tideland love song. Like Morning Land, she was beginning to sense her freedom now that the cat was gone.

White Bird turned with a load of wood in her arms, saw her sister, and began talking at once.

"Ehnn. I walked and walked, a long way. I was not afraid to be alone by the woods. Nothing was there to hurt me."

Morning Land nodded and stared at the items on the ground. There was pine gum which would help to cool the wound's redness, pine bark which could be boiled and used as a plaster, strips of willow bark that would brew into willow-bark tea—a certain cure for fever, some long thorns for clasping torn flesh together, some clumps of nettle, and several large puffball fungi. Morning Land glanced approvingly at her sister.

"You are the only one who helps me now. Continue to be careful. There are still things in the woods that could kill you," Morning Land cautioned. "This hunter has just lain here and slept, but taking care of him will make us both tired. All I have left is you, sister. Together we are strong enough to live a long time."

White Bird flushed happily. Her sister's approval was worth the effort of crawling naked over wet leaves. Only the sight of the wounded hunter soured her triumphant mood.

"It feels sad to see him hurting like this!" she exclaimed.

"I am trying," Morning Land said. "My hands have worked on his wounds, but the sickness may still refuse me."

"What hope will stay with us, then?" White Bird asked.

"Uhnn . . . he is the only one left," Morning Land agreed. "We will have to cure him of his pain. Ehnn, sister. Do not cry. Crying does not help the sick. We must build a hut for him and search for food. Only then will we be finished."

White Bird nodded. "I am without sense," she apologized. Mentally assessing the great amount of work still ahead of her, she added, "When darkness sits, it will be good to sleep on the ground again."

As White Bird left to cut down some long willow saplings to form the hut frame, Morning Land used her two rocks to pound the nettle roots to a powder. She worked until she was satisfied that the powder was fine enough, then set it aside on some leaves. The puffballs were much easier to pulverize, and their white granules were poured overtop the nettle root powder. Then Morning Land heated the pine resin on the hearth rocks until it was a sticky goo which could be stirred in with the powder to create a salve. By placing it on leaves close to the fire,

Morning Land was able to keep the salve warm and thickly fluid while she began the task of breaking up the willow and pine bark into small fragments.

She was still snapping the bark into pieces with her fingers when White Bird came up from the river with an armload of willow saplings. The Tideland girl put down her load of branches and stood silently for a moment, watching her sister.

Though Morning Land could not know it, she never looked more beautiful than when she was concentrating on some task. Her face softened from its usual sternness and there was no longer anything defensive about the way her body moved. As the early afternoon light fell across her smoothly tanned skin, she looked so perfect that White Bird wondered if this lithe woman could truly be her sister.

Morning Land glanced up. "Why do you look at me?" she asked.

White Bird flushed, embarrassed to be caught staring. "I do not know everything," she replied. "I wondered what you were doing."

"This will help to make the hunter strong again," Morning Land said, reluctant to explain in more detail. "Go to the river and clean yourself. Then we will build a hut frame."

White Bird grabbed up the empty clam shells and strolled off as quickly as usual, but Morning Land remained puzzled.

At the river, White Bird chose a place where the current was moving slowly and waded in. She moved tiredly, still thinking of the soft loveliness of her sister. As her legs sank under the surface, White Bird glanced down critically at her own naked form. Her breasts were as rounded as Morning Land's—bigger, in truth—but they did not make up for her thick waist and too-wide hips. Her legs were short, plump things, not long and sleek like Morning Land's. Her arms were strong but short, and her fingers seemed stubby compared with the graceful, skilled hands of her sister. It was difficult to imagine that the two of them had had the same mother.

Morning Land again noticed a change in White Bird's mood as the young girl returned from the river.

"What did you do that makes you so sad?" Morning Land asked. "Are you sick inside?"

White Bird shook her head and slumped down beside the hearth fire. She watched as Morning Land fastened the flesh of Laughing One's leg wound with long thorns.

"This work will soon be finished," Morning Land promised.

"We must spend the day doing things that will help the hunter. When the sun is near the ground again, we will have our rest."

When her sister did not respond, Morning Land brushed the salve from the fingers of her right hand and placed her palm on White Bird's leg.

White Bird stood up immediately. She took her digging stick and began drawing a circle on the ground to show the base of the hut frame. The work allowed her to avoid looking at her sister.

Morning Land was slightly hurt by the way her sister had brushed her aside, but she could think of no reason for White Bird's mood other than tiredness. She sighed and got to her feet to help White Bird with the hut frame.

In a strained silence, the two sisters began building.

They did not really speak again until that evening. When the hut had been completed and a supper had been gathered and prepared, the two sisters sat down next to each other in the entrance of their new home. Both were staring at the young hunter who was sleeping on the other side of the hearth fire, but their thoughts about him were very different.

"This frightens me," White Bird admitted. "I do not like to see him lying so still."

"He is not as sick as he was," Morning Land replied. "Soon we will bring him inside the hut."

White Bird said nothing for a while. She was sitting right next to her sister—so close that their hips touched—but her mind remained distant. Her knees were raised up in front of her as a support for her arms, which in turn braced her chin. In this hunched-over posture, White Bird had been staring across the fire at the sleeping hunter since early twilight.

Morning Land tried again.

"Pain frightens, but this day the sickness does not refuse. It has not pulled deep into his insides yet. Our medicine is strong enough. When he drinks the willow-bark tea, the fever will heal."

"I will get a piece of bark and wipe his face," White Bird said.

"Ehnn. Not this day," Morning Land replied. She was grateful that her sister was finally speaking, but wished White Bird would stop fussing over the stranger. His cure was her concern.

"Our work is finished." White Bird sighed. "When he sees us tomorrow, he will be stronger."

They were silent again, listening to the crackle of the fire and pulling the willow-bark capes tighter over their shoulders. Laughing One was protected from the wind by a pile of soft branches which the overly worried White Bird had heaped on in such quantities that his body now resembled a small, leafy hillock.

"Will we be able to leave with him when he goes back to his people?" White Bird asked.

"As we are living, when he goes, we will follow him," Morning Land said.

White Bird smiled at the idea. "My heart is happy to follow him. When we arrive at his village, we will have friends again."

"To get up and go after him is easy," Morning Land cautioned. "To live with his people is not. They may not find pleasure in seeing you. There will be other men, big and hurting. He has the weapons of the strangers. His tribe may kill us with their ways. Their women could hit and insult us. Their children could whisper against us. We will know nothing of their talk."

"We know his name," White Bird said. "*Tua-arikii* (Laughing One)." She spoke the odd-sounding word with the same reverent tone her people used when invoking a spirit.

Morning Land began breaking up small branches and feeding them to the fire. "*Shaa henaki,* poor sister," she said. "Sometimes a woman talks without sense. When darkness sits and the fire is warm, we think of the men who come to us in the night. The ahiri are strong in our minds then. They make us want to love again. But that one over there, that strange hunter, he does not worry about us. Who can tell what he thinks? Perhaps this is someone who is ugly inside, who will one day hurt us."

"I refuse that thought," White Bird replied. "His smile is so nice. His eyes are happy like a child playing. He cannot be a cruel man."

Morning Land grunted. "You want him, but will his family want you?" she asked. "He is only a boy. If other men start fighting over you, he will not be able to help."

"You do not know everything," White Bird grumbled. "If he were ugly inside and did not worry about us, he would have left us to die in the tree. Our Tideland men were the ones who ran away from danger. *Tua-arikii* killed the cat. Does someone who is only a boy do such things?"

Morning Land smiled quietly at the rebuke. White Bird was becoming very protective of the young hunter. She would have to be careful with her little sister. "*Siyemou,*" she said placat-

ingly. "He has courage, but there are older ones in his village
who will decide things. They will tell us which husband is mine
and which one is yours. We do not know enough about this
hunter or his people's ways."

"We can learn about him," White Bird insisted.

Morning Land lowered her eyes. "We will learn to speak as
he does," she agreed. Then she hesitated, trying to think of a
way of describing the uneasiness she felt. "We are alone now,
without any family," she said. "All our people are gone. Do you
understand?"

The confused expression on White Bird's face showed clearly
that she did not understand.

"When a woman is living in her own village, marriage is an
easy thing," Morning Land explained. "All her friends are there
to watch over her. Her husband will be respectful of her and
will not treat her badly because he fears her brother's anger and
her mother's scolding tongue. If he does treat her badly, she can
walk back and live in her mother's hut."

White Bird nodded slowly. "Our mother is dead," she whispered.

"There is no one to help us except strangers like *Tua-arikii*,"
Morning Land agreed. Then, remembering her patient, she
added, "He is lying on the ground under the night sky. If you
know what to do, help me bring him into this hut."

White Bird got up quickly and hurried to where Laughing
One was lying.

Drugged with willow-bark tea and the other herbs Morning
Land had given him, Laughing One was only vaguely aware of
the world around him. He wanted to sleep, but there were hands
touching and prodding at him, jostling him out of the gray haze
which had surrounded him since morning. Sleepy, tired, he felt
himself being lifted. Then a wave of awful sensations hummed
through him. His throat was blazing hot, yet his body was filled
to bursting with water. The pain was everywhere, aching and
throbbing all over. His eyes opened and closed, but he saw only
darkness. As the jostling continued, he urinated out into that
blackness. It was painful and only partially controlled.

While both sisters struggled to get him into the hut, Laughing
One tried to grasp what was happening. Feverish, puzzled, and
very tired, he could not understand why his body felt so light.
Twice he nearly plunged down onto his face, but the women's
strong arms kept him from collapsing. Then he was lying on the
ground inside the hut, and the women were covering his body

with strips of bark. One of the sisters lifted his head and held something to his lips for him to drink. It was a clam shell filled with willow-bark tea.

Laughing One's eyes slowly began to focus as his head was lowered back to the ground. A flicker of firelight showed the face of the younger of the two forest women. Then, as blackness filled the hut, he felt her cool hand press gently against his forehead. He heard the women's voices, but they were already becoming distant in his mind. He swallowed. His eyelids flickered and then closed. Knowing that he was not alone, he slipped back into darkness.

By the next afternoon, Laughing One had already grown strong enough to be bored with lying inside a hut. All during his struggle with the fever, the women had been there beside him, wiping his forehead with damp bark strips when he was sweating, giving him soft mush to eat when he was hungry, letting him drink as much willow-bark tea as he wanted, and then helping him outside when he needed to let the water out of his body. They had understood and accepted his sickness. He had seen their gestures, felt their kindness, and let himself be cared for.

Now though, with the fever gone and no sign of infection developing from his wounds, the sisters had left him alone while they gathered food and prepared meals. To a young man who had been active all his life, the stillness was intolerable. It was quiet and lonely inside the hut, with nothing to see but the thatched roof overhead, and nothing to hear but random bird calls and the ever present rush of grassland wind.

By late afternoon, Laughing One's need for company became greater than his fear of pain. Rolling over onto his uninjured leg, he slid out from the covering layers of bark and slowly crawled across the hut's dirt floor. His right thigh hurt when he moved it, but not unbearably. Even when he was crawling forward this way, Laughing One's training as a hunter prevented him from making much noise. He did not grunt as he moved, and when he slipped out through the hut entrance a moment later, he was so quiet that White Bird, who was working only a short distance away, did not notice him.

Squinting at the brightness of the lowering sun, Laughing One leaned back against the side of the hut and gazed about him. The camp would have seemed unbearably lonely had it not been for the naked form of White Bird perched on a small grassy hillock not far from the fire. Laughing One forgot his restlessness and decided to watch what she was doing.

   The young woman had already stripped off long pieces of the
willow tree's inner bark, soaked them in water, and pounded
them flat with her sister's rounded stone. Now she was inter-
weaving the strips to make two aprons; one for her front and the
other to drape across her buttocks. The task required full concentration, and it was because of this that she had not noticed
the young hunter. Her hands pinched, twisted, and sorted with
quick efficiency. The only wasted movements came when she
paused to straighten her back, shift her weight on her buttocks,
or stare whimsically at the sky.
   Laughing One enjoyed looking at her. She was of the age
when women in his own village were thought to be very desirable. Praised and pampered by the hunters, these girls of the
apron were among the most spoiled and difficult people of the
tribe. They were forever teasing men and stealing small "gifts"
of food from the hunters' fires. Assuming that they would not
be punished, they joked and flirted with married men in front of
those men's wives, annoyed young boys with insults about their
undeveloped bodies, and talked about older women in whispers
that echoed around the camp. Their loud laughing had embarrassed him in front of other men and made him shy from the
idea of ever taking a wife of his own.
   This forest girl seemed different, however. She was softer,
with her large, dark eyes, plumply feminine body, and smooth,
light brown skin. Young as she was, she seemed to know what
was wanted. The men of his village would be very pleased with
her. One of the older hunters would be certain to ask for her as
his second wife. Laughing One frowned as he thought about it.
   It was not until she had finished with her skirt and was ready
to slip it down over her hips that White Bird became aware of
her audience. When she finally quit pulling and tugging at the
bark strips, she felt someone else sitting behind her. Twisting
her neck, she looked back over her shoulder. There was no hesitation. She seemed to know exactly where Laughing One
would be. Seeing him there, she immediately stood up.
   Laughing One smiled and said her name. Though he used his
softest voice in an attempt to match the flowing Tideland
tongue, White Bird started slightly at the sound. Regaining her
composure, she stared at him for a long moment. Her large eyes
looked out fearlessly, for she knew he would not harm her. After another lapse, she smiled and gently nodded her head in silent greeting.
   "Tua-arikii," she said.

The hunter continued smiling, but inwardly he felt disappointed. Was there nothing else that could pass between them? Would he spend all the days of his recovery smiling at her and repeating her name? There had to be some way of teaching her.

Bolder now, White Bird walked toward the hunter, still nodding her head gracefully. As she drew near, Laughing One decided to ask her a simple question in sign language. He swayed his left hand slightly and pointed to the willow-bark skirt. Then he clenched the hand into a fist and pointed upward with his forefinger. Using his right hand, he gripped the extended finger and shook it back and forth. Finally he repeated the first gesture again.

He had asked her why she kept twisting the bark skirt in her hands. White Bird responded by giving him the round stone she had been using.

Laughing One shook his head and tried again. This time he asked her how long he had been sick with fever.

The girl offered him her willow-bark skirt.

Laughing One stared at her balefully, wondering why her sister was able to understand his signs when she could not.

Knowing that she had disappointed him in some way, White Bird knelt down beside him, keeping her thighs pressed tightly together out of modesty. Laughing One moved closer, with such a look of intentness on his face that she almost jumped up again in alarm. When he was in easy reach of her, he grabbed her waist skirt. White Bird dropped it in surprise and pulled back, shocked. She did not notice that Laughing One had said a word as he made the gesture.

Patiently, Laughing One lifted the skirt and held it so close that it was only a finger's length from her face. *"Kai-tama,"* he said, using the word over and over again.

Gradually, as her panic ebbed, White Bird began to understand. She repeated the sound, knowing that it was what he wanted her to do.

Laughing One smiled again and she felt a flush of excitement. There followed a short language lesson, during which Laughing One taught her his words for fire, water, tree, hut, sky, sun, stone, and woman. White Bird struggled valiantly to comprehend, but as the words kept on coming she began to fear that she would never remember them all. She had to think of a way to make the hunter pause.

Slowly an idea came to her. She would tell him some words from her own tongue. Holding up the waist skirt they had

started with, White Bird began to talk. First she said Laughing
One's word for waist skirt, then she said the Tideland equiva-
lent.

Laughing One frowned.

White Bird could see that her attempt was irritating the
hunter. On impulse, she lifted the skirt over her head and
slipped it on. The fit was good. As she stood up, the bark rib-
bons fell loosely across her hips and thighs, emphasizing her
figure. White Bird was so pleased with the work that for a moment she forgot about the young hunter. It had been a long time
since she had worn this type of skirt. After a hesitant step or
two, she began to pace back and forth beside the fire, assuming
her normal walking stride. The bark strips swished and shook
with each movement, making a soft rustling sound. White Bird
sighed when she heard herself.

Laughing One was impressed. In standing and walking,
White Bird had again shown the lithe suppleness which was
natural to her. Her slightly large belly and hips, her very
rounded breasts and arms, all seemed somehow right when she
allowed her instinctive mannerisms to take over. The waist skirt
only added to the sensual appearance as it balanced over her
buttocks, shifting and twitching slightly with each movement.
When White Bird again turned to face the hunter, she found him
looking at her with new interest.

She placed a hand on her skirt and repeated her lesson, saying the word in both the stranger's tongue and her own Tideland
speech. This time the stranger responded. With great effort, he
twisted his mouth and tried to mimic the Tideland word.
Though his rendering was crude, White Bird did not laugh. She
was beginning to realize how difficult her speech was for him.
When he finally had it right, she clapped her hands and shook
her hips with pleasure. Laughing One watched the swaying
waist skirt and smiled as well. With gentle coaching, White
Bird then taught him her words for fire, water, trees, hut, sky,
sun, stone, and man.

They were both still talking eagerly when Morning Land returned to camp. She strode in with her usual easy grace, her
shoulders slumped down slightly under the weight of an evenly
balanced load. Though she was surprised to see Laughing One
outside the hut, his presence did not embarrass her. Unlike her
sister, Morning Land had completed her willow-bark skirt the
day before.

Laughing One stared at Morning Land as she placed her

loaded basket onto the ground and he continued watching while she began talking to White Bird. He could see by the way her hair dripped water across her back that she had been in the river again. It did not surprise him. These sisters were always splashing about in the water. They bathed so often that their bodies took in the clean scent of the shore. Laughing One could smell the freshness of them whenever they came near.

After speaking with her sister, Morning Land returned her attention to the hunter, whom she had come to regard as her special patient. Without knowing why, Laughing One pulled back slightly as she approached him. He sensed that she was very different from her sister—not just in her proud beauty and aloof manner, but in some way that went much deeper. She was as gentle in her treatment of him as White Bird, but there was a cool efficiency about her actions.

As she bent close to examine his wound, Laughing One spoke her name. She looked up at him and smiled, but only from politeness. Her real attention was elsewhere. Laughing One watched while she loosened the bark straps which held the poultice in place and felt the flesh of his injured thigh. She seemed pleased with the healing. A moment later she rubbed grease on her hands and began to massage the thigh muscles around the wound. She pressed each of her hands against his skin in a circular rubbing motion which eased the soreness of the leg. Had White Bird been doing this, Laughing One might have become excited, but with Morning Land there was no sense of intimacy. For all the emotion her face revealed, she could have been working at a hide or a piece of meat.

While Morning Land was bending over him this way, Laughing One could not avoid noticing her well-formed breasts. Dangling just above his knees, they were soft but firm, and their nipples tilted upward in the manner of a woman who had never been suckled. Her abdomen was free of stretch marks, too, so it seemed likely that she had borne no children, despite the fact that slight wrinkles in the skin of her hands showed her to be well past marrying age. Laughing One wondered at the skill of those hands, for she rubbed life into his strained flesh just as Spear Maker carved life into stone. This quality was seldom found in a young woman.

For three more days, Laughing One and the Tideland sisters stayed at the camp beside the river. During that time, the young hunter worked at his weapons, exercised his injured leg, and taught the sisters as much of his language as he could.

Once he followed the vultures to the place where Morning Land had dragged the carcass of the cat. As he approached, several of the big birds ran awkwardly away over the grass, flapping their great wings until they were able to lift their heavily gorged bodies into the air. The area around the saber-toothed tiger was splattered with vulture droppings, and even the grass had been flattened and darkened by the fury of the birds' squabbling. The stench of death was now mixed with the stench of birds. Both got stronger as Laughing One neared the silent dark mass sprawled at the center of the mess. Flies still crawled over what was left of the cat's hair, but the animal's carcass had already been reduced to something even maggots would not have taken much interest in.

Laughing One shut his mouth very tightly and pulled out what was left of his two spears. The shafts had splintered and were useless, but the blades could be cleaned and used again. The cat's body turned as he yanked out the blades which had killed it. A caved-out shape of stripped bones, it had boiled with maggots and flies two days before. Now all the white crawling things had gone, leaving only these bones which were silent and unmoving unless something tugged at them as he was doing now.

Laughing One used a rock to break loose the cat's twin dagger-sized teeth. The heavily built skull of the saber-toothed tiger did not yield as easily to his pounding and had to be twisted and cracked before the tusks could be worked free. Then Laughing One shoved the carcass aside with a stick and watched the shattered skull bob uselessly against the grass. This thing which had almost killed him would soon be nothing at all.

Laughing One had taken the tusks as proof of his kill, for the claw scars he bore would not be enough to convince other hunters. Yet as he walked back toward the camp, Laughing One began to remember how other men in the village had given their women hair bracelets, horns, and even teeth necklaces made from parts of the animals they had killed. An attractive woman like Beautiful Star often had more of these than she could possibly wear and left most of them hanging around a pole in her lodge. Beautiful Star had never shown much interest in these things and had barely objected at all when her husband, Trusted Friend, had one day destroyed them, but Laughing One liked the idea. For the first time in memory, he had something worth giving.

On his way to the river, Laughing One met Morning Land. Before she could give her usual greeting, he dropped one of the dagger-sized teeth into her empty basket. With a few quick gestures, he showed her how she could bore a hole through the tooth and wear it suspended from a cord around her neck.

"Hunter's luck," he said, smiling, as if he had done something of great importance. Then he hurried on to look for White Bird.

Neither White Bird nor Morning Land liked ornaments made from parts of dead animals, but that night they worked conspicuously on their tusk necklaces. They would wear these things because the teeth had been given to them by Laughing One at their camp beside the river.

For Morning Land and White Bird, these days held a special peace. Without the lurking presence of strangers or the Devil Cat, the wilderness began to seem almost friendly, and the warm pattern of fall days gave the land a richness that was hard to resist. The sisters played in the river, hunted their meals amid the brush and reeds, wove new baskets and carrying slings, and added to their supply of tools. With no one to watch over them except a hunter who could neither understand nor condemn most of what they said, they felt a freedom which few grown Tideland women ever knew. They rested naked on sun-warmed shore sand, spoke mockingly of the elders who had once threatened them, and fed well on everything they gathered.

On the morning of his sixth day in camp, Laughing One awoke much later than usual, feeling uneasy. Lying on his back, with his left arm shading his eyes from the incoming daylight, he tried to remember what had happened.

The night had begun with a storm. There had been lightning, high winds, and hard rain. The downpour had steamed out the fire and whipped at their eyes until all three of them had huddled together under their one shelter. Even then, the rain had washed through, cutting holes in the hut roof and pushing aside pieces of straw and leaves until steady trickles of water dribbled onto the already wet humans who slumped beneath.

Both sisters had crawled about in the darkness of the inner hut, trying to repair leaks by tugging at the grass covering. Sometimes their efforts had worked, at least for a few moments, but equally often they had created new leaks while trying to

patch the old ones. More cold air and water had rushed in, drib-
bling down onto all of the occupants. At last the sisters had
given up their struggle and huddled close beside Laughing One.

Hugged against each other for warmth, they had lain in a tangle of interlocking arms and legs. With the belly of one sister
pressed up onto his back and the buttocks of the other touching
his groin, Laughing One had shivered through the worst of the
wind's gusts. Though there had no longer been any fire, all
three had been warm enough to fall asleep.

Later, in the calm that had followed the storm, Laughing One
had awoken to a dark, silent hut. Morning Land had continued
to sleep behind him, limp and supple at the same time, but
White Bird had not been sleeping. She had lain on her belly,
with her soft skin rubbing gently but persistently against him.
He had felt rather than seen that she was looking at him in an
amused, teasing way. While Morning Land had rested quietly
under a layer of bark strips, White Bird had wriggled still closer
until her belly had met his and her large breasts had been
pressed against his chest. Turning her head slightly, she had
whispered burning words into his ear, words so soft and swift
that even had they been in his own tongue he probably would
not have understood them. Then her lips had bent lower to nuzzle him, making pretend bites at his nose and cheek. This soft
nibbling with her lips had been done with such obvious pleasure
that Laughing One could only abandon his restraint and give in
to the passion of it. *Kairofa*, the dream woman, had come to
him in the night with her moving belly and hot heart. He had
been overwhelmed. He had not refused her. When the passion
between them had calmed, she had lain gently on top of him,
her plump body a comforting shield against the night. Snatches
of a soft warbling song seemed to spill out naturally from the
happiness inside her. Showing no more resistance to her affection than he had to her body, Laughing One had fallen asleep
with his arms around her.

Just before he had awoken, however, the dream had come. He
could not remember it fully, only as flashes of violence. He had
seen Morning Land being beaten and the two sisters shamed before the tribe. There had been something worse, out in the darkness that had threatened them all.

With these unhappy thoughts, Laughing One stepped outside
the hut into the morning sunshine. White Bird was grinding
acorns beside the hearth fire, but he barely nodded to her as he
limped over toward the bushes to attend to his body's needs. He

did not know how he should behave after what had happened, and there was nothing he could say to her. The flattering words that a man normally spoke in praise of his lover would mean nothing to her. Her very forwardness and the way she had enjoyed touching him would have been thought desirable in a married woman such as Beautiful Star, but could only bring trouble for a strange captive girl. Nothing a stranger did was ever acceptable to some of his people.

On his way back to the fire, Laughing One relented slightly. The girl's expression softened his feelings. She seemed worried by his apparent coolness to her. As he came closer, her wide, dark eyes watched him with such intentness that he had to smile. Somewhat shyly, he crouched down on the opposite side of the fire. To avoid looking into her face, he kept his eyes focused on her rapidly moving hands.

With a skill created by long practice, White Bird took each acorn and tapped it lightly with her stone, cracking the cap so that it could be quickly peeled off. Each shelled kernel was placed on a flat stone next to the hearth fire, where it soon became quite dry. When the last of the caps had been removed, White Bird would pound the hulled acorns with her stone until they became a fine powder. Then the flour would be placed in a basket and taken to the river for washing. Laughing One knew the process well by now. He had seen it done every day since his arrival there. His own people ate acorns, but never in the quantity that these forest women seemed to. To Laughing One, the resulting cooked gruel was an oily, tasteless mush which could hardly be worth all the effort that had gone into preparing it. He would eat the heavy, pasty stuff when it was offered to him, but he did not pretend to like it the way these sisters obviously did.

He was much less critical about the other food the women brought in, for he realized the skill that was needed. White Bird would leave each morning with nothing more than her basket and a fire-hardened digging stick. When she returned a short while later, her collecting basket always bulged with a surprising number of roots, berries, nuts, and greens. Laughing One had watched the young woman carrying her reed baskets and appreciated what she had done. A man had good reason to be grateful for such a girl. Whoever took White Bird as a wife would never feel hunger.

As he thought of the two sisters, Laughing One's hand reached down to touch the fringe of his new loincloth. It was made from strips of rabbit fur which were woven together with a skill that suggested Morning Land's work, yet White Bird had been the one who had given it to him. She had simply handed it to him one morning as he had come out of the hut. When he had tried to thank her, she had turned from him and quickly walked away. No reference had been made to the loincloth since then, but Laughing One had sensed that it had some special importance to the young girl. He wished he understood enough of her language to be able to guess what that importance was.

White Bird finished shelling the acorns and began grinding them to a powder. As she pounded away with her stone, she hummed softly to herself, trying not to let the hunter's silence worry her. The tactic did not work. Her task was not difficult enough to demand much attention, and she found herself feeling hurt and angry by turns. She had expected to be resting next to Laughing One and brushing her face against him. Instead she was left pounding acorns like an old woman.

To White Bird, the matter was simple. She had chosen Laughing One and he had been willing. If things continued this way, they would become married. What troubled her was the hunter's lack of politeness. At night, when they had slept close together, he had embraced her as eagerly as she had embraced him. Now, in the brightness of the day, he edged away from her. Perhaps he believed that she had tricked him. White Bird felt her eyes grow hot with tears whenever she thought of such a thing. She would have never tricked Laughing One. She liked everything about him. She loved to touch his shell-curved ears and run her fingertips along his skin. Most of all, she loved to see him smile. She would tease him, just a little, hoping for that smile. And sometimes, unexpectedly, he would laugh, letting his whole body shake with humor. It was wonderful to hear him then; more wonderful to touch him.

In coming to him the night before, she had only done what any other Tideland girl who was in love would have done. Women were expected to begin things. A man might call to his wife and ask her to come to him, but it was only by removing her waist skirt that she showed her willingness. Unless she were angry with him or having her time of blood, a wife would almost always do so, but if she chose to remain aloof, no man with honor would force her.

What was true for Tideland wives was also true for Tideland girls. A girl who felt anava, the great desire, would curve her arm around her lover's waist, look at him with obvious pride, rest her breasts against his back as he sat, nuzzle at the hollow of his neck. If he was gentle to her, she would go further, cooking small meals for him and sometimes giving him things. White Bird had done all this for Laughing One; had even spent a full afternoon trying to make him a loincloth. It had only been with Morning Land's help that she had finished it, but when Laughing One had accepted the gift, White Bird had gained enough courage to make love to him. Had Laughing One been a Tideland man, he could have refused her by spanking her buttocks instead of stroking them. But Laughing One had not refused, and a great joy had bubbled inside her there in the darkness of the hut. Had she been home in her own village, she would have shown her joy the very next day by building them both a marriage hut. Now, though, she did not know what to do. Laughing One was not treating her like his wife.

Impatient with just watching her work, Laughing One tried to teach White Bird more of his words. White Bird listened but was less eager than usual, and Laughing One began to wonder what was wrong with her. All through the lesson, the voices of the two young people were accompanied by the steady pounding of White Bird's rock. When the grinding was finally done, White Bird poured the white acorn powder into a basket made from tule leaves and stood up.

"Tua-arikii," she said, jerking her head in the direction of the river. "Uhuti (water). I will wash the acorns in the river."

Though Laughing One did not understand the words she used, he had seen White Bird wash acorn powder often enough to know what she meant. Smiling good-naturedly, he followed her to the river's edge.

At the river, White Bird scooped out a hollow in the sand so that her basket and its load of acorn powder could be nestled in a basin. With Laughing One watching every move, she poured water over the contents of her basket. As the water flowed across the powder, it took on a yellowish color from the tannin contained in the acorns. It would become still more yellowish as it gradually seeped through the closely woven sides of the basket and percolated into the sand. Three such washings were enough to take most of the bitter tannin away, and a final rinse would make the acorn mush edible.

While she was waiting for the water to drain away, White Bird thought of an idea. *"Yana* (swim)," she said, pointing first to the river and then to Laughing One's injured leg. *"Uhuti* (wa-

ter) . . ." She gestured helplessly when she failed to remember
the rest of the words.

Deciding that actions were easier to understand than words,
White Bird pulled her waist skirt over her head and waded in.
Now she was utterly naked except for the saber-toothed necklace which she had worn faithfully ever since Laughing One
had given it to her. She had even worn it while she had been
making love to him the night before. Laughing One remembered having been surprised by the sharpness of the tusk as it
had pressed against his chest, and having wondered how she
could bear to have it always nestled between her breasts.

White Bird waded out until she was waist-deep in the river
and looked back impatiently. Laughing One, who did not want
to get water on the poultice which covered his wound, stepped
out into the river very reluctantly.

As soon as she saw him enter the water, White Bird grinned,
turned, and dove straight under, leaving only a wake of bubbles
where she had been. For a short while the paleness of her body
showed clearly against the deeper blue-green of the river, but
then she passed into an area of shadow and vanished.

When she came up a few moments later amid a sputter of
spray, she held her arms above her head in an expression of triumph. Laughing One could see that she was holding something
in each hand, but it was not until she had crossed the distance
and swam back to him that he realized she was grasping two
mud-coated clams. Still panting for breath, White Bird stood up
in the water next to Laughing One and handed him this proof of
her diving skill.

Laughing One did not know what to do. He told her the word
for clam, but it was clear from the grin on her face that White
Bird expected much more from him than this. She waited there
a moment longer, breathing deeply while her dark eyes searched
for something in Laughing One's face. He must have disappointed her, for with a soft laugh she turned and plunged back
in, leaving him standing knee-deep in the shallows.

Frustrated at being teased in this way, Laughing One splashed
up onto the shore, dropped the two clam shells on top of White
Bird's collecting basket, and left.

When White Bird emerged from the water a second time, she
found herself alone in the river. With her long hair dripping
cold rain across her back and chest, White Bird watched Laughing One walk away. Her dark eyes welled with tears, but she

said nothing. She had failed. He did not find her beautiful. He did not think she was skillful.

As she climbed out of the water, White Bird's pride reasserted itself. She would not follow after Laughing One again. He would have no more gifts from her, and he could keep himself warm at night. Firmly resolved to be colder in the future, White Bird went back to rinsing acorns.

Completely unaware of the hurt feelings he had caused, Laughing One hurried up the hill. When he reached camp, he saw Morning Land bending over his weapons' pouch, studying the stone spear blades. She did not see him or sense that he was there, and for a long moment he stood motionless, watching her as she touched each weapon point, held it up to the light, and set it down again. This was something which never would have happened in his own village. Women there were taught respect for men's things. They knew that handling a knife or spear would take its luck away.

Laughing One hurried forward and grabbed his weapons' pouch so roughly that it stung Morning Land's hands as it was yanked from her.

"No!" Laughing One shouted at her. "Stop this! Leave these things alone!"

He wanted to say much more. He wanted to tell her that women must not behave this way, that it was dangerous for a woman to touch men's things, but their lack of common speech made it impossible to do more than shout commands at her.

Unlike her sister, Morning Land did not blush or look down when Laughing One shouted at her. She seemed surprised by his anger at first, but as he continued to yell and wave his arms about, she returned his stare coldly, her face showing contempt for his outrageously bad manners. After a few moments, it was Laughing One who shifted his eyes away, gave a disgruntled snort, and became quiet.

Then it was Morning Land's turn. Unable to answer Laughing One in his own tongue, she expressed herself in gestures as well as words.

"Shaaa!" she hissed. "Take your things. Take all of them!"

In a final show of scorn, Morning Land pulled the saber-toothed tusk from her neck and hurled it to the ground. Turning disdainfully, she walked out of the camp. Even the way she stepped conveyed a coldness that cut at Laughing One's pride.

Laughing One's outrage did not last, for anger never stayed with him long, but the sisters were not so easily appeased.

Without fully understanding what he had done, Laughing One soon sensed a change in the two women. Morning Land relented enough to retrieve her saber-toothed tusk necklace, and controlled her annoyance long enough to remove Laughing One's wet poultice and massage his thigh with grease, but she did so in such a coldly efficient manner that Laughing One was actually glad when she finally stopped. She did not replace the poultice this time, and Laughing One lacked the nerve to ask her why. Instead he stared down morosely at his healing thigh. The saber-toothed tiger's claws had left a puckered scar, clear proof of the last death struggle between them.

For the rest of the afternoon, the sisters refused to look at Laughing One or talk with him. Laughing One had begun to become used to being treated as a hunter rather than as a boy, and the sudden withdrawal of the women's attentions left him feeling very empty. He made several attempts to talk to White Bird, but each time she quickly turned away, without looking at his face. She would seem to become preoccupied with a chore or else suddenly decide to grab a collecting basket and go off in search of food. If Laughing One deliberately stood in her way, she simply sidestepped and continued on, her body often brushing past only a hand's spread from his. If she were looking in his direction, her eyes focused on something else that was either beside or behind him. And if he spoke to her, she seemed not to hear.

By nightfall, Laughing One was actually getting used to being snubbed. The sisters did not deny him a share of the food that evening. A meal mysteriously appeared on his side of the hearth during a moment when his attention was elsewhere. He did not see which sister had set it out for him, but his gratitude was short-lived. The meal was a poor thing, consisting of the usual acorn mush, roots, and tubers. Missing from it were the sweet berries and rabbit meat which he knew White Bird had collected. Laughing One said nothing about these shortages. He simply sat down gloomily and began to eat.

On the other side of the fire, the two sisters made a show of talking pleasantly to one another. White Bird ate little, which was unusual for her, but Morning Land chewed at the roasted rabbit meat as if she had never tasted anything better. When the last bit of it had vanished down her delicately formed throat, she lifted a string of cooked fat between her fingers and licked at it eagerly with her tongue, as if eating were something to live for all in itself. Then came the berries, slightly bruised and juicy as they were pressed between sensual, puckered lips. All the while she ate, her dark eyes mocked the hunter. When she had crammed in so much food that the sweetness of the berries no longer appealed, she lolled beside the fire with such a look of satiated pleasure that even White Bird wondered at it.

Laughing One tried to pretend that he did not care, but he did care. It was not the warm smell of the cooked meat or the sweetness of the berries, it was those trembling lips kissing food with the same eagerness that White Bird's lips had kissed his skin the night before. It made him want to hold this woman and do things that he had never wanted to do before. Surprised and bewildered, Laughing One almost cried out. Instead, he slipped quickly into the hut, without speaking to either of the women.

In the bitterness of that night, Laughing One began to think about his home, far away to the south. He thought of the village fires pushing back the darkness, of Spear Maker telling his stories while children lay near him in the firelight and men sat with their chins on their knees. Nearby, women would stare dreamily into their hearth fires, not listening fully, but lulled into their own soft harmony by Spear Maker's voice. After the day of quarrels and jealousy, the clearness of this memory brought tears to Laughing One's eyes. When the night grew colder, and neither woman offered to share her warmth with him, he decided to leave the river at daylight.

White Bird was the first one to awake and go down to the river the next morning. Out of habit she carried a collecting basket with her, but she showed no interest in hunting for food. She was tired and her limbs felt stiff. Without either Laughing One or Morning Land to snuggle against, she had spent the night curled into a tight ball. Even that had not kept the chill from her muscles. Now she felt twinges in her back each time her left foot thumped onto the ground. Never in her life had she seen such a thing. Three people in one hut, and yet no warmth shared among them. Each sister trying stupidly to keep her own body warm. It went against everything White Bird had been taught.

When she reached the shore, White Bird simply dropped the basket onto the sand and hunched down miserably. Even the bird cries seemed harsh and shrill this day. Their noise cut into her head, making it hard for her to think at all. She rubbed at her eyes, splashed water against her face, and slumped.

As she wondered what had happened to all the joy that had been in the camp, White Bird had a guilty sense that this was

true punishment for her impoliteness. She had completely ignored the hunter, keeping herself as lofty as Morning Land, and
now her sore back insisted loudly that such mannerlessness was
wrong. The prickling in her ankles and her spine would not kill
her, but it was matched by an anger in her chest. Oddly, this anger, which had begun because of Laughing One, was now
directed entirely at her sister. She had ignored him because
Morning Land had told her to do so. All her life she had always
obeyed her older sister. Morning Land had been so much wiser,
so much more beautiful, so much more willing to give orders.
But this time Morning Land had been wrong.

The idea was a shock to White Bird. The sister who was so
clever at healing, so certain about what should be done—this
sister could be wrong. The hunter would resent them and might
not want to help them anymore. It was wiser to treat him well.
Morning Land had been like one blinded. She had taken pleasure in driving Laughing One into a rage. She had been without
sense.

The soft sound of approaching footsteps made White Bird
turn her head. Morning Land was coming down the hill toward
her, clearly anxious to talk. At the sight of her, White Bird's expression hardened. She had nothing worth saying to her sister.
In a determined effort to avoid Morning Land, she slipped off
her waist skirt and rushed into the river. Cold beads of water
stung at her as her feet splashed up spray, but she ignored them.
After going only a short distance, she flopped onto her belly
and started swimming.

The piercing chill of the river was a quick cure for brooding.
White Bird twisted and churned in the water with grim earnest-
ness, heavy work being the only way to keep off numbness. For
a while she thought about nothing but swimming and was only
remotely aware of Morning Land in the water beside her. Finally, when her body could stand the cold no longer, White Bird
hurried up onto the sand.

The forest had been moist before, and a haze still hung in the
air, so the wetness clung to White Bird's skin even after she had
left the water. With the smell of wet autumn leaves strong
around her, she huddled down in the morning sunlight. She
wished she had thought to bring some of the dried rabbit skins
she and her sister had collected. A moment later, she felt a piece
of fur being thrust into her hands. Always mindful, Morning
Land had brought this for her.

White Bird glanced up at her sister with a look that was half resentful and half grateful. She could not think of anything to say.

"You are hard to find," Morning Land complained. "Why do you stay out in the bush alone?"

"Shiiwe," White Bird cursed, refusing to talk further.

Morning Land had found few things in her life that were as difficult for her as apologizing. Still, she persisted. "Do you want to go back to the hut?" she asked. "It will be warmer there by the fire."

"Shaaa," White Bird grumbled. "Why did we fight with the hunter? Are we still children? Here I am with my back ruined from the cold, and all because of your anger. You are a woman already, so what are you doing these things for?"

Morning Land grunted in surprise at this rebuke. White Bird's bitter words had sounded like the angry hissing of a goose.

"Who taught you to eat meat in front of a hunter and give him none?" White Bird demanded. "Soon we will be living with his people. He is our only friend and we have made him feel badly."

Morning Land rubbed at her chin, sensing that she was losing this argument. "A hunter can become too proud," she said. "This one is not our husband, yet we have gathered his food, healed his wounds, given him gifts, and warmed him at night. Does he thank us? No. Eh! this boy. His thoughts are those of a child. He thinks that what we do for him does not mean very much."

"You are still alive because he was there to help us!" White Bird exclaimed. "The cat is dead, but without *Tua-arikii* we would be the dead ones. Your heart is hard. You like hurting things. When are you going to be like other women?"

Morning Land rubbed at her wet limbs with a piece of rabbit fur in a show of calmness which she did not feel. "Dream men are always good," she said. "They do not trick a woman or leave her hurting, but real men must be watched carefully. They can treat you very badly. My heart refuses all men. The things they bring are not good for me. This boy you like may be strong, but he will make you feel terrible one day."

"It is you who makes me feel bad," White Bird growled. "This man speaks to me from his heart, and when a man speaks like that and looks right into you, you know things. My heart is saying I like this man. I will go inside his hut. You may stay alone and fight with the wind if you wish. *Tua-arikii* has no need of your food. I will give him what he wants."

Morning Land said nothing for a moment. She was feeling strangely defeated. "I have no more anger against *Tua-arikii*," she admitted.

"You are always full of bad thoughts," White Bird chided.

Morning Land sighed. "Yes, you are very much in love with that man now, and it is sweet for you, but he is not a Tidelander. His heart may change when we reach his village. Other women there may want him. Things may be different."

White Bird's fingers tugged at the saber-toothed tusk which dangled about her neck. She had been thinking these thoughts herself. It was clear that Laughing One had not understood the importance of making love to her under the shelter of their hut. "I am not a little girl," she said. "I know some things as well as you do. I could not pull my heart away from *Tua-arikii* even if I wished. He has become the important man in my life. But I will wait before I lie down with him again."

Satisfied that her necklace hung as it should, White Bird looked up at her sister and added, "You are also important to me, but do not make me choose between you. If you continue to treat *Tua-arikii* badly, I will know, and I will go with him."

After shaking the wetness from the piece of rabbit fur she had used for drying herself, Morning Land draped it across her shoulder with an indifferent toss of her head, trying hard not to show how much White Bird's words had hurt her. "*Tua-arikii* means little enough to me," she snorted, "but I will treat him well for your sake. I will jump up and run about and call him wonderful names if it will please you. I am the older woman. I have strength, and I know that there will be other men to choose when we reach his village. That will happen very soon now. We are leaving this camp today."

White Bird looked startled. Trembling slightly, she grabbed up her basket and hurried back toward the camp. Behind her, Morning Land followed much more slowly. She was worried, both for herself and her stubborn sister. There would be trouble when they reached Laughing One's village. There had to be. She still remembered how the warriors of the stranger tribe had raped her.

Morning Land was worried by other things as well, things inside of herself. White Bird had been right. Morning Land had enjoyed hurting the young hunter's pride. Without even intending to, she had turned the game they had been playing into something much more cruel. The only comforting thought was that White Bird would quickly undo any harm she had caused. Laughing One would be a well-fed man over the next few days. If anyone went without meat again, it would be White Bird, not the man she had chosen. Morning Land would try to help, too. It was important.

Resolved to control herself better, Morning Land followed the path up to the camp. The earth she stepped on had been well trodden by the numerous daily crossings of the two women, a clear sign to any stranger that there was a camp close by. But this was still a wild and empty land. Once the camp was deserted, it would be many lifetimes before humans settled near the river again.

CHAPTER SIX

The Way South

Laughing One and the Tideland sisters were not the only wanderers to come down into the Great Valley from out of the mountains. At a place where the river widened, a huge mastodon left the shelter of the deep trees and moved as quietly as a great brown shadow onto the open shore. Though it was more accustomed to feeding amid the silent timber forests of the high country, the mastodon descended into the valley lowlands during the colder weather of fall and winter. For most of the morning, this solitary bull had been foraging on elderberry bushes and cypress trees.

Waiting there in the sunlight, not trusting its weak eyes and refusing to move until its raised trunk had tested the air, the mastodon stood in complete silence. Its long hair was as dark as autumn chestnuts, its trunk and tusks as thick as tree roots. All the while it waited, yellowish membranes flickered back and forth across the surface of its dark eyes. At last the trunk was allowed to drop.

Now it waded out into the glittering river, moving deep enough for its belly hair to drag against the water's surface. As its trunk sucked in the cool water, the mastodon's long-lashed eyelids closed in a slumbering, dreamlike peace. Perhaps it would have waded still deeper, but something unexpected changed its mood.

In an instant the thick trunk rose up to smell the wind again. This time there was a trace of a new scent which made the mastodon let out a rumbling growl. The trunk twisted indecisively around one long tusk before lurching up into the wind yet a third time. With the new scent getting stronger, something in the mastodon's memory urged it to move back into the trees.

While the mastodon lumbered shoreward, creating its own tidal wash as it moved, three humans appeared on the river's opposite bank. All three stopped as soon as they saw the creature. The hunter, who was foremost, signaled for the two women to remain still, but his gesture was unnecessary. Neither sister had any intention of getting closer. They both stared wide-eyed at a beast which was unlike anything they had ever seen before.

Having gained a foothold on the opposite shore, the mastodon turned to face the intruders. Ragged ears flapped nervously; thick, dirt-encrusted feet pawed at the grass; the black, slithering trunk curled to rap against the ground with a rattling, snapping sound. An instant later the trunk was fluttering through the air again, and an angry trumpeting screamed into the wind; its one blast louder than a pack of howling wolves.

White Bird started and clasped at her ears. Morning Land lurched under her load. Aware of the unpredictable temper of these lone tuskers, Laughing One heeded the warning and hurried the amazed girls back up the path.

It was more than simple nervousness which prompted Laughing One's caution. He had seen the crushed limbs and mangled bodies of men who had been too slow around these giants. Every season some hunter from among the various valley tribes was killed by one of Ehina's kind. Like all the boys of his village, Laughing One would soon be forced to join such a hunt. Until now he had avoided these Ehina, but the women he was guiding had already forced him into doing things which he had never thought possible. To protect them, to claim White Bird as a wife, he needed the respect of his tribe.

Despite the problems they would cause him, Laughing One was glad he had found these forest sisters. During the days since they had left the camp by the river, the two women had followed him faithfully. All anger forgotten, White Bird had become full of teasing once more. Her laughter squealed forth explosively each time he teased her back, and whenever she was walking behind him, he could hear the soft warbling songs she made up to match the rhythm of her feet. Even the stubborn, willful Morning Land had deferred to him with a bemused tolerance, never eating until he had begun his meal, and never stopping until he had given the signal.

Though the country they were walking through seemed no different to the sisters from any other part of the river, Laughing One recognized every landmark. They did not understand why he had suddenly become so intent, preferring to wander about in the dust and sunlight rather than make camp. A while later he baffled them even further by walking over to a pile of rocks and crouching down beside it. With great care he placed his hands on the stones, touching the shape of each one as if some dreaming spirit lay hidden within.

Curious at first, the sisters soon became impatient. White Bird stood with her mouth partly opened, her face shiny with sweat, and wondered why Laughing One found this pile of stones so much more interesting than all the other piles scattered along the bank. Morning Land kept her lips tight and stared straight at the young hunter with an expression that clearly showed her annoyance. They were tired and their loads were heavy.

For the moment, Laughing One ignored the sisters. What they mistook for an ordinary pile of stones was both a marker and a signal. There were four tribes which shared the Great Valley, and signal piles like this one were what helped to keep peace among them.

Named for the chiefs who led them, the tribes of Black Snake, Wanderer, Stand in Camp, and Resting Moon followed trails which wound all across the immense open landscapes of the Great Valley. Sometimes they camped near the edges of the cliffs that fringed the valley, nestled in some tree-lined ravine amid blue ponds and downward tilting crags. On other occasions, they made their villages where the rivers ebbed and flowed over swampy flatlands, and hunted along the shorelines for flocks of migrating birds. Scattered this way across the wide savannah, the members of the different tribes seldom met one another, but during the warmest season, all four tribes journeyed toward the place where the game herds gathered in great numbers and joined their efforts for a single Great Hunt. Such meetings were the occasion for wide feasting and special ceremonies. The glories of the season were the marriages. Young couples from various tribes met at sundown after the hunts had finished and disappeared together amid the privacy of the woods. When the Great Hunt was nearly completed, many young women would leave their family lodges to live in a different village. Laughing One had always expected that he would find his wife during one of the ceremonies of the Great Hunt. Now it seemed things would happen differently.

All through other seasons, the tribes kept to themselves, staying in separate hunting areas that were marked by piles of stones like this one. Formed of fieldstones gathered in meadows all along the river, the stone pile showed the northern limit of the hunting ground for Wanderer's tribe. Laughing One and his two brothers had helped to build it. At its base was a great boulder that had been burned on one side by the power of a single lightning flash. Each season some hunters from Wanderer's tribe would come to this weather-polished pile of stones and turn that great central rock. The other irregularly shaped stones could be tipped any way that the hunters pleased. They were simply gray and white rocks set in the grass. It was the largest stone that was important. The burn mark on its lightning-scorched side always pointed toward the place where Wanderer's village lay.

Laughing One smiled when he saw the great rock had not been moved. This meant his people had not begun their winter journey into the south and were still awaiting his return. He would find his village where he had left it.

Laughing One felt grateful. His father had cared enough to risk the rains for him. Each fall, Wanderer's tribe had always been the first to reach the winter grounds, but this time it would be different. This time Wanderer would be late because he had waited for his son.

Laughing One finally looked up and saw both women staring at him. With a hunter to guide them, the sisters had adopted the tumpline method of carrying their loads, using a strap across their foreheads to keep the bundles in position on their backs. This made it easier to carry large objects, but after a day of hauling things over a hard trail, the tired women had bright red weals on their foreheads.

Laughing One tried to explain. "My village is near," he stammered. Then, adding hand gestures to replace words the sisters would not know, he told them that they would reach the village the next day.

This news did not greatly impress Morning Land. She stood as impassively as before, her expression clearly demanding that he give some signal. With a sigh, Laughing One ordered them to make camp.

The sisters immediately dropped their bundles and started down toward the river. Laughing One did not try to follow them. He knew they would swim until exhausted, then lie on the shore in the sun and talk quietly in their soft Tideland tongue until their skin felt dry again. After that they would take the stone choppers and begin cutting down saplings for their hut frame. The fact that they could build a hut so rapidly did not impress Laughing One nearly so much as their need for one. It was the same each night. Whereas Laughing One's own people would simply have lain in the open or dug small sleeping pits for themselves, neither sister seemed content until she had a shelter of grass and branches around her. It had meant stopping well before sunset to give them time for hut making and had slowed their arrival at the village by at least half a day.

Still, Laughing One was not that annoyed with the delay. He enjoyed watching the two sisters and had learned to love the gentle grace of everything they did. For a brief while, both these women had followed him, treating him as only the best of hunters in his own village could expect to be treated. In another day, they might both belong to someone else. As soon as they arrived at his people's village, things would be changed for all of them. Once home, Laughing One would waver under the scoldings of his older brothers and the disapproving scowl of his father. No one would think to serve him before the others.

For this reason, Laughing One almost hesitated the next morning, when the lifting ground fog revealed the first signs of his father's fall camp.

As often happened during this darkening time of year, cold air had moved down from the mountains overnight, blotting out the stars and leaving the ground covered in chill mist. Walking that morning had been like striding across a frost-encrusted bog, and the sisters were so glad to be stepping out of the mist into warm sunshine that they did not even notice a distant ridge rising above the grasslands. Only Laughing One knew what to look for. Wanderer's village sat atop that ridge. Beyond it, on the opposite side, lay a shallow lake that was fringed with marshes.

They were still a long way off when the outline of the ridge became visible through the haze. Laughing One quickly pointed it out to the sisters, but the women failed to understand its importance. Only later, after the haze had cleared and smoke trails from the village fires became visible against the sky, did the girls begin to grow tense and silent behind him. Their hunched shoulders showed their nervousness.

Guessing that the village hunters had already seen them, Laughing One decided to approach the ridge alone. One by one, he stabbed his three spears point first into the ground. Then he unstrapped his weapons' pouch and signaled for the women to wait.

"You must stand here," he said quickly. "I will return."

The sisters looked around them fearfully. As yet no other humans were visible in this great field of grass.

"Do not leave us here," White Bird pleaded.

"I will return for you," Laughing One repeated in a gently affectionate tone. "You will just stay here a little while."

White Bird reached out and grabbed his arm.

"Soon I will take you to my mother's hut," Laughing One promised. Then, dropping her arm, he turned and ran toward the ridge.

Laughing One moved with long, easy strides that covered the distance surprisingly quickly. As he came nearer, he waved his arms to show that he was weaponless. Finally he started to shout. Before he had reached the base of the ridge, five men suddenly emerged out of the tall grass beside him. They let out a great shout of recognition and rushed to meet the newcomer. They, too, were weaponless.

Watching from a distance, White Bird found the whole ritual difficult to believe. Suddenly six men seemed to be embracing each other and laughing together out in the midst of an otherwise empty field. The sight made White Bird feel forsaken and very lonely.

Laughing One no longer had time for such worries. He knew each of these hunters well. The wild-looking man with bushy hair and the trace of a chin beard was Fighting Eagle, Laughing One's tall and rather fearsome stepbrother. His slanted eyes and high cheekbones made Fighting Eagle appear more brutal than he actually was, for once away from the hunt, Fighting Eagle preferred to let others lead. Two of the other long-haired men, Bear Killer and Thunder in the Ground, were hunting partners whose quarrelsomeness did not prevent them from making more kills than anyone else. The finely proportioned young man with delicate-looking hands and long fingers was He Who Looks Up. He Who Looks Up had a trimmed appearance and easy good manners, both of which had resulted from his marriage to a woman nearly twice his age. Looking smaller than the others because of his slimness was Trusted Friend, Laughing One's only full blood brother and the beguiled husband of Beautiful Star.

Fighting Eagle was the first to turn his attention to the sisters.

"What children have the spirits given birth to?" he asked. "Do not hold it inside you, brother. Tell me how those women could be walking behind you."

"They are forest children," Laughing One replied, watching nervously as the other men retrieved their weapons. "A longtooth held them prisoner in a tree. They lived there until I came and killed the cat. That is why they follow me now."

Fighting Eagle snorted and glanced at the women again. He had a way of staring down at people from behind his sharp edged nose which made others very nervous around him, and Laughing One was no exception. Fighting Eagle's mouth seemed to turn down naturally at the edges, giving him the appearance of always being slightly angry. Now he picked up his own spear and began walking toward the place where the women waited. The sisters saw a tall, hard-looking man with prominent cheekbones and small, grayish-black eyes advancing toward them with a spear in his hand.

"Forest children," Fighting Eagle repeated incredulously. "These are not children. What happened to you that you tell me such things? Do you think you are the only man they have ever seen? Where is their village?"

"They have no village," Laughing One explained. "There was fighting; such bad fighting that these women had to leave. They were the last ones in their village, so they ran away."

"Who were they fighting? Where did these women live?"

Laughing One pointed north toward a distant line of mountains. "They lived beyond the Great Hills."

Fighting Eagle's eyes stared straight into Laughing One's, searching. "No one lives beyond the Great Hills. If you must say bad things, at least tell me lies I can believe."

"They were alone when I found them," Laughing One insisted. "They were hiding in a tree. The men in their village had been killed by the fighting."

Fighting Eagle's face showed his disbelief. "What fighting kills a whole village?" he asked. "Your story refuses you. Even if it is true that you found them alone, these women are more than children. They have grown up. One is very beautiful. She must have been married and given birth before this. They have treated you as an unimportant one, brother. They have not told you anything."

"We fought the cat together." Laughing One pointed to the puckered scars on his thigh. "This is where the cat clawed me when I killed it. Each of these women wears one of its teeth around her neck."

Fighting Eagle bent forward to study the marks on his brother's thigh. As a hunter, he had seen enough wounds to know that only the claws of a big cat could have left such scars. It made him realize the truth behind some of what his brother had told him. Without speaking, he walked up to White Bird and grabbed her necklace. The girl cowered at his touch, straining her neck as she tried to pull back from him, but Fighting Eagle's eyes stared only at the tooth. He recognized that the saber-toothed tiger's tusk was fresh. With a surprised snort, he let the tusk drop back against White Bird's chest and turned away.

"Do not wear me out with wondering. Tell me the way these things happened," he demanded.

Laughing One quickly told about his encounter with the cat. It was a story he had been preparing in his mind for days, but it came out almost too quickly, in a nervous flurry of words. When he had said all that seemed important, he finished with, "They have followed my tracks here. I have taken them back with me and have lain down in their hut. As I stand here now, I want to have them as my wives."

"There are many men who could be their husbands, brother. Why should the elders agree to you?" Having dismissed Laughing One's claim as nonsense, Fighting Eagle walked over to inspect the women more closely. "Do they understand us when we are talking this way?" he asked.

"I have taught them words," Laughing One replied.

"Then have them put down their bundles."

Laughing One gave the order and the sisters immediately complied. As Fighting Eagle came closer, White Bird huddled next to her sister. She did not want this grim-looking man to touch her.

She need not have worried. Fighting Eagle quickly dismissed her as an awkward, wide-eyed girl and turned his attention to Morning Land. Though Fighting Eagle had never worried much about feminine beauty, in the older sister he recognized the smooth lines of a perfectly formed creature. He admired her openly, as he would have examined a bull elk or a lone bison in its prime. It was only when he noticed her staring back at him that his attitude changed. Even when he looked straight into her face, Morning Land did not lower her eyes. Suddenly angry, he turned back to Laughing One.

"She is a bad one. She just stares. There is no respect in her. Can your heart really like such a woman?" he demanded.

"My heart does like her," Laughing One replied, "and I want to bring her to my hut beside her sister."

"Co-wives," Fighting Eagle snorted. "You are not even a man yet. Who will take care of them now and give them to you as wives when you are ready?"

"I am tired of being an unimportant one," Laughing One replied, his voice shaking with frustration. "When a man marries a woman, his heart is no longer fighting inside him. He has pride. I refuse to go back and sit with the children. Even if another man comes and wants to marry these sisters, I will not walk away."

Fighting Eagle was less impressed by Laughing One's words than by his manner. The brother he had known before would never have dared to speak to him this way in front of the other hunters. Somewhat more quietly, Fighting Eagle asked, "What kind of woman will this tall one be? Will she do what her husband tells her she should? Will she bring firewood and water? Will she make him furs for sleeping? I think she will be lazy and refuse. Ehnn, she will have lovers and refuse to listen to the man of her lodge."

"I do not fear her," Laughing One said. "I have seen how she does things. She is no worthless one. She saved my leg from great pain."

Fighting Eagle frowned in thought. It made his face look even more severe. "We will start fighting over these women. We will argue and yell about which man will marry which woman. You are not the only one who will want them."

"I cannot stand here and be quiet while other men go away with these sisters," Laughing One insisted. "They are important ones to me. We were together in the forest for a long time. We continued to stay at that river until my leg healed." Laughing One was surprised at how easily he was talking to his older stepbrother. The awe he had once felt when he had been around Fighting Eagle had somehow vanished.

Fighting Eagle was already tired of arguing. "Do not say anything more," he grumbled. "Our father will talk about these things with the elders until it is decided."

The brief silence which followed Fighting Eagle's statement was interrupted by Trusted Friend. "Just because your voice is loudest, brother, does not mean that all of us have to listen. I am glad to have my brother walking with us again. We could have stayed here only a few more days. Now we can all leave together."

Pointing toward the sisters, Trusted Friend exclaimed, "And these women! They are both beautiful and young. Only my little brother, with his wonderful luck, could have done such a thing. Who else goes out alone into empty forests and comes back with wives?"

Fighting Eagle glowered at Trusted Friend. Already the other men were smiling. If they stayed much longer, Trusted Friend would soon have them all laughing, and the situation was too serious for that.

Turning to the other men, Fighting Eagle said, "My younger brothers will stay here and talk until the sun is hot and burning on our backs. Young men's words do not mean much. Wanderer and the elders in the village where we live, they are the ones who decide things. We should bring these women to them."

Fighting Eagle gestured once and the other men began moving about through the hissing grass. Feet rustled against dry straw as the men passed the sisters on either side like prowling wolves. Even before Laughing One had given them the signal to start walking again, Morning Land realized that she and White Bird had been surrounded. As she heaved the load onto her back and refitted the tumpline over her forehead, she had the sense of being a captive.

White Bird's thoughts were less grim. She was curious about these strange men. She would gladly have looked around, but the tumpline kept her head pinned in one position, and her long hair fell back like a curtain, blocking out her view on either side. The only things she could see clearly were the legs of the three brothers in front of her. Even this view was enough to let her pick out Laughing One from the others. She knew the young hunter's walk, his shape, even his smell. Her mind had absorbed every detail of Laughing One in the days she had known him. Now, though, he seemed very distant from her. Though she could hear him speaking with his two brothers as they walked toward the village, the talk was too rapid for her to follow it. This was all the more frustrating since she sensed that it was her own future they were discussing.

After a while she gave up trying to listen and concentrated on other things. They were climbing the ridge, with the village just above them. The smell of food and smoke and human bodies was very strong. From somewhere overhead came an unmistakable high-pitched whoop. Alerted, people rushed forward to watch the newcomers. A baby was crying, a young woman laughed—but most of the talking was hushed and excited. White Bird could sense many people moving in a close circle around her. If only she could lift her head and see.

As if responding to her wish, the men in front of her suddenly stopped.

"*Supai,*" Laughing One said, without turning.

White Bird quickly dropped her load and straightened her back. A moment later she wished that she were under the load again. There were faces everywhere. One woman in the crowd shook her head, muttered disapproval, and pointed to White Bird's feet. Another woman nodded, making no effort to hide her distaste. White Bird flushed and turned toward Laughing One.

Something was happening. She could feel a growing tenseness in the crowd. Then a tall man appeared in front of the three brothers. He was not dressed any differently from the rest, but he did not need to be. His authority was obvious simply from the attitude of those around him. White Bird guessed immediately that this must be Wanderer, headman of the village and Laughing One's father.

While Fighting Eagle spoke with his father, White Bird tried to study the man's features. Wanderer looked stern. He had the same downturned mouth and sharp jutting nose as Fighting Eagle, but there was something less hard about his eyes. Perhaps it was only that she knew he was Laughing One's father.

As soon as Fighting Eagle had finished, Wanderer turned to his youngest son. He spoke sharply, but though his words sounded angry, his eyes were warm. White Bird guessed most of the meaning. Wanderer was saying that Laughing One had been wrong in breaking the solitude of his journey. He should never have brought these women back with him. It would cause new trouble among his people.

When Laughing One tried to explain, the headman seemed to barely listen at all. Wanderer's glance kept shifting from his son's face to the sisters and back to his son again. He appeared to be deciding on his own while Laughing One spoke, without any regard for what was actually being said. Evidently his instincts suggested something, for he suddenly nodded and placed his hand on his son's shoulder. Though Laughing One had not finished speaking, he had the good sense to become quiet. For a moment there was an awkward silence among the people as they awaited their headman's signal.

Abruptly Wanderer turned to face the crowd and began giving orders. White Bird heard something about food and water, but could not understand the rest of it. When the crowd did not respond at once, Wanderer spoke in a sharper tone. Then there was movement everywhere. Amid all the shuffling, a woman reached out and took White Bird's hand. At first the Tideland girl balked, but when she saw her sister was still beside her, White Bird allowed herself to be led toward a nearby lodge. Behind her, other women began picking up the bundles the sisters had left.

White Bird was halfway to the lodge before she realized that Laughing One was not with them. She spun around quickly and called his name, but there was no sign of the young hunter. He had disappeared amid the maze of lodges. White Bird stood on her toes to see better, and shouted several more times. No one seemed to notice. After a moment of this, the woman grabbed White Bird's hand again and tugged insistently. Reluctantly, White Bird followed her into one of the lodges.

Some distance away, Laughing One was slowly walking through his village. Despite the smiles, laughter, and clasps on the shoulder that had greeted his arrival, he felt tense and worried. Everything seemed the same as he remembered it. Racks of drying meat still hung between the mound-shaped lodges, drawing flies and giving off a smell that was too strong to be entirely pleasant. Beyond the lodges, new hides were staked out over the grass as always, their inner sides slowly drying under the autumn sun. Around him, he could hear snatches of excited talking as the details of his own adventures were mulled over by the tribe. He had often dreamed of this; of being the traveler returning home with important news. Now it had happened. He was the important one with exciting stories to tell, but he was not happy.

Like all of the valley people's dwellings, his parents' lodge had only one narrow entrance. To get inside, Laughing One was forced to stoop so low that he was almost crawling. Once past the entrance, he immediately felt for the stack of surplus hides which served as bedding and squatted down on them. In the dimness of the lodge, his light-accustomed eyes were nearly blind. He could only see the vague silhouette of his mother as she sat waiting for him.

Summer Wind did not rush to embrace her son. She wanted to, but she did not. She had been part of the crowd that had watched Laughing One and the sisters walk into camp, but the same reserve which had caused her to withdraw from the group before Laughing One could have seen her caused her to hold back now. She waited until his eyes had grown used to the darkness before she moved to greet him, and when she did touch him, it was only to place her hand against his cheek. Yet there was as much in that touch as in any of White Bird's passionate hugs.

During the silence that followed, Laughing One was finally

able to see his mother's face. Summer Wind had once been the beauty of her village; a bright-eyed, self-pleased girl whose flirting had worried her parents. Since her marriage, Summer Wind had grown calmer, but to Laughing One she had always seemed like his father's new bride. She had been much more beautiful and youthful than the other women her age. As he looked at her though, he noticed a change. There were trace lines on her brow and a puffiness under her eyes which he could not remember having seen before.

For the second time that day, Summer Wind wanted to cry. Now that her son was actually sitting there, with his elbows resting on his thighs exactly as they had always done, the pleasure and hurt were almost too much. She could feel the tears welling up again, but he was watching her and she held them in. With some difficulty, she began to talk.

"Ehnn. These days you have been away have caused me pain," she admitted. "But you have not been unhappy. You have been with strange women. Yes, they are your friends of the night. I have seen them walking behind you. Your heart has not been hurt."

Laughing One smiled at her. He pointed to the ugly scar on his thigh. "There has been pain, Mother."

Summer Wind sucked in her breath. "You are sick?"

"No, Mother," Laughing One answered. "There was sickness, but one of these women has healed me."

Before he could speak further, Summer Wind was up and examining the wound. The awareness that death had been close to her son made her suddenly animated. She wanted to touch him, to reassure herself by rumpling his hair and pressing her cheek against his face the way she had once done. It was only with great difficulty that Laughing One prevented her from making a poultice for him or brewing some herbal tea. As a way of distracting her, he began to tell her about his adventure. What he said was not like the carefully prepared story he had told his father and brothers. Every detail and emotion came out in a speech that became steadily more animated as his excitement built. While he continued to speak, Summer Wind grew quiet again, her brows frowning slightly as she tried to understand the change she felt in her son. When he told her about making love to White Bird, she grew suddenly cross.

"Ehnn. *Kairofa* has you trembling, even in the morning. Is this all a woman's work is? Does she not spend the whole day getting firewood, cooking, and treating hides? If she and her husband will stay together, she must work for him. Feelings are strong in a lodge at night, but dawn breaks this, and when morning is here the work of the day begins. Between a man and a woman, loving and lying down together in a lodge is only a small part. A woman who thinks only of her lovers and enjoys no other talk is never pleased with one husband. She just pretends to be a wife. She plays with her lovers in the forest behind the village and just stays there playing while other women work. When her husband comes, she tells him that her back hurts and she is too tired to work. He listens to her stories, but all the village laughs. Ehnn. I am already old from watching the woman your brother married. Trusted Friend, he married *Kairofa* herself. I am a woman, and a woman sees these things, no matter how sightless her son is. I have one sightless son. I do not want two such men in our village."

"Why are you saying these things to me?" Laughing One asked. "*Yi-quay-is* (White Bird) does not refuse to work. We have already lived together. My heart is happy with her."

"You have played together like children in the bush," Summer Wind chided. "In the center of the village it is a different thing. A woman from another tribe, she is never treated well. When she tries to speak our talk, others will laugh at her. They will say she has the voice of a small animal. She will be told her own people are not good. Other women will tease her and trip her when she goes to gather things. She will feel ashamed when young children speak to her and she does not understand. Soon she will hardly speak at all. There will be no friends to visit. She will just stay by herself near your lodge. Her life will be ashes and earth. It is a sad thing, but it is what people do."

"If that is what is going to happen, then *Yi-quay-is* and I will not stay here," Laughing One insisted. "We will return to the forest. But the people here are not so very ugly. They do not feel anger when their stomachs are full. If they see *Yi-quay-is* sitting here, in this lodge, with you teaching her, their meanness will be finished. Ehnn. Let her sit down with our family."

Summer Wind sighed. It made her sad to see how changed he was. "*Yi-quay-is*," she said, twisting her mouth as she tried to match the Tideland speech. "My face frowns at this woman's name. I do not like it. Where did she live that there were no men there? Only two women living in a tree—the strangeness worries me. Will she be good tempered? Will she listen? Or will she sulk, turn her back on me when I scold her, eat her food alone? Am I bringing one who steals into my lodge? I am too old a woman to deal with these things."

"*Yi-quay-is* is still a very young woman," Laughing One persisted, "yet she tried to pull the sickness out of my leg. She helped me with my pain. It is not long since she was a woman the first time, but she does not sit crying when there is no food. She finds it. I want this woman. Help me with her. Let her live here."

As she looked at her son, Summer Wind wondered how hard it would be for him before he finally wore the manhood markings on his brow. "I will not refuse you," she promised. "I will try to teach her. The last time I did this was long ago, but I will try. Still, I do not decide things. Your father, he and the elders, they will decide."

"If you say you will do this, my father will not want to hear anything else," Laughing One insisted. "The other elders will not care."

Summer Wind shook her head. "Your father knows how to talk, but this time his words will be thin. This time he might be refused."

Laughing One was openly surprised. "Spear Maker and the others?" he asked. "Why would they refuse my father?"

Summer Wind tried to think of a way to answer. There were so many unpleasant things which she did not want to talk about, and yet they were all part of it. "Before you returned to our village we saw others approaching," she whispered. "They were Passing Shadow and his two wives. Wanderer would rather have seen a true bear in his lodge than have greeted this bear shaman, but a chief refused no one. Passing Shadow and his women are still with us. They are not leaving until we leave. We will all walk south together."

"The bear shaman," Laughing One repeated. "Passing Shadow?"

"Passing Shadow, Belly Breaker, Eater of Filth—he has many names and many people who do not love him," Summer Wind said. "If my heart had what it wanted, he would go as far away as the sun, beyond even the Great Hills where these orphan sisters lived. He is a man who even your father would refuse if he could. He is poison in our village."

Laughing One was silent for a long moment. He had grown up listening to stories about Passing Shadow. The bear shaman was dangerous and unpleasant, a man avoided by everyone except the angry and unhappy ones. The younger brothers who were not favored, the ones who had no wives while older men had many—for these the magic of Passing Shadow held meaning. They listened when he promised them things. They feared his threats, for they knew that Passing Shadow could be cruel. Mostly, though, they admired his cleverness. Passing Shadow could outsmart many of the true village leaders, including his own brother, Black Snake. And where trickery and threats failed, there was always magic.

"I have walked far and come back to you," Laughing One said slowly. "I am among my own people. I am not still a child. Why should I fear this old shaman? The things he did, they happened long ago."

"Uhnn. I and those who know, we are afraid," Summer Wind answered. "The great cat that would have killed you and the wild wolf people of the night are without strength beside Passing Shadow. His magic will make you the one who tries to kill yourself. Look into his face and see the truth of Spear Maker's stories."

Laughing One frowned. "Why should I be afraid? I will just live beside his lodge and he will not see me at all. His heart cannot be jealous of me."

"He comes to put the marriage oil on himself," Summer Wind said. "He will stay nearby until he finds a woman who will follow him."

"He is old now!" Laughing One exclaimed. "He is as old as Spear Maker. He will not want these young sisters. He has wives already."

"He has two wives," Summer Wind answered. "They followed him when he climbed the ridge to our village. They are young women, but they were given to Passing Shadow. They follow the tracks of this ruined man. They would rather sleep in their mothers' lodges, but he has beat them until they understand. This is one who is not refused."

Summer Wind's words stirred other memories. Laughing One had heard of Passing Shadow's cruelty to his wives. At one time the bear shaman had had four women in his lodge, and every one of them had felt his blows. If a wife moved too slowly, if she did not prepare enough food, if she did not answer when he called, then she would know his rage. Any wife who ducked his fists or ran away was in very great danger. Passing Shadow would swing a club or cut with a knife when his fists were not enough. Perhaps he could be stopped by other men before he had hit a woman too many times or split her open with his knife. Perhaps not. No man with sense wanted his sister in the lodge of the bear shaman.

"He already has two young women, so what is he doing in our village?" Laughing One asked. "Why would he want to take still another and put her inside his lodge? Does his heart change so quickly? Do his wives no longer want him?"

Summer Wind did not answer. She knew her son would not understand. It was all still strange to him—part of the adult world he was only beginning to join. He did not remember the way she did. Finally she said, "Eh! Passing Shadow is not like other husbands. He is always hungry; always wanting. He will never let a woman rest until his whole body is tired. When it is dawn again and other wives prepare for the work of the day, his women are worn out. No woman can understand him. Something is eating his heart. It is strong, but has no warmth. The women he takes, they do not live long.

"That man!" Summer Wind exclaimed. "Every mother in our village fears him. They want to keep their daughters. They look for other women to please him, and you have these two sisters. Does *he* think he is too old for them? No. He is someone who knows about women. He will take one of them for his lodge."

"Why can I not also refuse him?" Laughing One demanded.

"I told you, he can make you sick," Summer Wind said. "His desire pulls the strength from women. His magic pulls the strength from men. The elders, they remember the terrible things he has done. They still fear his magic."

For a moment Laughing One did look as if he were becoming sick. "And Wanderer is also afraid?" he asked.

"Your father would kill Passing Shadow and think it was good," Summer Wind said quickly. "The husband I married does not fear shamans. But Passing Shadow is the brother of Black Snake, and Black Snake is a powerful headman. Yes, even though the shaman is bad, there are many who look after him. He does as he wishes."

Laughing One moved toward the lodge entrance. "It was better when we were completely alone," he said. "I will find these sisters. We will just leave this village and let Passing Shadow sit here with his wives."

When she saw that he was leaving, Summer Wind reached out and grabbed her son's ankle. It was the first time she had held him that way since he had been a boy, and he could have kicked her grip away easily if he had wanted to. He did not, though. She had known he would not. Instead, he crouched tensely in the entranceway, waiting for her to speak.

"Eh! Your father and your brothers watch," Summer Wind warned. "You have not married these women. They are not your wives. If you run away and refuse to listen, then the men will follow you. They will carry both of these women back to Passing Shadow."

For a moment Laughing One just stared at her. Then his uncertainty gave way to tiredness. He collapsed back onto the hides. "I should go away," he said, but his tone was despairing.

Summer Wind placed her hand on her son's knee. "Am I not going to keep asking for you?'" she insisted. "Wanderer will give something to you as well. Wanderer is a man who is strong. He will not leave talking until you have *Yi-quay-is*."

"And *Ir-yah-i-yah-ee* (Morning Land)?" Laughing One asked.

Summer Wind sighed. "She came the way of orphan children. She is completely alone. She will only leave this village by following the shaman."

CHAPTER SEVEN

Passing Shadow

Near the opposite end of the village, another lodge was being carefully watched. Three old women with black, soot-covered clubs served as an informal guard for the two forest sisters. Unlike the dreaded stranger tribe, Laughing One's people were unused to taking captives, and had only a vague idea of how such people should be treated. The old women with the ugly-looking clubs were not really expected to overpower Morning Land and her sister. Since the small opening to the lodge would permit only one person to pass at a time, and since that person would have to come out on her hands and knees, even one old woman with a club would be enough to discourage them. Should the sisters prove quick enough to escape the old women's blows, a single warning shriek from any of the guards would alert the entire village. All of the old women were skilled at letting out loud, earsplitting wails, and it was better to have them here at this tedious chore than moving about the camp stirring up trouble with their gossip. More than any guards, the land itself ensured that the captive sisters would stay in one place. The nearest village was many days' trek to the south, and with open grasslands in all directions, there truly was no place for the sisters to run to.

Encouraged by the silence outside, White Bird did try to thrust her head through the lodge entrance—once. She looked around tentatively and immediately found herself staring into three scowling faces. One old woman threw down her club and spat loudly. Another cursed, "*Katto aaan nataii* (Filth is food to you)" and waggled the end of her club in White Bird's face. The third woman simply glowered.

White Bird smiled back nervously and hurried inside.

"*Shiiwe*, the ugly ones have not left us," she told her sister.

Morning Land grunted acknowledgment between mouthfuls. While White Bird had been too upset to touch the food that had been brought to them, her sister was eating and drinking with perfect calmness. It did not help the younger sister's mood.

"Eh, I sit here itching," White Bird complained. "Why are we sitting like this when the sun is still high up in the sky? My belly hurts. Soon I will wet myself. Am I to just lie here in the place I have soiled?"

Morning Land was eating the thick mush the old women had brought them. She paused and began licking her fingers. "Then go. This is no bad thing. They will not kill you for it."

White Bird turned toward the entrance, hesitated, and then turned back toward her sister. Her face showed her indecision.

"What is doing this to you, making you hide in this hut?" Morning Land chided. "Go."

"The women outside this hut are not giving people. They will not let me walk past them. You come with me," White Bird pleaded.

"Uhnn. Then they will think we are trying to run away. If I sit quietly inside their hut, they will not be angered. You go. I will sit here and wait."

White Bird seemed to make up her mind. She stumbled out of the lodge awkwardly, banging her shoulder against the narrow entrance and making the frame shake. For a moment her form blacked out daylight. Then the entrance was clear again and she had gone.

With her sister's departure, a curious change came over Morning Land. The relaxed pose she had been assuming shifted to an alert tenseness. Dealing with her sister's nervousness had been a distraction, but with only the warm darkness of the lodge walls around her, Morning Land was again aware of her helplessness. Unlike the open huts of her own tribe, these closed lodges had a lingering musty odor, a scent she was beginning to recognize as the smell of Laughing One's people. She could not guess how long she and her sister would have to sit there while their captors discussed their fate, but she knew that the outcome would be unpleasant. White Bird, even in her worst fears, did not imagine the things that Morning Land remembered.

The entrance grew black again as White Bird reentered. Morning Land could see that her sister's face was flushed.

"*Shaa henaki,* these are ugly people," White Bird said indignantly. "Even when they give, they hurt. I went to the bush and they followed after me. I showed them what I wanted, but they refused. They watched as my water spilled itself. And when my water fell and kept falling, they laughed. These old ones, they shamed me. They said I smelled like dead things."

Morning Land shook her head. "Their hearts are not close to ours. Only *Tua-arikii's* heart comes near ours, and he is not listened to. But soon this will stop. They will talk until they have no strength left, and then they will decide things."

"The strangers, that is what they are like," White Bird said. "I miss *Tua-arikii.* When he was near, he always defended me. This waiting for him now will make me sick. I will not be given to another man. Without *Tua-arikii,* I will walk away from this village."

"Where will you walk to, senseless one?" Morning Land asked. "You can only follow your footsteps in a great circle and return here."

White Bird's voice took on a frightened tone. "This has caused me pain. We are living in this place of other people, not our own village. You should have listened and stopped walking when I asked. We could have gone back to living in the forest. We would still be free and living with *Tua-arikii.* What tricked you that you made us come here?"

Morning Land was spared having to answer when the lodge entrance darkened again. This time it was a young woman who approached them. Her slender figure slipped easily through the low entrance with an accustomed grace the Tideland sisters lacked. She brought a wooden bowl filled with thick, berry-sweetened mush, but it was obvious that this offering was only an excuse. After placing the bowl in front of the sisters, she sat back on a pile of hides, waiting for her eyes to accustom themselves to the dim light. Despite her curiosity, the woman made no attempt to speak. Her boldness startled the sisters.

"*Shiiwe,* this is one who will not stay in her lodge!" Morning Land exclaimed. "Keep your words in your heart, sister."

White Bird did not reply. She was fascinated by the easy way the woman had managed to get through an entrance which, to White Bird's thinking, seemed impossibly tight. Even more fascinating was the stranger's face. Her features were finely drawn when compared with the other members of her tribe, with a thin, slightly pointed nose and full lips that seemed to curve upward at the ends to form a self-contented smile. Her eyes were as wide as White Bird's but lighter in color and with a very different expression to them. Her stare had neither the coldness of the old women nor the warmth of Laughing One. It was something White Bird had not seen in a woman before.

Morning Land was less impressed. She saw that the stranger's breasts were too small, too easily hidden under a rawhide cape. The woman's arms and legs looked thin enough to seem bony. There was something in the way she moved which seemed to hide these faults, but it was not enough to make her beautiful—at least, not to Morning Land.

Though the sisters could not know it, they were staring at Beautiful Star, the lithe wife of Trusted Friend. Straight and slender, she was gifted in skills which seemed strange for a hunting tribe. Few women knew how to decorate themselves the way Beautiful Star did. Not content with bead ornaments, carefully fashioned aprons, or the scents of sweet-smelling leaves, she would sometimes dye her golden skin with black juice and trace out elaborate designs all along her legs, back, and belly.

Long before she had left her parents' village, Beautiful Star's laughing, teasing way with men had been a great worry to her mother. Once, when asked if she had had any lovers, Beautiful Star had smiled brashly, tossed a fistful of dust at the sky, and said, "There have been this many." Then she had giggled at her mother's troubled expression. Now, after four summers as Trusted Friend's wife, she had learned to taunt men with her wriggling buttocks nearly as much as with her wickedly restless eyes.

Beautiful Star was there to study the strangers and decide if they were a threat to her. White Bird's bewildered expression was enough to convince Beautiful Star that this girl was no rival. It was Morning Land who worried Beautiful Star. Vanity had made Beautiful Star very sensitive to the things her own body lacked. She had learned to cover weaknesses with movements and decoration, but this stranger could stand naked in full daylight without shame.

Beautiful Star was about to try speaking with the strange women when her thoughts were disrupted by a sudden movement near the lodge entrance. A moment later, one of the old women called out to her in a hoarse whisper.

"Get up and go away from this lodge if you want to keep your husband," the old woman warned. "The bear shaman is coming to look at these women. I can see him walking over there. If you stay and sit, he will put marriage oil on you. He will not care whose wife you are already."

Beautiful Star suddenly grew very rigid. She had been avoiding Passing Shadow for days. Having already angered many of the women in this village with her flirting, Beautiful

Star was worried. Even Trusted Friend's family had no love for her. There was always the chance that Wanderer might choose to rid himself of his son's unwanted wife by giving Beautiful Star to Passing Shadow.

Certain that no one would speak for her, Beautiful Star looked for a chance to escape. She bit her lip to keep it from trembling and glanced around wildly until her gaze settled on Morning Land. Then she stopped trembling and simply stared.

As a new idea came to her, Beautiful Star settled herself back and began to smile.

"*Yattee* (come)," she urged, adding a hand gesture to make her meaning clearer.

Morning Land glanced at White Bird. "How long will they have us climbing in and out of lodges?" she asked.

White Bird sighed. "I am glad to move. My leg hurts from crouching in this place."

As soon as she saw that the sisters were going to follow, Beautiful Star quickly crawled through the lodge entrance. Daylight blinded all three women as they stepped outside, but Beautiful Star was used to such things and recovered first. She realized Passing Shadow was close by and swung her head around until she could see him. The sight made her draw in her breath. He was every bit as horrible as she had imagined. For a moment she held her body rigid, unwilling that he should even look at her. Then she realized where his eyes were staring.

Beautiful Star had guessed rightly. Morning Land's appearance had overshadowed her own, and for once Beautiful Star was happy to be ignored. With a sly smile, she slipped unobtrusively past the old women.

White Bird's first awareness of Passing Shadow came from his smell. While her eyes were still blinking against the brightness of the sunlight, she noticed a strong, unpleasant odor not unlike the stink of decaying meat. As a man approached, the stink grew stronger. White Bird turned and looked up, frightened. What she saw only increased her fear.

At one time Passing Shadow had been well formed, but disease and excess had worked on him. His flesh sagged over the bones, leaving him with sunken cheeks and loose folds of skin around his mouth. Some sickness caught in a land far to the south had corroded his skin, leaving it scarred with bumps, lines, and pockmarks.

His upper lip had a peculiar bird-wing curve to it that seemed strangely soft against his other features. Worst of all were his eyes. Encased in bags and sagging lids, they showed a fierceness and intensity that gave no sense of age.

White Bird tried to back away, but he caught her jaw in his calloused hand and forced her to turn her face to him. For a moment their eyes met. Then he dropped his hold and turned to Morning Land.

Morning Land felt herself tremble as she watched Passing Shadow. This was something even she had not expected. While the shaman slowly walked around her, she saw his gaze shift to her stomach, her buttocks, her thighs, and her breasts. Each time something seemed to please him, for he would suddenly smile, revealing teeth that had been filed to sharp points. For some reason, the smile looked even uglier on him than his normal sternness.

Passing Shadow only stayed a short while. Then he said something to the old women, and the sisters were hurried back inside. The girls went willingly enough. The windless lodge, where day was as dull and dark as night, still seemed almost pleasant when Passing Shadow walked the other way. Once they were alone in the stillness, however, the understanding of what had happened deadened their spirits. Neither White Bird nor Morning Land could hide the repulsion she had felt. They simply stared at each other.

At the southern edge of the ridge, a fire had been lit and a circle of men was beginning to form around it. Only hunters came forward to sit quietly before this flame, for this was a council of men, removed from the sight and hearing of wives and children. Its rules were long-held rituals. Each man who came there would be allowed to speak, no matter how rambling or foolish his talk might be. The headman was obliged to stay and listen until every person had finished his say. Usually the elders spoke most often, with the younger men using a few short grunts to show their surprise, amusement, or confusion. Wanderer, who had lit the council fire and would snuff the blaze out again when it was time to leave, sat quietly beside it. He wore no special furs or beads and looked as poor as any hunter there. It was only the deference with which he was listened to that singled him out.

Old Spear Maker, whose gifts for storytelling and cutting stone weapons gave him an honored place beside Wanderer, had an unfortunate habit of urging the obvious in his speeches. He would ramble on, in a tone better suited to idle chatting than to a council of men. Often he would wander in his own thoughts even while he was talking.

Wanderer, whose own speeches were quick and controlled, sat patiently beside his old friend, frowning slightly in a show of careful attention. When the other listeners seemed most ready to laugh, Wanderer's frown and seriousness increased. If Spear Maker began to ramble or lose his way, Wanderer would quietly repeat phrases from what had already been said. This echoing had a calming effect on Spear Maker and tended to shorten the old man's speeches.

On this particular day, Spear Maker used the arrival of the forest sisters to express his thoughts about all women.

"A man is pleased to have wives," Spear Maker said. "They are comforting at night and walk far from their lodges each day to gather food. Many seasons ago, my own wife walked very far to bring me sweet berries and the roots I loved to eat. She never blocked the entrance of our lodge with her sleeping. Not her! We should eat together, tasting those sweet things, and other men would complain that their wives were not as good. But this was only joking. All wives are good, truly. They. . . ."

"All wives are good," Wanderer said softly.

"In this village we have many wives," Spear Maker continued. "We have already seen many children born. I know some men want more. I wanted more women myself, long ago. But life here is good. Our children are fat. Our women are growing fat with still more children. It could not be better."

"This village has many women already," Wanderer agreed.

Though Spear Maker continued talking in this fashion, soon even Wanderer had trouble listening, for now Passing Shadow approached the group. Hunters already seated by the fire grimaced and stared openly at him, but the bear shaman met their stares with a look that revealed nothing. Around his neck, the shaman wore three strings of bears' teeth. A cape of hawk feathers, held together by thongs and twine, covered Passing Shadow's shoulders. A bear's scalp protected his head from the sun. Passing Shadow had a long, wooden shaman's rattle, which he held as if he were ready to strike out at someone. He did not bother with greetings as he came near the group. He simply stepped in front of Spear Maker and Wanderer, momentarily blocking their view of the fire as he moved to sit, uninvited, on Wanderer's right side.

Wanderer responded to this rudeness by remaining just as he was, refusing to acknowledge the shaman's presence by so much as blinking. Spear Maker had become quiet when Passing Shadow had approached too closely, but now Wanderer grunted as a signal that the old man should continue. Somewhat hesitantly, Spear Maker began to speak again, with Wanderer nodding as attentively as he had before. Still, the mood had changed. Passing Shadow would not listen quietly to another man's ramblings. After staring at the headman and his friend for a long moment through half-closed eyes, the shaman stretched and edged closer to the fire. Though he was a humorless man, he began a hard, ironical laughing that made the other men visibly nervous. Gradually Spear Maker tired under this new strain. Unexpectedly insulted, he finally signaled that he was finished.

There was a sudden quiet around the council fire. The eyes of the hunters twitched as their glances shifted from Wanderer to Passing Shadow and back again. No one else would speak. All were embarrassed by the shaman's rudeness and wary of his bitter tempter. Even Wanderer's show of indifference could not last. With a sigh he turned to face Passing Shadow, giving the bear shaman his chance to speak.

Passing Shadow had been waiting for this moment, but was determined not to show his eagerness. In truth, he did not really understand the need that drove him to seek new wives so greedily. The sight of sloping bellies and smooth soft thighs had always been matched by the reality of frightened girls struggling against him or lying in shivering submission until his wanting had turned to anger. The momentary hope which he had felt with each new wife had always been frustrated by the girl's childish fear of him. Yet, despite these disappointments, he had fought and bargained for each new wife as vigorously as any young lover would have. Perhaps it was simply the struggle itself, the slow battle of wills between himself and headmen like Wanderer, which made him so relentless.

Passing Shadow began slowly, allowing his talk to build up strength as he reminded the men of their obligations and appealed to their vanity at the same time.

"You have a strong chief and do not waste strength fighting among yourselves," he concluded. "Your people do not suffer this way. Wanderer's wisdom keeps you safe. The whole village is like a family. But there are other villages and other chiefs. These people must be treated gently. They do not easily forget hurts. When they are angered, men are killed and women are carried off. A village can never be safe if others live who wish you hurt. Wanderer has not forgotten these things."

Wanderer accepted this flattery without comment, for he recognized the threat the words contained. Passing Shadow was reminding the council that Black Snake was the shaman's brother and that Black Snake's village was larger and more powerful than Wanderer's. These words could only mean that the bear shaman was preparing to make some demand. Wanderer sat rigidly, waiting.

"You have found two women—strangers—not born in our land. Their people have suffered. Men were killed. Women and children were carried off. They have lost their whole families. They themselves were attacked in the forest by a great cat which Wanderer's own son killed.

"What are these women? They lived like animals in the forest, like bears and wolves, led by no one. They have lost the secret of our talk. They can only make noises. Who will train them? Who will prepare them to be mothers and wives? There is much sorrow and anger in doing these things.

"To many, I am an old man. I cannot change this wrinkled skin or make my bones grow less tired, but I have other strengths. My magic will protect me from the bad things these women will bring. I can take these sisters from the outside and truly teach them. A young man could not be as sure."

Wanderer stared bitterly at the shaman. It was obvious that this greedy old man wanted both sisters for himself. Passing Shadow had come to steal the women Laughing One had found. Wanderer refused to let his son be treated this way, but he knew his position was uncertain.

"What you have said is not the only way," he replied. "You have wives already. My son, Laughing One, has been strong. He did not cry out when his arms and legs were cut by the claws of the great cat. He learned to kill. He went into the forest alone, and his hunting was good. He came back with women of value. Now he needs a wife to start his own family. I want to give him these women."

Passing Shadow stared quizzically at Wanderer. "If your son is ready for wives, why does he not sit here at council with the rest of the hunters? The boy may be brave. A woman may be brave, but this does not make her a man. If your son is not ready to sit at council, how can we listen to him? He has no voice."

"I am his voice," Wanderer insisted. "My son has passed his

test under the Moon of the Hunter. He has made a kill already, a great, long-toothed cat, but there was no one there who knew the rituals. His face was not marked. Soon he will kill again and I myself will see that it is done correctly. When our council sits again, Laughing One will be here."

Passing Shadow looked uncooperative. "This may be well, but until this is done, he cannot protect a wife. This will mean waiting. How will these women stay alive? Who will kill food for them? Who will hear when they are crying? Who will build a lodge for these women? It is not a little thing. This is more than helping. What man will do all of this and take nothing himself? What man will feed another man's wives?"

For a moment there was consternation among the other men. All of them knew what Wanderer wanted, and most liked Laughing One, but the shaman's words worried them. Then Fighting Eagle, the quiet man whom all agreed was the greatest hunter their village had ever known, chose to speak. Passing Shadow would not steal from the absent Laughing One while Fighting Eagle watched.

"I am the eldest child of Wanderer," Fighting Eagle said simply. "This son he speaks for is my brother. I do not think my brother will fail in his hunt. With his hunting and mine, these sisters will have more food than they need. No one will suffer. I will care for the women until my brother is truly a hunter."

Passing Shadow had not expected that there would be so much support for the boy. With the chief, the village elder, and the leader of the hunters all on his side, Laughing One had already won. Yet there was enough doubt in the expressions of those around him to convince Passing Shadow that he could still gain something from this.

"Great is the affection for this son," Passing Shadow admitted. "One of the young girls might make him a good wife, but you must send him away from her until he is ready. The woman must stay by herself until the marks of manhood are on Laughing One's forehead."

Wanderer nodded. "We will see it done. My own wife will teach this girl. She is a good wife, and the girl will be kept in a good family."

"There are many things that must be done," Passing Shadow continued. "We have spoken for the youngest woman only. Even a brave young man cannot have two wives. This is the mark of special skills. Everyone smiles when a young man marries his first wife, but two women? Ehnn. This is too strong a thing.

"Not long ago I had a dream that a new woman came to my lodge. I asked, 'Who is this beautiful child that does not speak?' I held her and called her wife. I took care of her and she started to grow in wisdom. There was magic in her, but this magic was full of pain. Taking this wonderful woman child almost killed me, but when I woke I understood. My magic had grown stronger.

"The oldest of these sisters is the one who lived in my dream. This woman is strong and important. She is a woman for a chief or a wise one."

Wanderer understood. The shaman was offering to share the women; to give the younger, unimportant one to Wanderer's son while taking the beautiful older sister for himself. In return, the friendship between Black Snake's tribe and Wanderer's village would remain strong. It was the easiest way, perhaps the only way.

"A woman can bring both life and pain to a man," Wanderer admitted. "But this dream of yours troubles me. There is trembling and hurting in it. Perhaps the spirits trick you."

"I know what I dream," Passing Shadow retorted. "This woman came and helped me. She helped me grow stronger. She made me alive again. The things she brought were good."

As Wanderer had expected, no one else spoke. Many of the men had been attracted by Morning Land's beauty, and several might have asked for her had there been no one to oppose them, but their fear of Passing Shadow was very real. The shaman's arguments seemed reasonable to them. Training a woman who knew nothing about their language or customs would be a difficult task, especially when there was a wife in the lodge already. Most of the hunters could guess well enough what their wives would say if they brought home Morning Land. It was better to let the shaman have her. His lodge was unhappy enough already.

Grimly, Wanderer acknowledged the silent will of the council. "Your heart will not be miserable," he said quickly. "The woman is yours." Then he began kicking dirt onto the fire, signaling an end to the council.

White Bird had fallen asleep in the lodge. Despite her itching skin and her worry over what would happen to them, she had slumped down against the lodge's inner wall and gradually let her head rest on her raised knees. Her body was too tired from three days of hard marches for her to do otherwise. At first she dozed in this semierect pose, with her soft snoring filling the lodge. Then she flopped over onto her side and sprawled across the hides. Her breathing became much quieter as she settled down into deep sleep.

A while later she began to have a frightening dream. She thought that a group of women had entered the lodge and were trying to take her sister. She could hear their insistent voices speaking in Laughing One's tongue, and Morning Land's frightened replies. These women smelled badly. They had an odor of dead meat about them that quickly filled the lodge. Through the blur of sleep, White Bird realized vaguely that she had smelled that odor before.

Suddenly her eyes were wide open. This could not be a dream. Even now Morning Land's legs were slipping through the lodge entranceway. There was a heavy, strong-looking woman close behind her, shoving at Morning Land's feet to hurry her along. With a frightened yell, White Bird struggled to wakefulness. Morning Land was already gone from sight before White Bird could think clearly enough to act, but this did not prevent the young Tideland girl from springing at the stout woman who was still inside. She grabbed the woman's leg and tried to keep her there.

Despite its smooth and fleshy appearance, the thigh White Bird grasped was surprisingly strong. It spun quickly under her grip when the woman turned toward her. As she saw her opponent's face, White Bird let out a startled squeal. The woman was cross-eyed. An instant later, the leg White Bird held slammed up against her jaw, sending her sprawling back onto the hides. Until that moment, White Bird had half believed that she had still been dreaming, but the sharp pain of the blow jolted her awake. She knew that what was happening was more terrifying than a dream.

The woman who had struck White Bird took advantage of the girl's confusion and made her escape through the entrance. By the time White Bird had gotten to her knees again, the lodge was empty.

"*Atoshe!*" White Bird called uncertainly. "Morning Land."

There was no answer from her sister.

White Bird hurried to the lodge entrance. It was painfully bright outside and she kept her face toward the ground as she started to crawl out, determined not to be blinded by the sunlight this time. She was halfway through the entrance when a stabbing jolt of pain cracked down across her head.

White Bird collapsed to the ground and clutched her throbbing temples. The blow left an aching in her head, but there was no blood. One of the old women had tapped at White Bird with her club; not hard enough to damage, but firmly enough to keep the girl back. As she lay there nursing her hurt, White Bird heard her sister shouting. There was a slap and a cry of pain. Someone had hit Morning Land.

The thought brought White Bird to her feet immediately. Not caring if she were hit again or not, she darted forward. The old woman who had struck her tried to stop the girl, but White Bird slipped past the crone and ran toward the place where she had heard Morning Land. Only then did she look up.

Morning Land was standing near the center of the village, surrounded by a group of silent onlookers. The burly-looking woman who had kicked White Bird was now standing behind Morning Land. She had Morning Land's hands firmly held. Another smaller woman—a girl really—was standing to one side, looking dazed and upset. Directly in front of Morning Land, with his hand held ready for another slap, was Passing Shadow. Morning Land watched him with the desperate unhappiness of an animal wedged in a snare.

White Bird hurled herself at Passing Shadow, but never got close to him. Her rush was stopped when the old woman she had avoided earlier kicked at her feet and sent her tumbling into the dust. As she fell to her knees, White Bird rolled and ducked. There was another shout from Morning Land, followed by a second slap.

Before White Bird could get up again, a club was placed against her throat. The old woman shook the club and muttered threateningly. When White Bird spat at the crone, the club was jabbed in, just enough to hurt. Morning Land screamed and was slapped a third time.

"White Bird," Morning Land shouted over her pain. "Sit there quietly. This is already finished."

"I cannot sit here and let him beat you."

"*Shiiwe.* Do not get up. This one drinks anger easily," Morning Land warned. "He came while I was sitting and grabbed and hit me. Do not say anything. Everyone here has fear of his anger."

Morning Land's voice seemed surprisingly passionless for

someone who had just been struck several times. Even in the Tideland tongue, her tone was cold.

White Bird stayed crouched on the ground, her head still aching from where the club had hit her. "I listen and I stop," she said. "They have caused me pain. Why do they strike at us? Are you going away with them?"

"I go with my husband," Morning Land said bitterly. "He has taken me and will keep me with him."

For a moment, White Bird just stared. "*Shiiwe*. Not this one. He is a husband who will kill you."

Though she could not understand what White Bird was saying, the old woman did not like the tone of the girl's voice. She pressed her club against White Bird's throat again. White Bird was too stunned by what was happening to offer resistance. She simply hunched back in an effort to draw her neck away.

"Go into the lodge," Morning Land said. "Leave me, and let these women take me with them."

"I refuse," White Bird said. "I will follow their tracks. You always helped me. If you cry, I will cry. I will find you."

"I sit alone this day." Morning Land was careful to keep her voice level and calm. While she spoke, her eyes were fixed on Passing Shadow's raised hand. There was nothing in her body pose to indicate resistance.

"If you cry, it will anger them," she told her sister. "I am afraid of this husband. This day I join his tracks, but soon I will run away. Do not think of me."

Passing Shadow was clearly bothered by the fact that these sisters were talking in a language he did not understand. After seeing the rage disappear from Morning Land's expression, he lowered his hand and ordered his wives to take her to his lodge. There was an awkward moment when Morning Land nearly stumbled under the sudden pressure Dreaming Place applied to her back, but the Tideland woman remained passively obliging and was not hit again. As she stepped along the path between the lodges, she called to her sister.

"Go back to living, little White Bird. Lie here this night and sleep in this hut. *Tua-arikii* will take care of you for a while. We are living with his people."

Still stunned and disbelieving, White Bird stayed as she was until the old woman started shoving her toward the lodge. For an instant the young girl thought of trying to run away, but then she remembered her sister's words and went back inside without a struggle.

CHAPTER EIGHT

First Kill

For the next six days, Wanderer's band walked southward through the Great Valley's dried grasslands. The savannah grasses shimmered like a golden sea during this Moon of Flying Birds. Their very dryness made the game herds turn away from the northern ranges and move toward the great shallow lake basins of the south. Winter rains would flood those lakes, turning their shores green with new grasses and young leaves while cold air and frost settled with a deep quiet over the north. Wanderer's band followed the game routes, with flocks of migrating birds moving above them. They awoke to the honks, trills, and hoots of waterfowl, and all day long the flocks of birds continued to pass like sudden clouds overhead.

There was beauty in this land, with its slow rising hills, lonely islands of trees, and distant pale blue mountains, but there was also a numbing sameness. With the sun hot on their necks, the dust stirred up by others' feet itching their nostrils, and the sharp-edged straw scratching their legs, few had time to enjoy what they saw. In other autumns, Wanderer had stopped for daylong rests wherever there was water, giving the women time to ease their aching legs and backs, and allowing the men time to hunt the area for game. This season it was different. The days lost waiting for Laughing One had to be regained, and all the tribe suffered because of it.

Things were worse for the women. Their days began when the first silver of dawn showed across the swaying hills of grass. First light was the time for taking down the makeshift camp, bundling all they owned onto their backs, and fastening tumplines across their foreheads. Whining infants added their struggling weight to the women's loads. Older children walked on their own, but ran themselves to exhaustion early in the day, and spent much of the afternoon crankily begging to be picked up. The thumping of tired feet on grassy soil, the dry rustling of hot straw, and the shadowless sky overhead—this was the sa-

vannah which the women knew. When Wanderer finally signaled the end of the day's march, the women threw down their
loads with explosive grunts and gulped in mouthfuls of dusty,
sun-heated air. Despite the red weals left by the tumplines and
the heavy aching in their backs, they would gather firewood,
build hearths and shelters, and cook a meal before sunset had
turned the grass silver once more.

The men were the hunters and protectors. They moved ahead
and behind the long line of women, ready to run forward with
their spears at the sight of game or drive off any cats and bears
which came too close. Since the overworked women had little
time for gathering, meat was needed every day on these treks.
The hunters relied on the migrating waterfowl, but killing the
birds was not so easy as it seemed. One careless move would
startle a wary flock, making it rise in a single great rush and
leaving the hunters breathing only dust and feathers. Kills had
to be made quickly, while all the village was on the move, and
only the best of men could do that.

There was food hidden in the great breathing flood of yellow
grass. Pigeons, doves, and turkeys all nested there. Rabbits,
ground squirrels, and hares darted about under the blazing veldt.
Some always fell to the hunters' spears and bolas.

More tempting game stayed at a distance. Pronghorn antelope
danced warily in the sweet-scented grass well beyond the range
of the swiftest hunter. Wild quagga horses hurried toward the
horizon as the band approached, leaving only their dust trails to
taunt the men. Once a solitary dire wolf was seen running
across the plain, with its tail raised and its tongue lolling, too
intent in its search to be bothered by humans. Such sights
seemed designed by a cruel spirit intent on teasing the hungry
men.

By the sixth day of their trek, Laughing One had begun to
slump behind the other men. The sense of ill-luck that had
trailed him ever since his return to his father's village made him
numb to what was around him. He was far different from the
alert, determined hunter who had wandered through the mist-
covered forests of the north. Remembering the two women who
had been so swiftly taken away from him, he became alert only
when ordered to hunt, and his eyes quickly grew dull again
once the task was finished.

Laughing One seldom brooded about Morning Land. She had
already refused him long before, back at the camp by the river.
Though she had once taunted him, Laughing One felt pity for

her when he thought of who she was with now. She had been thrown away.

His memories of White Bird were what caused the tears to start at the edges of Laughing One's eyes. Sometimes, when the wind was soft and steady as it was on this day, he could almost feel her breath against his ears and her short, biting kisses along the hollow of his neck. She had given him pride, and though it hurt him to remember, though she could never think of him now as she once had, he could not stop himself from wanting her.

Having to spend his nights with Trusted Friend and Beautiful Star did nothing to cheer Laughing One. Always moody, Beautiful Star began nagging as soon as she had slipped the tumpline from her forehead. She built no shelters. A simple hollow in the ground served as their sleeping place, but from the anger on her face she might have created a whole village of lodges. After the second night, Laughing One had learned to prepare himself for her yelling. Whatever ducks the brothers had snared were never enough for Beautiful Star. As she plucked the feathers and tied the birds to a roasting stick, she looked dangerously at the two men who shared her fire. They were no hunters, she told them. They missed the signs that others found. They were lazy and thoughtless. She had to eat raw roots while Fighting Eagle's wife grew fat with food and rubbed herself all over with sweet-smelling grease.

Trusted Friend and Laughing One would sit silently by the smoking hearth while Beautiful Star reminded Laughing One of all the pain he had caused his people. He had made them wait on a windy ridge while he found his way home again. Now children cried all through the camp, wives fought with their husbands, brothers refused to speak to their sisters, and all because of Laughing One.

The brothers' perfect silence under her harangue ended when the birds were finally cooked. Food quieted Beautiful Star as quickly as a mother's breasts calmed a squawling child. She snatched up bits of meat in silence until her belly grew tight and full. Then the smoldering anger was over. Her glaring ended and Beautiful Star felt happy again. Her voice grew soft. From the way she moved, it became obvious that a new desire stirred inside her. Anava always followed her meal.

As the land faded into night, the woman who had scolded and berated Trusted Friend invariably embraced him. Suddenly she appreciated what he had done and was grateful for his touch. Swift and soft caresses replaced the biting words. She had love for her husband once more. But none of this was shared with Laughing One. He was the person who tried to sleep while the muffled noises beside him grew into a shaking, ramming tussle, climaxed by a moaning from deep inside Beautiful Star's throat as she gave in completely to the call of her body. At such times, Laughing One's mind was again excited by the thought of White Bird lying in his parents' lodge only a short distance away. He wanted to call out into the darkness for her.

On this day, White Bird walked far behind Laughing One. She was part of a column of sweating women, all of whom stooped under their women's loads. Unlike the young hunter she would marry, White Bird had little chance to scan the horizon. For her the savannah was simply a place of hard earth and rustling brown grass that was forever brushing against her bare legs. Her view was confined to the muscular hindquarters of the woman ahead of her. For most of each day, she stared at those fleshy, well-fattened buttocks, not with the lusty interest of a man, but simply as a way of focusing her own regular stride. She knew every stain on the woman's knee-length apron and could have described her neighbor's legs and thighs better than the woman's own husband. The stained apron was typical of a people less used to cleaning themselves than White Bird's tribe. At this dry season, there was barely enough water for drinking, and the long walks had left layers of dirt on everyone. Strangely, the dust on her companion's body did not bother White Bird the way it once might have. More than anything else, White Bird admired the strength of that woman's plump, smooth thighs and the way she kept on at a regular pace long after White Bird's own legs ached with tiredness. Never in her life had White Bird walked so far for so long.

White Bird had little chance to feel lonely during these daylight marches. Apart from the dubious company of the woman in front of her, there was the knowledge that her own back was under the watchful eyes of Summer Wind. During the first days of the march, there had also been a flock of children, drawn by their curiosity about this strange woman whom the tribe had adopted. For a while the stares and grimaces of the young ones had been a torment. Even their friendly attention had been unnerving, for they had run in circles around her legs and sometimes nearly tripped her in their desire to get close. Gradually though, when they had realized that White Bird was not going to do anything unusual and did not resemble the screaming wild woman they had hoped for, they had drifted back to their usual games. After five days of marching, White Bird no longer held any special attraction for them. With the easy confidence of children, they had already accepted her as one of the tribe's adults.

It was only during the night that the strangeness of her surroundings truly bothered White Bird. Sleeping was so much harder when every sight, sound, and smell was new to her. The animals of the savannah moved about at night far more than they did during daylight. Just when White Bird was ready to drift off to sleep beside a smoking fire, she would see the flashing white bellies of antelope leaping through the deep grass and hear the whistling danger cry of a quagga horse. When the silver of twilight darkened to black, the coughing roars of great cats would echo back over the blowing grass. White Bird would clutch at her knees then, and huddle in her part of the chief's hearth, feeling hopelessly distant from Laughing One, her sister, and the warm Tideland waters of her homeland.

Morning Land would have calmed her at such moments, but she was gone. The shaman's family always kept apart from the rest, for no one wanted to be close to Passing Shadow. Even his lodge was on the outskirts of the camp. Respectable women might pity his young wives from a distance, but fear of the shaman kept them aloof. Men were also reluctant to talk with the girls, for the shaman's jealousy was nearly as great as his magic. Isolated and withdrawn into themselves, the shaman's wives' only contact with other people came through whatever news Passing Shadow chose to share with them.

Once, on the evening of the fourth day of the trek, White Bird had slipped away from the chief's lodge and searched the camp for her sister. She had seen Morning Land sitting beside Passing Shadow's other two wives, making them seem all the more wretched by her presence. Curiosity had made White Bird learn as much as she could about the two young women who shared Morning Land's fate. The older of them, a big girl named Dreaming Place, was the one who had kicked White Bird on the day when Morning Land had been taken. Dreaming Place came from Resting Moon's village and was known as a stupid girl. She even looked stupid. One of her eyes had twisted inward, making her perpetually cross-eyed, and the heavy, chunky build of her body simply added to the impression of slow wits. The other wife, Dancing Rain, who came from Black Snake's village, was by far the prettier of the two. She had a slim, delicate build, and the cleverness to avoid most of the sha-man's wrath. They were both pitifully unhappy creatures, cut off from their own families and not accepted by anyone else's.

When White Bird had approached their lodge, all three women had been working on a hide near the entrance. White Bird had tried to signal her sister, but Morning Land had not no-ticed. Morning Land had sat stiffly, her eyes focused on some-thing that only she could see. White Bird had watched as the muscles of Morning Land's face had begun to tremble, and sud-denly White Bird had realized that her sister was beginning to cry. White Bird had wanted to help, but before she had been able to do anything she had been discovered by Summer Wind and hurried back to the chief's lodge. Yet the sight of Morning Land's bitterly unhappy face had stayed with her. Whenever she thought about her sister, White Bird would begin to cry, much to the discomfort of those around her.

Deprived of the company of both her sister and her lover, the lonely girl turned to the only other person who showed an inter-est in her—Summer Wind. At first White Bird had been slightly afraid of the older woman. Even Summer Wind's early kind-nesses had not been entirely appreciated. White Bird had not liked it at all when Summer Wind had thrown away the girl's willow-bark skirt and forced her to put on a rawhide apron. White Bird had also been told to wear leather moccasins and leggings that wound halfway up her calves. Having always run barefoot before, she had at first refused, but Summer Wind had persisted. This time, though, White Bird's objection had been short-lived. After several days' march with the moccasins and leggings, her feet were much less scratched than they had been before.

Despite her fears, the Tideland girl had not been ill-treated by Laughing One's parents, and had found it hard to struggle against the weight of their silent kindness. During the first few days, she had been almost trancelike in her placid acceptance of this change in her life, but gradually White Bird had begun to respond to Summer Wind's orders and teachings in the same way that she had followed Sacred Dance's direction only a few moons before. Summer Wind had helped to fill a gap in the homesick girl's life, and White Bird had clung to her because of it. The results had been pleasing for both.

Summer Wind continued White Bird's language training by the simple expedient of pointing to objects or handing them to the girl while repeating their names. She would wait expectantly for White Bird to say the words properly. To relieve her loneliness, White Bird worked at these lessons eagerly. Within a few days she had become quite fluent in her newly adopted tongue and was rapidly learning what was expected of the wife of a valley hunter. For her part, Summer Wind was happy to have a daughter trailing after her. Beautiful Star had always been a disappointment to Summer Wind, but she found White Bird quite different. She felt that her son had shown sense in choosing the girl.

Now, after six days of walking, White Bird was beginning to take a certain satisfaction in the familiar chores of setting up camp. As the evening of the sixth day arrived, she was sitting before the chief's fire—her knees together and her legs tucked under her in proper woman's fashion—and slowly rotating a pair of ducks which had been skewered to a pointed stake. She and Summer Wind had finished the makeshift lodge a short while before. Now the older woman was off somewhere talking to the other matrons of the tribe. White Bird wished Summer Wind would hurry back. Evening was a lonely time for the Tideland girl, and turning hot meat was not a chore that required much thought.

White Bird stopped a moment to tug at the edge of her apron. It was still stiffly uncomfortable, and she seemed to be always getting stains on it. Then the wind shifted slightly, blowing smoke into her face. She coughed, rubbed the back of her hand against her eyes, and shifted position. When her eyes had stopped watering, she noticed a certain change in the camp. Expressions on the faces around her seemed to have grown more excited. Voices had risen, too. She could not understand the rapid flow of sentences, but the word "Ehina" kept being repeated.

"*Yi-quay-is!*"

The Tideland girl turned gratefully when she saw Summer Wind approach.

"*Yi-quay-is,*" Summer Wind said hurriedly. "The men will hunt in the morning. We will stay behind in this place a while longer."

"I do not know about these things," White Bird admitted. "We have killed and cooked many birds. Always the men have trapped them and dropped them for the women to cook, and always we have kept walking. Now the walking is finished? Women do not just sit in the village when men hunt. Why are we staying here?"

"You are still a young girl," Summer Wind replied. "We will stay behind when the men go on *this* hunt. It is Ehina they seek— Ehina, the moving hill. Only strong men know how to track and kill Ehina. Fighting Eagle has learned. Trusted Friend has learned. Now Laughing One will learn."

White Bird was very confused. She had no idea what Ehina was or why it was important that Laughing One should learn how to kill it. She knew that Laughing One was still an eeenuan, an untried hunter, and that they could not be married until this had changed. Perhaps the hunt Summer Wind talked of would change things.

"You are much older than I," White Bird said. "Should I be happy to hear these things?"

Summer Wind nodded. "The river we have camped near leads to a wide lake. If this hunt is a good one, we will stay in that place when the rains come."

"Ehnn. We will stay until the men have killed this thing," White Bird said agreeably. "Then they will come to us with the meat."

Though she tried to answer White Bird's questions, Summer Wind seemed worried. "Ehina is different," she said. "This is not meat a man drops in front of his women. We do not just eat it. When the men hunt Ehina, they walk and walk. They follow Ehina's tracks until the sun sets and they are walking again when the sun rises. It is more than one day's work to kill Ehina. Fighting Eagle, he is the one who truly knows how. He feels where Ehina is. He is the true hunter. This day he knows that Ehina is near. We women will stay and wait while the men go to where Fighting Eagle says."

White Bird frowned in thought. "I heard people talking. I listen, but I do not know things. Why are we just sitting in our village while the men work?"

"If they kill Ehina, we will have work," Summer Wind said. "Ehina is truly large. Ehina is huge with meat. We women will walk to where Ehina died. We will live there while Ehina is skinned and the meat is cut. It will be many days. Then we will return, carrying meat in our baskets and on our shoulders. We will live and live, eating the meat of just one Ehina."

"Tua-arikii will kill this Ehina?" White Bird asked. She had not liked Summer Wind's description of the beast the men would be stalking.

Again Summer Wind nodded. "Fighting Eagle will take him

with the men who will lead the hunt," she said. "If the kill is good, you will be married before the next moon."

White Bird was still confused. She should have felt elated, but Summer Wind's tone was not joyful. White Bird understood the chief's wife well enough to know that the woman was worried.

"We will sit and wait for the hunters," White Bird agreed. Then she asked, "Do the men fear Ehina?"

Summer Wind did not answer. For a moment she simply stared at the strange girl she had adopted. There was something in Summer Wind's expression that made White Bird's stomach twist inside.

"Will Laughing One be strong enough?" White Bird asked.

"The things you ask are bad," Summer Wind hissed. "Never speak of bad things before a hunt. That kind of talk will ruin us." Then, when she saw that she was beginning to frighten the girl, Summer Wind changed her tone. "Do not worry. Laughing One will come back for you."

While Summer Wind and White Bird fussed over the chief's supper, Fighting Eagle walked quietly past his parents' lodge. Though his stern features showed no emotion, the hunter's eyes shifted slightly as he passed White Bird. With luck, this girl would be a wife in a few more days. He hoped to be the one to lead his brother to her.

But Fighting Eagle was worried. Laughing One had already done most of what was needed to become a man. All that was left was for him to make a single large kill. A camel or bison would have been enough. Ehina were too dangerous. It took a special kind of hunter to follow the great beasts, and more than simple skills to kill one. Neither Wanderer nor Fighting Eagle had wanted Laughing One to be part of this hunt, but the boy had insisted, and the shaman had told everyone that the signs were good. Now Fighting Eagle had only one night to prepare his young brother for what might be the most dangerous moment of his life.

Fighting Eagle was nearing Trusted Friend's lodge and still muttering to himself when he noticed Beautiful Star coming up from the river. She was carrying freshly filled water pouches, but from the swaying, easy way she held them, it was clear that she felt no need to hurry.

In the set pattern of village life, a young wife was expected to simply nod her head politely and continue walking when she met her husband's older brother on the path, but Beautiful Star found it more enjoyable to provoke Fighting Eagle. She grinned up at him pleasantly, as if about to share some private joke. Fighting Eagle, who would normally have walked past quickly, now stopped in confusion. Once having stopped, he felt obliged to question the woman.

"Where are you going?" he asked, though the answer was obvious.

"I bring water for your two brothers," Beautiful Star replied, still grinning up at him.

"Ehnn. Then go," Fighting Eagle responded. This formality done with, he should have continued on his way. Unfortunately, at the moment, his path and Beautiful Star's were the same. He had no choice but to walk beside his brother's provoking wife.

"My men are at the hearth fire," Beautiful Star continued, her lips twitching with barely controlled humor. "Trusted Friend talks of the hunt, but Laughing One finds his talk terrible. Laughing One's heart is still very small this night. His skin itself seems to fear his touch. He cannot sit for trembling but gets up and walks and loses some water and sits again. Your young brother makes friends with the bushes this night."

Fighting Eagle grunted in annoyance and hurried on, angry at himself for having bothered to talk with this stupid woman. He would have been even angrier had he seen the expression on Beautiful Star's face as she stared after him. Beautiful Star knew that Fighting Eagle was everything a hunter should be—skillful, brave, and trustworthy. That was what made tormenting him so much fun.

Fighting Eagle found his brothers sitting beside their hearth and noticed immediately that Laughing One looked every bit as frightened as Beautiful Star had said. The boy was trying to assume the cross-legged pose of a hunter, but he could not keep his hands still, and his face was blanched an unnatural grayish color. Was this scared boy a match for Ehina? Fighting Eagle shook his head.

Trusted Friend looked up immediately as his brother approached. "You are here," he said gratefully.

"I am here," Fighting Eagle acknowledged and sat down.

For a long, awkward moment the three brothers sat quietly, forming a small circle around the hearth fire. As the eldest, Fighting Eagle should have begun talking first, but he simply stared into the flames. Trusted Friend made a few grunting noises to cover his uneasiness, while Laughing One sat with his fear and wondered why things had seemed so much easier when he had been about to face the saber-toothed tiger. Arriving silently behind Fighting Eagle, Beautiful Star set the water pouches beside her husband and stepped back. She stared at the three brothers bemusedly for a while, then shook her head and went to speak with the other women.

"Ehnn," Trusted Friend grunted, anxious to begin talking. "The sun is close to the trees. Soon it will be gone into its lodge and night will sit across this land. Another sleep and we will seek Ehina. You have been to that place many times before, brother."

"They are without number," Fighting Eagle said simply. He was not boasting. To the valley people, anything that could not be counted on ten fingers was without number. Fighting Eagle stared hard at Laughing One for a moment longer, then finally began speaking.

"Nearby are the feeding places of Ehina. Already men have found her droppings on the ground. Ehina walks on nights like this when the moon is large. In the morning she will be at the place where I will bring you. It is a lake with large trees. The small fruit on these trees is ripe, so Ehina comes in her hunger. Ehina is always first at the fruit, before the other animals. In the evening she calls to her sisters; calls to them unseen, and they come. Do you know the voices of Ehina?"

Startled at being asked a question, Laughing One simply stared at his brother.

"Ehina has many voices," Fighting Eagle said. "Sometimes she snorts and grunts like an old buffalo cow when it is ready to chew on grass. Sometimes her growl tricks even the great cats. When she is angry, the air shakes with her rage. But when she calls her sisters, her voice is soft; softer than a lover's whispering. It is strange, this soft voice. Only Ehina can hear it. Ehina stops to listen to her sisters when we hunters hear no sound. Ehina hurries toward places where we see nothing. If one of Ehina's sisters is killed by hunters, she will always know. She will leave the place without ever seeing where the dead one lies. She does not need to see. Her spirit tells her everything.

"Ehina is clever. She has more sense than the bear or even the wolf. An old woman Ehina leads the others. When this old one grunts, the others come to her. If she clicks her teeth, they stop to listen. And when she squeals her anger, her sisters rage. No man is safe then. If he even moves, he will be broken and scattered.

"There are things to remember," Fighting Eagle added. "When you see Ehina, she will look as big as the trees. Her feet will make the earth shake around you, and your spear will seem like a leaf in your hands. You will come close to her, so close you will be able to count the ticks on her belly and feel her hot breath in your face. I know these things. I have been under Ehina's belly before. It is like hiding beneath the shadow of a tree. Some men have no sense when they see Ehina. They do not act quickly. They just lie still until Ehina finds them. That is the thing to fear."

Laughing One stared at his brother, amazed both by what Fighting Eagle said and by the calmness with which he said it. This man had been there and come back to tell of it—many times.

"Ehina is the strongest thing that lives." Fighting Eagle continued. "She can walk faster than you will run. She will break a tree with her tusks. She will pick up thick branches with her teeth. A man with sense never tries to use his strength against Ehina. It is like a tree fighting the wind.

"But Ehina has weaknesses, and that is how we kill her. She hears everything. She smells things we cannot. But she sees little. A man who hides his scent and walks without noise can stand beside Ehina and she will not know him. That is what you will do.

"To hide your smell is an easy thing. You will take Ehina's droppings and rub your body with them—every part of it—until you smell like Ehina herself. For this hunt you will wear no hides. Everything you have smells of people.

"This thing will happen when the sun is high and the heat has made Ehina quiet. When Ehina is chewing on small fruits under the shade of big trees, she is less watchful. But if Ehina has her calf with her, she is never lazy like this. She is always turning back and forth, and then she is the most dangerous of animals. Though you hunt only one Ehina, you must never forget her sisters. Ehina is not like the buffalo or the deer. Ehina will turn and protect her wounded sister. That is why we hunt as a group. If you can approach Ehina and strike at her with your spear, we other men will run and shout to confuse her sisters.

"Always approach Ehina with the wind in your face. Remember, if you can hear her stomach rumble, then she can hear you. Always come from behind Ehina, for she can see a good distance if you are in front of her. Watch the way Ehina swings her trunk. If she uses it to bring fruit to chew in her mouth, then you can come nearer. But if Ehina turns, you must stop at once and stay perfectly still. Do not even breathe. Do not blink until Ehina has turned back again. Ehina only seems slow. She is not. Her trunk has the speed of a blinking eye. Let her grab you, and it is finished."

Beautiful Star had returned by this time and was listening to what Fighting Eagle said. Usually his hunting tales bored her, but on this night it was different. Instead of teasing or being snappish, she slipped quietly behind her husband and stared across at Laughing One. Until this moment, she had not realized that Laughing One might die.

After a long silence, Laughing One asked, "When I have my spear in my hands, where will I hit with it?"

Fighting Eagle picked up a stick and carefully traced the figure of Ehina in the dirt beside the hearth. The flickering firelight gave a curious shading to his drawing, making it almost seem to move at times. "There are many places," he said.

With his stick, Fighting Eagle pointed to a place just below Ehina's tail. "Sometimes a hunter will come up behind Ehina and drive his spear through here." The stick in Fighting Eagle's hand wriggled slightly to indicate a stab. "The cut must be deep. The spear must go in to the length of a man's arm. If it cuts this deep, Ehina will not be able to move." He shrugged. "If it does not cut deep enough, Ehina will turn in her fury. In such a place, a hunter has little chance."

Laughing One nodded. He hoped the other methods Fighting Eagle knew would be better than this. As if reading his thoughts, Fighting Eagle lifted the stick again and indicated a point just behind Ehina's ear. "This is better, if you can reach it. A deep cut here will bring Ehina to her knees."

"Often we strike at Ehina's belly," Fighting Eagle added. "A spear cut there will hurt Ehina, but the wound will not kill her. Ehina is too big. Only sometimes does the wound take her. Then she will only stay where she is, raising and lowering her trunk. When this happens, the hunter stays, too, and jabs Ehina many times. When Ehina turns to look at him, he grows still again."

"Ehnn. I will do as these other men have done," Laughing One said.

Fighting Eagle stared at his younger brother for a moment. The leader of hunters had been worrying about what Laughing One might truly do. The belly stab was the best for the open country they would be traveling through, but it left the hunter in easy reach of Ehina's trunk. Laughing One's fear might make him hesitate. He might even miss entirely. Fighting Eagle shook his head.

"This day we will blood our spears together," he decided. "I will walk here and you will walk here." Fighting Eagle used his stick to show two hunters approaching Ehina from behind and on opposite sides. "Follow what I do. When my hand moves this way"—Fighting Eagle raised his left hand and spread three fingers—"you must move also. Do not just stand and wait. Swoop down like the eagle and cut Ehina here." Fighting Eagle pointed to a place just behind Ehina's knees. "The cut must be deep and quick. Perhaps it is just a small one. Then Ehina will know what has happened. She will grab you—wah—like that. She will strike you down." Fighting Eagle slapped his hand forcefully against the ground. "You will be pushed down very hard and your bones will be broken. Never wait for Ehina to strike at you. Cut her leg deeply and jump away. If the cut is deep enough, she will die. Other men hiding in the bushes will come out then and cut her belly with their spears. Then it is finished."

"It will be finished, but I will not have killed Ehina," Laughing One concluded.

"Ehina is too big for you to kill her alone. If she dies, it will be enough," Fighting Eagle said.

"I will do what you have taught me," Laughing One promised.

"Do not talk until it is done," Fighting Eagle warned. "Many have died before Ehina's strength was broken. These men were not as fast as Ehina's trunk. Even with her legs cut and dragging behind her, Ehina always has her trunk. Sometimes the leg cut is too small. Ehina may suddenly come to her feet and trample a man to death. Watch all that I do."

As an afterthought, Fighting Eagle added, "If Ehina does grab you and throw you against the ground, do not struggle. Lie like a man who has died. Do not start to cry or moan. Be like the dead. If you are quiet enough, Ehina may leave you after a while."

Fighting Eagle was finished talking. The night had come, cold and clear, around the little camp, with each star distinct against a darkened sky. The brothers sat quietly for a time, listening to the night noises; the wolves, the settling flocks of ducks, a big cat coughing somewhere out across the plain, and the insects, chirping all around. The night would be mist cold, but without frost.

Gradually Beautiful Star began to move about, preparing the meal quietly this time, without her usual flow of complaints. Fighting Eagle sat motionless for a long while, looking up into the night sky. Finally, without saying more, he got up and went back to his own hearth.

The next day brought a mild morning, with the sweet smell of dry hay in the air and a steady wind. Amid a great golden ocean of grass which looked like it might go on and on forever, six men moved in single file. They walked smoothly, seemingly without effort, indifferent to the wind that blew back their hair, the grass seeds which clung to their legs, and the hopping insects which jumped about in all directions just ahead of them. There were herds of pronghorn and bison in the distance, but the men ignored these and kept on, saying nothing.

Bear Killer and Thunder in the Ground had added their skills to those of the three brothers. Rock Breaker, Fighting Eagle's usual hunting partner, was also with them. At the moment, Bear Killer served as tracker, walking well ahead of the others.

The trail itself was easy to follow. When Ehina moved through an area, the land kept her imprint for a long time afterward. Trampled areas where the grass had been worn away, splintered saplings, trees stripped of bark, and stones made smooth by the leather pads of giant feet, all showed that this was a well-used pathway for Ehina. What Bear Killer checked was the freshness of the tracks. Some signs were obvious. The dung was warm to his touch when he broke it open. A piece of bark he found still showed traces of wetness where Ehina had chewed on it. But Bear Killer was not content with these signs. He crouched down over the circular footprints, once testing the soil where Ehina had trod by touching it with his tongue. He checked the wind direction by crumpling dried grass and watching how it settled in his open palm. Finally he stood up and stared at a place where well-grown trees had formed a small woods.

His message to the others was told in a series of gestures. The Ehina were resting among the trees as Fighting Eagle had said. They were close enough to hear any loud noise the hunters might make, but the wind favored the men.

When Fighting Eagle gave the signal, the men started breaking apart piles of dung. With great care, the hunters rubbed the heavy smelling mush against their skin, making sure that every part of themselves was covered with brownish juice. Laughing One cringed at the feel of the steaming dung, certain that he would forever carry the strong odor of Ehina with him. The other men treated the dung as a talisman that was their greatest protection against Ehina's fury.

The wind Bear Killer had mentioned seemed to have died even as the men stood there. Everything was still and hot under the bright autumn sun. Even the flies were as active as any summer insects when they buzzed and hovered around the dung-soaked hunters.

Fighting Eagle approached Laughing One, studied him for a moment, and gave an approving nod. Then he began to separate the men. There was no more time to discuss strategies or trail signs. Trusted Friend and Rock Breaker went first, running silently through the tall grass in a hunched-over fashion so that only the tops of their backs were visible. They would circle about and approach the herd from a different direction, ready to drive off the other Ehina once the first strike had been made. Bear Killer and Thunder in the Ground would stay a short distance behind Fighting Eagle. They were the best spearsmen in the tribe, and the hunting leader wanted them close by. Should anything go wrong, a signal from Fighting Eagle would be enough to bring help.

Fighting Eagle nodded at Laughing One and the two brothers began running forward toward the trees. The woods the men were approaching bordered a shallow stretch of water which became a lake after every rainy season. Now, at the driest season, it was little more than a wide pool surrounded by layers of black mud. The water it held was essential to the animal life of the region, and made it a regular stopping place for the herds of Ehina that passed through the area. As the two brothers came nearer to the trees, Laughing One could hear the sounds of the feeding giants quite clearly. There was a whacking noise of wet mud being slapped against coarse skin, the cracking of branches, the heavy grumbling of massive stomachs, and an occasional deep-voiced grunt.

When the brothers reached the edge of the trees, Laughing One got his first glimpse of Ehina—pale gray shapes hidden in the deep shade of the woods. Amid the steady noise of moving leaves, trunks coiled and uncoiled, petal-shaped ears fanned against the still air, and great, gray-colored flanks heaved and shook, their sighs as deep and steady as the rustling of wind through treetops.

The two brothers were stepping silently forward through the brush when Fighting Eagle froze in place like a frightened deer. Though he could sense no reason for it, Laughing One held his breath and did the same. He heard a faint crunching sound. Vaguely, at the very edge of his vision, an enormous shape began to become visible. It was Ehina, less than a spear throw away and coming toward them with deadly quickness. In another moment her domed forehead had blocked out the trees behind her and there was nothing to see in that direction except this one great animal. Laughing One noticed the caked mud on her forehead, the glistening wetness of her eyes, even the nostril hairs on her upturned trunk. He knew that this was the old woman Ehina, the leader of the herd. Something had upset her and she was coming to search the area, with her trunk twitching warily and her ears flared out.

Fighting Eagle's instincts saved the two brothers. The Ehina shuffled past them, no longer certain of what she had seen. She stopped a short distance away and began to turn back and forth, her trunk still lifted in a half curl. Though she could not smell or hear the men, she was not deceived by the apparent calm around her. Her trunk remained raised for a long while. Finally, she broke the tension by grabbing a nearby bush in her trunk, ripping out its roots with an angry shriek, and hurling it at a tree. The tree cracked loudly from the blow, the bush splintered, and the brooding giant stomped away toward the lakeshore. Around her the other Ehina went on feeding. They were used to their leader's bad temper.

Fighting Eagle waited long enough to be sure she was gone, then started forward again. He had already decided on which animal he wanted. The two brothers slipped past several more cows—each one nearly as large as the old leader—until they came upon a young bull. This solitary male stayed near the edge of the female herd—a perpetual straggler. Too large to be treated as a calf any longer, the young bull was disliked by the cows, who only tolerated adult males during their breeding time. The young bull lingered as close to his mother as he could get, held there by warm memories of her milk and gentleness, but finding his present life very lonely. The irritable cows made rumbling noises in their throats and sometimes jabbed their tusks into his rear if he came too close, sending him away in an undignified retreat. Yet though he could have roamed the savannah safely on his own, the memories of his mother kept him tagging behind the older cows.

With the cold reasoning of the hunter, Fighting Eagle had chosen the bull calf because of its isolation. This Ehina was big enough to provide meat for the whole village, and was as inexperienced in its own way as Laughing One. There was less chance of its being able to turn on its attackers or avoid the hunters' thrusts. And while the old matriarch would come screaming to defend another cow or one of the younger calves, the unwanted bull was already an outcast. Its death would bring little reaction from the females.

The decision made, Fighting Eagle gave the hunters a signal and moved away to the right. For the first time that morning, Laughing One did not follow his brother. The young hunter knew that he was now on his own. He must slowly work his way forward until he was in position behind Ehina's left leg, ready to strike when Fighting Eagle gave the signal. But would he be ready? Laughing One had thrown his spear into a charging saber-toothed tiger and had cut its chest even while it had leapt at him. He had not trembled then, but now he shook. His spear shaft shivered in his hand. His eyes had blurred over. He kept wanting to pant and gasp, for it seemed as if there was not enough air in his chest. For a long moment he waited, motionless, while the blurriness in his eyes began to clear. Then he stepped forward softly.

The young bull Ehina showed none of the old leader's nervousness. At the moment when the hunters began their final approach, the bull had just discovered a section of grass which was still green and soft. With a pleased grunt, it curled its sinuous trunk in among the tempting blades. A moment later a clump of grass came free, pulled up along with a ball of soft earth. The bull banged the grass against its legs until the roots had been shaken clear of dirt, then lifted the clump to its mouth. It was still munching contentedly when Laughing One came to within a spear's throw of its flank.

The passiveness of the bull helped to calm the young hunter. This Ehina seemed strangely insensitive to danger. Laughing One was close enough to count the long, isolated hairs on Ehina's hindquarters, and still Ehina's only interest was in the grass it had found. Except for the steady swishing of its trunk and the accompanying crunching of its jaws, the bull could have been dozing on its feet. Still conscious of the snorts and rumblings of the cows that were hidden behind the neighboring trees, Laughing One crept forward until he was less than two spear lengths from the bull's left hind leg. Finally he was ready for his brother's signal.

It came quickly enough. Fighting Eagle suddenly stepped from the bush he had been hidden behind and raised his hand to show three spread fingers. Without waiting longer, Laughing One jumped up, swung his spear about, and slashed sideways against the bull's leg, using all his strength. The blade sliced through the thick outer skin and drove deep against the leg tendon, splitting it with a slushing crunch.

Nothing had prepared Laughing One for the wild scream of rage that erupted from the wounded bull. The shrieking blast seemed to cut into his brain, momentarily blocking out all other thoughts. He barely had sense enough to jump away into the bush as Ehina turned.

Though his spear tip was coated in blood, Laughing One was too dazed to think of using it again. It seemed that the forest around him had suddenly exploded. Ehina were everywhere, trampling and screaming in utter confusion. Suddenly tree limbs snapped and crashed as great bodies forced their way through the woods. Human shouts were barely recognizable in the midst of the din. Vaguely, in a back corner of his mind, Laughing One realized that Trusted Friend and Rock Breaker were trying to drive off the rest of the herd. Consciously, his eyes could only fix on the swinging black trunk of the injured bull.

The wounded calf did not have time to search for its attackers. Even as Ehina turned, another spear was plunged into its belly and withdrawn. The thrust came from Bear Killer, who had moved in as Fighting Eagle had drawn back. When Ehina spun about to face its new tormentor, Bear Killer had already ducked away. The bull's trunk was still trying to reach for this man as a fourth spear entered the bull's belly from the opposite side. Thunder in the Ground had joined the attack.

In the moments that followed, the three experienced hunters worried and harassed their prey with fierce intensity. Like wolves attacking a snowbound moose, the men leapt and darted around the huge victim. Each time Ehina felt a spear plunge into its belly, it responded by screaming loudly and reaching out with its trunk, but the hunter was always gone. Whenever the young bull turned to face one man, another would swing in to attack from Ehina's blind side. None of the spear thrusts were deep enough to kill, but all brought gusts of blood streaming over the loose hide. The wounds were weakening and infuriating Ehina, driving it into a blind frenzy of panic. In the space of a few moments, Ehina felt more than a dozen slash wounds, and its tortured belly became as red as a butchering ground.

Then a new fear seemed to enter the dying Ehina's brain. The sounds of other Ehina were getting fainter, for the herd was hurrying away, leaving the bull calf to face its tormentors alone. With desperate courage Ehina turned again, ignoring the hunter's thrusts, and tried to follow the herd. In bellowing agony Ehina pulled itself clumsily over the ground, its hind legs now a useless dragging weight. Once it tried to lurch to its feet by grabbing at a nearby tree, but the tree collapsed under the pull of its trunk and ripped out of the ground. With a groan of despair, the young bull crawled on.

Something in this agony touched Laughing One. He was not afraid anymore, nor was he enjoying the ugliness of a slow kill. He only wanted to put an end to things. Running silently forward with his spear balanced in his hand, he came close to Ehina's head, aimed at the spot behind the ear that would surely kill, and drove his weapon in with all his force. The blade cut deep, grinding into the vertebrae of the neck. For an instant the young bull grunted and staggered, and Laughing One thought Ehina would collapse. Then the trunk swung around and smacked against him.

It was only a reflex blow, but it sent Laughing One rolling away across the ground. The trunk was full of blood, which sprayed all over the young hunter as he landed in a heap amid the dust, an ugly red weal already forming along his left thigh. Bare-handed, he got up again in time to see Ehina die.

Badly hurt, bleeding from dozens of stab wounds, and with Laughing One's spear still sticking out of its neck like some strange growth, the young bull suddenly shuddered and went down. With a last reproachful sigh, Ehina slipped backward into a sitting posture, its front legs straddled, and its crippled hind legs spread wide behind its great belly. There was no further sound. Ehina could have been resting there in the midday heat. As Laughing One slowly walked toward Ehina, he half expected the giant to lurch up again. An impression of life was also given by Ehina's tiny eyes, which were still open and had a strange wetness around them, as if Ehina had been crying. The entire slumped form of Ehina held a sadness of unwilling submission to violent death.

Laughing One did not have time to brood over this. Trusted Friend and Rock Breaker were already running to join the others. As soon as he was near, Trusted Friend paused, gasping for breath, and looked around at the kill site. Obviously pleased by what he saw, he placed his right hand on Laughing One's shoulder.

"Ehnn. I see Ehina lying dead on the ground," he said happily. "This day my brother has made his first kill."

Laughing One nodded weakly. He was waiting for some sign from Fighting Eagle.

The hunting leader had been examining the carcass, poking at it with his spear tip to make sure there were no lingering traces of life. Apparently satisfied, he turned his attention to Laughing One. The red mark on his brother's thigh and the blood splattered across Laughing One's face and chest obviously worried Fighting Eagle. He frowned and shifted his gaze to the spear sticking out of Ehina's neck.

"Uhnn, senseless one," he said angrily. "Are you not afraid of anything? You are not the only one on this hunt. You should have kept your spear in your hands."

Without waiting for a reply, the hunting leader touched his bloodied spear tip to the wound on Ehina's neck. "When this happened, Ehina became so angry he struck at you and knocked you down with great force. Your leg shows where Ehina grabbed at you. What thoughts were in you that you were doing this thing? There is no cure when a man's neck is broken."

Laughing One could only stand there. He had not expected his brother's anger.

Relenting, Fighting Eagle placed his right hand on his young brother's head. "Ehnn. You went out into the forest this day and struck Ehina with your spear. You did not run. You did not wait until Ehina grabbed you. Soon we will find the others and tell them to go to where Ehina has died." Fighting Eagle pulled out his hunting knife and handed it to Laughing One. "This kill is yours."

Laughing One knew what to expect. Ehina was bleeding from dozens of wounds, but the young hunter would have to make one more. Walking up to Ehina's head, Laughing One plunged the stone dagger into the folded skin of Ehina's throat. As the warm blood flowed out, Laughing One caught some of it in his cupped hands and drank it. The blood had a strange, bittersweet taste that lingered in his mouth long after he had swallowed.

Then Laughing One daubed blood on his cheeks and forehead. As he did so, he noticed that Ehina's mouth had fallen open during the last moments of life. The tongue was thrust out;

a pink, fleshy mound that looked softer than any human skin. He wondered how a creature as coarse and huge as this could have such a delicate-looking mouth.

All the men were watching him now, even Fighting Eagle. Their faces showed their pleasure at what he had done. In the newly stilled woods, Laughing One raised his bloodied hands and sang,

"I have killed Ehina,
   shaker of trees.
I have killed Ehina,
   who strikes with curved tusks.
I have killed Ehina,
   whose breath is fire.
I have killed Ehina.
My spear was stronger than her.
I have killed Ehina.
This day I am a man."

It was a chant known to all the hunters of the great valley; a chant echoed around countless fires on the dark, windy nights when day seemed far away. When he had finished singing it, Laughing One at last understood that the hunt and the waiting were over. White Bird would be his wife. She had become his bride the moment Ehina had fallen. There was nothing left to be afraid of.

CHAPTER NINE

The Butchering

Up to their waists in lake water, the men became boisterous. As they rubbed off the dried blood and dung that clung to their skin, they splashed and insulted one another in a vigorous, almost hysterical way. Trusted Friend was teased for the size of his testicles. Rock Breaker was mocked for the way his face seemed to be always scowling. Thunder in the Ground was laughed at because he could kill Ehina but ran from the fury of his own wife. The high laughter hid the strain they had all felt, and each man took the teasing with a good-natured shrug. This rough joking kept away anger and the shame of fear.

Fighting Eagle was the first to leave the water. While the others were becoming more and more insulting, he went back to the kill and cut off Ehina's tail. In life the tail had been of little use to Ehina—being too short even to sweep away the flies which rested on its flanks—but to the hunters this was a valued talisman. The hairs on the tail's tip were considered the most powerful of love tokens, and a hunter who could weave his wife a bracelet from such hairs was sure of warm evenings for many moons afterward. Fighting Eagle's interest was much more practical, however. The tail was certain proof of a kill, something to bring back to their camp.

As Fighting Eagle turned to face the men once more, he made a quick judgment. Laughing One had rights to the kill since this was his first, but it was not good for the boy to expect too much. He must learn to share glory with the rest of the spear brotherhood. Trusted Friend, however, had long wanted such a prize and had a wife who would probably show gratitude. Fighting Eagle called his brother to him and placed the tail in Trusted Friend's hands.

Still dripping water, Trusted Friend stood motionless, his face muscles working nervously. Never an extraordinary hunter, he had long ago given up any hope of bringing back the prize of such a kill. Now it seemed that he would have it after all. For once the most vocal man in the village could find no words.

Fighting Eagle tried to ignore the gratitude he saw in Trusted Friend's eyes. He covered his own emotions by speaking quickly.

"Ehnn, brother. We have food here. You must go back to our village and talk to the people. Tell them something big has been killed. Let them come to where Ehina has died. The women will be slow. Hurry them. Soon the sun will be low in the sky."

Trusted Friend nodded and started running.

As he watched his brother go, Fighting Eagle felt a certain satisfaction in his choice. Trusted Friend would shout their triumph as lustily as he had shouted at the frightened Ehina a short while before. No other hunter could enjoy strutting in front of women as much as Trusted Friend did.

When Trusted Friend had gone, the men's mood became more somber. All could sense the great amount of work that lay ahead of them. With a signal to Rock Breaker, Fighting Eagle climbed up onto Ehina's back as casually as another man might have walked across a boulder. Rock Breaker pulled out his stone knife and followed the hunting leader. Together they began cutting through the skin over Ehina's spine, starting from a point above the chest and working their way back toward the tail.

Laughing One had never seen this part of the butchering. He had always arrived along with the women, when the best sections of Ehina's hide had already been stripped away. He knew that the men always split Ehina's skin along the spine and then pulled it down on either side, but he had not guessed that his brother's black knife could cut through the thick skin so quickly. Soon they would be peeling the hide back by punching at its underside with sharpened sticks. As he watched, Laughing One realized that part of this hide would be given to him.

He felt someone nudge his shoulders and turned to see Bear Killer standing beside him. Bear Killer held two stone choppers in his hands and was offering one of them to Laughing One. The message was obvious. As soon as he accepted the chopper, Laughing One became one of the men who would hack apart Ehina's head.

They began with the trunk, which turned out to be much less soft than it appeared. Its suppleness in life had been due to hundreds of specialized muscles. These same muscles had to be slashed through with stone choppers. Laughing One brought his blade down again and again, each time cutting only slightly deeper into the hard, toughened flesh. Soon his hands were red from the blood which splattered up out of the darkened skin. Before the sagging mass of trunk finally gave way under their efforts, his own blood seemed to be roaring in his ears.

Bear Killer picked up one end of the severed trunk and hauled it away, dragging it through the dust to a place where the women would later build a fire. There was something repulsive about the twisted gray mass when it was no longer attached to Ehina's head. It looked as if some soft, boneless creature that belonged in deep water had been accidentally churned up and washed ashore. Ehina's head seemed equally distorted with nothing below the eyes but a bleeding, gaping hole. Blood from the butchering had streamed out onto the giant tusks, giving them a savage, reddish hue.

Laughing One barely had time to wipe the sweat from his face before the next task began. Fighting Eagle and Rock Breaker had already folded the hide back from Ehina's shoulders, leaving a clear space for the other men to work. Thunder in the Ground climbed up onto Ehina's back, his bare feet making squishing sounds as they pressed down onto the red meat. There was little fat on the carcass. Once the skin had been pulled away from Ehina's upper back, his body seemed pinkish in color.

Thunder in the Ground immediately began pounding at the muscles on Ehina's neck in an effort to sever Ehina's head. Laughing One and Bear Killer joined him—one man standing on either side of Thunder in the Ground—and all three cutting slowly inward above Ehina's throat. It was a matter of battering, bruising, and slicing until the layers of outer muscles had been slashed off. Then bones and tendons had to be pounded loose. The amount of flesh that had to be cut through seemed enormous, for the muscles which supported Ehina's great head were massive.

Laughing One began to work blindly after a while; his body responding to a rhythm his mind was barely conscious of. Blood splashed out onto his chest, stomach, and thighs. His face became spattered with gore, but he did not truly notice. Already he was worrying about what came afterward. While his people were feasting, he would be in an isolated hut beyond the camp. It was the last part of the manhood rites he had begun in the Moon of the Hunter. For three days he would be isolated from everyone but the village shaman. When Laughing One had first left on his journey, Spear Maker had been the village shaman, but now it was Passing Shadow who would guard Laughing One's isolation hut.

A shout from Thunder in the Ground brought Laughing One's attention back to what they were doing. Most of the neck muscles had been cut away from Ehina's skull, and already the position of Ehina's head was changing. Pulled down by the weight of the tusks, Ehina's skull slumped forward, putting added strain on the frail neck vertebrae. Though huge in appearance, Ehina's head was actually much lighter than other parts of the body, for the skull was riddled with air-filled cavities. Only the solid weight of the ivory tusks made it top heavy.

More pounding finally crushed the neck bone and cut the tendons free. With a loud crunching sound, Ehina's mutilated head tumbled onto the ground.

Laughing One dropped the stone chopper into the dust and flexed his aching hands. Any thrill he had felt at killing Ehina had long since gone. All he wanted was to wash himself once more in that cool lake water and then rest under the trees until dark. When he looked up, he saw that the sun was already moving toward the western trees. The women should have arrived before this. He wondered what was slowing them.

Farther north, White Bird was again part of a moving column of women. With her head pushed forward against the tumpline once more and her eyes focused on the same wide buttocks that she had watched for the last six days, it was as if her interlude at the camp had never existed. The only difference was that now she could no longer let her thoughts drift. The present had begun to press in around her, and her mind felt muddled.

Her day had begun badly, with Summer Wind in a temper. When the last of the camel meat had been burned slightly on one side, the chief's wife had scolded so much that White Bird had felt hot tears welling at the edges of her eyes. Even then the older woman had not relented much. She had just snorted contemptuously and stomped off to yell at Beautiful Star for a while. Wanderer had been just as bad. He had thrown the meat down after barely tasting it and had begun to pace in circles around the camp, leaving the Tideland girl alone by their hearth. White Bird had felt a rush of self-pity which had left her sniveling throughout the morning.

Then Trusted Friend had appeared, brandishing Ehina's tail, and suddenly the whole camp had begun shouting.

"Eh-hey, our husbands, our wonderful husbands," some women had called.

"Everyone, Come here!" others had cried. "The men have certainly killed something. Now there truly will be meat."

The relief of the women had bubbled over in a continuous giggling. Even Summer Wind had been grinning. She had hugged Trusted Friend as if he had still been a boy. Then she had come back and hugged White Bird, all the while murmuring, "Daughter, daughter."

In the midst of a crowd of women, Trusted Friend had begun to reenact the story of the hunt. Beautiful Star, who had nuzzled her husband almost like a Tideland woman when he had first appeared, had stayed close to his side and added her own commentary to his steady flow of words. When Trusted Friend had stretched his hands wide to show the thickness of Ehina's head or leg, she had said, "Oh no. Not so big. Better let that one go. . . ." And Trusted Friend had frowned and pretended to be annoyed.

Surrounded by the soft, ready laughter of the women, he had been too preoccupied with his own storytelling to notice Passing Shadow. His first awareness of the shaman had come when Passing Shadow had suddenly snatched Ehina's tail from Trusted Friend's waving hand. Before Trusted Friend had been able to recover himself enough to speak, the shaman had demanded the prize of the kill for himself.

Passing Shadow had come close to dying at that instant. Stung and shamed beyond thought, Trusted Friend had raised his spear and prepared to thrust it into the shaman's back. It had been Beautiful Star who had stopped him. With a litheness and speed that had surprised even her husband, she had placed her own chest in front of the poised spear tip. Trusted Friend's arm had stiffened immediately. He had not understood why his wife protected the shaman, and she had not been able to explain.

Then it had been Wanderer's turn to grow angry. Frowning at what he had seen, the chief had pushed his way forward into the group. He had offered no comfort for Trusted Friend. With everyone silent and listening around them, Wanderer had refused to even look at his son and had acknowledged Passing Shadow's right to the prize of the kill. Glaring, biting his lip, Trusted Friend had continued to push forward threateningly until Wanderer had lost patience and told him to go away. Seeing that even his family sided against him, Trusted Friend had blanched and hurried off. He had remained by himself ever since, even when guiding the others toward the kill. Beautiful Star stayed far behind him, walking dejectedly. A live husband was worth more to her than any charm, but Trusted Friend would not believe that. She could not soften his hurt this time.

White Bird had not understood much of it. After it had happened, she had felt frightened and bewildered. Everyone had suddenly grown tense again. Later, in her confusion, she had asked Summer Wind.

"Mother, why does no one talk to Trusted Friend? There was so much happiness in his heart that we all laughed. Now his father has yelled at him and Beautiful Star is crying."

"You are not senseless," Summer Wind had grumbled. "Everyone feels unimportant now. I feel my son's shame. I would like to take this shaman and throw him into the fire."

"What is this anger inside the shaman?" White Bird had asked. "Why has he so much stealing in him?"

"He want's Ehina's tail for his new wife," Summer Wind had said.

Only afterward did White Bird remember that the shaman's new wife was Morning Land.

A shout from up ahead was the first sign that they were nearing the place of the kill. The woman in front of White Bird immediately began to increase her pace, her thick thighs pumping with speed that fascinated the Tideland girl. While White Bird struggled to keep up, she was aware of shouting all around her. The women were calling back to their men in high ululating wails that wavered through the fall afternoon. For a long while the women's voices and the swishing snap of grass against bare legs blocked out all other sounds.

When the halt came, White Bird threw down her bundle and quickly looked up, anxious to find Laughing One. What she saw amazed her. With its head cut off and most of its hide pulled away, Ehina lay before them like a hill of raw meat. After spending most of the afternoon under the hot sun, Ehina's belly was expanding with hidden gases. To honor the approaching women, one of the hunters now relieved the pressure by jabbing his spear into Ehina's bloated stomach. Immediately there was a hissing gush of gas and fluid that spewed up into the air like an eruption. The stink of the stomach and bowels spread in a moist cloud, enveloping the women and making White Bird gag from its strength.

The hunters were the strangest sight of all. It seemed as if they had deliberately painted themselves in the thick blood and black juices of Ehina. White Bird saw a man who looked slightly familiar and then realized with a shock that it was Laughing One. With his hair caked flat and his whole front covered with brownish-red filth, he stood beside the inert darkness of Ehina and waved at her.

She was jarred from her thoughts by Summer Wind, who pushed her forward none too gently.

"Supai, lazy one," the chief's wife said, laughing. "We will live, eating meat. My son always hits his mark. Do not go about pitying yourself. There is meat to be carried by the women. Come, little wife of my son. Here is your food. Eheeeyee."

With great reluctance White Bird allowed herself to be led into the area of slaughter. The smell was easing as the wind had picked up, but she was still frightened and nauseated by what lay all around her. Other women shouted happily, while White Bird only wanted to run someplace and be sick. She had barely controlled her stomach when she stumbled upon Ehina's severed head.

Some hunters had scraped off Ehina's skin and ears as well as Ehina's trunk, and Ehina's eyes stared up at her from out of a purplish, pink mass. The skin was still intact around Ehina's eyelids, and the tapering lashes added to the lifelike appearance. Something in Ehina's empty stare completely revolted White Bird's senses. Bending over, she retched onto the ground.

As she started to recover, she heard Laughing One ask, "Why is she so unhappy, Mother? Has the sickness touched her?"

Summer Wind laughed scornfully. "Your little wife is senseless. When she sees meat with her eyes, she just feels sickness. I take her with me where I go. The two of us do things together and gather food together, but her people were only good for chasing birds and rabbits. She should go back and live with her own mother. There is nothing here that frightens a true woman."

The words stung White Bird enough to make her forget her nausea. Summoning what grace she could, she stepped up to Laughing One. She tried to smile, but could only manage a nervous grimace.

Summer Wind was annoyed. "*Yi-quay-is,* why does your body shake so? Is this not what you wanted? Is your spirit unwilling to marry? Or is it the smell of blood that frightens you?"

Goaded by the older woman, White Bird pressed her cheek against Laughing One's grime-coated face and nuzzled him gently. The smell bothered her less than her own awkwardness.

She was truly glad to see Laughing One, but Summer Wind's badgering had made her feel guilty and stupid. Laughing One felt awkward, too, and did not hug her in response.

Summer Wind shook her head. "This girl has no sense now. Leave her alone. Do not spend too long on this young one. You are moving along the path, but she is a sweet, frightened rabbit that still runs in a circle. She will become stronger. Before night sits, her body will make yours look clean."

Summer Wind's anger with White Bird was sincere. It hurt her that the silly girl did not appreciate the glory her son had won.

White Bird was no longer listening. She was still staring into Laughing One's face and beginning to feel real joy at being with him again, when she felt Summer Wind tug at her arm impatiently.

"Soon you will truly be an adult," the chief's wife said. "Soon you will know how to work."

With an abruptness that shocked White Bird, the matron of the village pulled off her apron and stood naked before her son. Without any self-consciousness, Summer Wind bent down and began unstrapping her leggings and moccasins. Laughing One politely kept his eyes focused on White Bird. White Bird was too startled to notice the other women following Summer Wind's lead.

After a moment, Summer Wind looked up again and handed her things to White Bird.

"*Yi-quay-is,*" she said. "Another day and you, too, will understand things. Things will not always make you feel pain. Take these back to where you dropped your bundle. Then do as the women who live here have done." Seeing the incredulous look on White Bird's face, Summer Wind added, "When the blood splatters, there is nothing you have to wear. You need only your hands to work."

White Bird nodded and turned to go.

"*Yi-quay-is,* bring the baskets when you come again," Summer Wind shouted after her.

When White Bird had gone, Summer Wind turned to her son. "*Yi-quay-is* will do well," she told him. "*Yi-quay-is* still wants you, but this much blood makes her refuse. Sometimes a young girl makes herself weary with thinking. She fears something bad. After you left her, she felt pain. Her heart cried for you and for her sister. She is a kind girl. My heart agrees to her."

Laughing One only stared after the retreating form of the girl he wanted to marry. He had planned for this moment, but now he felt embarrassed and more than a little disappointed.

White Bird found the baskets Summer Wind had been carrying, and then began to take off her own apron. The changes were coming too fast for her, and she felt confused. When she had first put on her apron seven days earlier, she had hated the way it had felt. Now she was embarrassed to be without it. Nothing was making sense anymore.

On the way back, she noticed Laughing One watching her and immediately felt better. Without being too obvious, she slowed her walk a little and balanced the empty baskets on her softly swaying hips. For a moment, she almost forgot about the gore around her.

"*Niyate, Yi-quay-is! Niyate!*" Summer Wind scolded. "This day you cannot walk and dream. Give me a basket and watch what I do."

White Bird did as she was ordered, flushing slightly at being scolded in front of Laughing One. But the man she wanted was not looking at her anymore. He had his knife out and was waiting for a signal from Fighting Eagle.

When the signal came, eight men scrambled over the corpse. Laughing One and the others crawled up Ehina's sides, trying to keep a foothold on the slippery flesh. Once they had climbed to a good position, they began slicing off pieces of meat and tossing them to their wives. It was a boisterous kind of butchering. Each hunter threw the meat with deliberate unevenness, flipping one piece high so that the naked woman behind him had to jump for it, and heaving the next piece low enough to slap against her belly. The women were surprisingly agile, and it was rarely that a chunk of meat slipped past them to tumble in the dust. Then the wife responsible chased after the bouncing fragment, brushed off the dirt, and flopped it back into her basket, all the while vigorously scolding her husband. Summer Wind was older than the other women, for this was a game left to the younger married hunters, but she was also the most skilled. Though Laughing One tried to sail the pieces around her head, she caught every one, grabbing the meat and dropping it back into her basket with a single deft motion of her right arm. Laughing One smiled at her each time he made a toss. The butchering had become fun with the women there.

In a short while Summer Wind's basket was full, and she went back to get another. The meat she carried would be shared by everyone, for only a few of the women were filling baskets.

The rest were busy setting up drying racks, building cooking fires, or gathering poles for their new lodges. For the next several days the tribe would live beside the kill. Already the former pathway of Ehina was swarming with chattering, excited women.

White Bird proved to be nearly as good at catching meat as Summer Wind. At first Laughing One kept his tosses gentle, not wanting to embarrass the girl, but then he decided to test her a little. She did not disappoint him. Though slightly shorter than some of the other wives, she made up for it by springing about with a half-dance step whenever a piece seemed beyond her reach. The awkwardness had left her, and she grinned at Laughing One each time he tried to outwit her. The only apparent differences between White Bird and the other hunters' wives were her long hair and her tendency to scold at Laughing One in the more musical Tideland tongue.

Her basket filled very quickly. White Bird reluctantly stepped back to give her place to Summer Wind, but the chief's wife refused.

"I am old and my strength is small," Summer Wind said. "I have had my children. You are the woman who will marry my son. Stand firmly behind him. I will prepare our lodge."

White Bird was happy enough to agree. She changed baskets and rejoined the man she already thought of as her husband.

The game went on until the flesh had been stripped from Ehina's ribs and upper legs, and the carcass seemed to have a great wound in its side. When the men finally stopped, the first cookfires had begun to crackle in the fall air.

White Bird stood with a half-filled basket in her hands and stared up at Laughing One. Her body was sweaty and bloodstained, but to Laughing One she seemed very desirable, especially with the way her dark eyes glistened and the excited flush showed on her cheeks. Impulsively, he jumped down, set the basket aside, and embraced her. White Bird's nuzzling was not forced this time. She lifted her chest so that her breasts rubbed softly against him, and she felt Laughing One tighten his grip. They were stopped by Summer Wind.

"What do you two worry yourselves with?" the chief's wife demanded. Turning to White Bird, she added, "This day you still follow an old woman."

White Bird sighed when Laughing One let her go. She had not felt so happy since they had arrived at the village. Still caught up in the warmth of being near Laughing One, she qui-

etly helped Summer Wind pull their section of the hide away
from the kill and stretch it out, flesh-side up, on a nearby slope.
It did not matter what chores she had to do. She was a bride
now—a full wife—and that thought blocked out everything
else. Even when they were hammering in the wooden pegs
along the edge of the hide to keep it taut, White Bird never once
looked to see what Laughing One was doing. She forced herself
to wait, remembering that in a short while she would be back
with him again.

At last Ehina's ribs were broken free from one side and the
women were able to return to the butchering. White Bird arrived in time to see the men pulling the gray visceral mass of
intestines and stomach away from the body cavity. Ooze and
blood now seeped everywhere around the hunters' feet, but the
gore did not stop their enthusiasm. With a shout, they stepped
inside the open chest and began to cut at lungs, heart, and hidden areas of meat. White Bird was not bothered by the sight.
She would happily have gulped down the fluid just to stay close
to Laughing One. She hurried forward, her meat basket ready in
her hand, and then stopped, puzzled.

Laughing One was gone.

Laughing One had been staring after White Bird and admir-
ing the sensual rolling motion of her bare hips when Wanderer
had approached him. At the sight of his father, Laughing One
had quickly changed the direction of his gaze. Guiltily he had
remembered his promise not to be with White Bird until the
manhood ceremony had been completed.

If Wanderer had seen Laughing One embrace White Bird, he
did not mention it. Instead, he quietly took away the knife his
son was holding.

"I ask you to go," Wanderer said. "Do not refuse me. The
forest is your place this night."

For a moment Laughing One wondered what his father
meant. Then he remembered the isolation hut.

There was a slight frown on Wanderer's face, and Laughing
One could tell that his father disliked what he was asking
Laughing One to do. The chief's concern showed in his voice
as well.

"Hurry your walking," he said. "This black-haired girl you
want to marry will not die when you are gone. You will see her
again. For these three days you will have nothing."

There could be no arguing. Laughing One took a last look at

White Bird before he turned to go. She was bending over the hide, with only her full buttocks pointing in his direction. He doubted if anyone had told her what would happen to him now.

Wanderer led his son down to the edge of the lake, where Laughing One was given time to wash off the filth of the butchering. It took hard scrubbing, for Ehina's blood was like a paste over his hair and skin. By the time he was finished, his whole body was shivering from the chill of the water, and his hair was a dripping, plastered shell against his head. He wanted to cup his arms around his chest and crouch down to keep out the cold, but his father was watching so he tried to appear unconcerned instead.

Wanderer nodded.

"You have found the tracks, and they all lead this way. It is time to go from your people. We are taking you away, but your strength will bring you back again."

The words were part of a ritual, and Laughing One expected that his father would not talk to him again except in this fashion. He was wrong, though. They had barely begun to step through the woods toward the isolation hut when Wanderer added, "You will not be cold. There is a fire. The lodge is well built. Spear Maker set the frame and I myself found the secret coverings. Women think they are the only ones who know about lodge building, but we men do well enough when we have to."

Laughing One did not say anything to this, and the awkwardness between father and son deepened.

The hut had been placed in a small glade to the south of the camp. The fire Wanderer had mentioned was the barest of hearths, simply a pile of wood from which a few small flames flickered against the fading afternoon light. There was no need for any roasting sticks or baking stones. Laughing One would eat nothing for the next three days. His only nourishment would come from whatever the shaman chose to give him.

Two men waited for them in the glade. One was Spear Maker. The tribal elder's expression showed the pride he felt. It was a happiness mixed with the slight sorrow that all elders seemed to have when faced with yet another proof of their changing lives. Laughing One as a man made Spear Maker that much older.

But it was Passing Shadow who caught the boy's attention. The sight of his grim, ragged figure hovering next to the hut made Laughing One miss his step and nearly stumble. Wanderer caught hold of Laughing One's arm to steady him and felt the tremble that passed through his son's body.

"We wait for him," Passing Shadow said. "Let him walk into a man's dwelling."

The shaman's voice had a power that seemed to force obedience. Laughing One felt trapped. It was not just a ritual anymore.

As soon as Laughing One was close enough, Passing Shadow struck him twice across the face. The sting of the blows brought reflex tears.

"Let the spirit power teach you this. For a boy to grow up and live to old age there must be pain. Like all children, you have asked for things. You have wanted food to fall easily into your hands. You have thought only of laughter and lazy sleep. Now you must stand firm. Do not weep. The old leaves of childhood fall from you. New ones will grow. May you go through these changes correctly as your father has taught you to do."

They were the same words that were spoken to every hunter undergoing ritual cleansing, but now their meaning seemed very different. Laughing One stared into the flat blackness of the shaman's eyes and shuddered.

The rest went quickly. Laughing One half crawled and was half shoved into the hut while Spear Maker said a ritual prayer. A hide was placed over the lodge entrance to block out the daylight, and then the three older men left.

In the close darkness of the hut, Laughing One listened to their quick retreat. He knew that the butchering continued to go on, but none of the boisterous shouting reached him. The western wind kept blowing the sounds of the voices away. There was only the breathlike rumbling of wind through trees.

By twilight, most of the butchering had been done. A few men were still cutting the remaining strips of flesh from Ehina's legs, but they had to lump the meat on the ground beside them, since the last of the women's baskets had been filled long before. Another group, led by Fighting Eagle, was breaking apart Ehina's skull. They had begun by cutting out the tongue and giving it to the women to cook as a delicacy. Now the hunters hammered at Ehina's skull in an effort to pull out Ehina's brains for use in tanning and to free Ehina's immense ivory tusks. As their stone choppers pounded down through the hollow sinus chambers that surrounded Ehina's brain case, thin fragments of bone sprayed around them like wood chips flying from a hunter's ax. It was the last of the men's tasks, and already most of the hunters were resting in front of their new lodges. As butchering gave way to cooking, the women took control.

Summer Wind, Beautiful Star, and White Bird surrounded a single quivering fire, each doing a different task but sharing the company of the other two. Beautiful Star fussed over a pile of small intestines which had been dragged across the grass by one of the hunters and thus cleaned. Humming to herself, she cut the intestines into hand-length pieces and tossed them onto the coals at the edge of the fire. There they roasted quickly, twisting about like dying snakes until they had shriveled into circular rings. When she thought they were cooked well enough, Beautiful Star would scoop out the rings with a long stick and set them to cool in her basket.

White Bird was downwind from Beautiful Star, hanging thin slices of meat onto the drying racks. To be smoke dried, the meat had to be placed on racks that were close enough to the fire for every gust of smoke and heat to be blown across them. White Bird, who stood next to the racks, was often engulfed as well. She had to stop frequently, and her hands would fly about, rubbing at the stinging wetness in her eyes.

Beautiful Star could not resist chewing on some of the cooked intestine rings. She swallowed them eagerly, making loud smacking sounds as she sucked at the grease on her fingers. "I truly love this eating," she confided. "My heart rises when there is meat in my stomach. This is a good place to sit and eat until the pain of stretching makes you stop."

Summer Wind laughed. "The fat does not grow well on a stomach that always moves," she said. "Beautiful Star can never just find one place to sit and grow fat. She is always hungering for a man more than meat. If she should start to live like a true wife, with a baby growing inside her, she would become as fat as a slug."

The chief's wife chuckled, pleased with this image of her son's wayward wife. Summer Wind worked quietly, twisting cleaned pieces of large intestine inside out with her hands. Each piece was then stuffed with meat and tied at one end with sinew. Fresh blood poured in overtop of the meat made the fit tight, and sinew sealed the other end of the gut. Then the huge sausage was heaved onto the coals to roast.

Glad for any excuse to be away from the billowing smoke, White Bird sighed as she placed the last strip of meat onto the racks. Without saying anything, she picked up the empty basket, pressed it against her bare stomach, and hurried back to the butchering area. Summer Wind, who was lecturing to Beautiful Star about wifely duties, did not notice.

White Bird had another reason for hurrying away. Earlier that day she had seen Morning Land walking toward the shaman's lodge with a filled basket of meat in her hands. When the basket was empty, she would be sent back for more.

There was not much left of Ehina. White Bird arrived just as the last of the hunters put away his knife and began walking toward his lodge, leaving behind a rubble of cleaned bones. Ehina's feet had been cut off and rolled aside like unwanted tree stumps. They were the only parts with the flesh still on them. The rest of the carcass was a stripped ruin which cast strange shadows in the unsteady firelight.

This area of the camp was now empty. Fires had all been struck, and the same wind that was blowing smoke over the drying racks carried away the women's voices. When White Bird glanced about, she could see the others only as shadowy figures moving around faintly glowing hearths.

The hunters had left several piles of sliced meat next to the huge leg bones. White Bird crouched down beside one of these piles and began putting the slices into her basket. She worked faster than she had intended, her fingers scratching at the cold slabs of meat and slipping them unevenly into the basket.

It was the thought of meeting her sister that worried her. Morning Land had changed in the past few days, and White Bird sensed it. Though the shaman's lodge still remained apart from the others, White Bird guessed that this was not the only reason for her sister's silence. Morning Land seemed to be intentionally staying away.

A shuffling sound on the pathway behind her caused White Bird to turn quickly. She saw her sister coming toward the carcass.

Morning Land carried an empty basket just as White Bird had, but there the similarity between them ended. Morning Land move numbly, as if her body were walking without any conscious effort from her. Her feet were bare, but she seemed not to feel the coldness of the ground. When she passed by a cookfire where women shouted and laughed shrilly, her black eyes never moved at all. The expression on her face was not calm; it was empty.

Everything seemed quieter now. Morning Land had not noticed White Bird. Instead, she stepped toward another pile of meat some distance away and crouched down to begin her work. As Morning Land came closer, White Bird hunched over in the shadows, not wanting to be seen yet. She could not understand why the sight of her sister caused such a fearful tightening in her throat.

The night wind blew at Morning Land's hair, and White Bird suddenly realized that it had been shortened like that of the shaman's other wives. It scarcely reached to her shoulders. Whenever she bent her head, her bare neck showed through. There were black stripes tattooed on her upper arms. White Bird recognized these as the shaman's mark. More than anything else, it was the emptiness in those eyes which worried White Bird. Morning Land's face was still beautiful, but in a way that seemed dark and unfriendly. Morning Land's hands still moved quickly as she gathered the meat, but without the caring that she had always shown for even the smallest chore.

Has she forgotten that she ever had a sister?

The thought shocked White Bird, but not as much as the change in Morning Land's appearance had. Those marks and the shortened hair were the shaman's way of working her slowly free from the hold of others. He would crush her to himself until there was nothing left but this emptiness.

White Bird wondered if she should slip away unnoticed.

Morning Land was reaching for another piece of meat in her aimless fashion when her right hand banged sharply against a wedge of bone. The hand jerked back, her eyes opened quickly, and she cursed. It was a Tideland curse her mother had used, and saying it seemed to waken something in Morning Land. Her body trembled. Her face, which had been so stubbornly passive, suddenly looked alive again. She seemed desperate and very miserable.

"Morning Land!" The words left White Bird's throat like a cry of pain.

Morning Land looked up, as startled as if someone had hit her. She tried to get to her feet, but, before she could stand, White Bird was on top of her, embracing her. The impact knocked them both to their knees.

"*Shaaa!*" Morning Land gasped. "Why do you—? Why should you—? No. White Bird. Do not touch me. Do not—"

Morning Land tried to pull away, but her arms were pinned tight under White Bird's hug. Since she could not free herself without hurting her sister, she was forced to submit. White Bird went through the full Tideland greeting, placing her nose next to her sister's so that their breath was shared, and then squeezing Morning Land so firmly that, for a moment, neither could breathe at all. Morning Land's pretense at coldness could not last against the trembling excess of her sister. In another moment she was hugging White Bird back. They stayed like this— two figures huddled together in the shadow of the carcass—for a long time. Finally White Bird began to cry.

"I was afraid," White Bird sobbed. "What was this silence? I could not sit and wait. That is the way it is with me. I never know what I am feeling. I just take you with these two hands and hold you."

Morning Land stiffened slightly in her sister's grip. "You should not come and touch me this way. I have been thrown down. The feel of his hands is still on me. He touches me and my body is not mine. The insides of my body are dying from him. If you had sense, you would go away."

Far from drawing back, White Bird became more forceful, pressing her face hard against Morning Land's chest. There was nothing else Morning Land could do but rock White Bird in her arms and soothe her. For the first time in many days, Morning Land allowed her body to relax. The sudden release of strain made her own eyes wet with tears.

Gradually, both sisters began to breathe more gently. White Bird finally lifted her face to look at Morning Land. "Why this silence?" White Bird repeated. "I have trembled and almost killed myself with worrying. I will not just sit here, wondering, when shadows are hiding people who I care about. That is something I refuse to do."

Morning Land turned her head and stared into the darkness. "I am married to *Ahiri,* the night devil," she said quietly. "Such a woman does not speak what she feels. She hides it."

"This bad thing, this husband of yours, has he hurt you?" White Bird asked.

Morning Land looked into White Bird's big dark wet eyes and smiled sadly. "I am the wife who takes all Passing Shadow's attention," she whispered. "He is not the same with me as he is with his other wives. Last night he grew angry with Dancing Rain. She limps this day. He does not beat me, even when he is angry."

"He is too old to be so greedy for women," White Bird said. "You should have been given to someone else."

"I am glad the bear shaman is old," Morning Land replied. "I would not have wanted to see him as a young man. He does not need to beat me to teach me to be afraid of him. His touching me is enough. He hurts just by the way he rubs his fingers across my belly. When I look at him, all I want to do is be sick. Sickness is the only thing left in my heart now." While Morning Land spoke, her words seemed to become blurred, as if she were talking through a dream. "He is never finished with me. Every night he just pulls off my skins and reaches for me from behind. He just pulls off my apron and lays me down on the ground. That is what he wants. I do not refuse. I just lie until he is finished. I am too afraid."

"A man marries a woman and uses her body," White Bird said, unwittingly repeating words her own mother had told her long ago. "That is what a man does."

Morning Land shook her head. "The shaman wants more. This old man thinks I am food that he can eat. He has a hunger for everything I am. Before he is full, there will be nothing left of me."

White Bird frowned, trying to make sense of her sister's words. "When he lies with you and is finished, just get up and sit outside your lodge." she advised. "Just continue to live. When a woman washes herself in the river, the water sweeps the blood from her fingers and stays clean. A woman can give and give herself to a man and still be what she is."

Morning Land shook her head. "Come, old woman, with your wise talk. My little sister, the old woman." Morning Land was quiet for a moment. Then she sighed. "I am not as strong as a river. When I get up, I carry that man's sickness with me. My heart is never happy. I think, 'This night I will refuse him. This night I will be strong and turn away.' But in the darkness his hands are on me and I am not strong. I just give myself to him. When his other wives look at me, I see pity in their eyes. I am weak and afraid, just like them."

"Why should you be afraid of an old man?" White Bird asked. "Make the old one fear you."

"There is medicine in this shaman that makes him powerful," Morning Land insisted. She paused, trying to think of a way of explaining what she did not fully understand herself.

"His other wives, they have heard him in the night as I do now. This is what their lives have been like. Passing Shadow is the very big, very important thing in their lives. There is nothing else. Dancing Rain, the small one, she tells me things. When Passing Shadow took her from her parents, she was no older than you. She is thin and weak, but she is clever. She does not want to be with the shaman. At first she fought him. That was before she learned that she could not chase him out of her life. She has seen the death in him, the sickness that destroys women.

"Before I came, while Dancing Rain and Dreaming Place were still the shaman's only wives, they lived in Black Snake's village." Morning Land paused again, trying to remember the story as Dancing Rain had told it.

"One day the three of them were sitting near their fire. There was an emptiness in the shaman's face that Dancing Rain did not like. Something in her refused that look and she kept away. Dreaming Place did not notice. Dreaming Place was busy throwing wood on the fire. She hoped to please the shaman, but her hips kept brushing against him as she worked.

"The darkness was in the shaman then. He grabbed a log from the fire and hit Dreaming Place. He took hot coals and burned her. He hit her hips and struck her face. She fell and he kept on hitting. Dreaming Place thought he would kill her, but all she did was whimper.

"Dancing Rain yelled. She tried to pull the log from the shaman's hand. He threw down the log on Dreaming Place. Then he grabbed Dancing Rain's hands and held them in the fire. Dancing Rain screamed and fought, but she felt his strength. Her hands burned like meat. His hands burned, too, but his eyes stayed black and empty. Dancing Rain grew dizzy and fell down. When she woke, she was moaning. There was great pain in her fingers.

"We are women who have learned to fear our husband," Morning Land concluded. "We must be clever."

"Was there no one else near who heard them shouting?" White Bird asked. "The shaman made his women scream and no one heard this?"

"They heard," Morning Land said grimly. "They would not come near the lodge where the shaman has his wives. They did not want to face his anger. He is wilder than the cat."

"So no one helps?" White Bird asked.

Morning Land nodded. "No one wants to sit with the shaman's women. Some men sleep with other men's wives, but Passing Shadow's women have no lovers. They do not sit in front of their lodge and talk and laugh with others. They are always lonely. Dancing Rain and Dreaming Place have no choice. They must follow the shaman."

"They may continue to live that way," White Bird said, "but if you hate this shaman and he treats you badly, do not stay with him. Come to live in my lodge. The way we are sitting now, that is the way we should always be. Laughing One will not refuse you. When the blood was flowing from his leg and he was sick for days, you were the one who cured him. He will not just leave you to suffer."

Morning Land's voice remained toneless. "Laughing One is like a little brother to me. He would be killed if he tried to challenge the shaman."

"You should let us help you," White Bird insisted.

Morning Land shook her head and pointed to the tattooed stripes on her arms. "It would make no difference where I stayed," she said. "I am no longer a woman who men will respect. I do not have a full heart to give. I have only a small part of my heart left and that goes out to you. Passing Shadow has marked me. My flesh has become his. Other men will just leave me when they see these marks."

With deliberate quickness, White Bird rubbed her hands along the stripes on her sister's arms. Morning Land immediately pulled away.

"Shaaa! Is your mind crazy that you do these things?"

"These marks are nothing," White Bird explained. "Black juice dye covers them. I know what kind of a woman you are, sister. You have your own heart. You are not like his other wives. The shaman is only stealing with you. When your fear leaves, you will fight him. A mark on your arm will not break it."

Morning Land shook her head, but White Bird could see that she was uncertain.

"He is the one who has no sense," White Bird persisted. "He does not think about the woman he is doing these things to. He imagines you are stupid like Dreaming Place or a young girl like Dancing Rain. He must be taught that you are a woman who does not belong to him. You are the same person who escaped the strangers. You are the one who is going to kill him."

Morning Land seemed puzzled. Her eyes kept moving from her sister's face to the ruined Ehina. It was as if she were coming out of a daze. "I hear you talking, but I am still afraid," she said. "I am still the one who wears these marks on my arms."

"The shaman has no friends in this village," White Bird continued. "I see the vultures circling above him even now. You are going to use him like a ruined hide. For him, you are truly bad medicine. My sister—atoshe! There she is."

Morning Land got to her feet. "He waits for me in our

lodge," she explained. "He will not lie with anyone else there." She started to pick up her basket, but White Bird grabbed her arm.

"If this is something you truly do not want, refuse him," White Bird said. "Tell him there is sickness in you. He will be afraid that you will share your sickness with him."

Morning Land flinched from the idea. "What sickness could I have that would frighten him?" she asked.

"*Ojaii,* woman's blood," White Bird replied. "That is the worst thing of all for a shaman's magic. If you tell him that it is your time of blood, he will have to forget you."

Morning Land stared down at her sister. "He will not believe what I say," she whispered.

White Bird pointed toward the ruined carcass. "There is blood enough if a woman has cleverness," she insisted. "If you smell of it when you sit beside him, he will push you away. If you start to touch him, he will hit you with his fists. He will fear your *ojaii.* It will remind him that there are many other women in his lodge."

Morning Land blushed and shook her head. What White Bird suggested was something no Tideland woman would ever have done.

"We must live," White Bird persisted. "That takes cleverness. There were those who tried to kill us before, but we still live."

Morning Land suddenly bent down and hugged her sister. It was an impulsive nuzzling, and so unusual that it flustered White Bird completely. She flushed under the embrace, feeling a sudden rush of love for this strange sister of hers.

"The whole world is changing," Morning Land said wonderingly. "Even my little sister does not go about crying anymore. When she talks, others listen."

Then Morning Land picked up her basket and hurried back to the shaman's lodge. To the others watching her, she seemed the same as before, but White Bird noticed the difference. Morning Land was walking like a Tideland woman again.

Passing Shadow was not in the lodge when Morning Land got there. Instead, she found only Dancing Rain and Dreaming Place. Dancing Rain was cooking meat while Dreaming Place set other slices of it on the drying racks.

"Where has our husband gone?" Morning Land asked.

Dreaming Place simply glanced up dully and shook her head. As usual, it was Dancing Rain who did all the talking.

"You are a slow one," Dancing Rain said. "What were you looking for out there in the darkness?"

Morning Land shrugged.

"Our husband has gone to look after the boy, the one who made his first kill today," Dancing Rain continued, answering Morning Land's question even though her own had been ignored.

"Laughing One?" Morning Land asked.

Dancing Rain nodded. "He has gone to stay in a magic place, and when he returns they will tell us he has become a man. While he is there, Passing Shadow looks after him."

Morning Land did not like this idea. "Where is this sacred place?" she asked quietly.

Dancing Rain pointed toward the darkened woods. "Somewhere along the forest path," she replied. "Our husband went there carrying a bowl of medicine for the boy to drink. The medicine was all white and pulpy, and they say it has a bitter taste, but the boy will have to drink it anyway."

There was a nervousness to the way Dancing Rain spoke which Morning Land noticed at once. It gave her a bewildering sense of danger.

"The shaman is still there?" she asked, turning to face the night woods.

"He will be there a long time," Dancing Rain said. "I saw the vein throbbing in his forehead again. His eyes were empty. It is never good when that happens."

"Perhaps one of us should follow him," Morning Land suggested uncertainly.

Dancing Rain shook her head vigorously. "No woman ever walks to that place," she said. "If we went there, we would ruin its magic. Passing Shadow would kill us."

Morning Land shuddered. "He has a twisted heart," she whispered.

"A great anger fills him," Dancing Rain agreed. "Everything in him is always screaming. It will never stop."

Morning Land knew that this was true. As long as Passing Shadow was alive, he would go on hurting the women in his lodge, disturbing their peace even in the night, making it impossible for them to talk freely even with each other. More than anything else at this moment she wanted to be able to do something that would stop him.

Morning Land remembered what White Bird had told her, and a strange smile touched her lips. If she could not stop him completely, at least she could keep him from clawing at her. A little effort would prevent her from being touched by the old man.

With the barest of nods to Dancing Rain, Morning Land moved off to begin her plan. Yet, as she turned her back on the woods, she had the guilty sense of having abandoned Laughing One.

Much later, Passing Shadow found himself standing alone at the edge of the woods, looking up into the darkened sky. There was no mist that night, just a clear, cold sky in which every star shone bright and alone. While even a practiced hunter could not have seen far into the blackened forest beyond the camp, the stars above were plainly visible as they slowly moved in their circular paths across the night sky. It was possible to look up into an immense distance and imagine other eyes shining back, staring down through the cold. As he glanced higher into the star sheen of the sky, Passing Shadow did not stare at the fierce white stars themselves, but looked for the dark shapes between them. He knew that this was where the true night spirits dwelled. Now, before the night was spoiled by the brightness of a late rising moon, the shaman could see the great shadow lion seeking its prey, the giant sloth lumbering between the regions of light, and the herds of Ehina moving in a wide band of blackness. These were the seekers. On the nights of the black moon, they were the strongest spirits of all. Passing Shadow searched for the form of the great bear, found it, and grunted in satisfaction. His magic had not left him.

Passing Shadow did not remember how he had gotten where he was. In fact, he remembered very little. He knew he had been making medicine for the boy when a peaceful feeling had swept over him, almost as if he had been drifting through clouds of fog and shadow. A warning murmur in his mind had told him that the bear spirit always came to him this way, but he had gone on making his potion. He had intended to use only enough of the burning mushroom to give the boy the illusion of having had a spirit dream, but as Passing Shadow had been opening his pouch of mushroom fragments, the tingling sensations had grown stronger and stronger. Everything which had happened since then remained vague, for his mind had gone bad.

Passing Shadow staggered forward a few steps and clutched at his burning head. The sweating and shivering had passed now, as had the numbness which had swept over his body and limbs. Gone, too, was the sensation of being removed from his body, of watching his own actions from a long distance away. Having already drifted through darkness, his mind was returning, accompanied by the drumlike throbbing of his own blood.

Passing Shadow was uncomfortably familiar with these sensations. They swept over him like a storm wind at least once during every cycle of the moon. Pleasant at first, they always left him gasping and confused afterward. It had been different when he had been younger. Then he had gloried in this passionate violence. He had taken pride when the great bear spirit had swept over him, numbing his senses and leading him on blind, maddened hunts through the darkness. There had never been any hesitation. When the tingling sensations had begun inside him, he had welcomed them like an eager lover. It had not mattered if other people had been horrified by what he and his followers had done. The dreamy peace that had come afterward had been worth it all. There had been no memories to worry him then. It had simply been a need satisfied.

Now it was different. There was little that he did not see or feel in his dreams these nights.

Passing Shadow slumped, thinking of the spirits which had brought this change to him. There was no magic he knew of that could bring things back to the way they had been. He felt no great remorse for the killing he had done, only a desire to go on living as he once had. Sometimes he wondered if all great shamans felt this way. Did their youth seem as short as his had; over and gone with before he had scarcely begun to breathe?

Passing Shadow sighed and glanced up at the sky again. He did not like these nights of bright full moonlight. They were the worst for memories and dreams. That was when the things he had done seemed so much greater than the things he still wanted to do. On the nights of the Black Moon, it was different. There was no slow, quivering conscience to worry a man then. There was only magic.

Some people thought the moon never rose on such nights, but every shaman knew better. The Black Moon simply followed a different path from the golden one. The life of the golden moon was open and clear, but the Black Moon stayed hidden in shadow, cloaked in a mist of its own. Like a screened fire, it could not be easily seen, but a shaman could feel it. The Black Moon had the quality of death, and brought a restless stirring.

Already the night was changing. The great yellow moon had

risen and hovered just over the trees, making the lake sparkle under its light. Passing Shadow grunted disgustedly. This moon would ruin things. There was none of the magic, none of the promise, none of the spirit longing of those Black Moon nights.

Nodding slowly to himself, Passing Shadow began walking back along the path to the village.

The village had felt different before. The wind had made the hearths seem warmer. Fire sparks had made the night seem blacker. Now with the silver moonlight shaping things again, the villagers were reminded once more of their closeness to the earth.

Passing Shadow breathed deeply and coughed, disliking the taste of the air. In the woods he had smelled ragweed and sweet clover and autumn leaf dust. Here there was the rich smell of roasted meat, the scent of cooked fat, and the pervasive odor of burnt grease. Passing Shadow laughed emptily and noiselessly. It would have been an easy night for killing. By now most of the men had bloated bellies and were content to remain as motionless as possible. Everything around them was seen with glazed eyes. Against attack they were defenseless. Even walking became an effort when a man's belly was tight with food.

In the uneven firelight, people lay like bundles of bark cloth, gray motionless shapes amid deeper shadows. Some stirred, but it was only to wind or burp or relieve themselves in some other way before flopping down next to their hearths again. Loud belches echoed through the camp. Passing Shadow saw a young girl whose body seemed to jiggle when she twitched even slightly. She looked back at him as he walked past, but her dark eyes showed only a dulled, sluggish contentment. Passing Shadow wished that she had howling winds over her head and only empty trees to stare at.

Passing Shadow strode near Trusted Friend's lodge and saw the hunter and his wife sleeping together under a pile of hides. Beautiful Star was sprawled on her back, with her legs spread wide apart, as if inviting invisible lovers. As the shaman stepped near, she moaned and her eyes fluttered beneath their lids. With a loud sigh, she rolled sideways.

Passing Shadow felt an urge to kick her as she slept.

Perhaps Beautiful Star sensed this, for at that moment her eyes became wide open. As soon as she saw who was near, she sat up quickly. Enjoying the fear he had caused in her, the shaman moved on. He would let her go back to her dreaming, now that the terror had passed.

Passing Shadow knew he would not find any of his wives sleeping. He had taught them that a shaman's wives did not just lie down when the moon was full. "You insult the spirits with your snoring," he had said, and one look into his darkened eyes had been enough to convince them of what would happen should they disobey. Now none of them ever slept until he did.

Out of habit, Passing Shadow approached his own lodge cautiously, standing just outside the range of firelight and watching what each wife did when she thought he was not close enough to see.

Dreaming Place was at the fire, poking the ashes numbly with a stick. Her breathing was husky from tiredness, and her eyes looked very soft. It had been very easy for Passing Shadow to hate this stupid girl. Whenever he looked at her, he felt a meanness growing up inside him. Her very dullness was provoking. Her big, heavy body seemed meant for wounding. Whenever there was no reason for his anger, she seemed the one he should hurt. Even though he was getting old fast and no longer loved fighting for its own sake, there was an undeniable thrill to kicking at her fat buttocks with his heel or feeling his bony knuckles dig deep into the padded folds of her stomach.

Passing Shadow grunted softly and looked away. Just having Dreaming Place for a wife made him ashamed.

Dancing Rain was not asleep either. She lay on her side with her head propped up on one arm, idly making small toy lodges out of leftover pieces of bark. The toy lodges did not last long in the darkness, for each gust of wind blew in their roofs. With endless patience, Dancing Rain kept rebuilding them.

Passing Shadow felt a rush of pity for this young girl who had been so quickly forsaken by her loveless mother. Like him, she had not been wanted. Seeing her made him feel pity for himself as well, and for the bad things which had been done to him, for the insults and loneliness which all the seasons had brought. When he had first taken Dancing Rain as a wife, he had felt like crushing her to him, holding her in a grip of needing and self-pity. But she had been frightened of him just like the others. She had struggled in his arms. Her eyes had been cold and filled with girlish horror at the thought of being trapped inside a lodge with this horrid old man. That had taken the life from Passing Shadow's pity. Even thinking of it now left him empty.

Passing Shadow started to step forward into the light and then hesitated. Where was the other one, the beautiful golden-skinned girl he had wanted so badly? His fists tightened at the thought that she would sleep while the others waited, but then he saw her, moving about beyond the glow of firelight, nearly as much in shadow as himself. She was bending down to whisper something to Dancing Rain. Even in the dim light, she looked tall and slender and beautiful to the point of hurting. Passing Shadow did not know why just seeing her made him jealous.

He came forward quickly then, clearly expecting the women to stare at him in openmouthed amazement. None of them did. Dancing Rain hid her surprise by keeping her eyes downcast. With a quick swipe of her hand, she knocked apart the toy lodge she had been making. Dreaming Place frowned in obvious bewilderment. Morning Land did not even look up.

Passing Shadow moved closer to his new wife, thinking that she would soon realize her mistake and turn to greet him. Instead, she stood up quickly and hurried over to the meat rack. Passing Shadow watched her standing there amid the billows of smoke, pretending to be suddenly interested in checking the slowly cooking meat. Irritated, he came after her. For a moment they were both standing close together by the fire, but she was still refusing to look at him. Then she turned and scurried off into the darkness, heading for the bushes where villagers went to relieve themselves. Confused, Passing Shadow turned his attention to the others.

Dreaming Place still sat quietly beside the hearth, squinting at the red hot coals. Passing Shadow reached over and struck her on the arm.

"Lazy one, do not just sit and look," he demanded. "Are you senseless? Stand up and get a man what he wants."

Heavy and awkward, Dreaming Place struggled to get up. Passing Shadow snapped the edge of his fingers across her bulging stomach to hurry her.

"Do not insult me with your laziness," he grumbled.

Sensing the ugliness of his mood, Dancing Rain and Dreaming Place quickly scurried about the hearth fire, bringing their husband as much food as he could possibly wish for. When she returned from the bushes, Morning Land helped, too, but she managed to be always just out of the shaman's reach. Whenever he came too close, she seemed to suddenly need to do something at another part of the hearth.

No amount of dashing about could keep the shaman away forever, though. With their husband's meal done, the women began to prepare for sleep. Dreaming Place and Dancing Rain crawled into the lodge eagerly enough, but Passing Shadow remained by the entrance, waiting for Morning Land to come close at last.

She edged forward slowly, moving almost soundlessly. Her mouth was tight shut, and her eyes shone with reflected firelight. When she was just out of arm's reach from him, she squatted down and waited. This puzzled Passing Shadow all the more. They were alone. He should be pulling her to him, but there was something in her expression that frightened him a little. Held between wanting and caution, he simply stared.

Neither of them moved for a long time.

At last Passing Shadow grew impatient. "Are you senseless?" he asked. "Why are you waiting in the dark like this?"

Morning Land remained silent.

"What you are doing is foolish," Passing Shadow said. "Get up and come into the lodge."

Still there was only silence.

Suddenly angry, Passing Shadow raised his right fist. "Is this what you want?" he demanded. "Do you want to feel the thickness of this hand? Do you want to be thrown onto the fire? Shake your body and come inside."

Passing Shadow bent forward to reach for her, but Morning Land drew back quickly. "My stomach is sick," she said. "I truly feel miserable."

The sound of her voice made Passing Shadow hesitate once more. An exasperated look came into his eyes, but there was also a trace of concern. "What troubles you that you are like this?" he asked.

"Do not touch me with your fingers," Morning Land cautioned. "I am bleeding and have already ruined this piece of hide."

To prove her point, Morning Land pushed aside the front of her woman's apron. Passing Shadow saw a red smear along her upper thigh and realized it was blood.

"This hurts," Morning Land insisted. "My time of blood is on me." When Passing Shadow only stared, she feigned modesty and flipped the apron back down again. "Do not keep looking at it," she pleaded. "You are my husband, but you cannot be with me this night. This blood will ruin your magic."

Passing Shadow faltered, not entirely trusting her, but unwilling to risk being fouled by woman's blood. Sensing his uncertainty, Morning Land persisted.

"I will stay out here this night," she said. "I will sleep alone until this thing is over."

For a while longer, Passing Shadow simply stared. His passion had gone cold inside him at the sight of the blood on her thigh and he was already tired from the feeling that had swept through him earlier that night, but he was also stubborn. He did not want her to enjoy the thought that he had waited for her and gotten nothing. He studied her face, looking for any sign of triumph or defiance; any trace that she was questioning his dark power. Though Morning Land had been crying earlier, none of it showed on her face. All of her feelings were deeply hidden.

Giving in to his irritation, Passing Shadow finally jerked his head, grunted disgustedly, and crawled into the lodge.

Morning Land stayed where she was, not daring to show her relief. There was a thumping sound from inside the lodge as Passing Shadow grabbed one of his other wives. Somewhere in the dark, a woman groaned and rolled sideways. Her body began shaking viciously under the shaman's thrusts. Morning Land heard the girl's legs thumping against the ground. Suddenly frightened, she got up and moved farther away from the lodge.

The fur hide she would use to cover herself was where she had hidden it earlier. Morning Land quickly wrapped it around her and moved into the shadows. She would be cold but safe there, if there could be any real safety in a life which had become suddenly empty. Morning Land had always imagined herself as someone important, someone who would one day be respected by her whole village. But how could anyone be respected here? The best she could hope for was to be left alone.

CHAPTER TEN

Manhood

In the glade where his manhood ceremony was supposed to take place, Laughing One was lying in his own dirt. He had been that way since early morning, when Passing Shadow had made a quick attempt at cleaning him. Twisted and sweating, his body continued to expel its waste in an uncontrolled fashion. There was little other movement save for the soft hissing sound of air being sucked in through his mouth. Flies, lured by the strong body smell, alighted on his legs and crawled across his belly. His skin quivered at their touch, but it was a mindless response. Laughing One's brain was still encased in claylike unconsciousness.

A stake with feathers tied to it had been driven into the ground beside Laughing One's head. This was Passing Shadow's silent offering to the spirits on the boy's behalf. Judging from the stench, the flies, and the corpselike stillness of the boy's body, the spirits were not responding.

Under the warm midday sun, Passing Shadow tended the fire in front of the lodge and slowly prepared his medicine. He was trying to help Laughing One now.

Pieces of bitter mushroom, seeds from a wildflower, the root of a cactus, and the powder of a fungus. They all seemed harmless enough, yet each could blind the mind with the force of many scorpion stings. They had been strong enough to chase Laughing One's spirit away from his body, and now Passing Shadow was trying to call it back. Plants had caused the illness. With the simple logic of experience, Passing Shadow knew that other plants could remedy it. He was making an infusion of leaves and seeds that should lull the boy's tormented mind back into a curing sleep. The problem was getting Laughing One to drink it.

After chanting a prayer over his healing potion, Passing Shadow poured some of it into the same bowl he had used the night before. He shook the liquid slowly, tested its warmth with his finger, tasted it, and carried it into the lodge. There was a worried look on his face and a strange gentleness in his manner which would have shocked even his wives.

Laughing One still remained dangerously quiet. After staring at the boy for a long moment, Passing Shadow set the medicine bowl onto the ground. There was no use for it yet. Ignoring the flies which buzzed up at each movement, the shaman knelt beside the body of his patient and carefully cradled Laughing One's head in his hands. There were bruises on the boy's forehead from where he had banged his skull against the ground during the violent thrashing of his convulsive dreams. The skin around the bruises was very pale, and seemed unhealthily sticky beneath the shaman's fingers.

When Passing Shadow propped open the lid of one eye, Laughing One's glazed stare was so corpselike that the shaman's hands began to tremble. Half angrily, he slapped the boy's cheek. Laughing One's head lolled sharply to one side, unresisting. Passing Shadow slapped him again and again, but the only responses were the red imprints left by the shaman's palm. Except for the warmth of the body, he could have been handling a dead man.

The shaman was becoming frightened now. Still supporting Laughing One's head with his left hand, he reached down carefully and lifted up the bowl of medicine. When the brim of the bowl was pressed against Laughing One's mouth, his lips quivered slightly, but that was all. It was obvious that the boy could not be urged to drink.

Passing Shadow's actions grew more frantic. He let Laughing One's head rest on his knee and prepared to force open the boy's mouth. Hooking one of his fingers over Laughing One's upper lip, the shaman pulled the flesh back until the hollow of the mouth arced open below the bowl. The liquid poured down slowly across Laughing One's tongue. There were choking sounds as the flow of air was cut off, but still Passing Shadow persisted. He was thoroughly frightened now. If the boy did not swallow some of the medicine, both their deaths were certain. It would be the cruelest of tricks for the great bear shaman to fall victim over the death of a boy.

Enough of Laughing One's mind was awake to prevent him from being suffocated. He began to cough and sputter. His head twisted sideways in protest and, when the shaman continued to pour the liquid down his tongue, Laughing One started to swallow. By the time the bowl was empty, there were streaks of spit-tle and fluid all across Laughing One's face, but Passing Shadow was convinced that some had been taken. It might be enough. After letting the boy's head flop back onto the soiled hides, Passing Shadow hurriedly left the lodge.

He knew he was in danger.

It was the way of these rituals that a boy should never be truly hurt. However much the young hunter might be afraid of what he had to face, his sufferings were intended to be light. The shaman was expected to prevent things from going wrong. Now, because of one moment's blindness, he had poisoned the boy with too much of the mind-changing drug. Instead of having the boy take only a few sips, Passing Shadow had made him empty the entire bowl. Men had died from less than what Laughing One had drunk.

Passing Shadow's skin flinched when he thought of what Wanderer would do to him if the chief saw his son like this. Laughing One was well loved by the women and elders of this village. There were few men in the camp who would not be ready to raise a spear against the shaman who had hurt him. Even Passing Shadow's new wife owed something to the boy.

Passing Shadow ran a trembling hand across his forehead, trying to force a calmness on his unstable brain. Running would be useless. The hunters could track him in less than a day. His only choice was to stay and face them and hope for the boy's recovery. He did not think that Laughing One would die completely, but there was a chance the boy's mind would never be clear again. He might linger on for many seasons as a half-person; a burden to all the tribe. The medicine Passing Shadow had just given Laughing One was nearly as strong as the mushroom itself, but the leaves he was using were old, gathered many summers before. Their magic might have weakened. He wished that he could trust in them.

Two days later, the manhood ceremony took place. Though the shaman would gladly have delayed it, he could not, for he was as bound to the cycle of ritual and cleansing as everyone else in the tribe. The best he could do was pretend that nothing unusual had happened. Since he was the only one who ever entered the ceremonial lodge where Laughing One lay, he was also the only one who knew how close to death the boy had come. With everyone else in the village preoccupied with the butchering, it was not too difficult for the shaman to assume a calmness he did not feel. He slept with his wives, ate his meals, and spoke of spirit matters in a quiet, somber manner that aroused no suspicion.

Now, though, there could be no more hiding. Wanderer and Spear Maker were already dressed for the boy's manhood ceremony. Wanderer had put on his chief's robe and feathers. Spear Maker had dyed his lips black with berry juice and painted white rings around his eyes. When it was nearly sunset, they left the village together and walked quickly through the woods which sheltered the ceremonial grove.

The wind came out of the south that evening, bringing warm, earthy scents from the marsh-lined lake. To the men approaching the grove, it brought something else—a foul, unhealthy smell. The heavy, clinging odor reminded Spear Maker of the death stench that clung to a lodge after there had been a fatal sickness. There was something about the smell which weakened a man.

Wanderer noticed the stink as well, especially when they neared the edge of the clearing. The rank odor of human waste was too strong, too lingering. It might have surrounded a village whose tribe had spent the winter in one place, but never an unoccupied forest grove.

The two men entered the grove cautiously, with Wanderer in the lead. Wanderer could hear Spear Maker's harsh breathing close behind him, but he ignored it. His eyes were already searching through the grove ahead.

Laughing One had been propped up into a sitting position against the side of the lodge, but he looked dead. His cheeks were swollen like meat that had been too long in water, and his body was so limp that a simple push would have sent him tumbling to the dirt. Flies crawled through his hair, lighted on his hunched back, or buzzed noisily out through the lodge entrance. The growing coolness had not made them sluggish yet.

Incredibly, in the midst of this, Passing Shadow seemed unperturbed. The shaman crouched close to the fire, quietly stirring a bowl of ash paste which he intended to use for the ceremony. For all the worry he showed, Laughing One might have been quietly sleeping on the grass beside him.

Wanderer's shock was quickly replaced by a cold anger. It was clear that the boy had been badly treated; that he was very sick. The shaman had betrayed their trust.

As he walked toward Passing Shadow, Wanderer raised his ceremonial spear to a stabbing position.

A choking sound from Spear Maker alerted Passing Shadow.

The shaman glanced up to see a spear poised above his head. He also saw the wild look of anger in Wanderer's face. Another moment and the shaman would feel that spear's blade cutting into his flesh.

With a lurch of panic, Passing Shadow raised his hand in protest. "Go away!" he shouted. "Do not use a weapon in this sacred place."

"Aaan natai!" Wanderer cursed. "You have killed my son."

The chief's voice was strangely gentle, but there was nothing gentle in his expression. Passing Shadow knew that death was very close.

"Put down your spear," Passing Shadow urged. "No one wants your anger here." Passing Shadow's voice quavered slightly, but he hurried on in an effort to shake the hunter's concentration. "Yeane, the Black Moon, wanted your son, but I have freed him. He only sleeps. He will grow strong again."

Wanderer did not move. With the spear still held ready to strike, he called out, "Spear Maker, listen to my son's chest. If his breath is gone, this man dies."

Spear Maker hurried forward and knelt beside Laughing One. With shivering hands, he felt the boy's cheeks and chest. "He is breathing," Spear Maker shouted, "but he is very sick."

Wanderer slowly drew back his spear. A slight trembling in the wooden shaft showed how much the shock had affected the chief's senses. "It is you who will die now, shaman," he hissed. "Do not bother to cry out. Suffer this pain in silence or the women will laugh at you."

Passing Shadow felt himself starting to scream, but forced the sound back. He spoke in harsh, rasping gasps. "You are too quick. The boy is not dead. He was only a child, and Yeane was too strong for him. I have driven Yeane away."

There was no change in Wanderer's expression, but at least the spear had not plunged into Passing Shadow's chest yet. The shaman knew that this was his best chance. "Do not threaten me here," he repeated.

Before Wanderer could answer, Spear Maker called out, "The boy stirs. He is starting to move."

"Is he only asleep?" Wanderer asked.

"He has not been pretending," Spear Maker answered. "He shivers in this cold place."

A change came over the chief. No longer certain, he slackened his grip on the spear. Watching him, Passing Shadow began to feel more confident.

"The evil has been driven out of him," Passing Shadow urged. "Only his weakness is left. Put down the spear and help us save your son."

The chief scowled, but his spear was lowered. A moment later, Wanderer had crossed the grove and was crouching beside his son. Behind him, Passing Shadow got slowly to his feet.

For Wanderer, the worst moment came next. As he stooped to examine the boy, it was not the smell or the unhealthy puffiness of the flesh that sickened him. It was his son's eyes. They seemed full of pain. Seeing Laughing One now, Wanderer remembered the baby he had once carried in his arms, and the reality of what had happened came to him with terrible force.

Spear Maker was more practical. "Do not stay here. Go with him to the lake."

"No," Passing Shadow grunted. "This place is powerful. The magic has begun. I do not want to break it."

"It is dead," Wanderer grumbled.

"Stay in this magic place," the shaman insisted. "We must hurry. Laughing One's spirit has been carried on the journey to manhood. If it is not finished, he will lose the trail. He will weep for his lost manhood."

Wanderer frowned and turned to Spear Maker.

"Friend, we must wait," Spear Maker agreed. "On this day only can his spirit enter manhood."

Wanderer stared at Spear Maker and slowly nodded. "Fetch the ash paste and finish this thing yourself."

"What is making you talk this way?" Passing Shadow demanded. "I am keeper of this lodge."

The chief turned on him then, and the shaman could see the hate in Wanderer's eyes. "The boy who is my son is nearly dead," Wanderer hissed. "You are the one who brought ruin to him. I will not trust you."

Passing Shadow might have protested further, but he saw that Wanderer had drawn out his knife. Sensing danger, the shaman handed the paste to Spear Maker and stepped away.

"I have no knife," Spear Maker faltered.

Wanderer handed his knife to Spear Maker.

"This knife is powerful," he said. "Be quick."

Slightly bewildered, the old man took the blade from the chief. "Friend, your son is very sick. You must hold him. Keep his head just lying back. I do not know what is hurting him, but the blood from these cuts must not strike his eyes."

Wanderer did so, aware of how easily the boy's skull shifted under his strong hands. There did not seem to be any strength left in the muscles at all. Remembering the chief's mood, Spear Maker avoided the usual chants that preceded the marking. Gripping the knife firmly in his right hand, he made two vertical cuts in the center of Laughing One's forehead. A twist of the blade gouged bits of flesh from each cut. As soon as the blood began to flow out from the small wounds, the village elder filled the cuts with black ash paste. Later, when the cuts began to heal, the black ash would blend with the skin, leaving a permanent pair of marks on Laughing One's face.

"Spirit of this boy, you have been carried in the winds," Spear Maker chanted as he pushed in the ash pasted with his fingers. "You have scattered with the leaves and swept the lowlands. Now you must return. Your father, the strongest and kindest of men, stands waiting here. Do not be long in coming. The feast of manhood is ready. Now you will go and eat your meals from the place of importance."

There was a pause, and for a moment it looked as if the old man were praying. Then he quickly lifted his head.

"Now we must start caring for him," he said.

Oblivious of the smell and filth that dirtied their ceremonial clothing, the two men bent down to lift the body of the sick boy. They half dragged and half carried Laughing One from the clearing. Passing Shadow was left alone in the grove to do whatever he wished with what remained of the ceremonial gear.

A dunking in the lake seemed to revive Laughing One a little, but he started to shiver so badly that the two men did not linger there. They washed away as much of the dirt as they could. When they had finished, most of the smell was gone. There was nothing that could be done about the rest of it. Laughing One looked like a hunter who had been trampled. His head seemed too heavy for his neck to support. He tried to move his legs, but he was not able to keep pace with the men, and his toes dragged unevenly through the grass.

Summer Wind was in front of her lodge, explaining the marriage ceremony to White Bird, when the three men arrived. As she looked up, her lips had already begun to form a welcoming smile. The expression froze there.

"Light a fire here," Wanderer ordered. "The boy is cold. Come, woman. Get hides."

"He is dead!" Summer Wind wailed.

"No. He has struggled with spirits. Get hides to warm him."

Summer Wind stayed as she was, her surprise slowly turning to fear. She was unwilling to believe that the shivering boy being held up by the two men could actually be her son.

"My son!" she cried. "My beautiful child! The shaman has killed him!"

"No. Light the fire," Wanderer repeated.

This time Summer Wind responded by scrambling to her feet and hurrying inside the lodge.

The two men staggered forward with the weight of the boy between them. Wanderer's free arm almost brushed against White Bird's face as he passed, but no one noticed the girl. She was left crouching by the dwindling hearth fire, still in the same position she had held just before the men had arrived. Bewilderment and shock had kept her silent this long, but now, when there was nothing more to see, she started trembling.

White Bird stood up slowly, her face muscles still quivering, and forced herself to walk to the entrance of the lodge. Spear Maker's back was near the opening, but White Bird managed to slip in behind him, surprising herself with her own agility. It was dark inside the lodge, and bodies seemed to be pressed in close all around her. Summer Wind was crouched on her knees, holding her son's head in her arms. Her voice crooned out soft, muttering sounds as she rocked back and forth on her thighs. She had managed to cover Laughing One with hides, but his shivering continued.

"Rub life into him," Spear Maker suggested. "There is cold in his chest."

Summer Wind massaged her son's chest with her hands. The movement seemed to soothe her a little, for soon she was alert enough to notice her husband.

"Where is this shaman?" she demanded.

Wanderer was crouched over awkwardly a short distance away. He did not answer.

"Drive the shaman away from this village. Drive him away or something worse will happen," Summer Wind hissed. In her anger, she pushed her thumbs hard against the muscles of Laughing One's right shoulder. There was a looseness to the flesh which worried her. "My son's head is fiery hot. His skin is covered with wetness. He is in such pain that he cannot sleep."

Wanderer stared in surprise at the flushed face of his wife.

"Nothing more is going to happen," Spear Maker said. "The shaman has failed. If your son dies, we will seek revenge and go looking for him. The shaman knows this. He will not rejoice in his heart."

"My son is not a piece of raw fish to be thrown away," Summer Wind sobbed. "I know the call of this shaman. Among us lives Passing Shadow, the one who eats children. He is always hungry, that one. Drive him away. Pierce him with your spears. As long as he is near, the fear of this shaman will not leave me." Summer Wind's voice trembled as she stared at the expressionless face of her husband. Suddenly she gave up and let her head fall onto her son's chest. "I am weary of his deeds," she wailed.

Wanderer watched his wife slump down over Laughing One. In the thickness of the shadows, mother and son seemed to merge into one shape. Then the chief turned and stepped out of the lodge.

"Ehnn. Wait. I will go with you," Spear Maker said.

Wanderer kept on walking.

"Your child . . . his strength is not broken. He is not going to die."

Spear Maker was stumbling after the chief. In his haste to leave, he almost tripped against the crouching White Bird.

The chief saw his favorite hunting spear propped against the side of the lodge and reached for it. "I am going to kill this shaman," he told Spear Maker.

"Do not do this. Do not kill him."

Wanderer hefted the spear in his hand. As he turned to Spear Maker, his face looked older. "Can I remain here doing nothing? My wife cries in grief behind me. This child was near her heart. Soon other women will weep for a dead shaman. He will hear his own bones cracking."

Spear Maker understood the chief's anger, but he also knew the terrors of tribal feuds. Despite all he had done, Passing Shadow was still Black Snake's brother.

"Over there, upriver, is Black Snake's village," Spear Maker said. "Friend, go and kill them also. When they learn of the shaman's death, the laughter will stop on their lips. They also will want to take revenge."

Wanderer paused a moment, then shook his head. "No. The shaman ruined my child. I will not just wait until death comes. I will kill Passing Shadow and bury him in the ground."

"He has hurt your son and you must hurt him," Spear Maker agreed. The old man was having trouble keeping pace, but quickly added, "This shaman is one who has great desire. He has met a beautiful young girl and has tried to draw her into his lodge. Before you decide to kill him and pierce him with your spear, fetch this woman and carry her away. That will bite him so cruelly that he will taste bitterness."

"I want to kill him," Wanderer insisted. "You and the others will take his body and bury him."

"No. I will not go with you."

Wanderer continued hurrying down the path toward the shaman's lodge. Spear Maker hesitated. He had already smelled death once that day. Instead of following the chief, he went to find Fighting Eagle.

Three startled women looked up as Wanderer approached their hearth. Morning Land stayed as she was, but the other two quickly rose to their feet.

"The shaman, Passing Shadow, where is he?" Wanderer asked.

Dancing Rain pointed to a place in back of the lodge where Passing Shadow often went when he wished to avoid contact with his women. It was getting dark rapidly, and the chief could see only the silhouette of someone sitting amid the tall grass. He started forward, but the shaman had heard his request and was coming toward him.

"Have you come back to pick up your spear?" Passing Shadow asked, holding the short ceremonial spear that Wanderer had left in the grove earlier that day.

"No. Not for that. For my son." Even as he said this, Wanderer was angry with the weakness of his words. He owed no explanation.

"The spirits very nearly killed him," Passing Shadow said calmly. "I helped him fight against Yeane. I had to drive Yeane away, for the Black Moon nearly killed him while he slept."

"He cannot walk," Wanderer accused.

"I have cut a bone and split one end," Passing Shadow replied. "Yeane, the Black Moon, will soon be dead again. Then your son will grow strong."

"Yeane and those who live in the sky never hurt people," Wanderer retorted. "It is shamans who take life away."

"When you are awake, the day surrounds you," Passing Shadow explained. "Then it is the shamen who are moving about. You see only them. The sun blinds you. It is the spirits who truly hurt men. In the dark, in the cold places, when the air is heavy, they come. Their path cannot be seen. You see them only at night, when you close your eyes."

The two men were standing quite close, and Wanderer could see the shaman's face despite the growing darkness. Passing Shadow did not look frightened, but there was no outward show of disrespect either. Wanderer began to feel foolish. Passing Shadow acted as if he were talking to a worried father who had come to seek his help. His manner was one of passive concern.

"Your son was foolish to go into the forest so soon," Passing Shadow said. "Yeane is the bad one. The Black Moon blinds the sky. Then spirits approach those who are sleeping."

"You were there to wake him, to get up and stir the fire," Wanderer accused. "If you were truly a strong shaman, you should have opened his eyes."

"I saw the spirits come. I was standing underneath. They were not friendly toward you or your son. I uttered the call against them until my breath no longer passed through my chest. Then they went away."

"I no longer have faith in your ..." Wanderer began, and then stopped. Suddenly he realized that this was what Passing Shadow wanted him to do. The shaman had guessed that talking would slow the chief's anger, and already Wanderer could feel his rage deadening. He needed a way to break through the shaman's discipline, something that would upset Passing Shadow.

Wanderer's gaze shifted from the face of the shaman to the lodge behind him. All three wives were standing now. Their curiosity was obvious from the way they had bunched together at the edge of their hearth fire, anxiously listening to the talk of these two leaders. Wanderer guessed that they expected their husband to send the chief away in confusion as he had so often done before. But this time it would be different.

"I have heard your tales before," Wanderer continued. "When a storm is near, a man cuts leaves and makes a shelter. He does not expect a shaman's spells to keep the water from splashing him. I spit out these words of yours. Some shamen die when their magic is not good."

"These shamen are empty," Passing Shadow said, ignoring the implied threat. "I command the Great Bear spirit."

Wanderer was staring at Morning Land and remembering what Spear Maker had said about her. The hearth glow reflected in warm reddish shadows along the length of her slender body, reminding him of things he had almost forgotten. After a moment, she responded to his stare, looking up into his eyes. In that instant, Wanderer understood why the shaman had wanted her so badly.

"You are too old, shaman," he said quietly. "You have followed one path too long. You have lost your way and do not know how to see." Wanderer paused and then added, "It is these women. When a shaman makes love, he grows empty. You must begin tracing the path of spirits again. You must not go near women. Their pleasure is not good for you."

Passing Shadow's face showed his surprise. "I still feel the wind of approaching spirits," he protested. "I can still make out the smell of sickness."

"Some men only pretend to themselves. They are really empty." As he spoke, Wanderer saw his two other sons approaching along the path. That was good. He would need their strength to help force this through. "This day spirits almost killed Laughing One," he said. "You have grown too weak. It is the forest woman my son found. A dizziness rises from her body. Your magic will die if you do not drive her off."

As Wanderer started to move away, Passing Shadow reached out and grabbed his hand. "I hear the voices of the spirits on the path," he whispered.

The chief had been expecting this. His knife was already out. Fighting Eagle and Trusted Friend had raised their spears as well. Any violence from the shaman would have brought his own quick death.

"You must keep your eyes from this woman," Wanderer insisted. "You must live quietly, without anger. Only then will the spirits hear you." Wanderer paused, then shouted to his sons, "Look carefully, my sons. Take the woman Laughing One found."

Fighting Eagle immediately grabbed Morning Land's arm. She winced under his grip but offered no resistance.

Wanderer pushed the shaman's hand away and began walking toward his sons. The chief was still wary, for he had seen the wild hate in Passing Shadow's eyes. There was no certainty about anything this strange man might do.

"Take the girl back," he told his sons.

As the brothers started to lead Morning Land away along the path, there was a curious strangled noise from the shaman. Passing Shadow rushed up to the side of his lodge and shouted, "Your silence offends me! Why are you stealing my woman? She cannot just leave. She has my mark on her."

Wanderer stepped to within an arm's length of Passing Shadow's face. "She is still young. Keep your heart steady. When your magic grows and my son is strong, you will see this woman again."

For a moment, it seemed as if Passing Shadow might attack the chief after all. Then the shaman turned and hurried away into the darkness.

White Bird was not at the chief's lodge when her sister arrived there. She had been sent down to the lake to fetch more water, and was glad of the chance to be alone. Caught up in her own feelings of guilt and self-pity, she did not notice anything unusual until she was returning from the lake with the filled water pouches. As she neared the hearth, she could hear Summer Wind's voice, high and strident. White Bird stopped at the sound and listened, wondering what had provoked the woman's anger.

"*Katto!* This is that belly-filling, filth-eater's woman! I am to be the one who sleeps beside her? Eechnn! Her husband almost killed my son. His smell still rises all around her. Where she has been lying down, there she will continue to lie. Such people go to the earth."

White Bird's stomach lurched with expectation and she rushed forward. She was aware of Wanderer's voice, too, but she did not stop to listen. Her attention was on a familiar figure standing behind the chief.

"I have heard your talk," Summer Wind scolded. "Do you thing he has desire only for this woman? He does not want only her. Already he has gone to his other wives. We who are sitting here, we are the empty ones. We are the ones who hold nothing."

"Woman, you are like one who sings in the forest," Wanderer answered. "Your voice will not make the trees scatter their fruit. I alone must answer the others. The shaman is jealous of this woman. He thinks that he only may touch her, and this anger in his chest will make him weak."

Summer Wind bit her lip, fighting to control her frustration. For a moment she seemed to grow calm, but then she saw something on Morning Land's right arm which made her eyes become wide with rage.

"You should beat that shaman to death! He does not fear you! He does not care what you will see." Summer Wind reached out and grabbed Morning Land's hand, pulling her arm up into the firelight. Around Morning Land's wrist there was a neatly

braided bracelet made from Ehina's tail hairs. "Even here he
steals from you. This is just a worthless thing to him. He took
this from Trusted Friend to show us that he is the important one
and our son is not." Summer Wind curled her lower lip as if she
were smelling something foul, and then shoved Morning Land's
arm away. "Is this bad thing to stay at our lodge? Already the
smell that covers her body makes me lose my senses."

Stung by this treatment, Morning Land glared defiantly at the
chief's wife, who seemed ready to strike her. There was a
moment when the two women came near to fighting. Then
Wanderer stepped between them.

"Is this what you want? Do you want to insult me?" he
demanded. "This woman is not the one who has brought ruin to
us. You will not grab her throat or kick her. Keep her outside
your lodge if you wish, but she will stay with us."

Summer Wind saw the hardness that had come into her husband's expression and knew that her words would be useless.
She slumped visibly. "My anger is finished. I will not fight with
her."

Wanderer was not pleased. His wife had shown too much anger in front of his sons, and he felt shamed by it. With an abrupt
gesture, he dismissed her and began walking toward Fighting
Eagle's lodge. Trusted Friend and the hunting leader were quick
to follow. Neither son looked at Summer Wind.

The chief's wife was left with Morning Land. For a moment,
the two women just stared at each other, both still too angry to
speak. Summer Wind found it hard to believe that this stranger
could truly be White Bird's sister. It was not just the lack of
physical likeness. White Bird was an obliging, eager girl, while
this other woman seemed full of quiet rage.

"This sister is different," Summer Wind murmured to herself.
"For us to live together will not be good. Living that way, will
we not feel pain?"

As if by way of answer, White Bird hurried into the firelight.
She hugged Morning Land before her sister could protest, and
Summer Wind witnessed the curious ritual of a Tideland greeting. When the two sisters separated and stood side by side a
moment later, Summer Wind had thought of a plan.

"*Yi-quay-is,*" she called. "*Yi-quay-is,* daughter, come here."

White Bird quietly stepped around the hearth.

"*Yi-quay-is,*" come and take your sister away," Summer
Wind said. "A wife fears her husband, but my heart refuses this

woman. She will not enter my lodge. *Yi-quay-is,* I will share with you. Can you watch your sister?"

White Bird nodded eagerly.

"She must sleep outside the lodge. She must lie by herself. Then I will share with her." Summer Wind added, "When Laughing One is strong again, she will go back to the shaman."

"We will sit together and do things together," White Bird promised. "Living that way, Morning Land will not make you feel pain."

Summer Wind looked doubtful. Her glance shifted from White Bird to Morning Land and then she shook her head. "My face frowns at this woman," she said. "She must eat her food alone. If you have love for your sister, keep her from me."

Summer Wind took the water pouches from White Bird and went back inside the lodge, dismissing them both with a final shake of her head. After the chief's wife had gone, there was a silence between the sisters while White Bird decided what she should do. Less than a moon before, Morning Land had been the one to make decisions. Even now White Bird felt an urge to obey whenever she heard Morning Land's quiet, determined voice. It was hard for the girl to suddenly take charge of the woman.

"Do not fear her, sister," White Bird finally said. "She refuses everything because her son is ill. She is full of bad talk, but she will not kill you with her words. I understand your anger, but we are traveling together this day. You will not just stay by yourself. I will get you water and bring you food to eat. Do you feel hunger?"

Morning Land shook her head slowly. Her expression was carefully neutral.

"I will make a fire and bring you hides to sleep on," White Bird said. "Then we will just sit together and talk. Nothing will hurt you."

Without waiting for a reply, White Bird turned quickly and hurried into the chief's lodge.

Morning Land watched her sister leave. Then, when she was sure no one else could see, she slumped onto the ground, the stiffness suddenly slipping away from her arms and limbs. She started shivering a moment later. Morning Land's face held the miserably unhappy look that had startled White Bird many days before. It came back to her whenever she was quiet like this.

Morning Land felt something brush against her arm as she moved her hands away from her chest. It was the bracelet made from Ehina's tail hairs. She had barely noticed the ornament when Passing Shadow had given it to her. After seeing the anger it aroused in the chief's wife, she realized that the charm must have some importance. That was why Passing Shadow had looked so pleased with himself when he had slipped it onto her arm. She should have guessed that he had probably stolen it from someone.

Almost without thinking, Morning Land pulled the bracelet from her wrist and held it up before the fire. She was not really free of Passing Shadow—not yet—but somehow she felt that she was going to be. At least there was no reason for her to keep his gifts. With a quick flick of her fingers, she dropped the bracelet onto the glowing hearth coals.

Her expression hardened again as she watched it burn.

CHAPTER ELEVEN

White Bird's Marriage

For six more days, the grasslands were brightened by the sunlight filtering down through increasingly cloudy skies. On each day it might have rained, but some chance wind seemed always to part the clouds and send them drifting in lazy succession toward the horizon. The dreaded Moon of Snows had begun mildly, allowing Wanderer's people time to move the village to higher ground, where each lodge could be rebuilt in a place sheltered from the western winds and rains. The women dug out lodge floors that were below the level of the surrounding earth, and piled extra dirt in dikelike banks against the walls. Soon the winter village had become entrenched and permanent along the southeastern slope of a large hill.

On the seventh day, the first of the winter storms struck the coast. Far to the west, in the land that had once belonged to the Tidelanders, the storm came with hard battering surf that rammed up against the bluffs and pulled out layers of sand and dirt which had settled during milder seasons. The big wind pushed at the water relentlessly, stirring huge waves that worked against the shore. Trees were undermined and went down in a groan of snapping branches, and even giant rocks toppled into the surf, creating strange, shaking blasts of sound. As children, White Bird and Morning Land had known many such storms. The Tidelanders called them the Screaming Waters, and thought of them as wild spirit children.

The rain and wind that came with the surf went farther inland, pouring out cascades of water onto the coastal hills. In the forests where Laughing One had once fought with the great cat, trees shivered and split beneath flashing, lightning-filled skies. Some trees exploded from the impact of the lightning, but more fearsome were the mudslides which shifted whole areas of forest. Beginning as a deep sighing from within the earth, they soon rose to a booming roar that rumbled louder than the thunder.

By the time it had reached the home of Laughing One's people, most of the storm's violent strength had been spent, but there were still torrents of rain. The water poured down during the night, dousing the village hearth fires in a steaming hiss, and battering the lodge coverings like sprays of stones. Most wives had little rest as they struggled to stop sudden leaks in the roofs of their homes. Children cried uneasily while they slept, and husbands tried to calm the scoldings of their wives with promises that at daybreak they would make the mud walls higher and cover the roof with dead branches to keep the layers of grass and hides in place. By morning, when the rain had finally lessened to a continual drizzle, everyone in the tribe was miserable.

It was a chill, gray day, and for the people who were huddled together near their lodge entrances, there was little to see. A bluish mist created by the drizzle covered the land like cold steam, blotting out all but the nearest stands of trees. The ground around the camp was muddy, water-soaked, and dark. It gave off a strong smell of damp wood and ruined meat. As the women managed to get their hearths burning again, the odors of woodsmoke and cooking began to offset these other smells, and the village started to seem normal once more. Still, no one was in a good temper. Children quarreled in shrill, high voices, and wives scolded their husbands, who either shouted back or moved away. As the arguing grew more snappish, most men were content to let the wives fight among themselves and began to chew broodingly on dried pieces of meat. From the glowering expressions on the men's faces, it was obvious that they would soon leave the village and find more secluded areas.

Morning Land and White Bird sat side by side, with furs wrapped around their shoulders to protect against the drizzle. They stared out into the grayness with the same listless expressions that could be found on dozens of other faces. Anyone seeing the sisters from a distance might well have imagined that the two women had been born to the tribe. Summer Wind's solution to her problem with Morning Land had been to build a separate lodge for the two sisters, a lodge which would later be used as the first marriage home for Laughing One and White Bird. Already Laughing One's portion of Ehina's hide covered the lodge roof.

"This is the season of high waters," Morning Land said quietly. "Look how the river of rains is already in the sky. I will not be able to live like this much longer."

White Bird looked up from where she was staring at the fire. "Only sisters can live as well as we do. We no longer have our mother and father. We need to help each other. Why could we not both marry one man? We would not fight."

"I am already married to the crooked mouth," Morning Land insisted. "He makes evil faces whenever he sees us sitting together. He will not let this insult pass, and the people here fear him. Perhaps they will make a show of being fierce and brave, but it will do no good. You yourself know this. *Tua-arikii* is strong again. The shaman has killed no one. He will come back for his woman."

White Bird sighed with exasperation. "These people's ways will ruin us," she complained. She was still angry at having been shoved out of the chief's lodge as soon as Laughing One had recovered enough to speak to her. "These people are always afraid," she muttered. "I walk behind the chief's wife. The shaman caused her son's blood to flow, but I have seen her eyes widen with fear when she speaks of that man. And Wanderer has not done anything to Passing Shadow. He has let the shaman just walk away. Everyone here is fearful. Do you think they will just let this marriage happen? Oh no! They will fear the sickness that this rain can bring. All I have left now is you, my sister. What will I find to cure my pain when you are gone?"

"I remember how our people loved this rain," Morning Land said. "We girls hurried to play in the rain, splashing and running around the ring of huts. We would take the woman of importance, the one who was to be married, and make her run with us. Rain was her special form of luck."

"Our people had sense," White Bird reminded her. "These people only fear the rain."

Morning Land was not really listening. "I remember how we screamed," she said. "We truly shouted. We splashed each other as we danced around. The woman of importance made believe that she was afraid, but she was soon the dirtiest of all."

White Bird did remember. She had run the circle of huts, too, but she always remembered Morning Land doing it. After they had been around the village several times, the girls had pulled off their soiled aprons and run naked in the rain, giggling wildly as it had splashed over them. Even when she had tried to land as heavily as the others, Morning Land had come down on her toes. She had come down laughing in that high, clicking way of hers, while every part of her body had seemed to thrill with motion. She had always been graceful, but she had never been more beautiful than at those moments running through the rain. White Bird remembered, and the memory brought a painful rush of love for her sister.

"The sun is truly gone from this sky," White Bird said. "Perhaps these people are afraid of rain and will not touch us now. I truly had no sense when I wanted to come to this village. I will not marry *Tua-arikii*. I will just lay down beside my sister."

Morning Land's expression was so gentle that it made the young girl uncomfortable. To hide her awkwardness, White Bird picked up a stick and began tracing designs in the earth.

"The rain spills itself and will fall tirelessly until these lakes are full," Morning Land said quietly. "My heart cannot be happy. Even if you continue to live like this, it will do no good. The shaman has already taken me. Your marriage does not hurt me further. It does not change things. You must sit quiet and just wait. Perhaps a husband will make you stronger."

White Bird started to reply, but looked up and saw Summer Wind approaching them. The chief's wife carried two empty water pouches, which she quickly dropped beside White Bird.

"*Yi-quay-is,* daughter, the season of rains has come. Soon the lake will spill up onto its banks. Fill these skins now, while the water is clean."

White Bird got to her feet and picked up the empty pouches.

"Go downstream where the water is quiet and still," Summer Wind advised. "Wash yourself. You are growing up this day. Swim until all the dirt has gone."

Wondering, White Bird scowled at her adopted mother, but Summer Wind seemed not to notice.

"Feel beautiful, daughter," the chief's wife said. "This is the day that your heart wants."

Still puzzled, White Bird turned and began to walk toward the lake. The drizzle had lessened, and the thought of swimming was not unpleasant.

Morning Land understood what White Bird had missed. When Fighting Eagle and Trusted Friend appeared as soon as White Bird was out of sight, Morning Land was not startled. They would get no resistance from her.

By the time she had reached the place where the village trail joined the lakeshore, White Bird had forgotten about her sister. The misty drizzle seemed to have settled in close around her as she walked, blocking off the entire world except for a few nearby trees. It was muddy, and her bare feet squished against the soft earth. As she breathed in the clear scent of wet pines, White Bird felt like a Tidelander again.

There was a mist over the lake as well, covering it in the same way that the morning fog had sometimes settled across the mountain valleys. When she stared out over the bluish expanse, White Bird remembered her days in the camp by the river, in the one place where she and her sister had been entirely free. With a sigh, she let the two water pouches slap noisily against the ground. A moment later, her apron followed them, flopping down in a crumple over the pouches. With more care, she grabbed her saber-toothed tusk necklace and pulled the leather thong over her head. She left the tusk nestled amid the folds of her apron. Then she moved away quickly across the rocks of the shore, shifting her weight and changing her posture with each step.

White Bird hurried into the water and kick-dived below the surface. The lake was cold, but White Bird's pulse was racing, and she let her pumping thighs push her forward into deeper water. As she swam through the shallows, she remembered the Tideland girls she had known as a youth. Following a long-honored custom among her people, all of the girls who had been passing through womanhood rites had grouped into bands and gone about the business of tormenting any young men they could find. A group of boys trying to spearfish had been a perfect target. Sometimes the girls had dressed in seaweed, rolling their hips as they had stepped over stones, or dangling smooth young legs across sea-drenched logs. If the hunters had continued to stare out over the water, the girls had become more aggressive. Some had splashed noisily into the surf, cupping their small breasts in their hands and rubbing their nipples until these had become puckered and erect. Others had squatted down next to the boys in a way that had shown their buttocks and thighs. It had been a giggling, stumbling kind of courtship. If one of the boys had responded by grabbing at them, the girls had raced away, squealing insults. When they had tired of their game, they had made a fire to dry themselves and had huddled around it, suddenly only black-haired Tideland girls again, with smiles on their faces and their arms outstretched toward the hearth.

White Bird's own arms were beginning to tire, so she started swimming toward the shore. A short while later, dressed in her apron again and carrying the filled water pouches in her right hand, White Bird walked back toward the village. The drizzle still gave a blue haze to the world, but now the wetness only felt uncomfortable. By the time White Bird came within sight of the lodges, the pleasant, quiet feeling she had had was gone. In its place there was an uneasy sense that something had gone wrong. She had expected to find Morning Land waiting for her beside the lodge entrance, but Summer Wind and Beautiful Star were there instead.

"*Yi-quay-is,* are you afraid?" Summer Wind called. "Come here. Beautiful Star has a gift for you."

White Bird obeyed, but her expression was wary. "What are you doing, Mother?" she asked. "Where has Morning Land gone?"

Determined to be pleasant, Summer Wind ignored the question. "This day you will be happy, daughter," she said. "The things you dream about, the things your heart wants—this day you will have them."

"Has Morning Land gone?" White Bird persisted.

Summer Wind sighed. "The shaman has her."

White Bird's eyes showed her anger. "Why is my sister with the shaman again? *Tua-arikii* has been sick a long time and the shaman caused it. I have felt pain because of that shaman."

Before Summer Wind could answer, Beautiful Star interrupted. "There was nothing more a woman could do. We have left that blood behind us."

"Your sister has left you," Summer Wind said. "Laughing One remains. We must continue to live."

"My insides will not stop hurting with this," White Bird complained. "You have caused pain by having done this to me."

Summer Wind looked up angrily and recognized the same willful defiance she had felt in White Bird's sister. The girl might not be as tall or as finely shaped as the woman they had given to the shaman, but there was no mistaking her expression. White Bird's lips were pressed together petulantly, and her sturdy legs were spread wide in a stance that hardly suggested the modesty of a new bride. With an awkward grunt, the chief's wife got to her feet.

"*Katto!* Worthless one. Has your heart already died? Perhaps you do not want my son. When he was an Eeenuan, you were not afraid. But now, as a man, he frightens you. You with your unhappy face. Who would get you food if I stopped doing it? You would shiver with the cold or go die in the bush. You would sneak about stealing meals when others sleep. We are the ones who have to feed you. You are empty-handed, without friends or gifts. My son gains nothing by marrying you."

Summer Wind paused, anger having cut short the flow of words. To be insulted by a captive girl was something she would not endure, not even for her favorite son.

White Bird quickly realized her danger. She had already seen enough of Summer Wind's temper to know where it would lead.

"What is happening to make you so angry, Mother?" White Bird asked soothingly. "I do not refuse you. What I say is not important. The shaman is the bad one. He is the one who has caused this anger between us. I have no anger with you. You have treated me very well." In her eagerness to be obliging, White Bird clutched the water pouches she had been carrying. "Ehnn. I have brought you the water you asked for."

Summer Wind frowned. Her eyes studied White Bird with an intensity that flustered the Tideland girl. White Bird lowered her gaze and bowed her head submissively. After a moment, the chief's wife was mollified.

"*Supai*. You are going to anger many people if you do not learn to speak our tongue with care," Summer Wind cautioned. "Daughter, it is us you are insulting with your anger. Speak more gently. Do what the important ones tell you to. Daughter, the things we hear must be good things. Now, go into the lodge. Your apron is wet. Take it off."

White Bird hurriedly obeyed, promising herself that things would be different once she had Laughing One. There was still an angry flush on her cheeks as she pulled off her apron and removed her thong necklace, but she tried to keep her temper in check.

Beautiful Star came into the lodge a few moments later. White Bird was surprised to see that Trusted Friend's wife was nearly as naked as herself. Beautiful Star had taken off her robe to reveal a body which was painted with white, interlocking circles. In the dimness of the lodge, the patterning gave her an unreal appearance, making the traces of daylight glisten off her skin. She wore a short, rawhide apron around her waist, but the apron was so small and curved so tightly against her thighs that it seemed to be only one more part of the circle pattern.

Beautiful Star smiled. "*Anata*, shy one, your anger is useless. You must not be afraid of your husband. You are not an old woman who fears things. We are young, both of us. This day I have painted myself to honor your marriage. I have promised to paint you as well."

White Bird remained silent, and Beautiful Star seemed amused. "You can stare at me as much as you want. You cannot continue to just eat quietly and sit alone. This is your marriage day. I have only been covered with white clay," she said, pointing to a looping spiral below her right breast. "For you it will be poured out and pounded with red clay as well. Listen, if you would be as beautiful as I think you are, you will also be painted. Laughing One will see you and like you. His heart will be strong."

Before long, White Bird was quietly submitting while Beautiful Star and Summer Wind cut back her hair. The long, black tresses were wound around a wooden stick and sliced off with a sharp knife. Despite the crudeness of the method, the two women were skilled enough to give the hair an even edge. When they were finished, White Bird's hair fell only as far as her shoulders, and was square cut above her forehead.

White Bird looked down uneasily at the fragments of silken hair that lay in random piles across the hide where she had been kneeling. She had always prided herself on the flowing grace of her black hair.

"Mother, this hurts. What are you doing?" she asked doubtfully.

"Watch us, that you may know how this is done," Beautiful Star replied. "You have grown up. You hair smells so sweetly now."

Summer Wind began gathering the fragments of hair into a bundle. "We will collect these gatherings until we have enough to tie with thongs," she said. "A woman does not cast away her food. You will give your husband this. Just as we have treated you, you will also treat him. He will sit here with you and your heart will be happy. You will say, 'Oh my husband, take this beautiful hair.'"

"What I have to give is only little. Why would *Tua-arikii* want my hair?" White Bird asked.

Summer Wind shook her head at this new show of ignorance. "Sometimes a man is jealous," she said. "Sometimes his heart burns. When that happens, a wife does things. She gives her hair and he accepts this, as he accepts her. It is more than a friendly gift. It is a way of touching him, of touching his heart, which is a man's heart."

"My people do not do this," White Bird said. "Why does a gift of hair mean things?"

"There are many gifts a man receives from women," Beautiful Star answered. "If your husband visits a friend's lodge, that friend's wife will give your husband food. She will cook some meat and bring it to him. If your husband is cold, his mother will make him furs. If a man is courting, his sister will make him a beaded necklace. But only his wife will give him ornaments made from her hair. That is a sign that she has been well taken care of. Trusted Friend has all the hair I cut off. He has every piece of it," she added virtuously.

Summer Wind, who was bundling the cut fragments, snorted contemptuously. "There are other things a wife must do," she added. "You will live together and share many seasons. You will follow trails and go into the bush together. When it is your time of blood, you must refuse your husband and not touch his hunting things. That will ruin his *Uuuura*. The soiled pads of grass you use must be hidden. They must not be thrown where he will touch them with his feet. When your blood flows, your touch will make him weak."

White Bird nodded, wondering what other customs these people had. It seemed as if her life among them would be a difficult one, forever troubled by the fear of doing some wrong thing.

While Summer Wind wrapped leather thongs around the clumps of hair she had collected, Beautiful Star slipped out through the lodge entrance. She returned with shell cups full of red, white, and black dye. White Bird noticed that most of the cups were filled with red dye. The other colors seemed much less important. White Bird wondered at this, but did not ask. She was afraid it would make her seem even more ignorant.

"One time, when I was very young, my people moved far to the south, into the land of the people with long fingers," Beautiful Star said. "I was afraid of these people, and ran away whenever one came near, but I learned many things from them. As I am today, I remember what those people spoke to me long ago. That is the talk you will take from me now."

While she spoke, Beautiful Star used a small piece of hide to brush away any strands of cut hair that still clung to White Bird's body.

"In that southern place, where the sun is always strong in the sky, the woman of importance—the one who is to be married—must suffer many things," Beautiful Star said. "They do not just cut her hair as we have done. Oh no! They continue doing it and will not stop. Only when all of her hair is gone will they leave her. This young woman, she is very fearful. She does not like what they are doing. She cries, but they do not listen. They cut her arms and legs to make her blood flow. When they finish, they mix ash paste in the cuts to leave a lasting mark."

"*Katto!* Those people with long fingers are just animals," Summer Wind snorted. "Do not speak of their ways."

Beautiful Star ignored Summer Wind's crossness. Dipping her hands into a cup of red dye, she said, "This red paint is a very good thing. It is strong. This is the birth color that heats inside you. As you begin a marriage, this color takes your childhood away. Things will start to change for you now."

Like most Tidelanders, White Bird was able to sit motionlessly for long periods of time, and she called upon that skill now. She tried to keep her body passive as Beautiful Star's smooth, dye-covered hands moved in soothing circles over her skin. This time it was not easy to stay calm, for there was something very disturbing about Beautiful Star's touch.

"These people with the long fingers, they have many strange ways," Beautiful Star continued. "In the night, when darkness sits, all the young women come and stay in one great lodge. The women talk and wait. Then their lovers come. Each man lies with a woman until morning breaks. Then they separate, and the man just leaves."

"What a bad one you are to talk of these things," Summer Wind interrupted. "Be quiet if you are going to talk without sense. No lodge could hold so many women."

Beautiful Star hid her annoyance by concentrating on her painting. Her graceful fingers left crisscrossing marks over White Bird's neck and shoulders. Gradually, as more and more dye was applied, the skin became coated in a solid, deep color.

"I have not seen such a lodge," Beautiful Star admitted. "But every woman in this tribe has many lovers. There is never only one man who sleeps beside her. No lover says, 'This woman is mine.' It is only when a woman grows big with her first child that things change for her. Then she must leave the great lodge. The man she has been lying down with most often, the one who her heart goes toward, that is the one she chooses to marry.

"Some women walk another path. Their insides never grow big with child. For them, one man follows another. Such a woman may learn much and tell the young men how they can be strong lovers. Such women are not afraid of anyone."

"Women are not that way," Summer Wind snapped. "Women refuse to give their lovers to another. If men keep asking for others and not for her, a woman grows angry. Being without a child makes a woman sad, not happy. There is nothing truthful in what you say. Finish this."

Beautiful Star continued to smile, but fear of the chief's wife kept her silent for a while. With steady persistence, she worked her hands over the round smoothness of White Bird's breasts, stomach, and thighs.

"Stand up," she said at last.

White Bird did so, and was aware of how red her body looked. The smell of red clay was stronger in her nostrils than the pine smoke from the hearth. Beautiful Star finished White Bird's buttocks and the backs of her legs very quickly, for the clay paste was becoming thicker now. Soon every part of the Tideland girl, from her face to her toes, was covered in red dye.

Finally Beautiful Star stood up. "Ehnn. It is good. Your skin does not give way. You do not call out in pain. You are truly a woman."

"This is how one does things," Summer Wind agreed. "If it were not for the rain, we would take you around the village so that everyone could see you."

White Bird thought the painting was finished, but she was wrong. Beautiful Star paused only long enough to wash her hands in rainwater before returning to her shell cups of black and white dye. This time she used brushes made from dried milkweed stalks that had been chewed flat at one end.

"You are the important one here," Beautiful Star told White Bird. "Now sit as other women do."

As the Tideland girl obeyed, Beautiful Star squatted next to her, somehow managing to make even this position seem graceful. With the black dye, she traced two straight lines down the center of White Bird's forehead. Reflections of the manhood scars now found on Laughing One, these lines continued all the way down across the nose and upper lip. Next, dark circles were drawn around White Bird's eyes and on her cheeks. These circles would later be filled in with white dye.

Beautiful Star was serious and calm while she worked on the young girl's face, but the lodge was not quiet. Summer Wind had begun to lecture again.

"A young girl often fears men," Summer Wind told White Bird. "She fears the hurt and pain that they can bring. That is what is wrong with young wives. But a woman learns things. When I was married to Wanderer, I feared him and his ways. He asked for me and I refused him many times. Now my heart is much stronger. That is a woman's way."

Beautiful Star was quickly painting lines and stars across White Bird's back. She seemed to follow no organized pattern, but responded to whatever shape came into her mind. "There are many things a chief's wife does not see," she said. "She does not see the young men who creep from behind when a young girl is lying at her family's fire. These men are truly senseless! They do not care that elders are near the same fire.They make love through the girl's legs. Sometimes the girl is so excited that she kicks and shouts. Sometimes the man hurts her and she sobs. Then the elders discover what is happening. Oh, what fights there are!

"Older women are very different," Beautiful Star added wryly. "They are not small inside like young women. Uhnn. They are big. Their insides are stretched wide. It takes much for them to find pleasure. The old woman wraps her legs around her lover's waist and holds him there. She wants to feel him beating deep inside her. They are face to face. Her legs are wrapped around him and she tells him he must eat."

"Why are you so full of bad talk?" Summer Wind asked angrily, aware that Beautiful Star was mocking her. "This is not something I want to hear. White Bird is very young. For her it will be different."

There was a strained silence after that. Beautiful Star went on to paint a wide-winged bird across White Bird's chest and abdomen, but she did not seem pleased with the work. When the last snaking lines had been traced over White Bird's thighs, Beautiful Star threw her brushes down with an exhausted grunt. Summer Wind, who had been waiting for this moment, held out a loose, leather robe and placed it over White Bird's shoulders.

"This robe is very powerful," Summer Wind insisted. "It will help you not to feel pain."

"I will be cold," White Bird protested.

"You will have the warmth of the fire and the warmth of Laughing One," Summer Wind replied. "A man's warm skin is very pleasant. Sit quietly. Let him see how you are painted when he comes for you."

White Bird remained silent while both women embraced her and left. She wanted to thank them, but she felt too awkward and confused to speak. This was not the way she had planned to greet her new husband. Beautiful Star's designs had suited her own body, but on White Bird's heavier, more robust form, they seemed distorted. White Bird did not feel like either a Tidelander or a valley woman. She was just an awkward girl who had somehow been misplaced.

It was Fighting Eagle who brought Laughing One to his marriage lodge. The two men had waited in their parents' lodge while Summer Wind and Beautiful Star had prepared White Bird. For most of that time, neither had spoken, but as they approached the marriage lodge, Fighting Eagle felt a need for talk.

"One moon dies, another appears," he grunted. "Great anger is often followed by peaceful days. Our hearts feel pain, but after that we live as always. Your wife sits down a little distance away. Take the trail that leads to her."

Laughing One nodded. Unable to make much sense of his brother's words, he kept his mouth shut and his face down against the rain. The weather was worsening. Already the air had darkened to a thick gray, and the hearth fires provided only a weak glow through the wetness. Most would probably go out before dawn, despite the efforts of the women to keep them lit.

"It is a young woman who waits for you this night," Fighting Eagle continued. "She has just begun to learn things. When she meets you, she may start to tremble. When you lie down with her and make love, she may start to cry. She may cry each time you touch her. You must take care of her, touch her gently. Help her when she trembles. This is a lovely young woman who does not yet know things."

The two men were close to Laughing One's lodge, and Fighting Eagle abruptly stopped. "I leave you by this lodge," he said. "Learn how these things are done. Lie beside her and teach her. Make noise now, before you enter. Do not let her be frightened."

There seemed to be something else that Fighting Eagle intended to say, for he placed a hand on Laughing One's shoulder and stared into his face, but when a woman suddenly thrust her head out of a nearby lodge, the hunting leader quickly turned and left. His hunched-over form soon blurred into the surrounding grayness.

Laughing One stomped his feet against the ground to make a warning noise, but he did not hurry forward. For a long while he only stared at the lodge in front of him, both wishing that Fighting Eagle had come with him all the way to the entrance and feeling a shivering thrill of expectation. He might have lingered there even longer if the rain had not felt so cold against his skin. Finally he coughed loudly and crawled into the entrance of his new home.

White Bird looked up as he came in, but did not move. Laughing One slipped quietly past her without uttering a sound. She heard the thump of his fur robe as he dropped it onto the ground near the entrance. It was followed by the clatter of spears and the heavy thud of the weapons' pouch. Still he said nothing. She remained sitting as she was, but her arms began to tremble.

"There is food," she said quietly. "You must eat. They tell me you must eat."

The musical sound of her voice, with its strange Tideland accent, cut through the dizziness in Laughing One's mind. He stared at her more closely, trying to recognize the girl he had once made love to. Beautiful Star's painting made White Bird seem strange. Her black eyes were completely hidden in shadow, and the darkness of the ocher made her undyed lips appear too lush and full. There was nothing familiar about her cropped hair or the earthy scent that came from her. Even the shape of her body was mostly hidden by the loose marriage robe.

"The sun was well hidden this day," she said. "It is hard to do things when there is little light."

It was not really an apology. White Bird simply spoke to relieve her inner trembling. With a half-fearful expression on her face, she held up a wooden bowl filled with mashed berries and acorn mush.

Still slightly shaken by the familiar softness of her voice, Laughing One crouched down beside her and began to eat. He felt no hunger, and the mush slipped awkwardly over his fingers as he tried to scoop it up, but the eating implied acceptance. He was anxious to make things right again.

"I will learn how to do these things," White Bird promised. "Do you have enough food?"

Laughing One nodded. He wanted to speak, but his throat was choked with the tasteless acorn mush.

"My leg is trembling," White Bird complained. "They told me we would meet again this day. They rubbed oil on my skin and I just sat here until it was finished. I have sat here so long that my leg is trembling." As she said this, White Bird finally shifted position, and Laughing One noticed the strong, rounded calf that suddenly protruded from beneath her robe. Like her voice, it was something familiar, but also something that seemed strangely out of place.

"There is water here," White Bird said uncertainly, holding up a pouch.

Laughing One took the pouch and gulped the water eagerly, for he could not have swallowed the mush without it. His throat felt wonderfully clean as he set the pouch down.

"Are you strong again?" White Bird asked. "The shaman is powerful and he stole your strength from you. People wanted to kill him, but Wanderer refused. When you were lying down sick, it hurt me very much."

"The shaman only made me slightly sick," Laughing One answered. "I have been given my life back again." His voice was raspy, and he realized suddenly that he did not have anything more to say to her. In a forced attempt at politeness, he chewed on some of the dried meat. As the silence between them grew more obvious, neither could understand the shyness that they felt.

White Bird was becoming desperate when she looked down and noticed the bundle of hair that Summer Wind had prepared. She hurriedly picked it up and held it out to him.

"I am only a young woman, but your mother and your sister have started to teach me. They told me to give you this."

The move was so unexpected that Laughing One nearly dropped the meat when he attempted to grab the bundle. As his fingers closed over the silken texture of White Bird's hair, she lifted her face to him. For a moment he wanted to touch her, but the white rings of paint over her skin were too distracting. His hand hesitated.

"*Siyemou.* Why do you go looking for things?" White Bird asked quickly. "You are afraid."

He looked at her blankly. "No, I am not afraid," he said.

"*Shiiwe!*" her voice rose in anger. "You refuse me! You do not like the food I bring you! You do not want the water I bring. I am not a child without sense. I still see things. You do not want me! Have you married me only because everyone told you to? Were you afraid to refuse them? Now speak truthfully. If you do not want me, I will just leave." As White Bird said this, she began to turn away. In another moment, she was getting to her feet.

Laughing One grabbed at her to keep her from going, and his strong hand gripped the edge of White Bird's bridal robe. The robe came off easily, for the bark strips that held it in place had only been loosely wound around White Bird's upper arms, but the Tideland girl pulled away from him before he could touch her further. For a moment they crouched on opposite sides of the lodge, staring at each other.

White Bird was naked now, and Beautiful Star's wild patterns seemed to wind in snakelike coils across her skin, emphasizing the tensed fullness of her strong body. Laughing One was afraid that she would run from the lodge if he came closer. Instead, he held out his hand to show that he had not wanted to hurt her.

"This painting has made me ugly!" White Bird gestured contemptuously at the layers of dye on her face and breasts. "I smell of dirt! Everything itches!"

"Why are you shouting?" Laughing One asked. "What are you saying? Why do you talk like this, saying my heart is not strong for you? Your thoughts may be angry, but mine are not. My heart became yours before I married you. I do not understand your anger. Do Tideland women refuse to paint themselves?"

White Bird nodded and moved closer. He could have touched her easily now.

"I do not want you angry," Laughing One said. "I want you to tell me about the things your people do."

White Bird was quiet a moment. Then she explained.

"*Tua-arikii,* a man of my people does not just leave his woman alone. If he has a full heart, he accepts the gifts she brings. She lies down inside his hut and he makes love to her in the night. He is the important man in her life then, and they are married. She builds a marriage hut, and when it is finished, she brings him to it. That is my people's way."

It was said simply and quickly, but as she spoke, Laughing One realized that she was describing what they had done in their camp beside the river. He remembered the quarrel they had had and how she had refused to sleep with him afterward. Now he finally understood how much he had disappointed her.

"After all that has happened, I did not understand," he said awkwardly. "As I am now, I have been without sense."

"I thought your heart had changed," White Bird told him. "I thought you no longer liked me. You do not refuse me?"

Laughing One shook his head and reached for her. "What has happened before is not important. I have married you and you are my wife. The two of us will just sit beside each other, in this lodge. That is how it will be."

White Bird waited until his hands touched her shoulders, but then seemed to change her mind. "My skin is hurting," she said hurriedly. "I feel like a woman whose skin has died. I will go and wash myself in the lake."

"The rain is hard now," Laughing One told her. "Even the hunters stay in their lodges when the wind is hurting like this."

White Bird stared at him for a moment, and he noticed that

the anger seemed to have gone from her. When she spoke, her voice was soft and gentle again.

"*Tua-arikii*, a Tideland woman does not fear the rain," she said. "We do not cover ourselves with furs when the mist comes. We swim in the cold pools. The wind circles above us, and we play until the treetops snap. My people, they love the hard rain." She wanted to tell him more; about moonlit surf that seethed back from the tidepools, and the long strands of seaweed that lay lifeless across brownish-red beaches, but his language had no words for any of these things and she knew he would never understand them. Instead, she stood up and slid her bridal robe back over her shoulders. "I ask you to let me go."

Without a word, Laughing One picked up one of his spears and his fur robe. As soon as she realized that he intended to go with her, White Bird smiled at him. It was the same wide, open grin she had used long before, when she had been hunting shellfish for him in the river.

Outside, the last moments of daylight were accompanied by a downpour of rain. It splattered into Laughing One's face and made the black dye streak along White Bird's arms and legs. Laughing One felt a desire to return to the lodge, but when he saw his new wife hurrying over the wet grass, his pride forced him to follow. With his face down against the rain, and his feet sinking into the soft mud at each step, Laughing One ran beside White Bird.

When she reached the shore, most of the red dye had already been washed from White Bird's legs, and her plump thighs shone with the same film of moisture that shimmered across the surrounding leaves and bushes. For a moment she stood still, catching her breath and breathing in the rich earthy scent of the forest. Then she let the bridal robe slip from her shoulders as she waded into the lake.

Laughing One stayed on the shore beside the rock where she had laid her bridal robe. The rain did not bother him so much now. He was content to watch White Bird's sleek, tanned form wading through the waist-deep water.

The downpour had already washed much of the dye from White Bird's skin, and she plunged into the waves to get rid of the rest. Foamy bubbles frothed through her hair as she forced her head down toward the lake bottom in the first part of a long, spiraling dive. As she sped forward through the cold water, she was reminded of similar days when she had played amid the great breakers that had rolled against the headlands of her

former home. She had floated on her belly while the white water had pushed her toward the shore, feeling her body being
gradually lifted by the current. When the wave had finally broken around her and had seethed into white rivulets against the
sand, she had jumped up again like a porpoise, leaping out toward the deeper water. High breakers had meant nothing to her,
and after having been tossed about amid the wild surf for most
of a morning, she had staggered up onto the rocks, feeling numb
but satisfied. If her mother had been watching, the older woman
would have shaken her head and called her "*Apaia* (otter girl)."

White Bird kicked to the surface, gasped in deep lungfuls of
cool air, and began to tread water. *Apaia anava* (sea-otter love).
That was how her people had spoken of days like this, when
there had been uncertain rain and heavy surf. At such times, the
sea otters had left their homes amid the seaweed to chase the
foam and churning water of the breakers. It had been anava that
had driven them; anava that had only grown stronger with the
tumult of the windy rain. White water seething over rocks had
seemed to cause apaia anava, the special passion. The otters had
mated and mated and had turned themselves together in a
rolling love swim that had been as flowing as the incoming
waves.

White Bird smiled to herself. Laughing One was where she
had left him. A small figure against the deep gray-green of the
misty woods, he stood guard over the shapeless mass of her
bridal robe. The rain had flattened his hair around his face, his
fur robe fluttered with each gust of wet wind, and something in
his expression made her want to rush toward him.

She came out of the water quickly, her form momentarily sil-
houetted against the dull light of the overcast sky. Laughing
One watched as her feet padded noiselessly across the shore,
and then suddenly she was embracing him, and he was aware of
a dozen sensations at once. There was the soft, pulsating little
"*hai-ai-ai-ai*" noise which her lips made as she nuzzled him in
Tideland fashion, the beating softness of her breasts next to his
chest, the tug of her arms around his shoulders, and the sleek
coolness of her skin under his hands. She would have pulled
him down onto the sand with her, but he resisted.

"*Supai.* You must listen," he said. "You cannot just sit down
and make love in this place. I hear noises of breaking twigs.
Something approaches. Sometimes an animal comes to these
waters. They are often here at dawn. They hide all day and then

come again when darkness sits. Though now the whole part of my body says 'wife' we must climb away from this shore."

His words cut through White Bird's amorous mood. She remembered another river and the great cat that had hunted around its edge. With a shudder she picked up her bridal robe and followed after her husband.

Their hearth fire had nearly gone out when they reached their lodge. While Laughing One tried to stir it up again, White Bird dried herself, wrung some of the wetness from the ruined bridal robe, and prepared their sleeping hides. Then she squatted near the lodge entrance and began using a dry piece of fur to brush off her husband's back. Many wives massaged their husband's shoulders at night as a matter of habit, but for White Bird the newness of doing these things held a fresh excitement.

"Eat. You must eat," she said.

Laughing One shook his head. He frowned slightly as he stirred at the hearth ashes. "This night will be cold without a fire."

"*Siyemou.* You are not completely alone. Your wife is still alive. I will stir the hearth. Another woman has taught me." As she said this, White Bird arched her back so that her breasts were pushed against Laughing One's shoulders. He could feel their soft pressure on his skin each time he prodded at the embers.

"There is much I still do not understand," he admitted.

"Knowing how is important," White Bird agreed. She was leaning so close that he felt her lips against his ear as she spoke. "But when a woman has her husband and her heart goes out to him, nothing will trouble her. You are the man of my lodge. I will not pull my heart away from you."

"I do not think of what happened before," Laughing One said. "This day is another season."

White Bird shifted her position in a way that brought her body still closer to his own, and suddenly Laughing One was reaching for her. She stiffened slightly when he touched her, then pushed herself into his arms. A short while later, White Bird had her moment of sea otter love.

CHAPTER TWELVE

Winter Rains

Soon after White Bird's marriage, Passing Shadow and his wives left Wanderer's village. Though he had Morning Land again, Passing Shadow could not forget what had happened. The tension between himself and the chief continued. Worried that there could be more anger against him, Passing Shadow took his wives and walked out of the village one morning at first light. Few saw him go. The hearths of his neighbors were still barely smoking and there was only a vague mumbling of sleepy voices from the darkened lodges as he left. Two days later, the shaman and his wives stumbled into Black Snake's winter camp.

Few of Wanderer's people regretted this change. Some men wondered about the fate of the beautiful, golden-skinned woman with the flat belly and high breasts, but their curiosity was not strong. The women said only that Morning Land had gone the way of orphan children and dismissed her from their thoughts as surely as they would have dismissed anyone who had died.

For most, simply getting through the winter was worry enough. The first winter storm was followed by a second and then by a long series of wet, overcast days. This was the gray, low-sun season, when the hiss of rain and the feel of gliding mist were never far away. It was the coldest, longest winter White Bird had ever known. There were times when even she could not swim in the near-freezing waters of the lake. Like other valley women, she remained hunched under damp robes, cooking meals, decorating hides, grinding dried seeds, and waiting for a spring warmth that seemed to be forever delayed.

While the women were sometimes able to avoid the tule fogs and chill backwaters, the men were not. Under the rain-gray skies of midwinter, they stalked the marshlands and the groves at the water's edge, seeking the hordes of ducks and geese which made the shallow lake their winter home.

It was because of the ducks that Laughing One and Trusted Friend waded through the quiet waters of a cattail marsh in the predawn chill of a rainless winter morning. They held a carefully meshed rope net between them. Ahead of them, barely visible in the pale light of the setting moon, were the black forms of countless sleeping ducks. Guided by sight and by the occasional squabbling noises which the floating birds made when they bumped against something in their sleep, the two men cautiously waded out from shore. They were already knee-deep, but the water would be up to their thighs before they were ready to make a toss. It had to be done carefully, for any loud noise would send the entire flock darting upward into the morning sky.

Of all the types of hunting which he had done in the three moons since his marriage, Laughing One hated this the most. Submerged under the surface of the bristling cold water were root masses, stems, and half-buried branches. The root masses and dead branches were often sharp enough to cut a hunter's foot. The stems could tangle between his toes and send him floundering forward into the sheets of duckweed and green pond scum that layered the water's surface. And though the cattails looked like a tempting screen which could hide a hunter's approach they provided better shelter for the birds. Often the shadowed areas were so overgrown with interwoven stems, matted leaves, and other plant clutter that a man could not force his way through. It was better to remain in the more open water, even though this meant shivering under a cold night breeze. It was more than discomfort which threatened the men. The fog-swept backwaters bred bone-chilling sicknesses. Many an old hunter who had escaped being crippled during the hunt died from slower pain. His enemy was a sickness that had struck at him unseen while he had waded past floating plant masses and watched the dawn sky grow pink and gray behind the bare branches of the woods.

At last they were close enough. Just as the first glow of dawn began to show in the east, the two men came within arm's reach of their prey. Things had to be done quickly, for the ducks were already beginning to wake. In a single flow of movement, Trusted Friend gave the signal, tensed, and prepared to throw. Laughing One mirrored his actions. For an instant the net was falling through the air, its webbed shape caught in the growing light. Then it descended over four of the closely packed sleeping birds.

The ducks awoke just as the trap tightened around them. They lunged upward in a squawking flutter of wings, but already the men were pulling the edges of the net together. Laughing One held the ropes secure while Trusted Friend killed the trapped birds with quick, bone-crunching thrusts of his stone chopper. Around them, the rest of the flock burst into flight. Calling frantically, they darted toward the glow of the eastern sky; a swarm of frightened birds moving in unison, their swiftly beating wings flashing back reflected light as they circled around over the water a second time.

Other hunters were also netting at the moment, and soon the alarm spread from flock to flock as countless birds called their warning over the stands of tule and cattail. Like the roar of a waterfall or the rumbling of distant thunder, the ceaseless flapping of their wings engulfed all other sounds. Wings glittering with sunlight, this windstorm of birds circled through the air above the lake. Separate flocks dove together, spun about, and crisscrossed the flight paths of other flocks so closely that it seemed as if they must collide, but they never did. Gradually they began to fly lower, and to divide into smaller groups again. By the time the two hunters had reached the shore, some birds were already landing.

As soon as the two men had dropped their bundle onto a grass-covered ledge, Trusted Friend looked up at his brother, raised four fingers, and smiled. Both knew it had been a good hunt. Then they unraveled the net, examined the dead birds, and strung them together on leather thongs. They were silent as they worked, but it was a different type of silence from the tense quiet that had come before the hunt. This was a peaceful moment, when each man was preoccupied with his own thoughts.

For Laughing One, this winter had not carried the hardness of other seasons. He was married now, as was shown by the black hair which his wife had weaved along the upper edge of his waist cloth, and which he himself had attached to the handled end of his spear thrower. By simply living beside him, White Bird had taught him more about a woman's complaints, depressions, and sudden passions than he had ever guessed from all his seasons in the lodges of his parents. It sometimes startled him to realize how much he had already come to depend on her. As he approached his lodge, he would find himself listening for the Tideland songs she sung. The nuzzling, sniffing way she had of greeting him no longer seemed strange. Nor did the fact that, for all the clinging eagerness of her lovemaking, White

Bird rarely touched anyone apart from himself. Even when forced to crowd in next to other women, she would slip past each of them without jostling.

As Laughing One finished wrapping a leather thong around the leg of a duck he was holding, he remembered the quarrel that he and White Bird had had the day before. There had been a few harsh words, as there always were when they talked about the one subject on which they could never agree, and then White Bird had spent the rest of the afternoon in total silence, becoming so passive that even the twitching of her fingers had stopped.

Laughing One handed the bird to his brother and asked, "Did you ever want to take a second wife?"

Trusted Friend was busy tying the thongs together so that all four birds would dangle from a single carrying strap. He looked up questioningly. "What are you saying?" he demanded. "Have you already grown tired of the wife you have?"

"No," Laughing One answered quickly. "White Bird is the only woman I want. She is the one who talks of these things. She is always worrying about her sister."

Trusted Friend finished tying the thongs together and lifted his bundle into the air. The four ducks dangled below his hand, with their legs pointed upward and their heads flopping limply back and forth each time he moved the strap.

"A wife's crying and anger do not last," Trusted Friend said. "The winter season often makes a woman full of tears. When spring comes to these woodlands, she will be happier."

"My wife's feelings for her sister are very strong," Laughing One insisted. "She tells me that the men of her tribe often married two sisters, and she does not understand why I cannot do the same. If I keep refusing, things could become bad between us. She might even run away to be with her sister."

"Your wife is already growing a child in her belly," Trusted Friend reminded his brother. "Soon her stomach will be standing out, and she will be too tired to run away."

Laughing One shook his head. "This thing worries me," he said. "Even when White Bird does not talk about it, she is thinking of her sister. She wants the three of us to be together, the way it was before."

Trusted Friend carried his bundle to a nearby tree. "What kind of a woman is White Bird's sister?" he asked. "Is she ready to turn her back on the shaman so quickly? If you go and fetch her, will your lodge still belong to you? Will these sisters do what you ask them?"

While he spoke, Trusted Friend reached up over his head and hung the carrying strap around one of the tree's lower branches. With the ducks safely beyond the grasp of the foxes and coyotes which prowled the lakeside thickets, it was possible for the men to relax.

"White Bird says that Morning Land hates the shaman," Laughing One replied. "That is why she refuses him."

Trusted Friend turned and walked back toward his brother. "The shaman lives in another village now, and your wife's sister is there with him. Do not go looking for her. Leave her where she is."

When he saw the startled look on Laughing One's face, Trusted Friend explained, "All of the things which belong to the shaman are dangerous for other men to touch. Leave this one alone."

Laughing One crouched down and began stretching the net out across the sand. The morning sun was already rising through the trees and would soon be strong enough to dry the ropes. "The shaman is an old man with wrinkled skin," he said. "No young woman could have pleasure in him."

Trusted Friend crouched next to Laughing One. "You are too young to be involved with these things," he said. "If you talk against the shaman, no one will listen to you."

"I have said this to my wife," Laughing One protested, "but she refuses to believe me. Worry about her sister has made her sullen. Often she refuses me. Her heart is very brave when she talks of Morning Land. She is afraid of no one then."

"All women are afraid of death," Trusted Friend said grimly. "White Bird will learn to be afraid if her husband dies and she is left with nothing. This shaman's anger does not come only from his mouth. If you quarrel with him, your life will be short."

"Perhaps he will tire of Morning Land," Laughing One said hopefully. "The shaman has two other wives. If he were given a gift for Morning Land, perhaps he would be willing to let her go."

Trusted Friend shook his head and stood up. "What gift can you give?" he asked scornfully. "The shaman does not give up his women when he lives in his brother's village. If you were to go there and try to take his wife, you would die in that place. The men would come at you with their clubs and spears."

"I will not have to steal Morning Land," Laughing One said. "White Bird says that if a woman of her tribe tires of a man, she just leaves. She hides at the edge of the path and follows a trail back to the people she loves. Morning Land has left other husbands this way."

Trusted Friend spat and shook his head. "I talk and talk and you do not listen to me," he grumbled. "Even if this woman left the shaman's lodge, even if she came to me on her own, running as fast as she could, I would not want her."

Laughing One looked surprised. "She is very beautiful," he said.

"Your wife's sister is a bad woman," Trusted Friend insisted. "To her a husband means nothing. She will not follow a man or carry a child in her belly or bring food in her basket. Oh no, not her. She cares nothing for you. Keep the wife who holds your baby in her stomach. Let her sister find another man to marry."

"White Bird will not listen to me," Laughing One persisted. "She will start to cry again if I tell her I do not want to marry Morning Land."

"Then let her cry," Trusted Friend grumbled. He picked up his weapons' pouch and began sorting through his spear blades. "You are not the one who will decide this thing. Stay quiet and say nothing to your wife. All this talk is useless anyway. Her sister will never come back to your lodge on her own. She will just stay married to the shaman."

As the hunger moons of winter slowly began to wane, Laughing One decided to follow his brother's advice. He never talked of Morning Land when he was with his wife, and gradually White Bird became less sullen. As long as she had expected Morning Land to return to her with each new day, White Bird had been prepared to fight with Laughing One on her sister's behalf, but when one moon followed another in the sky overhead and there was still no sign from Morning Land, White Bird found it harder and harder to continue the quarrel. She was too well satisfied with her new husband to think so much about unpleasant things.

Before the winter was over, there were signs of other changes in White Bird. Her large breasts grew even fuller. Her rounded hips grew even wider. Once Summer Wind realized what had happened, she began giving White Bird advice on how to prepare for the birth, but Beautiful Star, who regarded pregnancy as a kind of illness, just shook her head knowingly. Sometimes, when she was sure she was alone, White Bird would feel the new hardness in her stomach, or rub her hands across her swollen breasts until the pleasure of it brought an involuntary smile. At such moments, Morning Land and the shaman seemed very far away.

The Moon of Frosts was followed by the Moon of Storms, and then, one night, during the middle of a rainstorm, White Bird felt that spring was very near. Out in the darkness, a wind had shifted, blowing new warmth that tingled and prickled at her skin. The next morning she looked outside her lodge expecting to see mist shrouds or stone gray clouds overhead, and found sunshine instead.

Though the rain did not end there, the showers which came afterward had a fine clean softness to them. This rain of spring which tapped at the dry leaves of the lodge roofs also worked steadily through the earth of the lakeshore, bringing shiny new shoots of grass up from out of the muddy soil. Soon there were fields of new grass rolling under the wind and moving easily in the even sunlight. It was the Moon of Clover.

Now, more than at any other season, it was the women who kept the tribe fed. The great flocks of ducks and geese had moved north to summer nesting grounds near the edge of the great glacier, and the larger game animals had left the lake area for the green meadowland of the open savannah. The men had little to do. Women and girls were the ones who strolled up into the hills and fields where the honey smell of clover blossoms thickened the air.

There were plenty of grasses and roots a woman could pick, but clover was always the favorite. A skilled wife could hook her forefinger around a clover blossom, snip it off at the base of the stem, and have it rolled into a tight ball in a single quick movement. The blossoms did not always go into the baskets. Many women ate nearly as many of the honey-sweet blossoms as they collected, and some fat nursing mothers would quit their work early, flop their wide buttocks down onto the new grass, and chew contentedly on clover. There was a price for such gluttony. Clover created gases that could make a woman burp and wind throughout the night. Children who followed their mothers' example were often left moaning from the pressure in their bellies. Then it was time for the mothers to administer soaproot remedies, rub grease over swollen stomachs, and knead at their children's bellies with a heavy massage until the gas pains had ended.

By early afternoon, families had had enough of the clover meadows. Wives and older daughters would put on the furs and aprons that they had taken off when the sun had grown warm around them, and heave the filled baskets onto their backs. Children who had gotten a ride on the way out had to content themselves with toddling along behind the women. Many became cross, and the high giggling of the morning was often replaced by whimpering cries.

Back in the village, the children slept while the women either rested or prepared meals. The quiet rarely lasted long, however, for spring evenings created other passions besides hunger. During the Moon of Clover, the young people made love as much as possible. Girls who had been lured into the lush meadows came back in the early darkness with grass-stained knees and happy smiles. The valley people understood the urgency of this season, and as the moon grew large over the crests of the hills, they welcomed it with their best-loved ceremony. At dusk, on a day when the moon was full, they began their Clover Dance.

The sun seemed slow in setting that day, for the men had been strolling restlessly about the village since midday. They had spent much of their time gathering wood for the great fire which would form the center of the dance, and gradually a huge pile of wood had been built up on the hill above the village. There were few women about. All but the oldest had gone off into the fields to help prepare grass skirts for the dancers.

As the sun finally began edging toward the western trees, groups of men climbed the hill once more, walking slowly and easily in the cooling afternoon breeze. Spear Maker was to lead the ceremony, but he was one of the last to reach the top of the hill. When he got there, he stopped and stood in front of the huge pile of wood, listening to the small sounds the wind made as it brushed through the hollows in the woodpile. Then, suddenly, as if responding to some unseen signal, he lowered the burning torch he carried and started the fire.

The dry wood flared up quickly. Flames seemed to jump and frolic in the spring air. Within moments, the yellow flickering had spread across the entire wood pile and heavy billows of smoke were surging into the darkening sky. Somewhere out in the grass not far from camp, the waiting women would see that signal and begin to move closer. There would be much giggling and excited whispering among them as they attempted to sneak up on their own village.

On the hilltop, Spear Maker sat alone, looking very little be-

side the great fire. He glanced about and nodded when he saw
that all of the other men had formed a wide circle around the
dance area. When the last of the hunters had sat down, Spear
Maker cocked his head to one side, blinked, and began a loud
chant.

His words came slowly at first, as if he were remembering
each one of them from some distant moment in the past. He
spoke of the feast that had been prepared, the women who had
been sent into the fields, and the night that was just beginning.
His words described the wonder of melting ice and lifting fog,
of a warmth that burnt away the last of the cold. Then, with a
long sigh, he grew suddenly silent.

There was a murmur of agreement among the waiting men.
The tribe had survived another winter, a mild one this time,
without any deaths. They had not always been as fortunate.
Some of the older hunters wondered how many more times they
would be able to smell the spring clover and watch the women
dance. Not everyone who was with them now would be there
the next time Spear Maker spoke this prayer.

Spear Maker stared at the men for a long moment, then began
again. This time the song was one that all of them knew, and
other voices were joined to his. A hunter with a hollow log
started thumping his hands against the wood. Other men added
to the pounding rhythm by clacking sticks together or swishing
grass brooms across the earth in front of them. From their hiding places, the women would hear the ringing musical sound
and know it was time to approach.

Now the words spoke of the easy drift of shadows through
sunlit fields, of flowers rising above dew-soaked leaves, of the
softness of clover and the love of women. The chant ended with
the line, "Let our women come to us."

From what seemed a long way off, a female voice called
back, "We are near. We have heard your singing."

The voice was high and nervous, and every man on that hill
stared in its direction. Nearby, a large bush shivered as if something were moving under it, but the hunters pretended not to notice. For a while longer, Spear Maker and that solitary woman
called back and forth to each other. Then, finally, the rest of the
women appeared.

They came out from behind the bushes in two rows, walking
with slow dignity toward the crest of the hill. The older women
formed a line to the right of the dancers. With them were one
heavily pregnant wife and several very young girls. Like all of

the women, they had greased their hair to a shiny blackness and scented it with sweet grass to give it the smell of open fields.

The dancers themselves were naked except for fringed grass skirts which sloped outward around their hips. Shaken with each step the women took, these skirts rustled and swished noisily in the evening wind. It was a sensuous sound, and one which could be heard clearly by the silent circle of men.

Though all of the women advancing toward Spear Maker held their heads high in an outward show of pride, many of the younger ones seemed shy. Some trembled when they felt the men watching them. A few might have lost their nerve entirely and retreated back into the bushes had it not been for the stern-faced matrons who walked beside them. Summer Wind and the other senior wives had little patience with timid girls. They knew the importance of this ceremony. They had learned the songs and steps of these dances when they were children, and had worked at the skills all their lives. The dance was a kind of magic and was to be taken seriously by everyone. No giddy youngster would be allowed to spoil it.

Not every dancer was reluctant, however. Beautiful Star, who led the line of young women, moved with a balance and a fineness of step that delighted all who saw her. She had been the center of many clover dances; the woman everyone remembered, the one all the men wanted to chase out across the grass. Even when walking slowly, she managed to twitch her thighs suggestively and smile at those who watched.

Behind her, White Bird was much more uncertain about what was expected from her. No Tideland ceremony had ever been so filled with gestures and rituals. When Tideland women wanted to dance, they simply stood up from where they had been sitting and started. There was no hiding or walking in rows. All of this seemed very strange.

The women stopped a short distance away from the great fire. After a moment of uncertain shuffling, the two rows separated. Matrons and very young girls quietly slipped back to rejoin the men in the outer circle, leaving the dancers alone with Spear Maker at the edge of the fire. In an attempt to reassure themselves, the young women linked arms and faced the men as a group. Some nervously placed their hands across their bare stomachs, while others looked around to see if their men were watching. All waited anxiously for Spear Maker's signal.

When he saw that the women were ready, Spear Maker crouched down beside the fire. His body suddenly began shiv-

ering as if some winter's gust had swept across his skin. In a
tired voice he called,

> "There is no warmth in this fire.
> I lie awake through the cold night.
> I shiver like a leaf which lives
>   near the heart of the wind."

Beautiful Star responded. Stepping forward and smiling almost shyly this time, she chanted,

> "Do not feel uneasy.
> Your thoughts are known to us.
> A woman's skin has the warmth
>   Of clover in the sun.
> To touch her is to put your hand
>   From snow into the fire."

As she sang this, Beautiful Star started to move sideways,
tugging at the other girls' arms to encourage them. The rest of
the dancers followed after her, and soon they were walking in
a small circle inside the larger circle of the watchers. The
women who sat with the men began to clap their hands in a
sharp rhythm. The men added the high clatter of their wooden
instruments, but the pace of the dancers remained sluggish. Too
many of them were new to the clover dance ceremony.

With sudden impatience, Beautiful Star dropped her arms to
her sides. She stopped so quickly that White Bird nearly
bumped against her. Confused, the rest of the girls stopped as
well.

Beautiful Star kept her eyes shut while she listened to the
thumping rhythm. Her hands moved first as she began clapping
out the beat with her palms. Then her mouth opened and she began making sounds to match what her hands were doing. *"Aaa
yaya, aaa ya yan, aaaa yhan ya yaba,"* she called, over and
over again.

It was like the cry of a cicada in the summer heat. The other
girls stared at Beautiful Star for a moment and then began making tentative chanting noises of their own. This was slow work
at first, but Beautiful Star would not let them stay sluggish. Her
voice rose and fell in an increasing frenzy, its high anger driving away their silence. White Bird added her voice to the cry,
as did the women who sat with the men.

Beautiful Star countinued to work at the group of dancers, banging her hands together until her palms hurt, singing until the muscles stood out on her neck. Her voice was aggressive and demanding, crying still louder until it held each of the girls with its strength. She made them forget the watchers long enough to let the beat and the chanting mingle with their own voices. Soon all of the girls were chanting very hard. Their mouths were open wide and their eyes were shut. Their shoulders shook until their breasts trembled. No longer just a group of girls standing awkwardly before a fire, they were becoming balanced and eager.

Beautiful Star's eyes were open now. She glanced over at the others, shifting her gaze down the line of girls and noting how easily each was moving. Satisfied, she began to lead them again. This time the women moved quickly around the dance circle, first sweeping past in one direction, then wheeling about and going the other way. The shuffle became a jump step. It might have resembled running had it not been for the dancers' arched backs and the constant shivering of their hips. Darkness had made the watchers invisible. All the girls could see now were the great clouds of heat and smoke which the fire sent above their heads and the panting shapes of their fellow dancers. They felt the warm night wind blowing softly around them, fluttering their grass skirts and the loosened strands of their hair. With nothing left to inhibit them, they gave themselves completely to the rhythm of the dance.

Her work done, Beautiful Star released the arms of her partners and moved in closer to the fire. When she was near enough that a single leap would have landed her in the flames, Beautiful Star stopped, flung her arms high, and began a shuddering, pulsing dance of her own. Washed in the flickering colors of a high fire, her body moved faster and faster. She seemed to be drawing strength from the steaming heat of the flames, letting their warmth excite her the way a man's touch would have. Had she been any closer, she might have burnt her hands or seared her chest. Instead, she shrieked, turned herself, groaned and writhed. Her sweating skin shimmered in the fire light. Her eyes grew quite wild. She knew that the dance now centered on her.

Hurried on by Beautiful Star's example, the other dancers whirled, turned and swayed beside the fire, pummeling the dirt with their feet and shaking so much that the grass skirts thrashed and clattered around their thighs. White Bird had been carefully watching every move of Beautiful Star's, but now she forgot about the dance leader. She was aware of the heavy pounding of her heart and of how even the grass skirt felt too tight around her. She was not aware of the wide darkness of her eyes or the high crooning sound she was making as her hips thrust back and forth. The leaning, wheeling bodies of the other dancers were the only things she noticed outside her own frenzied dancing, and even then she missed the final signal.

Without warning, the high, pulsing rhythm ended and the air no longer seemed alive with voices. It was as if everyone had suddenly grown tired and stopped singing at the same time. White Bird looked about for the other dancers and found that they were gone. Arms waving, the rest of the girls had hurried off into the darkness.

While White Bird stood there, wondering what to do, she was almost knocked over by Trusted Friend, who had leaped around the great fire ahead of every other man. Gaining speed even as he bumped past her, Trusted Friend continued his wild dash after his wife. In another moment, he had disappeared into the dark.

This confused White Bird more than ever. She did not know that a woman was free to choose her lover once the dance was finished with or that Beautiful Star could not always be trusted to wait for her husband. White Bird was only aware of the other hunters who were coming behind Trusted Friend and of the women who were giggling as they rushed far out over the dark grass. Each girl seemed to be fleeing in a slightly different direction. There was no leader this time.

Thoroughly bewildered, White Bird also began running. Around her, the chase did not last long, for the women made no attempt to duck aside and were quickly caught. When she heard the joking and laughter of the other dancers coming from out of the dark grass, White Bird slowed her pace to a walk. There seemed no point in going further. Ahead, she could see the darkened shape of the forest, and no amount of goading would make her enter that.

She was about to turn around and walk back dejectedly toward the fire when someone grabbed her. The shock she felt was only momentary. Even without seeing his face, White Bird knew that the man who held her was Laughing One.

Laughing One had been surprised by White Bird. She had danced as well as any of the village women. Swaying back and forth amid the bright shadows cast by the flames, she had seemed just as sensual as Beautiful Star, and much less willful.

Now, as he held her next to him in the dark, Laughing One felt pride, excitement, and a strange contentment. With White Bird in his arms, things seemed balanced and right. At that moment, he could not have denied her anything.

Without talking, they walked down to the lakeshore. The clover moon was full and pale over the eastern trees and its light gave the lake a strange haze. White Bird hurried into the shimmering water, splashing about to wash the sweat from her body. Laughing One could just see the paleness of her skin each time she dove under the surface.

Cold water seemed to reawaken the passion White Bird had shown during the dance. After she had bathed, she came out wet and laughing onto the shore, looking very innocent and beautiful. Before he could slow her, she was hugging his chest with a tight embrace. Her body felt cold next to his, but he did not have a chance to pull away. Her weight overbalanced him, sending them both sprawling onto the sand. That was what she wanted.

White Bird crouched over Laughing One, pushing him down with her newly swollen stomach to keep him beneath her. When Laughing One tried to hold her, she shuddered and shook away his grip, her wet shoulders simply slipping from under his hands as she slid her head down across his chest. With her cheek pressed against him, White Bird made soft little pulsating noises through her lips. She was *Kairofa,* the passionate one. Her buttocks were lifted high, and she kept them rocking very gently to and fro. Her breasts were rubbing invitingly against his stomach. Laughing One could feel the wildness growing in him as he reached for her a second time. Then she settled into his arms with a yielding eagerness that left him gasping.

Later, as they walked back toward the village, White Bird was quiet, trying to keep this feeling of peace and happiness. The moon shadows lengthened, the night cooled, and still they stepped slowly. Even the warmth of their lodge was less important than the contentment that had come to both of them. Human sounds would intrude up on their quiet soon enough. For the moment, the rustle of leaves and occasional noises of the darkness were enough. They would both remember this clover dance for many seasons. Though neither could guess it, their time as a young couple was already over. By the following night, everything would have changed.

CHAPTER THIRTEEN

The Shaman's Quarrel

While Wanderer's people had been preparing for their clover dance, the people of Black Snake's village had whispered among themselves as they brooded over things which they had witnessed but did not understand. Behind their troubled expressions and their nasty words was an honest confusion. None truly knew why their bear shaman had gone to live apart, had chosen to sit still in a makeshift lodge on a hilltop well away from the home of his wives. In that lonely place, where only the noises of the woods and the constant beating of rain droplets against his lodge roof could disturb him, the shaman had sat brooding through much of the dark season.

The old women of Black Snake's village felt they had an answer. To their thinking, it was the shaman's proud and willful new wife who was to blame. She, with her beauty and her unfriendly eyes—she was the one who had ridiculed Passing Shadow and sent him away in smoldering anger. The old women had many unflattering names for Morning Land. Sometimes they called her "Ugly Mouth" because of the way she twisted her lips whenever the shaman was near. Sometimes she was named "Cruel Eyes" for the way she stared at people without seeming to see them. At still other times, she was simply known as "The Deceiving One" because of the way she always seemed to have trouble doing even simple chores while the shaman watched her, yet proved far from senseless when the women were by themselves. Whatever names they used, the old women shivered with indignation over Morning Land's boldness. They believed that the shaman should have met her constant refusals with the pounding of his club. When blood covered her shoulders, the old women grimly asserted, his wife would not feel such pride. Hot coals on her thighs and buttocks would remind her that she could not do as she wished.

Not all of the women saw things so coldly. Some of the younger ones had been unwilling brides themselves and still remembered the fear of their wedding night, when a stranger's relatives had surrounded their marriage lodge and a husband's brother had kept them from escaping. The shaman's quarrel concerned a young woman like themselves, and they felt he deserved the tricks she played on him. They understood why Morning Land had ruined the shaman's sacred red powder by leaving it out in the rain one night. When his prized eagle feathers had been found crushed and dirtied in the mud; when she had sewn bits of shell onto his shaman's robe during her time of blood and had thus ruined its magic; then he had felt the price of his stealing. Though their fear of Passing Shadow made these young women stay at a distance, they noticed the things which Morning Land did and said nothing.

In his lonely place on the hill, Passing Shadow was as confused by what had happened to him as any of the other members of Black Snake's tribe. Morning Land was truly desirable, and none of the women he had owned before could compare with her. He still felt excitement each time he saw her. Like a throbbing hurt that would not heal—that he did not want to heal—she lingered in his thoughts. He had come near to killing her many times that winter, but something in her wide dark eyes had made him weaken. Something in the coldness of her appealed to him. She gave him nothing, not even when he was thrusting himself into her and filling the lodge with his harsh breathing. She tugged at him when he wanted to be peaceful and she threatened his shaman's power—and he liked it.

Two nights before the night of the clover dance, Passing Shadow had kept watch in his place in the forest. He had been awake all night, chanting and praying to the one force he still worshipped. But even Yeane, the Black Moon, had seemed deaf, for this was not the season when Yeane was strong. As the blue-gray light began to show in the east, the shaman fell silent. When growing light pushed back the shadows, the terrible hidden force that lay behind the darkness lessened its grip on the land. This was when a shaman's powers were weakest. Passing Shadow stared broodingly into the spiral patterning of the hearth flames.

Finally the shaman spat and got to his feet. He had decided to go back to the village and face this woman. As he entered the makeshift lodge that had been his home for so many days, Passing Shadow glanced around quickly to decide what to bring back with him. There was not much. The sleeping hides he had used had grown moldy with the dampness and were not worth carrying. Neither were the stone utensils or the spear he had used. He had broken the spear shaft one day while trying to evoke the protection of the great bear spirit. Since the ceremony had failed, the spear must have been unlucky. Apart from his hunting knife, the only thing Passing Shadow truly needed was his medicine bag.

The bag was a crude-looking sack made from untanned otter skin, but Passing Shadow regarded it as the source of his power. It held the essential items of his trade, the ones which his guardian spirit had told him to use whenever he tried to cure a patient. There had been no need for these tools since his departure from the village, but though he had not opened the bag in more than a moon, he had always kept it with him. Each time he had prayed, he had slid his hands over the bag's magical contours, and each night he had slept with it resting beside him.

As he lifted it, though, something felt strange. There was a new heaviness. He had first noticed this difference on the morning he had left the village, but his mind had been so troubled then that nothing had mattered except escaping from the problems of his lodge. Now though, in the quiet of near dawn, he had time to wonder. He opened the bag and began sorting through its contents.

At first, everything seemed right. The eagle feathers he had used as padding were still in place and, when he brushed them aside, his fingers felt the greased willow handle of his deer-claw rattle. As he pulled the rattle out, the string of deer hooflets made a sharp clattering sound in the morning air. Beneath the rattle, in a layer of duck's down, were the bear-shaped stone he had once found, a curiously twisted blue shell, a string of bone beads, and some loose bear claws. The order was exactly as it should have been.

Passing Shadow sighed and sat back on his haunches. He was about to repack the bag when his finger touched the last item in it. This was a beautifully shaped hollow legbone taken from a giant condor which one of the village hunters had killed that winter. After polishing it and decorating it with symbols, Passing Shadow had decided to use the bone as a whistle during his curing rituals. To protect it, he had stuffed the bone with eagle feathers. It should have been one of the lightest items in his pouch, but it was not. As soon as he grasped it, he realized that this was the source of the bag's new heaviness.

Carefully, he brought the bone closer and examined it. There were no feathers inside. They had been removed. In their place was a red muck that looked like dried clay. When he sniffed it, he realized that it was not red powder which had been mixed with the clay. It was blood—woman's blood.

The shock of this discovery kept Passing Shadow motionless for a long moment. Then he hurled the bone away from him, stumbled out of the lodge, and began frantically brushing his hands across the dew-soaked grass. Even the morning wetness could not ease the burning sensation in his fingers.

The terribleness of the deed almost overwhelmed Passing Shadow. He felt as if the earth would grow soft beneath him and swallow him up. Foulness seemed to ooze on all sides. To be stained with the childbirth blood of a woman was unspeakable. Even an ordinary man never made love to a woman in her time of blood. To do so brought frightful things. For a shaman, it was much, much worse. How could he expect to meet Yeane when such decay coiled around him? The strange odor of a woman, the smell of her childbirth blood, drove off all spirits. The taste of it scorched the spirits and made them afraid. A shaman who had touched such things could not expect the spirit guardians to hear him. His magic was finished.

In a barely conscious daze, Passing Shadow used the broken spear shaft to push each of the items from his medicine bag into the fire. The last thing to burn was the bag itself. Then he threw the wooden spear on top of the coals. His discovery had chilled him, and he shivered even as he watched the flames. His wife had tried to kill him with her evil charm. She had refused him and repelled him, and now she had tried to give him a sickness from which he would never recover. She had tested her skill against the power of a shaman. Passing Shadow knew that he could not linger in this place. The spirits he sought would never approach it again. As long as he stayed, he could have no faith in his own powers.

While setting fire to his solitary lodge, Passing Shadow decided to kill Morning Land. There was truly no other choice now. Phlegm formed in his mouth each time he thought of how her filth had touched him. Only when he had rid himself of her would he be clean again.

It was almost full day when Passing Shadow stepped down from the hillside and followed his own pathway back to the village. He was stumbling and finding it difficult to keep walking. Several times he had to rest until the dizziness left him. Finally he reached the place where he had hidden his weapons.

Armed with a club, he approached his lodge. When he

stepped inside, his anger flared forth, but he found only his two
other wives. Each received several heavy blows to her back and
thighs before the truth reached his senses. Even then he very
nearly killed them both in his frustration. Only Dancing Rain's
desperate pleading gradually slowed his hand. From her, he
learned that Morning Land had already run away.

In the early daylight, Passing Shadow silently left Black
Snake's village. He was prepared for the hunt this time. In all
the wild land, there was only one person foolish enough to help
his evil wife. Passing Shadow knew where he could find both
of them.

Already a day's walk north of Black Snake's village, Morning Land was truly afraid. Running away had seemed a simple
thing during her long stay in Passing Shadow's lodge. She had
remembered her flight from the strangers' camp, had taken
comfort from the fact that she had found her way through empty
forests once before. But the land here was different. The grass
was full of thorns. She had to walk carefully, and it took a long
time to go only a little ways. Instead of rivers and forests, she
saw only hills and open grassland. One low hill followed another, with little change. It was not good country to hide in.

She had run away at night, while the moon had cast its quiet
light across the land. For a while she had listened to the voices
of Black Snake's people far behind her. Each time a man
shouted, she had waited in silence, preparing to run, but there
had been no sounds of pursuit. Later, when she had been much
farther away, she had rested under the trunk of a large tree. It
had seemed a long time before morning had come.

The return of daylight had brought no comfort. She had carried little food with her, for fear that others would guess her
purpose, and the few things she had brought were gone completely before the sun moved toward the trees once more. She
had found some roots and the eggs of a bird, but her stomach
was far from full. With darkness approaching once more, Morning Land began to wonder if she should have stayed.

At best, her thinking had been muddled. During the moons of
rain and frost, when the winter darkness had surrounded her
lodge, a desperate loneliness had seized the Tideland woman.
Without even her sister for comfort, her grief had grown into a
numb desire for revenge. She had wanted the shaman to be as
dead as her own hopes. She had wanted him to die as her own
people had. In this dulled, weeping mood, Morning Land had

acted almost without thought. Fouling Passing Shadow's magic had seemed such an easy thing, for she had never truly believed in his powers.

With the coming of spring, her mood had begun to change, but by then it had been too late. The medicine bag had been out of reach, and she had not been able to undo her work. For many days she had waited, wondering when the shaman would discover the deed and come to hurt her. Finally the waiting had proven too much. She had simply started to run.

The foolishness of this act was becoming apparent. Morning Land did not remember the country she was crossing through. Each hill looked so much like the one she had climbed before it that she had lost her sense of distance. She knew a wide, shallow lake lay somewhere to the north of Black Snake's village and that if she followed the shore of this lake, she would eventually reach Wanderer's village. The problem was to find the lake. Morning Land had thought she would reach it easily after one day's walk. Each time she had climbed the hill, she had looked eagerly for signs of water on the other side. Now, as the second nightfall approached, her fear mounted. Something was wrong. The beautiful, blue lake did not show in the distance as she had expected. She recognized nothing.

With this final uncertainty came a deep sadness. She had no father or mother to run to. Her only hope for life lay in her sister. If she could not reach White Bird before the shaman found her again, she would be truly lost. She knew of no place else to go.

Morning Land walked along the crest of a hill, trembling and looking expectantly toward the north. This time she saw a line of distant trees. Perhaps they bordered the shore of a lake. Urged on by the hope, Morning Land began to run down the northern slope of the hill. She wanted to run quickly, to reach the trees before the land grew dark, but the thorns in the grass hurt her too much. Tiredness had made her footsteps heavy. At the bottom of the slope, she stopped and sat on a rock. Several thorns that had broken off were stuck in her flesh. Panting from her run, she squeezed at them and tried to pull them out. The moccasins she wore were little protection against thorns as long and spiked as these.

Morning Land was too sore to go much farther. Instead of standing up again, she began cleaning the thorn cuts with rotten leaves until the blood no longer flowed from them. Then she looked about for a place to sleep. There was no real shelter. In the end, she chose to sit beside some broken tree trunks and covered herself with dried grass to keep out the cold.

In this lonely place, Morning Land huddled close against herself. Her feet kept hurting, so she brought them under her thighs for warmth. Her mouth tasted very bitter, perhaps from the roots that she had been eating earlier. Morning Land had no fire or water, but there was no time for gathering. Already the sun's rays had ceased to light up the place where she was sitting. The calls of evening birds echoed out longingly over the empty hills. Morning Land wondered why she had seen no large animals moving about, and decided that the thorns under the grass made grazing here unpleasant for them. With this last thought, she fell into an exhausted sleep.

In the morning, she heard the sounds of water beating against a shore. Her body felt cold and cramped from its sitting posture, and her feet hurt even more than they had the evening before, but she ignored the pain. She stood up in the morning sunlight, staring north toward the line of trees.

It was a hazy morning, the kind which always preceded a hot, humid day. The air had a thick, golden texture that made distant trees look fuzzy, and in places only the upper branches showed, as if the treetops were hovering over the mist-layered ground. It was already warm enough to make the thought of water very pleasant.

Moving toward the trees at an ever quickening pace, Morning Land soon found herself among them. She stepped across layers of fallen pine needles and down onto sand. Without any wind to ripple its surface, the lake stretched out in a featureless blue plane ahead of her. When she reached the water's edge, she stopped and drank heavily. The bottom showed clearly enough from up close, but anything distant quickly disappeared in the white blur over the horizon. When she had drunk as much as she wanted, Morning Land pulled off her apron and stood naked in the morning light, enjoying the sensation of having at last reached her goal.

Then she heard a branch snap somewhere behind her.

It was a quiet sound, barely noticeable even amid all the stillness, but with no wind, there could only be one cause. Something was moving up in the woods.

Morning Land turned quickly, her muscles suddenly very tense, and stared into the trees. There was nothing she could see, not even a twitching of leaves. Whatever it was had become silent again. Was it watching her, or had it already slipped back into the shadows?

With effort, Morning Land forced herself to breathe easily. Perhaps uca, the porcupine, had wandered down near the shore, sensed her, and gone back again. She might even have imagined the sound.

Sighing at her own foolishness, Morning Land stepped out into the water. It felt cold and good on her sore feet, sending a slight shiver up her back. She slipped farther in, until the level rose past her ankles and up her calves. When she was knee-deep, she stopped and waited for the ripples to fade. The lake's surface was very smooth. Looking down into it, she could see a perfectly mirrored reflection of herself, from her smooth thighs to the pointed shadows cast by her breasts. She allowed herself to linger, loving the shape of her own body.

More sounds came from the woods. There was another snapping of branches.

Morning Land wanted to pretend that she had not heard them, but she knew the sounds were real. As she stood there, up to her knees in water, trying to probe the shadows for signs of movements, she remembered that there were people who wanted to kill her. Soon Passing Shadow would come to seek her out and take his vengeance. She could not stop near this shore. Wanderer's village and her sister were still a long way off.

Morning Land waded out of the water and continued walking. Her feet were giving her less pain, so she increased her pace as she followed the shoreline. Sometimes, when thick growths of trees blocked her way, she waded back out into the lake to circle around them. Toward midday, she paused long enough to bathe her feet and gather food. Then she started walking again. In the evening, Morning Land heard a distant shouting and took comfort in the sound. After searching all day, she was at last nearing Wanderer's village. The shouts came from far away, however, and night arrived before Morning Land could find the village fires. While White Bird and the others celebrated their clover dance, Morning Land went to sleep hungry.

The first predawn light cast a bluish haze across the forest, giving new energy to the chirping chorus of birds. In Wanderer's village by the lake, everything was still. Even the most passionate of lovers had finally yielded to sleep, and none of the older hunters felt like following a trail. On this morning the women were as quiet as their men. Some hugged the sleeping forms of their husbands with unusual possessiveness while others lay sprawled out awkwardly on the earth floors of their lodges, their legs and arms splayed out in heavy slumber.

Still lying in the dimness of her marriage lodge, White Bird was stirred from her sleep by the change in sounds brought by the coming day. The noises of darkness were suddenly gone, and in their place came the startlingly loud chorus of birds. The cooing of the forest doves formed a soft undertone for the pulsating, high chirrups of the true songbirds, and the chattering of crows and jays added a lively melody of its own. White Bird pushed herself to a sitting posture with much rustling of the sleeping hides. She smiled at the still sleeping form of Laughing One and then straggled out into the morning air.

The smells and warmth of the new day excited White Bird. Across every field, young grass shone in the sunlight. Gusts of wind made the fine blades flutter in soft waves that took on a silver glint amid the green. White Bird felt a strong desire to be at the lake again. A simple plunge into the cool water would wash away the hearth smoke and lodge sweat that seemed to cling to her skin.

It did not take long for White Bird to give in to the impulse. She had become used to indulging herself. Since the beginning of her pregnancy, Laughing One had been flatteringly attentive. White Bird knew she was being treated very well.

There was a pungent odor to the air in their camp, but as soon as she had passed the last of the village lodges, the wind began to carry the clean scent of new leaves. The deep green of the forest closed around her when she hurried down a special path which led to a private part of the lake, where she would be well hidden from the watchful eyes of other villagers. She did not fear the woods anymore. On this late spring day, it seemed as if the water, the young earth, and the haze-shrouded air were all the world she could ever desire. White Bird began singing a soft love chant which kept time to the pace of her walk.

At the lake, she took off her apron and stood naked while the morning breeze rustled against her skin. White Bird did not hurry into the water. Instead, she stayed as she was, with her mouth held open to taste the wind. She was facing the woods, and everywhere she looked, the bright green of new growth was spreading across the browns and reds of winter. For a long time, she was content to stare at nothing but trees and shadows.

Then something moved.

It was at the edge of her vision, but it was enough to change her mood. Cautiously she turned to stare in the direction of the movement. Though there was nothing visible, White Bird trusted her senses.

A short distance away, Morning Land crouched on her hands and knees, not daring to shout a greeting. She felt the fineness of the white mud under her fingers and this gave her an idea. Squeezing some of it into a ball, she tossed it out beside her sister. White Bird looked around frantically, but only seemed more confused then ever. Morning Land took a second handful, squeezed it into shape, and threw again. This time the mud ball landed at White Bird's feet.

"Atoshe!" White Bird exclaimed. "Who sneaks through this forest like a weasel? What are you doing? Why are you trying to hit me with this mud?"

When she got no answer, curiosity made White Bird move closer. At last she recognized the form of her sister and hurried to her. The two hugged and wept together for what seemed a long time.

"Suyemou," White Bird muttered at last. "Sister, what are you doing here? Why have you come to this place?"

"Ehnn." Morning Land was almost reluctant to talk after her two days of silence. "I have run away," she said quietly.

White Bird simply stared. She felt fear growing in her as she looked into her sister's eyes. There was something about all of this which brought a strange taste to her mouth. "You came here from Black Snake's village?" she asked doubtfully.

Morning Land nodded. "I walked across the thorn hills and then followed this shore," she said. "I was not waiting here long before you came."

"What were you thinking of?" White Bird asked. "Were you trying to kill yourself? There are wolves and great cats living in those hills. It is no place for a woman to sleep alone."

Morning Land looked at her with such intenseness that White Bird was forced to turn her head away. They both knew. A shaman might have talked about calling spirits, but the sisters never needed words to explain these things. They reacted as the birds or animals did, simply yielding to a stronger force than good sense.

Finally White Bird asked, "Do you hate the shaman this much?"

Again there was something in Morning Land's expression

which made White Bird uneasy. She had seen the look some-where before, but could not remember when.

"I have lived in Black Snake's village for a long time," Morning Land said. "At first I felt brave and strong. There was still a fire inside me. but by the time the second moon had grown small in the sky and vanished, I was weaker. It seemed that something would happen if I could not drive him away. I tried to hurt his magic objects, but soon I knew that nothing was going to happen. Another moon came and went, and the rocks by the shore sparkled with cold. My strength was failing. An-other moon came and went. For nights I thought of dying. The shaman would clutch at me and enter me and suck at my breasts. My body smelled like a carcass. Even my mouth was filled with the taste of him."

Morning Land shivered at the memory of it. "The moons continued to change in the sky. Birds flew north and the clover began to grow. I thought of my beautiful sister. I thought of your smile. Then I remembered how far away you were. By the time the winged flies had gathered in the sky, I knew that I must reach you. I chose the moment and ran far away.

"They cut my hair the day the shaman married me. Now if I throw it in front, it reaches my chest. When I swim, it covers my back."

Morning Land untied the bark cord which held her hair tight behind her head and let the dark tresses fall down onto her chest. It was visible proof of the time that she had spent in the lodge of Passing Shadow.

"The shaman will not just let you run away," White Bird warned. "He will come back to find what he has lost. Then the people in this village will make you return to his lodge."

"Perhaps he will follow me," Morning Land admitted, "but if he comes here, it will not be just to find me. He thinks I have ruined his magic. He will beat me on the head with his club un-til I am flattened like a leaf. Killing me, that is what he truly wants."

White Bird sensed the hopelessness in her sister. She wanted to say something comforting, but there was no comfort for this kind of hurt.

"Have you come to ask my help? I can get you food and help you build a shelter," White Bird offered.

Morning Land looked down for a moment. "I do not know what to do," she admitted. "I do not know how to end this thing."

As she looked at her sister, White Bird felt tears coming. "I will not leave you alone here in the forest," she decided. "You will stay with me in my lodge."

Morning Land shook her head. "I have the shaman's mark on my arms. I cannot lie in your lodge and pretend to be free of him. I feel him following me even now. He is ready to sink his teeth into my flesh. I have not driven him away. He will come here to kill me."

"Let him come," White Bird hissed. "You are not alone. This is Wanderer's village, and he has no love for Passing Shadow."

Morning Land was not convinced. "The men here still fear Passing Shadow," she said. "They will listen and believe what he tells them. The shaman will take me away, and when I am beyond their sight, he will kill me. Shiiwe. This time he will kill me."

"If the shaman hates you, then he also hates me," White Bird said. "Laughing One and I will not let him take you away."

Morning Land did not feel like arguing. She was noticing how rounded White Bird's belly looked and how dark her nipples had become. "You have been eating too much meat," she observed. "Your insides are too full. And fat. Your stomach is very fat."

"I just continue to live," White Bird muttered, her voice trailing off in embarrassment. She had hoped to see delight in her sister's face. Instead, the thing she had been so proud of seemed unimportant.

"Your nipples are dark," Morning Land persisted. "Your eyes look white. Your stomach is very big. You must have a baby inside you. Now tell me."

"Ehnn. It is the truth," White Bird admitted apologetically. "After you left our village, this baby just grew. I have watched my stomach get bigger and bigger until it is standing out."

There was a choking sound in Morning Land's throat that slowly developed into a chuckling laugh. Then, before White Bird was aware of the change, Morning Land wrapped both arms around her. The two women's chests were pressed together in a sudden embrace.

"I truly have been far away," Morning Land murmured. "I did not guess this. What should I tell you? You must sit here with your husband and let your stomach grow. If you try to run away with me, it will ruin this baby."

"Why should a sister's help be refused?" White Bird demanded. "If childbirth is something that hurts, then I do not want you to be far away from me when it happens."

Morning Land did not say anything. She just stared at her sister with a bewildered expression on her face.

White Bird stood up slowly, reluctant to leave Morning Land's embrace. "Wait here," she urged. "Stay by the water. Do not run into the forest again. As soon as it is quiet, I will bring you food and some hides to wrap yourself in."

Morning Land nodded as White Bird started back up the path. She continued to watch until her younger sister was out of sight. Then she stepped off the path and hid behind a tree trunk.

Time passed slowly, for Morning Land had never been able to sleep when the sun was high overhead. As soon as she would start to breathe heavily, some noise or movement would startle her to wakefulness. The rustlings of insect wings, the croaking of frogs, the persistent chittering of birds, all jarred her strained senses. Once awakened, she could not relax again. Crouched in the gloom of the forest shadows, Morning Land stared out uneasily at the sun's hot glare off the lake. Staying behind to wait for her sister was proving much harder than she had imagined.

Hoping to ease her restlessness, she moved closer to the water. She stepped silently amid the moss-covered roots, her feet seeming to instinctively avoid the small branches that might crunch under her weight. After a quick glance to either side, Morning Land slipped off her rawhide apron and began wading into the lake. It took her only a few moments to reach waist-deep water. She dipped her head under and stood erect again, with the cool droplets flowing softly down onto the golden warmth of her back. Staring at the open horizon of the lake, she began to feel a peaceful mood returning. Then some final sense of danger made her turn toward the shore.

Passing Shadow was standing in the pathway.

He was naked, and it was the first time she had ever seen him that way in daylight. She had almost forgotten how ugly he was. The pockmarks that cratered his face descended along his neck, across his shoulders, and down most of his chest, giving his skin a decayed appearance under the harsh sunlight. In contrast, his body did not seem at all shriveled. There were hard muscles on his arms and legs. Even during that first moment of shock, Morning Land realized that his strength could easily match hers.

The Tideland woman trembled involuntarily. It was not revulsion she felt, but simple terror. When she saw the heavy wooden club her husband carried in his right hand, she knew that he had come to kill her. The thought made her cringe.

Though he had her trapped, Passing Shadow did not strike at once. When he began to come toward her, his feet moved slowly across the shore sand.

Morning Land wanted to scream, but fought down the impulse. There was no one near enough to help her, and the sound would probably have made him attack her at once. She had to find a way to keep him at a distance while she tried to think.

"Ehnn. I did not hear you coming, old one," she said. "Go back to your lodge. It will do you no good to hurt me."

Passing Shadow did not answer. He moved forward until his feet were stepping in water. Without realizing she was doing it, Morning Land began moving backward into deeper water to keep a distance between them.

"You should not have come to this place," Morning Land continued. "I do not like being with a man like you. My heart does not agree to you. Go and find another woman. I will not return to your lodge."

Passing Shadow was wading into the water now. She was moving, too, but at a much slower pace. For each step she took, she had to feel back with her heels to make sure that the bottom was safe. A stumble would have left her helpless.

"This marriage is finished," Morning Land persisted. "My heart is miserable when I am in your lodge. You have other women who do not take fright when they see you. Build your hearth apart from me and live with them. You do not need me anymore."

Passing Shadow screamed. Then he began coming for her, wading through the water with a quickness that seemed impossible. He would stop her mouth with his club. He would pound at her until she lay shuddering.

Morning Land had hesitated too long. Before she could turn away, he had caught up with her. As he seized her left arm, his own right arm rose to strike a blow with his club, but Morning Land fell backward and pulled him with her. Off balance, the shaman slipped on the bottom mud. He fell splashing into the lake.

Underneath the water, Passing Shadow was less agile than Morning Land. She turned around and caught her hands onto his throat. Though he tried to pull her off, Morning Land squeezed as hard as she could. Her grip held tight. After a moment, the shaman began to choke. He might have fainted and drowned. Then a sudden blow from his club knocked away Morning Land's hands.

With his face flushed purple, Passing Shadow stood up, swaying uneasily in the waist-deep water. Breathing badly, he slowly moved back toward the shore.

Morning Land turned and dived deeper.

She kicked out with both legs, forcing herself under. The cold water flowed swiftly around her chest and head, and she thrust her arms forward frantically in a wild effort to get away. At any instant, she expected to feel Passing Shadow's hands clutching at her again, and this gave her body a strength she had never realized before. She stayed under for a long time, until her chest ached for air and the world was reduced to a dark pathway in front of her. Since all sounds had faded as soon as she had begun to swim, she had no idea of where Passing Shadow was.

At last Morning Land was forced to surface, but even as she took in air with gasping sobs, she kept swimming. Her long legs flashed through the water. Her arms pumped steadily. As soon as she had gotten her wind, she went under again.

When she rose to the surface a second time, she was too tired to go any farther. She had to rest. Reluctantly, Morning Land slowed her pace and looked around.

She could not see anyone.

She had gone out so far that the shoreline was only a fuzzy shadow behind her. There was nothing moving around her, but she did not know how far her vision could be trusted in the glare. Morning Land stopped swimming entirely and shook her head to free her ears of water. There were no sounds other than her own splashing.

Where was he?

Any happiness she felt at still being alive faded as she realized her position. His brief taste of drowning would keep Passing Shadow from following her into deep water, but she could not stay out forever. That was the thought that which kept the blood pulsing heavily in her throat. Passing Shadow would be watching her from the forest. It might take most of the day to force her out of the water, but he was a trained hunter. He could wait. She imagined him up there already, hunched comfortably under some thick growth of scrub, his eyes scanning the water for signs of movement. He would be resting while she exhausted herself. As the day wore on and the sun's glare lessened, he would be able to watch everything she did. Finally, when her body had begun to shiver uncontrollably from the cold of the water and she was forced to come out of the lake in a stumbling, exhausted stagger, he would be ready. There would be no defense against him then. Her body would collapse like a wounded duck's under his pounding club.

Morning Land stayed as she was, slowly moving her hands and feet back and forth in the water while she tried to think. Her left hand reached for the stone knife that swung from the thong around her neck. Her nipples were puckering with the cold, and there was a cramped feeling in her stomach. Fear had shaken her resolve. She could not stay in deep water.

Morning Land realized that her best protection was the villagers. In a short while, some hunters or a group of women would walk down to the lake's edge. If she were close enough to shore, she could call out for help. Passing Shadow would not be able to attack her. She could follow the women back to the village and tell Wanderer what had happened. Then she might finally be free of the bear shaman.

With her pulse jumping and her breath coming in frightened little gasps, Morning Land forced herself to move closer to the shore. It was a cautious paddling, very different from the fierce, area-covering strokes that had brought her out into deep water. As she pushed herself forward, she kept her head lifted above the surface and her eyes focused on the outline of the woods. Any abrupt noise or movement would have sent her whirling around in a panic-stricken flight, but there was nothing. She swam to a place where her toes could touch bottom and stopped.

She was still too far out.

Morning Land began to walk along the bottom, feeling the mud squish against her feet as the water grew steadily shallower. The sense of being watched was very strong. When she was close enough to see the details of the shore, she stopped again. No amount of urging would have forced her any nearer. Her gaze shifted indecisively along the shorefront. There was no movement.

She waited, up to her chest in water, for what seemed a very long time. Despite the heat of the air, her body began to shiver. When the trembling started, she hunched down and wrapped her arms around her chest in a vain attempt to hold in her warmth. She kept her legs moving, pushing her feet up and down against the bottom. The muscle cramps she feared did not come, but she still felt sick and shaken.

Finally someone did come down the path. Morning Land

heard the rustle of bark cloth and the sound of gentle singing. As she listened, she recognized the song, and suddenly realized that the person approaching along the pathway must be her sister. She had forgotten White Bird's promise to return with food and hides.

When White Bird stepped into view, a new kind of terror gripped Morning Land. Passing Shadow could not be far away, and White Bird was alone on the pathway. The shaman might decide to kill her as a part of his revenge.

Without hesitating, Morning Land began to wade inward again. As her waist emerged from the water, she reached for the knife on her neck thong. The feel of its handle under her fingers was little comfort.

White Bird stopped singing when she saw Morning Land's apron lying against a rock. She leaned forward questioningly, and then shifted her gaze to the lake. As soon as she saw Morning Land, White Bird set down her bundle and waved.

"I have tied up these things," she called. "I have taken the hides from inside our hut!"

"*Atoshe!* Go back!" Morning Land shouted. "The forest is not empty. Passing Shadow is very near. Go quickly!"

Confused, White Bird stepped closer to the shore. "There is no one here. I have come with food. You have not had anything to eat."

"Do not come this way! He is here!" Morning Land shrieked, pointing frantically toward the woods. "Go away! Run back to the village!"

White Bird spun around and started to obey, but she was too late. The shaman had already slipped out onto the path behind her. With a high scream that cut through the silence of the midday calm, White Bird made a desperate plunge sideways into the underbrush.

The tactic did not work. Passing Shadow kicked at her feet as she tried to dodge him, bringing her to earth with a heavy thud. White Bird rolled away from him, but Passing Shadow had the quickness of a trained killer. His club came down against her thigh. She cried out in pain and began scrabbling to regain her feet. She was on her knees when the next heavy blow slapped down across her buttocks, flattening her against the ground. As Passing Shadow struck at her back and shoulders, a wild agony cry of "Ah . . . ah . . . ah . . ." escaped from White Bird's throat. She grasped her stomach with both hands. In sick horror, Morning Land realized that the girl was trying to protect her unborn child.

No conscious thought had stirred in Morning Land since the beginning of Passing Shadow's attack on her sister. Without realizing she was doing so, she had been half wading and half running toward the struggling figures on the beach. As Passing Shadow prepared to finish White Bird with a skull-crushing blow, Morning Land was less than an arm's length away. Her knife, which she had already ripped free of her neck thong, whizzed through the air in a stabbing thrust. Its cutting edge struck Passing Shadow above his right shoulder blade and plunged in. Deflected by the force of Morning Land's blow, the shaman's club whirled past White Bird's head and crunched in the sand.

Passing Shadow grunted in pain. For a moment he staggered off balance. But when Morning Land tried to pull her knife free, he spun around and jarred loose her hold. His strength was even greater than she had expected. Her clutching fingers could not keep a grasp on him long enough to slow his movements.

Though she had stopped his attack on her sister, Morning Land was no longer able to escape from Passing Shadow. In a moment he had regained his weapon. This time the club was aimed at Morning Land as it swung through the air. It caught against her left calf, hurling her sideways into the brush. A sharp branch scraped the skin from part of her right cheek, but she managed to keep on her feet. With a quick backward jump, she dodged the shaman's second strike.

She was not as quick the next time. The club hit her on the hip, making a crunching sound as it dug against her flesh, and sending her tumbling down the pathway. As she felt herself losing balance, she screamed, "Aaaatta! Run, sister! He is trying to kill us! He wants to break everything. Go up the pathway! Go to the village!"

Morning Land's knees landed on the sand just as Passing Shadow's club cracked against the small of her back. This time the pain was a blinding jolt that seared through her. She had to get out of reach. Through the blur of pain, she saw that the water's edge was less than a hand's spread away.

The club bounced off her shoulders, but she ignored the pain and leapt into the shallows. Passing Shadow followed, still certain of his victim.

Until then everything had favored the shaman. Now, though his right foot slipped on the wet sand and once again he started to fall forward into the water. As he came down, Morning Land rolled to one side and kicked at his face. Her foot missed, but the impact of her heel on his left shoulder was enough to jar the club from his hand. It spun free of his fingers and was hurled sideways, churning up water as it landed. Passing Shadow was quick to follow after it. He had risen to his knees and was making a plunging grab for the weapon when Morning Land kicked at him again. This time her foot slid under his belly and smashed his groin. With a scream of pain, the shaman clutched at his vitals.

Morning Land tried to reach deeper water. She knew she was hurt. The scrape on her cheek had sent blood streaming down along her neck, but this was nothing compared with the awful stabbing throbs that came each time she moved her legs. It was an agony even to take a deep breath. A short while before, she had leapt across this distance. Now she could barely stagger. Her hobbling gait was not fast enough to put a safe distance between her and her husband.

Passing Shadow recovered much more quickly. Without his club this time, he hurried after her. Morning Land's knife had not cut anything vital, and the pain of its gash seemed to be goading him on. While Morning Land stumbled awkwardly through the shallows, his own legs were as strong as before. He was quickly within reach of her again.

Morning Land let out a wail of despair as she felt his weight pound down on her already throbbing back. She tried to keep balance, but her muscles refused to obey. In an instant of intense pain, she collapsed into the water with her husband on top of her.

All her efforts seemed feeble after that. She turned in the water and began scratching at her husband's face and neck, but he brought his knee down against her stomach with a force that pushed the breath out of her. Before she could breathe again, his hands were around her throat, shoving her head below the surface. For the first time in her life, the terror of dying came to Morning Land. She clutched and tore, ripping out pieces of skin with her nails, but nothing could stop that choking grip. She was gagging; drowning beneath him. Her eyes did not seem to see very well anymore, and there was something whirling in her head. Everything seemed far away from her. Her enemy was too strong. It would be easier just to let go.

Morning Land did not hear the hunters who ran down the path from the village. She could not know that her sister's screams had finally brought help. When Fighting Eagle felled Passing Shadow with a crunching blow to the head, she was aware only of a faint jarring. And when Laughing One lifted her from the water, the joy of being able to breathe again blinded her to everything else. She shivered weakly in his arms, her throat hurting with each soblike gasp.

Soon the whole village knew what had happened.

"Come quick," people called to one another. "The shaman is killing his wife."

They gathered near the edge of the lake, forming a crowd on the pathway. Many were frightened. Those who had only been curious at first soon grew angry when they saw the injured women. They watched Summer Wind and Beautiful Star place healing poultices on White Bird's wounds and whispered, "What is wrong with Passing Shadow? Why does he want to kill all these women?"

"The bad spirit has taken his mind," others whispered. "He came during the night and stayed by these woods, waiting to insult us by fighting with our women. He must be tied up."

"He should be killed," others insisted.

No one seemed to care much about Morning Land. Summer Wind had covered the older sister's shoulders with a fur robe which helped to hide the blood-streaked bruises and swellings on her body, but no further effort was made to comfort the woman. While others fussed over her sister, Morning Land was left to crouch in a painful huddle.

Passing Shadow remained surrounded by a tight circle of armed hunters. He had regained consciousness and sat in furious silence, grasping his own wrists.

In the midst of all this, Wanderer tried to question the two sisters. Most of the story came from Morning Land, who described her attempt to run away from Black Snake's village. She spoke slowly, aware that her words would decide her future, and only occasionally would she stop to wince as some jolt of pain shot up through her leg, her back, or her hip.

"I crept to this place by the lake," she concluded, "but the shaman wanted me dead. He knew that I would never come back to this lodge. When he found me, he almost killed me. I saw him and took a fright. I tried to go away into the lake, but he found my sister instead. He did not care whose wife my sister was. He threw her to the ground and began hitting hard. When I tried to help her, he returned to beat me."

No one looking at Morning Land's face could question the

truth of what she said. Her hair clung in a damp shell around her head, its lower ends matted with dirt and blood. Part of her right cheek had been ripped open, and though the wound was clotted now, its scar would stay with her.

Wanderer turned his attention to White Bird. "Why did the shaman come here to do you harm?" he asked.

White Bird could add little to Morning Land's story. "The shaman is to be blamed for all of this," White Bird wailed. "He only wanted to kill. He was very angry. He felt a desire to kill us both in this place. Now I and my sister have been left to suffer. My child is quiet inside me. The shaman's club has sent my child to its death. He has taken the fruit and left me suffering here."

The chief felt great pity for the Tideland girl. He also felt pity for his youngest son, whose face showed how much White Bird's pain was affecting him.

"Why did you bring these bundles?" Wanderer asked.

"We had to go through the forest to be safe," White Bird answered. "We did not want to sleep in the forest, but we knew the shaman would be following us. Now my child is dying and I cannot walk."

Satisfied that the two women had nothing more to tell, Wanderer turned toward Passing Shadow. For a moment he stood quietly in front of the shaman, trying to decide whether it would be best to kill the man at once. Then he seemed to change his mind.

"Those who strike at others should have their own bodies broken," Wanderer said. "That way they will learn what pain is. Why did you come here, shaman? Did you think we would not be angry? Do you imagine that women are everywhere to be killed as you please? You, who will not fight with men, are only able to hurt these women. You have struck them because I and the others were not there. If I had been there, I would have broken your arms."

Passing Shadow placed his left hand over the wound Morning Land's knife had made. He checked to see the gash in his shoulder was no longer bleeding before he looked up at the chief. "She is not of your family," he said quietly. "She and her sister are different people."

Wanderer pointed at Morning Land. "The wounds on this woman are still open. Her blood is still flowing. I gave her to you because she was grown up and you wanted her. But you, you treat your women too badly. This is why they run away from you. Now you have traveled far over the thorn hills only to kill her. Why do you want to kill this woman?"

Passing Shadow answered in a dull, listless fashion, without the usual power in his voice. "She was beautiful that day when she first sat down next to me, in the same lodge," he said. "She looked like one who was still alive, but she was not. There was a deadness in her. Her words were ashes. Her touch burned me like hot coals. I tried to treat her well. I ignored her insults. I pretended not to notice when she refused her share of the women's work. My other wives were blamed for things she had done. Nothing pleased her. Others warned me that she would take all my strength. You yourself had said these things. But I refused to listen. All was silence in my mind. She waited until the words had ceased and the darkness was around her. Then she did her work. I very nearly died from her."

There was a murmur from the crowd of listeners when they heard this. Some glanced nervously at the Tideland woman to see her reaction, but Morning Land's face remained impassive.

Wanderer shook his spear angrily. "Be on your guard, shaman. This is the spear that comes for you. Make a sudden movement, and my point will strike you. Your words are empty. I myself told you only to leave this woman. I told you not to get near her. Instead, you came here to look for her. You surprised two women and wounded them. You were thinking only of killing them."

Passing Shadow waited until there was complete quiet. He knew that Wanderer's people were curious, and he would work at them. "You shout against me," he said. "You think I like to kill only women. You have not drunk the poison that fills my stomach. I want you to hear these things she has done. She is a wild spirit, not a woman. If she comes too near to you, you will be wounded as I was. You who look at her and weep for pity, you yourselves would kill her."

Wanderer was already regretting his decision to let the shaman talk. "You have told us nothing, shaman," he shouted. "We have heard the words of these sisters, and we are waiting for you to give us yours. If you had killed this woman, I would kill you this very day. Now you tell me you still want to kill her. My sons and I will not allow this. We do not find women just so you may kill them."

"Ehnn. Then listen," Passing Shadow answered. "I have warned my wives not to touch my sacred things. This woman here, she only pretended to listen. When I was lying peacefully, she crushed my sacred feathers." The shaman paused, then added, "We are men. We do not take a woman by the arm and draw her to us when it is her time of blood. We do not go to the women then. No. We do not touch them. But this one, she steals away from that path. When her flow of blood comes, she touches my sacred robe and ruins it."

Before Wanderer could reply, Passing Shadow raised his hand to prevent himself from being interrupted. "Do not say that she did not know, that she was truly ignorant. Before we fight one another over this woman, know what she is. Do not think evil of me."

Passing Shadow paused again, but it seemed to be from real emotion rather than for dramatic effect. Even Wanderer had to acknowledge that the man looked shaken.

"I went away from her then," Passing Shadow continued. "I went into the forest to a place where the souls wander. I had only part of a shelter to keep the rain away. In that dwelling, I kept my sacred medicine bag. But this young girl, who should have died long before, she poisoned my medicine. She took a bone whistle and filled it with her ajaii. Katto aaan nataii. Her aijaii, it ruined me. It gouged my eyes. It pierced my mouth. I am not a coward. I came to take revenge."

There was a shocked silence among the listeners. Some women blushed and looked away. Others hid their faces. The hunters stared in disbelief at the forlorn figure of the Tideland girl. This was truly a shameful thing. For the first time, some began to think that the shaman had been right in beating her.

Wanderer studied the shaman carefully. "We have found this woman almost dead. You say you tried to kill her because she choked your magic with her *aijaii*. Now show us this ruined bone whistle."

"This man could have died," Passing Shadow said, pointing to himself. "The day I found that thing, my brain howled with pain. My fingers were burned by it. I threw it into the sacred fire."

"Men who are truthful, who want to be friends, they speak openly," Wanderer said. "They send to tell you they are coming. They greet you with gifts. Men who think only evil, they remain silent and surprise any person who comes near them. You are a man who was hiding. When I look, I see this woman's wounds. I cannot see where your magic is broken."

The insult cut as deeply as Wanderer had intended it should. Passing Shadow's face darkened with blood. Before the shaman could protest, the chief raised his hand for silence and turned toward Morning Land once more.

"Woman, we are told what you have done. Does the man who said these things speak truthfully?"

Morning Land knew that to answer yes would mean her death. Without hesitating, she stared directly into Wanderer's eyes and said, "That man is not good. I do not understand how he thinks. He says that I am bad and that everything which I touch grows bad. When my blood is flowing, I do not stay together with my husband. I do not want to stay near him at all. He has not treated me well. Who does not think a wife should continue to feel anger when her husband treats her cruelly? If I knew where to go, I would run far away from him."

Passing Shadow leapt to his feet. Had there not been several spears aimed at his chest, he would have attacked his wife a second time. "She is without shame!" he cried. "Fear her lies more than anything else! I have been bitten by them before. She would tell you I was dead if it pleased her." Passing Shadow looked frantically at the faces of the crowd. "I do not fear women, but this one is different. You can throw hot coals on her and she will walk calmly away."

"This woman cannot take revenge on you," Wanderer retorted. "She cannot return the blows she has received."

Despite the chief's words, there was an awkward silence. Wanderer's gaze shifted from Morning Land to the hunters who surrounded Passing Shadow. He could sense that the tribe was becoming confused. Many were more likely to believe the shaman than Morning Land. The Tidelander's aloofness had made them distrustful of her.

Laughing One had been kneeling beside his wife, content to let Wanderer deal with the shaman, but he, too, sensed that the mood of the villagers was changing. "Passing Shadow always steals," he shouted. "Even with his words, he steals from you."

As the attention of the crowd turned toward him, Laughing One stood and faced his father. "We will grow old listening to this shaman talk," Laughing One said. "His wife has no father or brother to defend her, yet he says she is a threat to us. He says he fears what she will do, but he will not let her go. Oh no. Not him. He must kill a woman before she can have even one child. He thinks you will not remain angry with him. He thinks you do not understand that he has beaten more than his own wife."

Laughing One pointed at White Bird. "Look at this woman.

She is already badly injured. He has left her here to die by herself. Does this woman have no husband that he treats her so badly? I have no other wife. He took his club in both hands and broke her, but he says it is not his fault. He waited by this path and tried to kill her secretly. Now he pretends that it is only his wife who has been hurt."

Again the crowd was grumbling, and once more their anger was directed at Passing Shadow. With deliberate slowness, the chief turned to face the shaman. "My son loves his wife very much," Wanderer said. "He loves the child that grows in her stomach. He has never treated her badly. Now she has been left lying on the ground. Her wounds are hot. She was not your woman, but you could not leave her alone. You were going to kill her."

Passing Shadow saw that the chief was determined to finish him. Somewhat over quickly, he said, "Anger blinded my eyes. I was disgusted with that woman." He pointed at Morning Land. "I came to strike only her, but I was like one asleep. I hit blindly at the woman in front of me, thinking she was my wife."

"You wanted to kill my wife also," Laughing One shouted. "You did not just strike her once. She has wounds all over her body. You tried to club her to death."

Wanderer nodded toward White Bird. "This woman can scarcely breathe. She thinks she is about to die. You were never afraid of her, but you were waiting in ambush on the trail. It was no spirit that she met on this path."

Before Passing Shadow could reply, Summer Wind interrupted the men with an angry curse. "*Katto aaan nataii!* We cannot wait here, listening to the crooked-mouthed one. He has very nearly killed *Yi-quay-is*. She is worn out. The flesh in her legs is hardening and stiffening. So great is the pain that she cannot stop moaning. We must take her to her lodge and care for her. If she cannot walk, some of the men must carry her."

Laughing One, Trusted Friend, and Rock Breaker quickly came to help. Under Summer Wind's direction, they carefully lifted White Bird in their arms and began carrying her up toward the village. Beautiful Star went with them, but Summer Wind remained. Like the chief, she wanted to see this quarrel with the shaman finished.

"Tell the shaman that he no longer has a wife here at our village," Summer Wind said, pointing toward Morning Land. "He left this woman here to die. That marriage is ended."

Wanderer showed his agreement by raising his spear. "You

made war on these women," he said to Passing Shadow. "You beat my son's wife. Now come here with your club and strike me. Do you think I will let this insult pass? I will give you an answer."

The expressions on the other men's faces showed Passing Shadow that he had lost. He stepped back, away from the circle of spears. "That woman will make you howl with rage," he warned. "She should be killed."

"You attacked my son's wife," Wanderer repeated, "and now you must fear my anger. Go and live in Black Snake's village if you want to escape me. If you stay, I will be one of the hunters who will attack you."

Passing Shadow pointed at Morning Land. "What will you do with that woman?"

"You almost killed my son's wife," Wanderer replied. "Now he will have your wife as well."

"That woman ruined me!" Passing Shadow shouted. "She has death in her. No child can ever grow in her stomach."

Several hunters shifted their spears uneasily.

"Do not stay here any longer," Wanderer said to the shaman. "We are tired of your talk. Go away."

Passing Shadow quickly retreated into the woods.

"Go into the forest and follow him," Wanderer told Fighting Eagle. "Do not let him come back."

CHAPTER FOURTEEN

The Great Hunt

In the early afternoon, a great herd of Ehina fed peacefully on lush grass near the upper end of a widened river valley. The blue water of the river itself glinted in the distance. At a season when most smaller streams had already gone dry, the grazing giants were drawn to this one valley, where lingering dampness and rich soil gave the grass roots a succulent, sweet taste found nowhere else.

Out beyond the rolling hills that fringed the valley, the land looked very different. There, white hot sunlight had baked the grass to shades of bronze and brown. These dry grassy plains, with their crusted earth and thorn scrub, offered no water to the thirsty Ehina. Dust and hot winds pushed past small trees where the leaves had already grown brown in the sun and yellow light. This was a place for pronghorns and bison and striped quagga horses that did not mind the dryness. While they darted about in the high, bronze grass, other game followed the old paths of Ehina, paths which crossed the black rocks and bronze plains to descend into this one valley, where green meadows were still bathed in humid light.

All down the long slopes of the valley, high grass and bright green bushes stretched out beneath the summer sun. The banks of the river led down further to shallow water, where groups of Ehina circled about or stood motionless under the sun's heat, their ears and trunks extended to catch the cooling western wind. The air was filled with crunching and snapping sounds of constant eating. Needing little sleep, the massive creatures had been munching steadily since before sunrise. They would go on feeding until late afternoon, when the sun's full heat would cause a brief pause. Then it would be more eating that would last well into the night. With such immense appetites, the Ehina would have the entire valley grazed out in a few more days.

This was not truly a single great herd. The gathering of Ehina was only temporary. Amid the blur of constantly moving trunks and jaws, there were many separate family groups, each one led by its own dominant female. There were a few great bulls mingling with the adult cows, and a small bachelor group of young males grazed near the outer edge of the valley, but most of the Ehina were female.

When the summer season was as dry and hot as it was on this day, even a brown river would have been carefully guarded by the Ehina. Here, the grateful giants drank easily, leaving big footprints in the mud, rubbing their rumps against water-darkened logs, or resting on their knees for a long time in the warm current. Shining wet backs, flared, foam-specked trunks, gleaming big tusks and submerged foreheads, all showed that the growing heat would bring little discomfort to these huge animals. Up on the bank, the feeding continued in a good-natured but destructive fashion. One old cow was using her massive, bone-crowned forehead as a battering ram to topple a large tree. Her own heavy body shook with the impact of each lunge she made, but the tree shivered and cracked like a sapling. After several blows, its roots began breaking apart. Then, with a final crunch, it toppled. Joined by her family, the cow moved to the top of the felled tree and began chewing on its upper branches. Other Ehina ripped the bark off neighboring trees. Bracing themselves against each tree with their tusks, they used their trunks to pull off long, chewable strips. None of the trees they attacked would survive another season.

Amid the rumbles, squeals and sighs of the feeding herd, there was also the harsh breathing of one injured female which stared at her companions with glazed eyes. This large cow moved uneasily over the trampled grass. Her huge body surged about in a tense sideways shuffle as she paced back and forth near the edge of her family group. Her spread ears and lifted trunk were a warning to the others, as were the low growls which quaked in her belly. The rest of the Ehina watched her cautiously and turned aside apprehensively whenever she approached, for they feared her uneven temper.

The cow's weaving and anger had an obvious cause. Claw marks showed on her wide back, and near her swollen shoulder there was a great tear which opened like a pale flower of ruptured flesh. Separate cuts on the left side of her head and trunk accounted for the uneasy, groaning sound of her breathing. The off-yellow color of the wounds and the foul smell they gave off were proof that they had not started to heal. Flies' eggs had added to the infection, and the hatching maggots ate her opened flesh. The sabertoothed cat which had caused these wounds was dead—crushed against the earth under the weight of Ehina's huge forehead—but the cow's misery remained. Maddened by pain, she slapped wet mud against those places she could reach with her trunk and threw dust across the rest, but the dirt would not stop the hungry maggots. For her, this was a time of pain and death.

Death was near for the others as well. Though none of them was aware of it, the Ehina were feeding at the mouth of a great natural trap. Downwind, to the east of them, the river valley deepened and grew so narrow that its walls were too steep for the Ehina to climb. At the point where the walls were highest, humans were building hunting platforms in the trees. The wind and the day were perfect. In a short while, the Great Hunt would begin.

One human hunter was much closer than the rest. Crouched low in the tall grass, Bear Killer remained as still as a rock while he studied the movements of the herd. Though he was too far away to see more than a few of the great beasts, others revealed their presence by thrown-up clouds of dust. Bear Killer could not count beyond the number ten, but he had already guessed that this herd was larger than any they had chased before.

Keeping at the edge of the grass, he began to move away downwind. His feet sped lightly across the ground in a series of short bursts. Each time he stopped, he sank from sight, always a little further off than before. There was no reaction from the herd. The Ehina were peacefully oblivious of him, and were likely to remain grazing in the river valley. Only one of the creatures had shown nervousness. Bear Killer took this as a good omen.

Farther east, Stand in Camp, leader of the four tribes of valley peoples, had carefully chosen the killing area for the Great Hunt. It was a place amid the steepening valley walls where the men had their best chance to slay Ehina. There were many large trees with branches that were too high to be grasped by the Ehinas' trunks. At the shore of the fast-flowing river was one enormous pine tree with a crown that reached well above the surrounding woods. From a place high in its branches, a single, keen-sighted hunter would watch the movements of the approaching herd and signal to his fellow men.

The men had arrived at the site before sunrise, traveling in single file up from the south. While the forest had been still and cold, with mist dripping in chill drops out of the leaves, each hunter had chosen the tree from which he would strike at Ehina. Throughout the morning they had prepared small platforms for themselves. It was rarely enough to simply climb a tree and wait for the giants to pass beneath it. The hunter needed to see the Ehina as soon as they arrived within range of his spear. Thick leafy vegetation that blocked a man's view or interfered with his throwing arm had to be cut away. In other trees the branches were too exposed, and the hunter had to create a screen of cut boughs to hide behind. All of the men were naked, having bathed in the river and rubbed their bodies with leaves and bark to deaden the human smell.

Organizing the building of these tree platforms was Stand in Camp's main task. While every hunter knew how to make a barricade of leaves around himself or clear out vegetation with a stone chopper, few were comfortable in the company of so many other men. During most seasons, hunting was a solitary business. Lying in wait was also unusual for the men. Following a trail was the accepted way of making a kill. To chase after an animal and run it down brought each man a sense of pride. Waiting like this offered no release for straining muscles. As soon as they sensed the Ehina, these men would grow tense. Their eyes would glisten with eagerness and restraining them would be difficult.

Now that the men were sitting in their trees and the watcher of the forest was perched high in the crown of the old pine, everything seemed strangely quiet. Hunters called to one another in hoarse whispers, already staring excitedly up the slope of the valley, as if expecting the gray bulk of the Ehina to suddenly appear before them. Stand in Camp sighed. The plan was a good one, but these men would never be good at waiting.

The men were not the only ones who found the routine of the Great Hunt difficult. Even normally pleasant and friendly women grew quarrelsome after only a few days of living in the Great Village. This was really four separate villages arranged within signaling distance of each other, with each chief trying to manage his own people. Yet even that much closeness strained the patience of these wandering tribesfolk. It seemed as if the complaints were endless.

The women bathed several times a day, approaching the river in small groups. Such an act was of little importance in true village surroundings, where privacy was assured by the isolated nature of the bathing places, but in the Great Village, women suffered from a sense of being constantly watched. They were fearful that strange men might shame them by spying through the trees. Already the women of Black Snake's tribe had complained that they could not even pick berries without being followed by young hunters from Resting Moon's camp. In Resting Moon's village, the stories were very different. His people insisted that there were young men from Black Snake's tribe who only lingered around village hearths and watched women all day. Black Snake's men, it seemed, refused to leave. Even if a girl went out only to gather firewood, these men would try to sleep with her. Worried and jealous, the two rival groups of women repeatedly screamed insults at one another whenever they were near enough to shout.

Stand in Camp had tried unsuccessfully to settle the matter, only to be accused of favoring Resting Moon's people. In truth, the leader of the Great Hunt did prefer the company of Resting Moon, for Black Snake's village was the home of a very troublesome shaman. Passing Shadow's quarrel with Wanderer had grown so loud that now the peace of the four villages was threatened by it. Only Black Spear still supported the bear shaman. Passing Shadow's repeated attempts to gain back the wife he had lost had turned the three other village chiefs against him. When all of his demands had been refused, the deserted shaman had moved off to brood by himself and mutter his threats to the wind.

Such quarrels with shamans were bad at any time, but even more so before a Great Hunt. People knew that an old shaman rarely fought openly as other men did. It was too difficult to hurt a young man that way. In such struggles the old shaman might easily be killed, and shamans, like most old men, did not truly want to die. Instead, the shaman would use bad medicine to sicken his enemy or cripple him from afar. Shamans, it was said, could turn a rotten log into a poisonous snake, and the bite of such a snake would make a man weak forever. A shaman's medicine could turn aside a spear or break a stone knife into small pieces. If a shaman's powers were strong enough, his enemy might fall into a river and drown.

Men who worried every day about the uncertainties of weather and game had a great fear of magic. The dread grew worse when a Great Hunt was near. With a shaman's curse on a man, any number of terrible things could happen to him. His spear arm might suddenly grow weak, dust might blow into his face and blind him, or he might be unable to move when Ehina turned. Perhaps he would be trampled by Ehina and have his bones broken like little pieces of reeds. Many of the men in this very woods believed that Laughing One's luck had already changed. They refused to stay in the same tree with him. Only Wanderer's other sons had been brave enough to risk the shaman's curse. Even Stand in Camp felt that the boy would suffer badly before this hunt was over. It was all the woman and the shaman's fault.

Stand in Camp paused to check the wind again. It was still coming in strongly from the west. There should be no sudden shifting this time, nothing to give away the hunters' presence. The great chief smiled as he thought of it. Despite Passing Shadow's bad medicine, the spirits had sent them a perfect day.

That dawn, the women, children, and old men from all four villages had left to circle northward around the Ehina. Soon these people would form a long, curved line to the west of the river valley. Their human scent, the loud noises they made, and the fires they set would be enough to panic the herd and drive the Ehina eastward toward the trees. Some of the old hunters in the line would bring torches to burn the dry grass. The other three village chiefs—Black Snake, Wanderer, and Resting Moon—would also be with the line, organizing the beaters and making sure that the fires were properly set. Stand in Camp felt sympathy for them all.

While this chief was staring hopefully toward the west, Fighting Eagle and his two brothers scattered leaves across the lower branches of their tree platforms. These were small shelters, with barely enough space in each one for a single man to sit or stand upright. Like roosting birds amid the sunlight of the treetops, the brothers listened to the sounds from the woods below. Though the mist and dew had gone from the forest, the scents of the undergrowth were still strong in the air around them. There was nothing in these sounds or scents to indicate trouble, but an uneasy feeling persisted. All three men understood why theirs was the least crowded tree. Just a few trees away, men had been forced to break loose foliage simply to make room for themselves, snapping off dried limbs and dropping them in piles onto the ground beneath. The tree where Laughing One and his brothers sat could easily have held six more, but the other hunters were so unsettled by Passing Shadow's threats that none even dared approach.

Fighting Eagle was silently furious at the other men's cowardice. He had trained half of these hunters himself, yet now they avoided him and chose to stay in different trees. Even Rock Breaker, his oldest friend, had remained on the ground below, supposedly to help Stand in Camp prepare the other men. Now, though, when every hunter had found his place, Rock Breaker could not be seen. It was an insult that Fighting Eagle would not soon forget.

With his feet placed securely in the crotch of the tree, he stared out over the forest like the eagle he had been named for. From his position, he could see the other men working, but they carefully avoided his glance. Perhaps it was shame at their own fear which made them shy. Perhaps they realized that ignoring their hunting brotherhood was as bad as any shaman's curse. To Fighting Eagle, it seemed as if they had scattered at nothing, like a herd of too easily frightened deer. Did they really expect the shaman's evil to come swooping down on them with yellow talons? Whatever their thoughts, Fighting Eagle knew he could not expect help from any of them.

Grunting in disgust, Fighting Eagle turned and spoke to his brothers. "Stay in place," he ordered. "This is one day when you must sit quietly. And do not be found sleeping when Ehina comes. Look for the signs."

"We are ready," Trusted Friend replied. "The Ehina will not reach us here."

Fighting Eagle nodded and pointed at the ground beneath them. "When the Ehina steps there, we will throw our spears. If the Ehina still stands tall after she has been hit, we will just continue to sit and watch her. Only when the Ehina has fallen down onto her knees and is just lying there, only then will we climb down to kill her. No hunter will be hurt unless we climb down too quickly. The Ehina that have not been wounded will soon go away, but sometimes one just stays nearby. Sometimes that one comes back again. In the dust, she is hard to see. Hear what I have to say, brothers. Stay in this tree until you see me climbing down."

Laughing One stared up the ravine, trying to imagine what it would be like. He had heard many stories about how the earth shivered under a hunter's feet when the Ehina passed and how a man was deafened by their shrieks, but he had never believed it all. Even now he could not quite believe. The valley was still and lifeless except for the worried-looking hunters perched in its trees.

Unlike many of the others, Laughing One was not greatly

worried by the shaman's threats. Passing Shadow had already tried to poison him and to kill his wife, and both times the old man had failed. Laughing One did not believe that Passing Shadow could destroy him just with bad medicine after failing the other way. What hurt was the trouble this shaman's curses had caused him and his brothers. He felt ashamed of the way men made excuses and grew surly when he approached them. His name had become a bad thing around the camp.

Laughing One's love for White Bird had barely been enough to get him through the grim days since her sister's return to their village. Aside from the quarrelsomeness and murmured insults of his fellow villagers, Laughing One had been confronted with the problem of dealing with two difficult women in a very crowded lodge. For half a moon after the shaman's attack, Laughing One's home had been filled with the odor of grease and poultices. In making her cures, Morning Land had left piles of roots, leaves, and bits of bark all around the lodge. During the first days of their marriage, White Bird had always woken as soon as he had risen from her side, but now all she did was roll over gratefully and stretch out to fill the space he had left. She no longer waited to see if Laughing One liked her cooking. As soon as he had his food, she went to sit beside Morning Land. Each morning and night they swam in whatever lake or river was nearest the village, and Laughing One would watch them go, remembering the times when White Bird had begged him to come with her.

Many other things had changed as well. Whenever Laughing One came back to the lodge after a hunt, White Bird would be talking with Morning Land. Their high singsong Tideland speech did not seem as pretty to him as it once had. It was a language he could not understand, and in speaking it the sisters excluded him from their thoughts. "Do not tell me it does not matter," Laughing One had once said to White Bird. "I have just sat here all night and understood nothing. This lodge has become a bad thing, full of sweat and the smell of sickness." White Bird's reply had been soft spoken and quick, but little had changed afterward.

All of this would have been hard enough had Morning Land shown him any gratitude for giving her this home, but the stubborn woman remained as aloof and hostile as ever. Laughing One guessed that Morning Land knew at least some of his own language, yet whenever she had something to tell him, the message came through White Bird. For all the talk which passed between Morning Land and himself, he might have been a shadow cast by the fire. She had been given to him to marry, and he had married her, but he had come away with a stranger, not a wife. At night she slept on the opposite side of their lodge, with her back toward him. It was always the time of blood with this woman.

Laughing One did not know what he could do to change these things. He was not a man who could force a woman down in the dark. If he had gripped her arms or blocked her mouth with his hands, he would have been ashamed to look at her in daylight. What pleasure could he have from her fear and anger?

He was also aware that she had been terribly treated by the shaman. The pain from her wounds must have been so great that even the thought of being touched would frighten her. Sometimes she would whimper in her sleep when she put weight on an injured muscle or let out a sharp cry of pain when she twisted her arm a certain way. He could still see the bruises where Passing Shadow had clubbed her, and the marks around her throat where the shaman had choked her until she could not breathe at all. He remembered how even her eyes had been swollen and bruised; how she had been thrown down for dead.

"Everything hurts with us," White Bird had told him. "At night we just lie there and cannot sleep. The pain is always trying to keep us awake."

Laughing One could understand some of this. Three people crawling about in the same lodge could not always be pressing noses and making love, but Morning Land's coldness hurt him, and when he saw her naked, he sometimes wished for her. It had grown so difficult in his lodge that he had begun to be glad to stay away from it. Even here, on this tree platform, waiting for the Ehina to come, things seemed easier and simpler than they did when he was facing Morning Land.

By this time, the women had already reached their position northwest of the herd. Black Snake, Wanderer, and Resting Moon were busy talking to the older men who would carry the torches and light the grass fires. Organizing the rest of the people was the job of the village matrons. Summer Wind knew exactly where every woman of her village wanted to be placed, and soon she had them lined up and ready to march. After that, there was little to do except wait.

Each woman would walk beside a partner. White Bird had been teamed with Morning Land. To the right of the Tideland sisters were Rainbow Pool and her daughter. To the left of the sisters, Summer Wind and Beautiful Star stood together silently. For a long while the women stayed in place, speaking only in whispers and wondering when the hunt would truly begin.

"*Shiiwe*, this sun is too hot," White Bird complained, raising the front of her apron in a way that showed the bruises on her thighs. "Why is there so much talking with these men? What can they be saying? This heat is hurting me. Even if we were walking slowly it would be better."

"Be quiet, sister," Morning Land whispered. "We will be starting soon enough." With a long hide draped across her back, Morning Land's bruises were shaded from the sunlight and seemed like a strange pattern on her tanned skin. It was only when someone looked more closely that her body showed how cruelly she had been beaten. The swollen areas on her back, hips, and legs had gone down again, but the skin was still badly discolored by small ruptured veins. There were patches of red, purple, and black, and yellow, and all of it looked sore.

"I do not like to be just standing here," White Bird persisted. "These people's ways will ruin my heart." Like her sister, White Bird had dark purple bruises extending from the upper part of her right arm all down across her front and back. Below her waist, the apron she wore hid most of the other marks left by the shaman's attack except when she was lifting it to cool herself as she was now.

"Is there a thorn in your foot that you refuse to be quiet?" Morning Land demanded. "Are you the only one who is standing here in the sun? Look around you. Women are standing way over there. Some carry children on their backs and they do not refuse to be patient."

"I cannot wait forever," White Bird grumbled. "I am looking in the direction where our husband has gone, and I am worried. This hunt is something I am afraid of. Everyone talks of how the shaman has cursed Laughing One."

"That old one no longer has any power over us," Morning Land replied. "I am no longer married to him."

"Then why do you act as if you still were?" White Bird demanded.

Sensing trouble, Morning Land glanced at her sister warily. "What are you saying?" she asked.

"Why do you act as if you were a guest in our lodge?" White Bird persisted. "It is as if you had only stopped to sleep for one night before walking on. Laughing One married you, but you do not sleep with him or sit with him. You never even speak to him. You offer him nothing. Your silence hurts our lodge. It makes all of us unhappy."

As she listened to her sister's rebuke, Morning Land's expression hardened. Her lips were pressed thin, and there was the beginning of anger in her eyes.

"You could help Laughing One, but you refuse," White Bird continued.

Morning Land sighed. "The shaman I was married to was older than my father," she said. "Passing Shadow hit and kicked his wives. We would crawl away from where he was lying and try to hide in the corners of the lodge, but he always found us. Even in daylight we were sad. We were always afraid of what he would do. It is not easy to forget the shame of that life."

"Laughing One has given you a home," White Bird insisted.

"I have nothing to give him," Morning Land replied. "I am still too weak and bruised. I cannot do anything for a man anymore."

"You cannot just marry a man and then leave him for someone else to care for," White Bird grumbled. "Listen to me. Do not refuse Laughing One. Do not just leave him alone."

Before Morning Land could reply, the other women started moving. Still quiet, the beaters began to walk in a great line which would place a human barrier between the Ehina and the open land to the west. For a while, White Bird amused herself by watching the chief's wife try to match strides with Beautiful Star. For Summer Wind this was strict, difficult work, but Beautiful Star swung her hips even when there were no men to notice. She glided along with the suppleness of a dancer, completely uninhibited by Summer Wind's scowling glances or grumbles of disapproval. After a while, White Bird found it harder to watch the pair, for the teams of beaters were gradually spreading apart as they moved. When the line stopped a second time, the Tideland sisters were more than a spear's throw away form the chief's wife.

White Bird could see the entrance of the valley now, though the Ehina were still so far distant that they showed only as a brown spotted line against the grassland. After staring at them for a moment, she turned her attention back to her sister.

"Even if you do not have a full heart to give him, you should let a small part of your heart go out to Laughing One," she said.

When Morning Land stared at her but did not answer, White Bird placed her right hand protectively over her bulging stomach. "I thought this baby had died," she murmured, "but it continues to grow. When I feel the strength of it, my heart is happy."

With a quiet smile, White Bird grabbed her sister's left arm and placed Morning Land's hand over the unborn child. Morning Land jerked her arm back uneasily at first, but White Bird was insistent. Soon Morning Land's palm was spread gently across White Bird's belly.

"Laughing One is the father of this child," White Bird said, staring up boldly into her sister's wet eyes. "This child is the reason you must not refuse him."

Morning Land sighed. Her mouth twisted into the resigned smile of someone who knows she has been beaten.

A few moments later, the second signal was given. Now the line of women beaters started to walk directly toward the herd. White Bird noticed that Summer Wind and Beautiful Star had begun singing and clapping their hands. As White Bird listened, she heard a soft chanting coming from all of the women around her. There were no loud banging noises or blazing fires yet. That would begin later. At the moment it was enough to let the women's scent reach the Ehina.

Farther east, most of the Ehina had stopped eating and were shifting about nervously. The comfort of their secluded valley had been intruded upon. Some stood motionless with their trunks raised, sniffing at the air suspiciously and making curious grunting noises. Others weaved about in front of the family groups, but always kept their heads facing west. Calves huddled against the sides of the cows and twirled their trunks in uneasy imitation of their mothers. None of the Ehina could see the approaching humans. Their eyesight was too poor. For them, the line of women was an odor in the wind, a smell so strong that they could almost taste it. The chanting was something they could hear quite clearly, but the fact that it came from so many directions confused them.

Gradually, as the noises and smells grew closer, the Ehina began to bunch together into family groups. The mothers with young calves moved toward the back while the larger cows formed a living wall to protect them. There was a lot of shuffling and sideways rocking among the adults as they tried vainly to find a target for their anger. Every animal in the great herd was agitated, but none of them had trumpeted or turned to flee. Instead, the huge creatures were unnaturally quiet, with only their trunks and tails twitching nervously.

The injured cow was the first to start moving. This particular
Ehina had been pacing near the edge of the herd when the scent
had first reached her. It had made her instantly immobile.
Standing as tall as she could, with her head lifted into the wind,
she had remained as motionless as a sentinel. The nervous
snorts and shuffles of the others had gradually acted as a goad,
keying up her own tension. Finally she pointed her trunk to-
wards the west, as if something upriver had caught her attention. Then she rushed forward in a stiff-legged walk that looked
like a run. She stopped amid a great cloud of dust, lifted her
trunk high, and let out a squeal of rage. Her trumpeting blared
across the grasslands.

Under the bright, almost blinding sunlight, the straining cow
surged to and fro trying to bluff her hidden enemy. The hideous
squalling she was making seemed to increase her anger.
Screaming shrilly, she grabbed a bush in her trunk, uprooted it,
and hurled it back to earth. Again she shuffled forward toward
the still distant line of humans. For all her noise, she was floundering blindly, and in her efforts to frighten the humans away,
she only panicked herself. Indecisively, she spun around, retreated a short distance, and repeated her ritual charge.

This threat display provoked the others to action, but instead
of charging their invisible enemy, the cows turned and hurried
away. With their trunks held above their heads, they fled along
the banks of the river, unaware that the sides of the valley
would gradually become steeper around them. It was not a full
panic yet. They were still moving at a fast shuffle.

White Bird was enjoying herself. It had been two seasons
since she and Morning Land had walked side by side without
having to carry bundles or loaded baskets on their backs. This
day's march reminded her of the trips they had made through
the salt marshes when they were girls. It was that same kind of
perfect day. There was a summer smell to the tall grass which
brushed against her legs, and the wind felt cool on the back of
her head. Lulled by memories, she had almost forgotten about
the Ehina. They were just a moving dust cloud that blotted out
part of the landscape in front of her. Once or twice she had
heard some trumpeting, but those noises seemed distant compared with the chanting voices of the women.

White Bird did not notice the tension of the other beaters.
Beautiful Star was swaying and prancing as before, and Morning Land had a pleased expression on her face, but the rest of

the women looked grim. Their memories were different from those of the Tideland sisters.

The pace of the drive began to speed up. The chanting changed to a chorus of shouts, with each woman making as much noise as she could. Some sent out ululating screams that wavered shrilly in the wind. Others had brought along sleeping hides and fanned them over their heads to increase the human scent. Beautiful Star had found two pieces of bark and was clapping them together to produce a loud whuffing sound.

Lacking these tools, the Tideland sisters improvised on their own. White Bird, who had been chanting Tideland love songs before, changed from singing to cursing. Amid the wild noises around her, she screamed out against Passing Shadow, wishing him every kind of fearful death she could imagine. She was surprised at her own inventiveness. Morning Land's method was more energetic. After taking a few normal steps, she would suddenly leap into the air, spread her arms wide, and shriek out something that resembled a whoop. The sweeping motions of Morning Land's arms looked ridiculous and would have made White Bird laugh a short while before, but now she was becoming worried.

When the women reached the area where the Ehina had been feeding, White Bird began to realize what the men were faced with. She noticed the ripped-out stretches of grass, the ruined trees, the huge piles of dung, and the flattened, compressed look of the trampled shore mud. The land seemed almost leveled in places.

The moving line around White Bird suddenly stopped. At a signal from Wanderer, everyone began to collect whatever scraps of wood or clumps of dried grass she could find. It was time to light the fires.

On the open savannah, the men might have simply set fire to the bush. High grass always burned easily during the summer dry season, and it took only moments to torch small leafed trees or blacken the ground. In this river valley, however, conditions were very different. An open fire could quickly sweep uncontrolled along both banks of the shallow river. Hemmed in by the valley walls and pushed on by canyon winds, it might soon engulf every tree, including the ones where the hunters themselves were perched. Trees did not grow back in a single season the way high grass did. Rather than ruin the valley for generations and risk entrapping their own men, the hunting leaders chose a different tactic. They built a series of large bonfires which, when linked together, sealed off the upper end of the valley. It was hoped that the stink and sting of the smoke from these fires would be enough to panic the Ehina.

As the fires were lit, one by one, the tension among the people eased a little. The piles of grass and deadwood fed the flames until they boomed and reverberated in great crackling roars, sending columns of deep black smoke up into the wind. Already the clear sky was becoming dirtied with a dark haze. People had to step back to prevent their skin from being singed.

The women continued to shout and jump about, but the fires themselves became the greatest goad. No animal could smell this much smoke without becoming panicked. The wind would soon grow hot on the Ehinas' backs. The stench of the smoke would sicken and almost smother them. All they would want to do would be to get free of the fire.

The great herd had slowed down while the humans paused to light their fires. No longer pressed hard from behind, the older Ehina had begun to grow suspicious of the steepening valley walls. Apprehension made them reluctant to move into a narrower space, and with the humans already out of sight, the Ehina shuffled forward uncertainly. There was much trunk twisting and angry trumpeting as the great beasts tried to decide what to do.

Then the black smoke rose up behind them in the western sky.

The stink came heavily, and all at once, its sour taste filling the suddenly hot wind. The odor of burning grass and wood was mixed with the harsh snaps and crackling sounds of things catching fire. It seemed as if flames had leapt along the very sides of the river valley. Already crowded by the narrowing valley walls, the huge herd began to sense its doom. Nothing in the beasts' memories was worse than the fear of being burned. Whatever caution the giants had felt was forgotten in a sudden wild need to escape.

A young bull abruptly turned and fled downriver, trumpeting fear as he shuffled forward at the greatest speed his legs could manage. The other Ehina snorted and grunted uneasily at the bull's wild screams of alarm. Faced with sudden heat, a heavily blackened sky overhead, and the stinging taste of smoke, the frightened Ehina could only try to withdraw to safer sections of the valley. They were being driven in an unequal struggle. During that awful moment of panic, they hurried frantically across the soft earth of the river's flood plain, kicking and trampling any bushes or trees that blocked their way. Panicked beyond reason, they fled in a trumpeting mass. No living thing could have stopped them.

The pressure inside the herd was tremendous. Pushed shoulder to shoulder, the huge beasts were oblivious to everything but the blinding urgency of their own fear. Bellowing cows banged against one another as the herd swept along. Most kept their trunks tightly curled, but tusks were cracked, ear flaps were ripped open, and toenails were smashed when the giants piled up against their neighbors. In the uncontrolled flight, the calves were in great danger of being trampled by their elders. Some mothers tried to protect the young ones by keeping the calves under their bellies.

A few adults tried to escape the pressure of the herd by climbing out of the ravine, but the herd was moving too fast for them to get a safe footing. One cow's ridged foot pads could not keep a grip on the sliding earth of the ravine wall. Rearing up on her hind legs, she fell badly. One leg snapped and buckled as she crashed back into the valley. With a wild cry of pain, she collapsed onto her chest. Her ivory clacked against the ground and her head became locked in a low position, but she lifted her trunk as a signal to the others. For a while the herd split around her, with huge beasts passing her on either side, but her squeals could not drive them off indefinitely. When the rearward pressure became too great, the rest of the herd simply climbed over her, the heavy blows of their big round feet slowly trampling her to death.

With trunks curled and ears spread, the badly frightened animals continued their wild rout. In the trees ahead of them, the hunters waited.

There had been no talk among the hunters for a long while. The Watcher of the Woods, perched high up in the crown of the huge pine tree, had been the first to observe the rising smoke in the west. His signal had called the attention of the others to it. Soon all could see the great, soft purple smoke cloud that spread across the western sky. As the air continued to darken, the sun grew pinkish in color. The wall of fires gave off an oily stink not at all like the wood-burning odors of the hearth. It seemed as if the entire forest was being destroyed.

Chased by the hot wind, startled birds fluttered up from their roosts and flew downriver in squawking, frightened flocks. Jays and crows swooped low to catch insects which were also fleeing. There was more than smoke driving the insects. The ground was shaking with the footsteps of something huge.

All of the men were alert and listening. Specks of soot and ashes were visible in the wind around them. Farther away, they could hear the sharp trumpeting of the Ehina. Even the trees had begun to tremble with the vibrations of the approaching herd.

Staying in a tree all through the morning had been difficult enough for Laughing One. As he heard this great deep rumble echo through the forest, he felt an urge to flee for safer ground. The tree seemed a poor refuge from the largest and most dangerous animals in his world. The explosive fluttering of the birds and insects around him had only increased his uneasiness. Then, climaxing the build-up of tension, there came a wild cat wail from the Watcher of the Woods. It was the signal that the Ehina were close—almost on top of the men, in fact—and were approaching from every western edge of the valley.

The treetop caller changed signals again, this time to a high-pitched bird trill. It was the final alert and was hardly needed. Blinding dust had already swept in among the trees, stirred up by the feet of the herd. Suddenly, as if from out of nowhere, a tremendous crowd of huge, dust-shrouded bodies filled the open spaces below the trees. Spears were hurled down from different directions, penetrating the necks of the stampeding giants. It was all frightfully quick. Some Ehina fell back, groaning, onto the ground, but most continued on.

The overcrowded tree to the left of Laughing One proved a death trap for the hunters perched amid its branches. Eight men suddenly found their shelter toppling as a huge tusker smashed head on into its trunk. The tusker was killed instantly when the tree fell on him, but the men had no chance to jump free. They were suddenly engulfed by the herd's final rush.

Straining to escape, one man received a terrific cut through his stomach as a broken branch fell back into him. It was as if he had been speared by a great stake. A second hunter was gouged through his chest by the tusk of a frightened cow. While the hunter jerked and twitched in a vain attempt to get free, the cow cleared her tusk by brushing it against the earth, crushing the man's chest cavity as she did so. Another cow struck out with her trunk a moment later, and a third man fell to earth with his neck broken. The other five hunters were able to scramble away from the ruined tree.

Even then they were not safe. The terrified herd was all around them. As he tried to climb for higher ground, a fourth hunter lost his footing. Laughing One saw him fall into the stampeding herd, but no trace of him was ever found afterwards. While trying to avoid an angry bull, a fifth hunter stepped into the path of a large cow. Without making a sound, the huge female slapped the man to the ground with her trunk and stepped on him. Five men were dead in a moment, and the oncoming herd never paused. The Ehina heaved forward through the heat and dust.

Laughing One had thrown his spear at the same instant as the other men. On impulse, while the herd had been milling past and trumpeting in utter confusion, he had hurled his weapon down into the neck of the nearest Ehina. The strike had seemed a good one, but he could not be sure, for billowing dust clouds had covered everything a moment later.

After that, it had been a matter of waiting and hoping that their tree would hold up under the pressure of those gigantic, shoving bodies. The three brothers crouched motionless while the rest of the herd thundered past beneath them. All were sickened by the fate of those men who had been caught on the ground. Laughing One could see his own apprehension reflected in the faces of his two brothers as they crouched beside him on the lower branches. Trusted Friend was clearly frightened. His eyes had the wild look of someone who wanted to run and could not. Fighting Eagle's expression was more controlled, but even his eyes showed worry.

Then, as suddenly as they had appeared, the Ehina were gone. The rumbling tapered off abruptly as the last of the herd fled the valley. Very cautiously, Laughing One and his brothers peered down through the settling dust. All Laughing One could taste as he moved his tongue about in his mouth was dirt.

The massive stampede had completely stripped the valley of every small bush and shrub. White dust still blew about like a flurry of snow across a land that was startling in its ruined appearance. Grass blades had been pounded into flat shadow patterns against the ground. Small trees had had both leaves and branches ripped from them, leaving them to stand like shorn skeletons in the sudden stillness. All around lay the great carcasses of fallen Ehina, some still moving and filling the air with their groans. The brothers' own quarry was a dark, humped shape on the ground directly below them. A half-grown cow, it had fallen to its knees only a short distance from the trunk of the tree. All three brothers' spears were embedded in its neck.

The Ehina was so still that Laughing One guessed it must already be dead.

Deciding that the area was safe, Fighting Eagle slithered down the trunk of the tree. When he was standing on the ground, Trusted Friend and Laughing One followed. There seemed to be an emptiness to the place now. It was almost as if an earthslide of loose soil had slipped downhill and buried everything. No insect, lizard or bird remained on that ruined shore. Even the Ehina tracks were half filled with dust. As the men walked, a finely ground powder rose in little whirlwinds around their legs. The ground still felt warm to step on.

Like vultures, the men cautiously approached the huge gray shape of their victim. Now that they were on the ground, the cow seemed much bigger. Her tusks were as long as one of Laughing One's outstretched arms, but it was her eyes that the young hunter noticed. The Ehina's dead eyes seemed to stare out at him from beneath dust-caked lids.

Fighting Eagle searched over the collapsed form of the Ehina, looking for any lingering signs of life. After a moment, he approached a small, moundlike bulge in the Ehina's side and punctured it with his knife. Blood rushed out from the Ehina's flank with surprising force, but there was no other movement. The glazed eyes did not shift. The caked eyelids did not flicker. Though the beast's skin was still warm to the touch, its spirit was truly dead. Fighting Eagle reached up and pulled one of the spears out of the Ehina's neck. He examined it for a moment, then tossed it to Laughing One.

While Fighting Eagle was freeing Trusted Friend's spear, three other hunters approached the kill. Rock Breaker, Thunder in the Ground, and Buffalo Tongue had been less fortunate than the brothers. Buffalo Tongue's spear had disappeared along with the bull Ehina he had thrown it into. Thunder in the Ground had missed entirely, only to have his spear shaft crunched to splinters under the herd's pounding feet. Rock Breaker had held onto his spear. Somewhat shamefacedly he walked alongside Fighting Eagle. Both men knew it would take a long time to repair their friendship after this day's insult. To cover his embarrassment, Rock Breaker crouched beside the kill and pretended to examine its hide. He kicked the Ehina's folded leg with the toe of his moccasin while Fighting Eagle handed Trusted Friend's spear back to its rightful owner.

Rock Breaker drew away when Fighting Eagle turned to look at him. The rest of the men watched uneasily, aware of the tension between these two former hunting partners. Any hostile move from Fighting Eagle would have ended the friendship completely but the hunting leader was no longer angry. Behaving as if nothing had happened, Fighting Eagle offered his knife. Gratefully, Rock Breaker quickly used it to cut the dead Ehina's throat and thus complete the killing ritual. Preoccupied with their own problems, none of the six men noticed the silent approach of a huge, living Ehina.

It was the same cow which had battled the saber-toothed tiger several days before. She had escaped the hunters' spears and should have been far away, hurrying after the surviving members of the herd, but something had kept her back. She had been lingering close by, hidden behind a nearby tree where the leaves were still green.

Laughing One was the first to see the second Ehina. Some premonition made him glance up from the carcass just as the huge cow stepped around the tree that had hidden her. For a moment he watched in astonishment as she threw her head up and flared out her ears. There was no trumpeting or threat display this time. The cow did not move back and forth indecisively. Her forefeet shuffled briefly against the ground, as if she were trying to test her footing, and then she came straight for them.

Laughing One screamed, "Ehina!" and pointed frantically at the oncoming giant.

With no tree to hide in and no fire to drive the Ehina back, the men scattered. Aware that the Ehina was much too close, Trusted Friend fled along the valley toward Black Snake's men. His two brothers stayed where they were, but while Laughing One was too frightened to move, Fighting Eagle continued to pull at the handle of his spear. The weapon's tip was stuck in the dead Ehina's neck vertebrae and would not come out. Rock Breaker and Thunder in the Ground both ran for the side of the ravine. Buffalo Tongue took too long to realize the danger. He never had time to react properly.

The Ehina came on relentlessly, moving with a speed that Laughing One could not believe. Still quiet, with dust spraying out from under her feet, the Ehina seemed momentarily unsure of which man to follow. When she was less than a spear's throw away, Buffalo Tongue turned and started to run, unwittingly focusing the cow's attention on himself. Buffalo Tongue was a strong hunter, but he had no chance of escaping. The cow was traveling at full speed, almost twice as fast as he could run. He had gone only a short distance before she was on top of him.

At the last instant, Buffalo Tongue threw himself sideways, hoping to gain time as the cow turned. The Ehina was not distracted enough to be slowed down. Her trunk swung out to catch him and smashed hard against his rib cage. It was like colliding with a falling tree. Two ribs caved in immediately, and Buffalo Tongue skidded sideways across the dirt. Completely winded by the blow, the hunter rolled onto his back. There was no hope of getting up again.

Stunned by the first blow, Buffalo Tongue stared up helplessly as the dark blur of the cow's head descended toward him. The hardened tips of her crossed tusks pushed in just below his rib cage with bone-crushing force, popping open his abdomen and snapping his spine in a single thrust. A sudden rush of blood stained the white ivory dark red. Buffalo Tongue began a wild, agonized screaming. His crazed shrieks did not last long, for the cow drew back her head and slammed into him again. This time her thick tusks clacked hard into his chest cavity, squashing ribs, muscles, and lungs in a single terrible crunch.

While Buffalo Tongue's body was shaking and trembling under the impact of the cow's tusks, Fighting Eagle managed to free his spear from the carcass. As soon as he had the spear balanced in his grip, the hunting leader hurled his weapon at the Ehina's neck.

It was a good throw, enough to have crippled a smaller beast. The blade slashed in behind the cow's right ear and sent a burst of pain through her system, but it did not stop her. She let out a high, terrifying scream and spun around to face Fighting Eagle. As the Ehina turned, one of her hind legs kicked at what was left of Buffalo Tongue, shoving the bleeding corpse down into the mud-filled river. Then she came toward Fighting Eagle.

The hunting leader had not waited to see the effect of his thrust. As soon as he had thrown his spear, he had fled for the side of the ravine. With the Ehina behind him, Fighting Eagle ran straight on at full speed, but the squealing giant was already moving faster. The infuriated cow held her trunk out as she charged, homing in on Fighting Eagle's scent. When the hunter tried to turn, the cow swung at him. Her trunk slammed against his ribs. Hurled sideways by the blow, Fighting Eagle was tossed back toward the carcass of the dead Ehina. Unlike Buffalo Tongue, he did not wait for the cow to sweep down on him again. Instead, he dove forward behind the body of the dead Ehina. Puzzled by his abrupt disappearance, the cow hesitated.

Fighting Eagle wriggled his way under the side of the carcass, forcing his body into a tight space between the dead Ehina and the earth. Several of his ribs had been cracked by the cow's trunk, and the pain in his chest was intense, but he did not moan or cry out. He knew that his only hope lay in silence. As soon as he had pushed himself as far in as possible, he made his body stay perfectly still.

It was a small chance. The cow's long tusks could easily reach him where he was. Unless she accepted his quick disappearance as real, she would soon be pulling and prodding at him again, crushing him the same way she had crushed Buffalo Tongue. Already he could hear the ominous rumbling of her belly close at hand as she tried to find him.

Laughing One was alone now. He had stood motionless while the giant cow had crushed the life from Buffalo Tongue, and he had watched his brother dive behind the carcass to avoid the Ehina's charge. Incredibly, the cow had not noticed him. By staying motionless, he had saved his own life, and instinct told him to remain as he was.

Everything had been happening so quickly that the frightened young hunter could barely understand it all. A few moments before, they had been standing peacefully beside the carcass of their prey. Now Laughing One's whole sense of things had been disrupted. The huge cow did not belong there, turning to and fro as it tried to find another victim for its anger. In moving out into the open, the Ehina had left Laughing One no time or space in which to leave. He could only stand paralyzed, hoping that the cow would not sniff him out and run him down.

For a moment it seemed as if the cow might return to her hiding place amid the trees. She was obviously tiring. Her breath came in heavy, deep gasps, and her sides shivered slightly as she stood staring at the fallen Ehina. Laughing One could smell the hot, steamy scent of her body. When he saw her sway sideways and take a step back, he felt certain that she would leave, but then her trunk suddenly swung up over her head. An instant later, her hideous trumpeting pounded against his ears. Startled, he threw his spear at her.

Though the throw was made on blind impulse, Laughing One's aim was good. The blade hit with a heavy thump and cut deep into the Ehina's throat. An eruption of blood spurted out of the cow's neck, streaking down across her chest and forelegs.

The cow's squalling grew even louder. Laughing One saw her feet move forward in a blur of dust. He leapt sideways and started to run down the valley just as Trusted Friend had done a short while before. There was no time for dodging or turning. There was no place to hide. He could only keep going in a headlong flight, with the Ehina closing in behind. Once he turned his head, but the sight of the huge black form towering an arm's length away made him afraid to look again. He forced his legs to go even faster and struggled against a wild urge to scream.

There was a terrible, shaking blow. Everything around him seemed to move. He had been struck midway along the back by the enraged cow, and he felt himself being lifted, moving forward without effort. Strangely, he did not panic. His body was limp and unresisting as he slapped onto the ground like a plunging diver an instant later. Clumps of dirt forced their way into his mouth. His face became buried in a pile of earth. Knocked down and totally winded, he still remembered Fighting Eagle's words and remained as he was.

Whether the cow would have continued her attack on the motionless hunter or eventually backed away was something Laughing One would only be able to guess at, for the Ehina's attention was distracted by the arrival of other hunters. Shouting warnings as he ran, Trusted Friend had roused the other tribesmen. From all sides of the valley, armed men came running toward the enraged cow. Before the Ehina could do further damage, two spears jabbed into her upper trunk. She shrieked from the unexpected pain and pulled back just as a third spear penetrated her left eye. Oozing blood from many wounds, she shook herself in a vain effort to push out the spears.

The stunned Ehina had no time to flee. She was completely encircled. Spears began to hit her from all directions. Still trumpeting, she swung her trunk about like a flailing fist, but her great strength, which could shatter bones so easily, was of no use to her. The men stayed at a safe distance. Whenever she started to charge one section of their line, spears from the rest would slash at her head or flanks. A second eye-piercing thrust left her totally blinded. Standing in the center of the circle of men, with their spears bristling from her head, neck, and stomach, she whipped her bleeding trunk back and forth in soundless protest.

The Ehina was badly hurt, but death did not come easily for her. Covered in her own blood and no longer able to defend herself, she remained standing long after she should have collapsed. Several of Black Snake's hunters, who had driven their spears into her bulging stomach, grew bold enough to run up and pull out their weapons. Since she could not smell or see, they were able to use the same spears to jab her again and again, until the blood drizzled out in steady streams from her sides. It was only after one hunter shoved his spear in deep enough to burst a main artery that she finally fell. With her collapse, the last kill of the Great Hunt was accomplished. The hunters began to drag away their wounded.

No one wanted to touch what was left of Buffalo Tongue. The mangled corpse lay half submerged at the side of the river, its feet and legs curiously unharmed. From a distance, the hunter looked as if he were simply resting stomach down on the mud. But there was no stomach, and no chest either, only a ripped-open torso from which dark red patches flowed out into the dirty water. Eventually one man, who was either braver or less sensitive than the others, quickly grabbed onto the two moccasined feet and pulled the corpse up the side of the ravine.

Fighting Eagle tried to stand up, but sharp pains in his chest made him gasp deeply and double over. With his arms folded across his ribs, and his thighs pressed tight against his stomach, he huddled next to the Ehina carcass that had saved his life. Rock Breaker and Thunder in the Ground reached down to help him, but he shook his head.

"When I see a hunt that is so cruel, I feel like being far away from this valley," he said. "Where are the others?"

"Buffalo Tongue is dead," Rock Breaker answered.

Thunder in the Ground provided unasked-for details. "He was nearly crushed to pieces. His flesh was torn deep. His stomach and chest were torn open. That was what killed him. He bled everywhere. Even his back was gashed."

"My brothers," Fighting Eagle interrupted, "where are they?"

"Trusted Friend walks," Rock Breaker replied. "Laughing One tries to crawl. The Ehina just left him, thinking him dead. It tossed him to the ground. Now he can hardly move."

"My brother is wounded?" Fighting Eagle asked.

"We fled to the side of this valley and waited for the Ehina to leave," Thunder in the Ground explained. "We waited and waited. We saw how the Ehina killed Buffalo Tongue. We heard you yell and knew you would hide yourself. Laughing One was just standing there. He was unable to move. When the Ehina screamed, he threw his spear at her. She ran after him and nearly crushed him. That Ehina just tossed him to the ground."

The others protested, but Fighting Eagle stood up and started to walk to where Laughing One lay. The hunting leader held his chest, and there were pain lines in his face, but he walked without help.

Laughing One was still where he had fallen. He had remained motionless all through the final killing of the Ehina, keeping his eyes tight shut and barely breathing. When the great cow's screaming had finally stopped, he had opened his eyes and twisted his face free of the dirt. Most of the dust had settled, leaving a clear midday sky above him. As he had stared up into the open blueness, he had been surprised at how beautiful it had looked. He had found he could move his arms and wriggle his toes and feel the wind blowing against his back. His stomach had hurt and he had still felt winded, but it had only been when he had placed the palms of his hands against the soft earth and tried to push himself up onto his knees that the true pain had come. He had been unable to stand up. Whenever he had flexed his leg muscles, the pain had become worse. He had writhed to one side and then another, desperately trying to find a position that would not hurt. Finally he had collapsed onto his stomach again.

"Brother, where are you hurt?" Fighting Eagle called.

"Ehnn. I do not know," Laughing One groaned. "I ran from the Ehina, but I did not run fast enough. I pretended I was dead and the Ehina left me."

"You are not bleeding," Fighting Eagle told him. "Have you tried to move?"

"Eh. I can move," Laughing One grunted, "but I cannot stand. I have tried to crawl and I cannot. My body feels like it is very nearly in pieces."

Fighting Eagle nodded to Rock Breaker and Thunder in the Ground, who quickly lifted Laughing One to his feet. When Laughing One tried to move his legs again, the pain was so great he cried out. "Ehnn. The pain digs deep in my back. I am almost torn open."

"Carry him on your back," Fighting Eagle told Rock Breaker. Pointing up the side of the ravine, he added, "Take him to the top of that hill."

Supporting Laughing One's weight on his back like a mother carrying her child, Rock Breaker staggered up out of the valley. Fighting Eagle and Thunder in the Ground stayed by his side.

It was a slow journey for the four men. At each step, Laughing One felt pain. Twice the effort of carrying the young hunter became too great, and Thunder in the Ground took over the burden. Laughing One asked to be left on the ground, but the other men ignored him. In this back-and-shoulder fashion, they finally reached the top of the ravine. At last the men did leave him to rest under the shade of a small tree.

For a long while Laughing One refused to move anything for fear that the wild jolts of pain would start again. He ached and hurt all over now. After a while, he began to realize that his brother, Fighting Eagle, was close by. Neither of the two men spoke. Each was in his own private world of hurt. Laughing One wondered if they would be left there to die. He had heard of such things. Eventually, he began to worry about White Bird and Morning Land. A crippled man was no good to any woman. Someone else would have to marry the sisters.

CHAPTER FIFTEEN

Morning Land's Cure

White Bird had had enough of Ehina and hunting by the time she and the other women reached the killing area. Her legs ached from stepping over the mounds of rubble turned up by the herd, her hair smelled of smoke, her eyes stung from dust, and her skin was itching from where she had brushed against twigs, thistles, and tall grass. After so much shouting, she could barely speak at all. The husky dryness in her throat made her look longingly at the river, but the water there was still muddy from where the Ehina had churned it up. The huge beasts seemed to have ruined everything in their path.

White Bird's eyes searched over the ground. The further below the hills they walked, the worse the damage grew. The land in this lower part of the valley had been nearly ruined. Clumps of grass and vines were flattened onto the ground, crushed and covered in powderlike dust. Small whirlwinds of dust continued to spin through the standing trees and the upflung roots of those that had fallen. White Bird walked under a tree that had partly collapsed from the pressure of the stampeding Ehina and was now braced up by another tree. Its ripped leaves shivered like grass when the wind touched them. Though the day had grown clear again since the herd had passed and the fires had gone out, the air here still carried an oily stink of burning plants.

Because she was so tired, White Bird slowed down as she saw the first of the dead Ehina. This was the cow that had lost its footing at the edge of the ravine and fallen back in, only to be trampled to death by the animals behind it. The huge creature lay on its side, half buried in gray mud. There were crusts of dried mud on the exposed areas of its legs, head, and flank from where other Ehina had stepped on the cow as they had hurried past. Blood flowed out from a gash in the cow's neck that a hunter had cut with his spear to make sure the beast was dead. Apart from this one wound, the Ehina's body had been left untouched.

There was a smell of death about the carcass that caused a momentary wave of nausea in White Bird. To steady herself, she pressed both of her hands against one of the cow's huge tusks and bent over. The ivory had a polished gleam in the sunlight, but she felt grooves and scratches under her palms, and there were brown areas on the tusk that showed the use it had gotten. Being this close to the cow, White Bird could see its opened eye staring up at her. Something in its lifeless gaze frightened her, and she felt a sudden urge to get away from this place. As if guessing what she was thinking, Morning Land came up and placed a protective arm around White Bird's shoulders.

"Ehnn. Now it is finished for this one," Morning Land said.

"When I look at this Ehina, all I feel is sickness," White Bird told her. "It rises within me and grabs my heart."

Morning Land smiled. "Your heart will not be ruined by a dead Ehina." After a pause, she added, "There must be many animals killed or the hunters would not have just left this one. We will soon be eating meat again."

"My heart will only be happy when I greet *Tua-arikii,*" White Bird grumbled.

"What is doing this to you, making you so sullen?" Morning Land asked. "You cannot just sit here and wait. Some women are already greeting their men. We must stay with the others."

But it was too late for that. The line of beaters had split into random groups as soon as the women had reached the killing area. Wives from various villages had hurried forward to greet their hunters, each woman anxious to reassure herself that her own family was safe. Distracted by the sight of the dead Ehina, White Bird and her sister had lingered while Summer Wind and the other women from their village had rushed on ahead. Now the Tidelanders were left alone amid shouting strangers.

At first the shouts around them sounded excited and happy, but while the two sisters were slowly weaving their way forward past various Ehina carcasses, an ululating wail of grief echoed out across the valley. It was followed by a second cry, and soon many women were wailing in chorus. White Bird looked questioningly at her sister, not knowing whether this was real grief or simply some new hunting ritual. Morning Land just shrugged.

"There is blood on the path ahead," someone yelled. "There are dead men. We have seen them. This is a place where men die."

"*Kai* (come down)!" White Bird called. "Why are you saying these things?"

No one answered her.

"I will take a look," a second woman shouted.

"No, it is farther downstream," the first woman told her.

A third woman ran by holding some object in her hands. There were tear streaks on her face. "A great Ehina, hidden by the trees," she cried. "It came and grabbed the man. It tore him to pieces in front of the others."

"How many of our men have the Ehina killed?" White Bird asked, but the woman was already hurrying up the slope.

Morning Land held onto White Bird's arm. "We do not know what is wrong," she cautioned. "We must not lose our strength until we have seen these things."

The two sisters quickened their pace. White Bird felt herself becoming more and more anxious as the cries spread around them. People were shouting at each other, and their words were often garbled, but White Bird knew enough of the language to guess at most of the meaning.

"Many men have been hurt," she told her sister. "Already they are speaking of the shaman and saying that he caused these bad things."

"That old man sits alone in his own lodge," Morning Land said. "He has no magic. If he had such medicine once, it is dead by this time. He is a man whose strength has died."

"My back was ruined by this man who you say has no strength," White Bird retorted. "The scars you have now were not there before you sat at his fire."

The two sisters hurried on until they reached a place where a crowd of people had gathered around the carcass of a dead Ehina. The bulging mound of the creature's body was partially hidden behind the circle of curious villagers. White Bird recognized most of the people in the group. Wanderer was there, along with Trusted Friend. The two men were talking anxiously, and Trusted Friend kept pointing toward a second Ehina that lay dead nearby.

"Someone is very frightened and runs without thinking," Morning Land said, pointing to where a young woman was hurrying down the side of the ravine. "Who is running like that?"

As the sisters watched her, the woman skirted around a break in the pathway, jumped down onto the valley floor, and darted toward them across the trampled ground.

"Ehnn. My eyes try to fool me," White Bird grunted. "That woman is Beautiful Star."

She had never seen Trusted Friend's wife move so quickly before.

Beautiful Star slowed down to a walk as soon as she came near the two sisters, and allowed herself a few panting breaths before she started to speak.

"Do not just stay here," Beautiful Star shouted. "You are not the one who feels pain. Come and help us."

White Bird glanced questioningly at Morning Land. "Ehnn. What is this woman saying?"

"Do not stand there crying," Beautiful Star interrupted. To emphasize the importance of her words, she grabbed White Bird's hand and pulled insistently. Before the Tideland girl fully realized what was happening, the two women were already climbing up the valley wall. Morning Land hesitated for a moment, then slowly followed after them.

Beautiful Star did not slacken her pace when they crossed the steeper sections of the ravine. Her long legs stepped easily around rocks and scrub that would have given a hunter trouble, proving that there were hard muscles in her apparently delicate frame. Behind her, White Bird was finding it difficult to keep up. Her pregnancy was reaching a stage where it had begun to slow her actions and she often tired quickly. Finally, when they were two thirds of the way up the slope, she stopped and leaned against the side of the ravine.

"Uhnn, this hurts," she gasped. "There is pain in my breast."

Beautiful Star turned and looked at her impatiently. "Do not stand there shivering and crying. Your baby will not be born today."

"What is wrong that you hurry me this way?" White Bird asked petulantly.

"Some men were killed," Beautiful Star said. "Some women will come home this night with nothing. Your husband lives, but he has been hurt on one side of his body."

White Bird just stared at her, not really understanding.

Beautiful Star pointed down the slope toward the carcass of the cow Ehina. "That Ehina went after the men," she explained. "It killed Buffalo Tongue, but Laughing One is still alive. You have not lost your husband. You must help take Laughing One home. We cannot just leave him here."

Beautiful Star stopped speaking, for White Bird had closed her eyes and was shivering. For a moment, Beautiful Star thought the girl might collapse. She placed her hand on White Bird's arm. "*Yattee* (Come)," she said firmly.

White Bird shook off the grip. "I am frightened when I hear your talk. If *Tua-arikii* is near, I will hurry."

Laughing One and Fighting Eagle were still under the tree where the other men had left them. Fighting Eagle had raised himself to a sitting posture, with his back braced against the tree, but Laughing One was lying down, with only his head lifted. Around them, three worried women were hurrying to get things ready. While Rainbow Pool bent over her husband and tried to wash his body clean with a wetted section of her apron, Summer Wind tended to Laughing One. Behind them, Rainbow Pool's daughter was lashing together two long poles that would eventually become some form of carrier. Beautiful Star left White Bird's side and went to help the girl.

Feeling useless, White Bird slowly walked up to where her husband lay. Laughing One smiled as soon as he saw her, but she could see the worry in his face. As she knelt down and touched him gently on his chest, she realized that she did not know what to do next. Her husband was hurt, and all she had to offer him was a leather pouch half filled with water that had already become warm and bitter tasting from the day's march. It was Morning Land and Summer Wind who knew how to help an injured man. All White Bird could do was get in the way.

Summer Wind did not allow White Bird time to brood. The chief's wife tugged her adopted daughter's arm until White Bird turned to face her.

"My daughter, do not refuse to help," Summer Wind said. "Laughing One cannot move. He has tried to crawl but he cannot. Take these pouches ... take them ..." She handed two empty water pouches to White Bird and added, "Do not just stand there. Go to the river. Find a place where the water is clean."

"I will build a shelter," White Bird offered.

Summer Wind stared at her. "What use could a shelter be here, so long a walk from the river? We will bring him back to the village."

White Bird nodded, but she was not fully aware of what Summer Wind had said. Though she tried to listen, the words slipped by her. Everything seemed blurred inside her head.

"*Kai!* Hurry, girl," Summer Wind scolded. "He is not dead. You must help him get stronger."

White Bird took the water pouches Summer Wind had

handed her and walked back toward the side of the ravine. As she started down the path, she nearly collided with Morning Land, who had just reached the top of the slope. The stunned expression on White Bird's face immediately told her sister that something frightening had happened.

"Why do you cry like this?" Morning Land asked. "Has *Tua-arikii* been hurt?"

White Bird nodded.

"Where was he hurt?"

White Bird started to speak, but then shook her head. There were wet tear streaks around her eyes. Morning Land felt an urge to hug the girl, and said, "If he is still alive, we are the ones who will look after him." When White Bird continued to back away, Morning Land asked, "Why do you walk like this? Where are you going?"

White Bird held up the pouches she was carrying. "*Tua-arikii* needs water."

Slightly puzzled by the way White Bird was acting, Morning Land stepped off the path to clear the way for her sister. Neither woman said anything else. White Bird started to descend the slope, clutching her water pouches all the way down. When she reached the bottom of the valley, she finally gave in to the nausea in her stomach and vomited. Everything that happened to her afterward became even more hazy.

Left alone at the top of the slope, Morning Land turned hesitantly toward the other women. She did not know what she was expected to do. She had learned about treating wounds, but no one was going to ask her for help. Without White Bird to act as a go-between Morning Land was still an unwanted stranger.

Morning Land might have stood there indefinitely had Laughing One not smiled at her. That one friendly gesture amid the hostile indifference of the others affected Morning Land more than she would have believed possible. She had never disliked Laughing One, and had become quietly fond of him for the way he had treated her sister, but in that instant when he smiled, she felt something entirely new. Suddenly she really did care, and decided not to let the others push her aside.

As she came forward, Morning Land's heart was beating rapidly. She half expected to be spurned and sent away, but she crouched down beside her new husband with a surprising show of confidence. Before Laughing One could speak, Summer Wind scowled and said, "*Katto!* There is no place for you here."

Morning Land pretended not to hear the village matron. She

reached out and ran her hand gently over her husband's chest, feeling for breaks or swellings. Laughing One stared at her in amazement, especially when she began to touch his back and abdomen, but Summer Wind grabbed her hand before she could explore further.

"Why do you continue to bother him like this?" she hissed. "Be quiet and just sit."

Morning Land turned to stare at the chief's wife. "I will not sit quiet while my husband is still alive."

Summer Wind glowered back. For a moment, the two women seemed on the verge of fighting. Then Laughing One intervened.

"Leave her, Mother," he said. "She is a healer. She will try to cure me. Perhaps I will not get stronger. Perhaps no woman can make me strong again. Let her try."

Summer Wind's gaze shifted from Morning Land's face to that of her son and back again. *"Aya,"* she grumbled. "I will help the others. We will send you to the village, and you will stay there until you get strong."

As soon as Summer Wind stepped away, Morning Land had Laughing One roll onto his stomach and try to move his feet. While he did so, she checked his legs, buttocks, and back with her hands. There seemed to be nothing broken, only pulled or ruptured muscles. There was a good chance that he would be able to walk again. Grimly, she realized that he would have to be able to. Both sisters' lives with this tribe depended on that.

It was much later before Morning Land had time to think about anything beyond the immediate needs of her injured husband. Only at dusk, when the sisters tended their fire in a deserted section of the Great Village, did she begin to brood about the feelings she had kept hidden within herself. A deep stillness had settled over the village, for all of Wanderer's people were away, working in the killing ground. They would stay at the river valley for days, feasting on the Ehinas' softer parts while the women tried to cut and smoke as much meat as possible before the carcasses began to decay. Despite the efforts of nearly everyone in the tribe, there would be wastage this time. With so many kills, it would be impossible to make full use of everything.

The Tideland sisters had no part in either the butchering or the feasting. The only red meat they had seen all day had been in a basket that Summer Wind had brought up for them during the afternoon. The chief's wife had been gruff almost to the point of rudeness, but her actions had kept her son's family from going hungry. Now Morning Land began cooking some of the meat while White Bird cut and dried the rest.

Morning Land glanced away from the fire, letting her eyes explore among the maze of empty lodges. There was no movement to catch her attention. Staring intently, she listened for any small sounds that might be made by birds or animals moving about near the edge of the village, but all she could hear was the fluttering whisper and crackle of her own hearth fire. As she nibbled at a half-cooked piece of meat, she was reminded of the great forest she had once traveled through. In that perfect stillness between the heavy-barked trees, the sharp cracking of a dried branch had seemed heart-stopping in its loudness. Such a silence held the village now. The softly flickering fire in front of her was its warmest part.

Looking into the fire reminded Morning Land of how tired she was. Everything she had done that day was making itself felt in her aching muscles.

The trouble had begun as soon as they had tried to move their injured husband back to the village. Since none of the men could be spared from the butchering, the six women had had to take turns pulling Laughing One on the litter. They had worked in pairs, with Summer Wind and Rainbow Pool doing the bulk of it. Beautiful Star and Rainbow Pool's daughter had been too lightweight to make much of a team, and White Bird's pregnancy had kept the Tideland sisters from dragging their husband for very long. Laughing One had not helped matters by repeatedly insisting that he could walk. Twice he had crawled out of the litter and had tried to limp along while his two wives had braced him. Both times he had collapsed in agony after only a few steps and had had to be carried again. Finally Fighting Eagle had told him to stop pestering the women, and Laughing One had remained sullen but cooperative for the rest of the trip.

When they had reached the lodges, Fighting Eagle had upset everyone by resting only briefly and then going straight back to the butchering. He had said that if he could not cut up the animals he had killed, he could at least watch while others did so. His bemused wife and daughter had followed after him, protesting all the way. Summer Wind and Beautiful Star might have stayed longer, but Morning Land's habit of ignoring everything Summer Wind suggested made the village matron grow flustered and angry. This time it had been Beautiful Star who had prevented a fight by reminding Summer Wind that what her son had really needed was food. It had been a relief for everyone when the two had returned to the butchering.

For Morning Land, their departure had meant the beginning of her real work. With Laughing One lying on his stomach, she had massaged his injured muscles until they had felt loose again. Then she had covered her husband's lower back with a poultice of wet clay. Spliced willow saplings had served as back splints once she had strapped them on with rope cords and locked them firmly in place with another layer of wet clay. The bark stripped from the saplings had been used to make willow-bark tea. After several portions of this tea, Laughing One was now sleeping soundly inside their lodge. The back brace would keep him from twisting his injured muscles while he slept. In the morning, she would remove it, massage his muscles again, and give him time to exercise his legs. The treatment would continue until his strength improved.

The smell of cooking meat reminded Morning Land that their meal was almost ready. She smiled as she realized how hungry she was, and looked over to see if White Bird had finished with the rest of the meat. To her surprise, she found that her sister was still trying to make the drying racks. None of the meat had been hung up or even sliced. It still lay in a mound where Summer Wind had left it. With the impatience of someone who was overtired, Morning Land turned on her sister.

"*Shaa henaki,* lazy one. Have your hands stopped working? My stomach hurts and I want to eat. I will become thin, thin to death, waiting for you. Your husband is still alive and he, too, needs this meat. We are here to take care of him."

White Bird looked up, clearly bewildered. She fumbled with the knot she was doing and had to rework it twice before the cord finally held. The frame she had made was an awkward structure, not at all like her usual work. "My hands do not work well," she admitted. "I do not know what is making them shake and shake."

Morning Land would have said more, but tears were already starting to flow across White Bird's cheeks. The girl was obviously too tired to be of any further use.

"Your hands do not have the trembling sickness. You are only tired," Morning Land said softly. "The meat is finished. Take some for yourself and bring another piece to *Tua-arikii.* The sun is already late in this sky. I will tie the racks."

While White Bird shuffled past her to tend the cooking fire,

Morning Land went over to the half-completed drying racks and studied them. At first she thought she could fix the frames White Bird had already begun, but then she changed her mind, cut all the knots, and started over again. Her graceful hands had none of the problems with knot-tying that White Bird's stubby fingers had experienced. In a few moments, the drying racks began to take shape. While she worked, Morning Land could hear White Bird yawning and pushing at the ashes with her digging stick. Morning Land hoped that the girl would not burn herself.

When the drying racks were finished, Morning Land noticed White Bird crouching beside her again. This time she was carrying a cooked piece of meat on a flattened stone.

"I took this meat, which cooked well, and brought it for you to eat," White Bird said.

Morning Land smiled and took the food. It was not until she started to eat that she realized how desperately she wanted it. As she chewed, she noticed again how tired White Bird looked.

"There is much more meat," White Bird said. "You told me to give some to Tua-arikii, but he is sleeping. I could not wake him."

Morning Land nodded, swallowed, and said, "Let Tua-arikii sleep." She paused long enough to take a drink from her water pouch before adding, "Do not let Tua-arikii just lie by himself. Cold must be chased away when a man is hurt. Go and be with him."

White Bird knew that she was being pampered, but her body ached too much for her to object to it. Instead, she smiled gratefully and hurried inside the lodge.

Morning Land finished her meal slowly, enjoying the quiet. It would be a still night, without the usual rushing of wind amid summer leaves, for the western breezes had dropped off during the afternoon. In the red light of sunset, the trees around the camp were almost motionless. The silence had deepened, until even the dying sizzle of cooked meat sounded loud, and a squirrel running among leaves seemed as big as a deer. The family of crows that had alighted in a nearby tree were making all manner of bird noises, some harsh and guttural, others very soft and caressingly intimate. Sacred Dance had once told Morning Land that, while most birds only sang or called, the crows of the forest truly spoke to one another. Behind her, Morning Land could hear the more immediate sounds White Bird made as she settled for the night. Unlike the roosting crows, the Tideland girl was soon still, joining her heavy breathing with that of her husband.

After licking the grease from her fingers, Morning Land stood up and stretched until the tension in her back began to ease. She hesitated a moment, and then pulled off her apron. As her outstretched arms lifted the sweat-soaked hide over her head, Morning Land had the guilty feeling of doing something improper. She had kept her apron on dutifully each day, ever since White Bird had told her of the village customs. As she placed the apron on the ground beside her, she could not prevent herself from glancing around nervously to see if anyone had noticed. But there was no one watching her, only the unseeing lodge fronts. She was completely alone. Relief swept over her as she realized that for once no one could disapprove of what she did.

The sunset gave Morning Land's skin a reddish glow, emphasizing her slopes and curves with deep shadows. She noticed that the ugly bruises had begun to heal. Only discolored marks still showed. Her body was strong, strong and beautiful, even after men had tried to hurt it. She had not been humbled or shamed. Passing Shadow had left a scratch-shaped scar on her cheek and had carved his bands of dye on her upper arms, but even he could not harm the perfect smoothness of her lines. Morning Land gently touched her breasts and ran her hands lovingly along the soft areas of her stomach and hips. It was a pleasure she rarely allowed herself, but in the warmth of the quiet sunset, it seemed right. She knew she was beautiful. She had not seen a single woman in the four villages who could match her. Compared with her, they were all trail-worn females.

After a short while, Morning Land tired of her self-love, picked up her knife, and crouched down beside the pile of untended meat. In cutting the meat from the Ehina's hindquarters earlier that day, Summer Wind had used her stone chopper to unroll sections of muscle. These had been flattened and left in a pile inside the basket. Morning Land cut the sections lengthwise and divided them into thin slices. If she had had enough water, she might have washed the slices before hanging them, but it was late and there was no time. The meat would have a slightly bloody taste.

While she worked, the sunlight continued to fade around her until her fire was a thin line of brightness against the dark. Long, deep shadows filled in the spaces between the other lodges, making the hump-shaped roofs look like a series of small hills. Even the crows had stopped their noises. The branches of the tree they roosted in rose as black silhouettes against the brilliant twilight purple of the sky behind. Night had already reached the woods, a clear night that would have a full summer moon. Without a breeze, sounds carried far through the motionless trees, and nocturnal voices began to intrude over the earlier silence. From a hillside above the village, the soft fluttering call of an owl mingled with the faraway strumming of frogs. There was a great squealing and flapping of excited ducks that had settled on some lowland pond to the east. Then Morning Land heard a blowing snort that came from somewhere deep inside the encircling trees. She listened intently, staring out into the black shadows. The sound was not repeated.

The Tideland woman quickly began adding wood to the fire. She did not stop working until the blaze was well up and flickering warmly. Then she put her apron back on.

To steady her nerves, Morning Land started draping slices of meat across the rack frames. At first she let the thin meat slabs simply droop down over the cross poles. Then she decided that the flies would find it too easy to lay their eggs inside the meat folds. To prevent this, she propped the hanging ends of meat apart with small twigs so that the smoke could reach the meat's underside as well as its upper surface.

Morning Land tried hard to be efficient, but fear and tiredness were beginning to wear at her. Despite the reassurances she had given White Bird, Morning Land had suffered too much at the hands of the shaman to no longer fear him. For whole seasons she had seen how he had delighted in frightening and hurting his wives until they cowered from his kicks. Each time she felt the bruises on her neck, she remembered how he had clubbed her and her sister so that they could not even breathe. Such a man would never allow a wife of his to be taken away. He would use his bad medicine to make death come upon all of those who stole from him. When Dancing Rain had first told her of Passing Shadow's powers, Morning Land had only smiled. She could not believe that the ugly old shaman had the magic to drive a man senseless or make him weaker and weaker every day. Now she was no longer certain. The Ehina *had* turned and killed many men. Laughing One *had* been struck down. What if Laughing One's injuries were truly caused by the shaman whom Morning Land had angered? Perhaps strength would not come back to Laughing One. Perhaps other bad things would happen to her family.

While Morning Land was searching around for more splinters to open the meat with, she heard a wolf howl. Its voice rose and fell, seeming to go on and on, and fading out only to be followed by the barking yips of a second wolf and then by the answering howl of a third. Their wild chorus became louder until it filled the night. With the smell of death strong in the air, wolves from all across the neighboring savannah were moving in to feed on the dead Ehina in the river valley. The human fires would keep wolves away from some piles of butchered meat, but the packs would feed well wherever a trampled Ehina lay dead on the open ground or some rack of meat was partly concealed by shadows. These were not the timid forest wolves that hunted after deer and small game. These were the big plains hunters, scavenging, heavy-boned beasts that came in great numbers. Too stupid to have much fear of man or any other creature, they would not be driven away once they had tasted meat.

Morning Land had never known such beasts. Coyotes and small packs of forest wolves had sometimes hunted through the coastal hills, but their howls had never seemed so threatening. Nothing she had ever experienced before had prepared the Tideland woman for what she heard this night. The snarling began almost as soon as the packs closed in. Though the Great Village was a long walk south from the valley kill sites, the wolf yelps, snappings, and thick growls seemed much closer. Morning Land could hear the wolves feeding. The wet, slapping sounds of meat being ripped off bones, the crunching of teeth against gristle, the licking and slurping of mouths swallowing liquid entrails—all echoed back through the darkened trees like some wild feasting of hungry spirits. Morning Land had a sense of great skulking forms streaming through the black woods, ready to pounce on anything they found.

Morning Land began to feel abandoned and alone. Though she told herself that none of the wild beasts were as bad as Passing Shadow, she wondered what she would do if the wolves came her way. The deserted Great Village, with its old hides and bags of dried meat, might seem like an easy feeding ground, where wolves could lope undetected through the shadows between the lodges, tearing at hides or gnawing old food until they found something better. Morning Land's hearth offered them that. The meat on her drying racks was fresh and tempting.

Morning Land checked her fire. She had enough wood to keep the hearth burning until morning. All that was needed was someone to tend it. Smoothing her apron under her buttocks, Morning Land sat down again. She had brought Laughing One's spear out of the lodge, and now she set it on the ground beside her, within easy reach.

Morning Land stayed as she was, listening to the night and wondering if any wolves would suddenly appear in the shining, moonlit clearing around her lodge. If the packs were running about, they never came near the village, which remained quiet under the silver light and shadow of the moon. For a long while Morning Land doubted that it would ever be day again. The world had become muffled and empty, a place of rustling leaves and deep shadow.

By the time the sky began to grow pale with predawn light, Morning Land was shuddering. The wolves had finally stopped howling, and the chirping of birds were echoing from the tree-tops instead. Even the crows had begun their cawing talk, but at that moment Morning Land did not really care. After tossing the rest of the wood onto the fire, she got to her feet and stepped over to the lodge entrance.

Her sister and husband were still sleeping. Laughing One had been sprawled on his back all night, snoring softly. White Bird had both legs draped across her husband's. She was lying stomach up, with her hands resting on her rounded belly, and her head turned so that she faced Laughing One. In her contortions, she had managed to kick off the sleeping hides.

Morning Land stooped down next to the pair, intending only to cover them up again, but when she felt her sister's warm breath against her face, her mood changed. Pulling off her apron, she moved in beside White Bird. White Bird stirred but did not wake, and Laughing One only snorted in his sleep as Morning Land pulled the robe back over all three of them. Soothed by the warmth of the sleeping group, Morning Land finally slept.

A long while later, a solitary female figure passed the outer circle of lodges and entered the village. It was Summer Wind, bringing yet another basketful of meat for her injured son. Bloodstains along the bare sections of her legs, arms, and face remained as traces of the heavy butchering work that she had done for most of the night. Her walk was strained, and not made any easier by a lock of greased hair that brushed against her face with each step. Summer Wind promised herself that she would chop the lock off as soon as all the butchering was over. Valley women had good reason for keeping their hair short.

It was more than simple kindness that made Summer Wind cross the distance between the killing ground and the Great Village. She was worried about her son's family. The wolves had been very active during the night. They had ravaged two of the Ehina carcasses to the point where little more than bones remained, and had knocked down and ruined several drying racks in their search for more meat. All through the night, as she had listened to their howling and snarling, Summer Wind had kept thinking about Laughing One and the sisters. By morning she just had to know if they were safe. The meat she carried was only an excuse.

When she neared her son's lodge, Summer Wind slowed her pace and searched the area for signs of trouble. She did not like the silence. Being careful was a habit for the village matron. Though it looked as if no wild animals had been nosing about for food, she did not know what form of creature might suddenly come sweeping around the corner of an empty lodge. As she reached the edge of Laughing One's campsite, she noticed that the meat racks the sisters had set up were still untouched. Gaining confidence from this and the absence of animal tracks, she finally approached the hearth.

With disciplined thoroughness, Summer Wind studied the setup of the hearth and frowned disapprovingly. Valley women did things differently. There was far too much meat on the flimsy racks. A strong wind would collapse the whole thing. Worse still, both wives were asleep, having left the hearth fire to burn out on its own. When camping in a lonely place, one person should always sit up, watching for trouble. Concluding that the Tideland sisters were both slow-witted, Summer Wind set down her basket and peered into the lodge.

The intimacy of what she saw made Summer Wind draw back slightly. Three tanned bodies were cuddled together in a comfortable bundle, with Laughing One at the center. Draped over him like a second sleeping robe was White Bird, and snuggling up beside both of them was the second Tideland sister. Summer Wind's own tiredness made her impatient, but when she saw the contented expression on Morning Land's face, she hesitated. Morning Land did not look hardened now. With her eyes closed and the wary expression gone from her features, she seemed quite young, almost as much a girl as White Bird. For a brief moment, Summer Wind wondered about the woman. Then she sniffed and shook her head. These Tideland sisters were as lazy as buffalo cows.

Summer Wind went back to her basket and began slicing more meat.

This was the last time that Morning Land sat up all night watching for wolves. Though the packs returned to the valley, their numbers were never again as great, and they continued to avoid the village. By day, Morning Land was too busy with lodge tending and treating Laughing One to brood over much else. Perhaps something would happen to them sooner or later, but for the moment the two sisters followed a daily routine of walking around the empty village with Laughing One braced between them. At first he could only move his legs feebly while the sisters supported his entire weight, but gradually his walking became more confident. When he had exercised as much as he could, Morning Land would have him lie on his stomach while she massaged his back muscles. Unsure about which cure to use, Morning Land tried everything she had learned. She had White Bird bring her the leaves and bark of the red cedar so that she could boil them and make a lotion for rubbing onto Laughing One's muscles. When the lotion was used up, Morning Land pounded clumps of chickweed into a poultice, and left it clinging to Laughing One's back all through one hot afternoon. After that, she tried making a poultice from the leaves and bark of birch trees, but with less pleasing results. There were potions, too. Laughing One grimly drank concoctions made from boiled bearberry plants and various other leaves and roots. Sometimes he willingly swallowed the entire bowlful. On other nights he gagged, spat it all up again, and stared reproachfully at Morning Land. Whether any of these cures helped or not, one thing soon became obvious. The young hunter was growing stronger. Well fed, well rested, and well loved, Laughing One had a contented expression on his face as he limped around the village with his wives. Soon he only needed Morning Land to brace him while White Bird simply walked beside them for company.

After several days, the rest of the tribe returned to the village with their new hides and bundles of meat. They brought with them news of Passing Shadow's latest attempt to ruin the Tideland sisters.

It was Fighting Eagle who told his brother what had happened.

Laughing One was lying on his stomach in his lodge one afternoon, waiting for Morning Land to start her massage. His wife had smeared pine sugar over her palms and was holding her hands above the hearth coals so that the sugar could melt and soften. When she was finished, these same hot, sticky palms would be rubbed across Laughing One's back. Laughing One did not mind the pine sugar. It was better smelling than the bone grease or meat fat Morning Land sometimes used. What bothered him was the shock of her hot hands against his skin. He needed to brace himself for that, and he was doing so while he listened to White Bird ramble on about the problems of her pregnancy.

"Summer Wind keeps telling me that I am a child," White Bird complained. "Why is she always saying things like this to me? Even when this baby is born, I will still seem little to her. Why does Summer Wind worry so much? Does she think this baby will make me sick?"

Laughing One nodded. He had learned that most of what White Bird said did not require a reply. She only wanted someone to listen to her. White Bird was sitting beside his head, with her legs tucked in so that her buttocks rested on her feet. Even in the dull lodge light he could see the changes in her. Her breasts were larger and now sagged against the top of her abdomen. Her stomach itself seemed very round and large for a woman who had only been married for a few seasons.

"It is a strange thing, this growing," White Bird said. "When I was small, my chest was thin. I walked and played and never thought of these things that happen to a woman. All the while I played and ran, my breasts grew bigger and bigger. I never even felt them swelling. Then one day I woke and my breasts seemed very large. They were huge and suddenly hurting me. While I had slept and dreamed, I had grown into a woman. Now my breasts still just continue to grow. They are heavy with milk. My breasts will make a child strong."

White Bird tapped her protruding belly with obvious pride. "My stomach has also grown very large. My stomach is much too big. I wear myself out just walking. I ask myself, 'What is wrong? Why is my body so heavy? Why are my legs not strong enough?' This stomach is huge and stands out above my apron. It pushes away the hide."

Seeing where his eyes lingered, White Bird took Laughing

One's right hand and placed it against her belly. "Ehnn," she crooned. "This baby is moving around in my stomach. It will not lie still. It does not want to leave my stomach."

Laughing One did not hear the rest of it, for at that moment Morning Land's hands came down hot and sticky against his back. He winced and gasped as she began rubbing with a circular motion. Morning Land did not believe in warning her patient. It pleased her to see him jolt. Yet there was no sense of meanness in the way she worked at his hurt muscles. She applied a gentle pressure with the palms of her hands, and the soft rubbing made a warmth flow out through his whole body. Perhaps it was only wishfulness, but Laughing One thought he felt a certain love in those soothing hands.

His thoughts were interrupted when a shadow darkened the entrance of the lodge. He looked up and recognized the silhouette of his brother. Fighting Eagle was crouched in the entranceway, waiting for his eyes to adjust to the darkness before coming inside, and totally oblivious of the fact that he was blocking out the family's light by staying where he was. Like Laughing One, he wore a brace, but his was made from hides and lashings, and was wrapped around his chest like some form of body armor. The uncomfortable gear made him irritable, as did the constant fussing of his wife and daughter. Never a good patient, Fighting Eagle longed to be out on the open savannah again.

Though he grunted polite acknowledgment of Laughing One's greeting of "Ehnn, brother, you are here," Fighting Eagle's presence made the Tideland sisters uneasy. White Bird stopped talking and huddled over in an unsuccessful attempt to cover her naked breasts and stomach. Morning Land's soft humming faded into silence. She kept up her massage, but her palms pressed a little harder against Laughing One's back. Like White Bird, she did not enjoy being stared at by the hunting leader.

Fighting Eagle had reasons for centering his attention on Morning Land. She looked very beautiful, with her long dark hair forming spiral patterns across her bare shoulders, and her perfectly formed breasts swaying gently each time she moved her hands along Laughing One's back. Fighting Eagle wondered at the strange chance that had given such a woman to his youngest brother. She would have seemed much more at home in a chief's lodge.

Morning Land felt his stare and turned her head so that she could face him. Her eyes looked up at Fighting Eagle with a bold curiosity of her own. Both studied each other for a long moment. Then Fighting Eagle pointed to the pine sugar Morning Land was rubbing onto Laughing One's back.

"Old women have taught you skills," he said approvingly. "You have learned to do everything that a woman does." Thoughtfully, he added, "Since the hunt, there is much grease from Ehina in this camp. Grease and clay are good. Rainbow Pool rubs my back with grease and clay before a long hunt. Then the skin does not hurt from the sun."

Morning Land smiled quietly and lowered her gaze. Her hands continued to move in steady circles over Laughing One's skin.

"Ehnn, brother, there will be no long hunts for me," Laughing One said. "I will walk only a short distance from this lodge before I will sit down beside a tree. I will sit there and wait for strength.

"When there is pain, Morning Land rubs my back—all over. She places many strange things on my skin. I do not know my own smell any longer."

There was a long silence. Impatient with his wives' awkwardness, Laughing One asked, "When will we go from this village?"

"We have gathered too much meat to carry," Fighting Eagle replied. "We will stay close for some days until most of it is finished. Then the usefulness of this place will be over."

White Bird got to her feet and slipped out through the lodge entrance as soon as Fighting Eagle was no longer blocking it. As first wife, it was her duty to serve all visitors to her lodge.

Fighting Eagle sat down on the hide where White Bird had been kneeling a moment before. "Ehina hit you on your back and you will feel pain for a long time," he said conversationally. "Still, your heart shows no anger. You have stayed here for many nights with two women to cut away the hurting. My chest also keeps hurting, but I do not live alone either. When I came back from this hunt, I brought another wife to my hearth. Turtle Shell was married to Buffalo Tongue and did not want to just sit alone in an empty lodge. Now she works beside Rainbow Pool."

Laughing One jerked his head up in surprise. "Did you tell Rainbow Pool you were going to do this? What did she say? Was she angry?"

Fighting Eagle shrugged. "Rainbow Pool has no reason to be jealous of Turtle Shell. Turtle Shell and I were not lovers before and we are not making love now. Her husband is dead. She will wear ashes on her face for three moons. Even now, Rainbow Pool and Turtle Shell are sitting close to each other, talking together."

Laughing One could readily believe this. Rainbow Pool was a gentle wife who would have suffered a great many things without ever speaking against her husband. Her own father had been a man who had beaten his wives. Rainbow Pool had watched him turn on her mother again and again. She had expected little better from her own husband, but Fighting Eagle was never cruel. He could not insult or hurt his wife without also offending himself. Rainbow Pool loved him deeply, and their lodge had a calmness that many men envied.

Laughing One grinned. "Turtle Shell will not always wear ashes," he said. "Perhaps she will soon begin to think of you in other ways. Perhaps she will begin to come to you in the night."

Fighting Eagle looked offended. He did not want to talk about wives with his younger brother. "The shaman has killed the Great Hunt," he said. "Even as he sat beside his own fire, he sent out his bad medicine and broke the circle of villages. All of the men who died were from Wanderer's village and Resting Moon's village. None of Black Snake or Stand in Camp's hunters were hurt at all. Some say the shaman did this just to insult us because we took his wife away. Some say that only those who live with Black Snake or Stand in Camp will be truly safe."

Laughing One did not see Morning Land's face, but he did not need to. The way her fingers pressed into his back told him how she felt. White Bird, who was just re-entering the lodge, let out a frightened gasp.

"The shaman did not cause any of those deaths," Laughing One said. "His medicine is too weak."

"When so many men die at the same time, people always think of a shaman," Fighting Eagle replied. "Now the chiefs no longer trust each other. The Great Village has been torn to pieces like a rotten log. Wanderer's people will go on alone. If we meet Black Snake's people camping on the grasslands, we will just walk away again. We will not camp there with them. This is what Passing Shadow has done."

As Fighting Eagle spoke, White Bird crept next to Morning Land for comfort. The hunting leader looked up to see two frightened women facing him. Belatedly, White Bird offered him the bowl of ground meat she had brought, but he did not seem interested. He set it aside without touching the food.

"Do all of Black Snake's people think like this?" Laughing One asked.

"They are very cruel to Wanderer," Fighting Eagle replied. "Stand in Camp's people are also that way. They want to stay away from us."

"I will be happy to go back to our own village," Laughing One said. "Let Passing Shadow stay with those people who are truly afraid of him. His magic has only touched me lightly. After days of walking around this village with my wives, I am becoming strong again. If he cannot kill me or Morning Land, who he hates, why should anyone else fear him?"

Fighting Eagle shrugged. "You and your wives mean nothing to Black Snake's people. They are only thinking of the men who have died. They know the shaman is angry and grieves for his lost wife, and they expect him to take revenge."

Morning Land's tensed fingers were hurting Laughing One's back. He shook himself to loosen her grip, but she seemed unaware of what she was doing.

"This Passing Shadow has no sense at all," Laughing One grumbled. "All he does is make people want to kill each other."

"Passing Shadow has sent a message to our own village," Fighting Eagle continued. "He says that the people should go away and leave you and your wives to starve here alone. He says that if they do not do this, they will also starve. There are many who listen to what he says."

When he heard this, Laughing One struggled to get up. He pressed his palms against the earth of the lodge floor and pushed, nearly knocking Morning Land off balance as he did so. Seeing what he wanted, Morning Land shifted position and helped support him with her arms. In a moment, he was sitting cross-legged on the ground, facing his older brother.

"So the shaman's breath is still in my face," he said. "The old man could not kill me himself, so now he must frighten away the other villagers."

Again Fighting Eagle shrugged. "Many of the women in our own village have families who live with Black Snake and Stand in Camp's people. Those women are very angry. They want Wanderer to give the shaman's wife back to him."

Laughing One could feel the tensed silence of his wives. "This is Morning Land's lodge," he said. "She came here by herself. I did not bring her away or steal her, but she is staying with me now. She has cured my back with her medicine. If she had not helped me, I might have died here in this village. Now

I will not just sit and let her be given back to the shaman, who only wants to kill her. Even if all of the people in this village do go away and just leave us here to starve alone, I will not give up this woman who has helped me. I do not believe that the shaman is strong enough to kill with his magic, but if you and the others are afraid, then go ahead and leave us."

Fighting Eagle shook his head. "I am not going away. I hate the shaman for what he has done. He is not fit to live. I wish I had killed him on the day when we drove him from our village. My spear would have finished this thing. Instead, he is still talking and laughing about the trouble he has caused."

Laughing One tried to understand it all, but he found himself thinking about Morning Land instead. She was right next to him. He could feel her strong arms helping to brace his weight and her breasts brushing gently against his back each time she breathed. It did not seem possible that she could be taken from him.

"What will the others do?" he asked.

The stricken look on Laughing One's face made Fighting Eagle regret the tension he had brought to this lodge. On impulse, he reached out and grasped his young brother's hand. "No one is leaving this village now," he said. "Their angry talk is like the humming of stinging flies, but it will not cause this woman's death."

"Will the other men help us?" Laughing One repeated, unable to believe that men like Rock Breaker and Thunder in the Ground would ever allow their families to suffer because of him when it would be so much easier to give Morning Land back.

Fighting Eagle nodded. "We are not so weak that we cannot fight. We belong to one village and the shaman belongs to another. Does the shaman think we will not answer his insults? The next time we meet, I will kill him."

Laughing One could guess what Fighting Eagle would do. No one else but Fighting Eagle and Wanderer could ever have talked these superstitious hunters into defying the shaman. Laughing One knew he was lucky to be the chief's son. An ordinary hunter would have been forced to give up the woman long before this. Even now, he was not safe.

"I thought it was finished with this old shaman," Laughing One said, sighing. "I thought he would leave us alone."

Fighting Eagle got to his knees, grunting slightly as his chest brace dug against the skin of his stomach. "You are young and the shaman is old," Fighting Eagle said. "You have the woman and he does not. Of course you are the one who wants it to be finished."

CHAPTER SIXTEEN

Waiting Child

It was a circle of small fires tightly guarded against the night. There were no skins to lie on, no round shallow hollows scooped out of the dirt to rest in, no lodges to protect them from the heavy dew of the dawn, and no women to stir the coals of a hearth. This was a hunting camp, where men lay on the ground, listening to the sounds of the night and telling each other stories while the one on guard tended to the fires. The guard would change several times before dawn, but every man was expected to keep aware of the night creatures that moved about in the surrounding darkness.

"The roosting places of the Racciss are close by," Rock Breaker told the other men. "Fighting Eagle and I saw where they have slept." He pointed eastward. "Over the ridge there is a large tree that once had leaves and fruit before the Racciss began to come. Now it is broken. Every leaf it has is spotted with droppings, spotted white like the hide of a young fawn. Around its trunk, the ground is white like snow. You walk and walk, and still the ground is white. The Racciss are without number. There are enough to roast and eat for a full moon, enough for all the villages that have ever been."

"Before this night is finished we will bring you to them," Fighting Eagle confirmed.

None of the men in the camp doubted the truth of Rock Breaker's claim. All had seen the immense flocks of Racciss moving over the lakeland area that formed the tribe's new summer home. For many days, ever increasing numbers of birds had been seen swooping and gliding through the trees bordering the lake. A single Racciss flew so swiftly on its powerful wings that it might have passed unnoticed. But the Racciss never traveled singly. They came in incredible numbers that awed the people who watched them. Flying from east to west each morning, the flock spread out across the lake like a gray cloud. From a distance they resembled swirls of spinning dust. Though each bird flew past quickly high above the hunters' heads, so many birds passed that their droning wings made a numbing sound. It took most of the morning for the entire flock to pass, and by early afternoon they were coming back again, flying west to east this time. Women gathering in the marshes would look up when they first felt the shadow of the returning flock sweep across the ground. For a while, the women would stop talking and shake their heads at the wonder of these spiraling columns of flying birds. But when the Racciss kept coming in undiminished numbers, the women grew overwhelmed and returned to their work. The flapping sounds over their heads became like the rumbling of distant thunder.

Hunters were frustrated by the great flock. No spear or tossed stone could reach the birds at the height they flew. A man had to stand and watch more meat than he could eat in a lifetime soar past overhead. To ease their hunger, Wanderer had had his men spread out around the shallow lake and scout for signs of the birds' roosting place. After five days of searching, Fighting Eagle and Rock Breaker had found the site.

"You cannot kill Racciss during daylight," Rock Breaker said. "You can only watch as they turn back and forth over your head, never coming within reach of your sling. But when it is getting dark, they are soon hurrying for the trees. The Racciss will not sleep alone. At sunset their calling and calling comes from everywhere. They wander the sky with great speed, swooping and darting until the air roars with their numbers. Then they land mightily on all the big trees that grow close to one another. The Racciss have great need to be close. Even when they have landed and are sitting on the branches, they move closer and closer together until each tree's back bends with their weight. Even for a big tree it is dangerous when the Racciss roost. Branches break in the wind from their fluttering wings. Leaves and berries are pulled apart by their grabbing claws. The clicking of their beaks is louder than Ehina's squeal."

"The ways of the Racciss are strange to us," Wanderer admitted. "All my life I have been watching and watching for them. They are not like other birds. Their flocks must travel with great caution, for they are so many in number that they cannot calmly set down in one place. When they embrace the land with their great hunger, only its bones and ribs are left. It must be many summers before they come back to the same place. A hunter can grow old hoping to catch the Racciss."

Fighting Eagle gave a slight smile. "We will not grow old with waiting," he said. "Less than a day's travel to the east of here, the Racciss are resting. Rock Breaker and I will show you where. We have prepared our nets carefully and will leave from here before the sun rises again. On the way, you will see the signs that the Racciss have left. While we are walking, we will not talk. The Racciss are faster and stronger than most other birds, but they are not smarter. We will find them sleeping."

Wanderer nodded approval. "When you were a young man, I tried to teach you everything I knew. You wanted to learn about the forest and grasslands. Now you have taught these others how to understand the signs." Wanderer paused, momentarily overcome by his own unexpected show of fatherly pride. Then he quickly added, "We should rest. Soon we will be ready to walk toward the place where the sun rises."

With one man on guard, the rest of the hunters gradually settled into sleep. Alone in the darkness, Laughing One let his attention shift away from the other men. He had camped in the forest on many nights and was well used to feeling hard ground under his back, but he missed the company of his wives. Each time he shifted position, he thought of how White Bird would have brushed the sand clean with her hands and then spread out a skin over it. Her lodge pride was very strong. Even when she had nothing to offer, she greeted those who came to her hearth with a graceful bow of her head and with polite greetings spoken in that expressively soft voice of hers. The kind sparkle in her dark eyes was all the comfort Laughing One had ever needed. He missed it now, as he missed the soft feel of her body against his own and the burning love words she murmured in his ear.

His memories of Morning Land were slightly different. In his mind, she always seemed to be farther away, working somewhere near the edge of the camp. Morning Land had done well that summer. Impressed by the way she had cured her husband, many wives had grown curious enough to seek the Tideland woman's advice about methods of healing burns and wounds. Secretly honored by their interest, Morning Land had listened patiently to her neighbors' problems and had answered with a politeness that had surprised Laughing One. If the remedies she had spoken of had not always been helpful, at least none of them had caused any harm.

Laughing One had reason to be grateful that there were two women in his lodge. Within a moon, White Bird's child would

be born, and every villager knew that birth was a very dangerous time. Far too often sickness followed a new mother, taking
the strength from both her and her child. Laughing One grew
restless whenever he thought of White Bird straining to give
birth alone in the forest. It was something he would never wit-
ness, for no man could ever disturb a woman in such a place.
His one assurance lay in Morning Land. All the restraints that
held him back would not trouble her. She would be there in the
forest with her sister, using her secret cures and healing ways.
Though he did not understand Morning Land or the moods that
drove her, he knew that she loved White Bird. There was no one
else in all the village better able to help the young Tideland
mother.

While thinking about his wives, Laughing One fell asleep.
His next awareness was of Fighting Eagle shaking his shoulder.

Laughing One opened his eyes to find that it was still dark,
but that the darkness was filled with movement and murmuring
voices. Most of the other men were already awake. There was
a clicking of spears and a shuffle of nets as the hunters' tools
were taken up once more. By the time Laughing One had staggered to his feet, the others were preparing to leave.

Wanderer and two other men stayed in camp to douse the
fires. The rest left with Rock Breaker and Fighting Eagle. They
hurried off in single file through the forest undergrowth. Near
the end of the line, Laughing One struggled to keep pace, his
senses becoming more alert even as he walked.

The men moved quickly until they reached a small valley on
the other side of a steep ridge. There were fresh signs of the
Racciss all around them as they climbed down into that valley.
Thick bird droppings splattered parts of the earth, and at times
the ground felt spongy, giving Laughing One the unpleasant
feeling that he was stepping across soft mounds of bird droppings. The farther he walked, the greater the stink that rose up
from the densely littered ground. It became a choking, heavy
odor that made his eyes water and brought mucus to his throat.
Covering his nose with his free hand, Laughing One fought
back an urge to cough. He was grateful when the line of men
swung away in a different direction, where the Racciss had been
wider spread and the ground was slightly clearer.

As the sky was just beginning to grow light, the men entered
a place where the normal sounds of the forest seemed deadened.
The wind, which had been pulling at Laughing One's hair a moment before, was abruptly left behind. His breath felt heavy in

his lungs. There was a stifling warmth there, radiating down from the branches overhead and from the bushes on all sides—the warmth of living bodies. A liquid fluttering of feathered wings echoed through the trees. Laughing One could hear the creaking and tappings of overloaded branches and the softer, melodious cooing that rustled in the foliage like a sighing wind. Along with the ripping noise of leaves being torn aside, there was the clatter of countless droppings falling through the foliage. The men had found the hollow under the roost.

Almost wearily, Laughing One looked up into the trees overhead. The maze of branches rose in black silhouette against the growing blue light of the sky, and side by side, clinging to every branch in numberless rows, were the Racciss. There was an urgency now, for even this much daylight produced high squeaks of excitement from the awakening birds. Abrupt and short-lived, their "Cuh, Cuh" sounds flowed in quick succession, accompanied by a sideways scurrying of clawed feet. These small shuffling movements shook every branch like a strong breeze. The pink streak of dawn continued to descend through openings in the leaf canopy, awakening other birds farther down. Soon the entire roost would be scattering. All around, the air was filled with the rank, stirring, animal smell of the Racciss.

Acting on common impulse, the hunters began their killing. Some men threw their nets over the lower branches, relying on a single swoop to entangle as many birds as possible. Others leapt in among the waking Racciss and swung wildly with their spears, knocking down a great number of startled birds before they could break free. The hot stillness of a moment before was drowned out as quickly as if a sudden gale had blasted the forest. Bushes and trees writhed in the uprush of panicked birds. The Racciss shot straight up through the branches, their squealing cries accompanied by the booming flutter of countless wings. Some became entangled amid the upper leaves and pitched back down again to flounder on the ground with broken wings. Most of the flock escaped from their roosting place unharmed, sweeping back and forth over the treetops before lifting cleanly in high flight against the brightening sky. Soon they were a great cloud of birds once more, gray and slim-winged, with silvery white wing tips catching the tinted glow of the sunrise.

On the ground, running men and thrashing birds merged in utter confusion. While most of the scattered flock reformed and drifted slowly away toward the west, others could no longer lift their wings or dart upward in a wide climbing curve. Held down by the vicious threads of human nets, they could only struggle and call out as their fellow Racciss passed directly over them, rising higher and higher in great sweeping circles until they were lost in the sky. For the pinned birds who only followed the retreating flock with their eyes, the end came quickly. Suddenly frail and stiff-feathered, they did not resist the killing blows of the men. The nets vibrated with their wild bird plunges, but their straining wings were not strong enough to break through the hunters' ropes. Instead, they fell back quivering, knocked down with spears and sticks until their bones were crushed. Soon the jerking and the high, frightened calls were all silenced.

For the hunters, it was like being caught in a nightmare storm, with swirling bodies instead of clouds and falling feathers replacing rain. Laughing One felt frightened by the great power of the moving swarm. The Racciss that floundered in his net were weak, vulnerable things which he could kill, but the torrent that swept past overhead seemed indestructible. Winnowing, fluttering sounds came from all directions. The air was a whirlpool of wing-stroke gusts. Caught in the vortex, the hunters were spattered with green droppings and white feather tufts that clung to their sweating skin. When the last of the wounded Racciss lay dead at their feet, the men stared at each other in astonishment.

Before midmorning, they were walking back toward the village. Each man had made vine slings and carried a load of dead birds across his back. On the way, some hunters lingered, and soon the disciplined line of the early morning dissolved into isolated groups. Laughing One and Trusted Friend went on together, no longer mindful of the other men.

Laughing One would have liked to remain silent. He wanted to think about what they had seen, but Trusted Friend was in no mood for brooding. After a night away from his wife, his mind was preoccupied with lovemaking, and he shared his talk with the only one who would listen.

"The woman I have is full of pleasure," Trusted Friend began. "Her heart wants me and rarely refuses. I cannot find another like her—another with such skin and eyes. My heart is miserable when I am away from her. I mourn for what she has. She is someone who lies with me all the time. When we are in the lodge, she pulls off all the skins that are covering us and pushes her belly next to mine. I feel her warmth and the way she pulls at me. The wanting never dies in her. She needs a man

who is strong. If I refused, she would find someone else who
would give her what she needs. She does whatever she has to to
feed her wanting."

Laughing One said nothing. Listening to Trusted Friend brag
about his wife was one of the disadvantages of having him for
a hunting partner. On another day, Laughing One might have
shown more interest, but the men were carrying spears, nets,
weapons' pouches, and a heavy load of bird carcasses. The dead
Racciss were held in place by rawhide thongs tied to their feet,
and hung across the hunters' backs like bundles of hides. With
the sun growing steadily hotter, Laughing One guessed that he
would soon be sweating heavily. Already he itched from where
the Racciss's oval-shaped bodies jiggled against his skin, and
the birds' ticks were a special torment. Compared with this,
Trusted Friend's love stories formed only a mild annoyance. It
was easier just to let him talk.

"She has the food I want," Trusted Friend continued, "but for
her this is a food she can eat and eat and never be full of. We
do not just live in our lodge. We do not just lie there. We make
love. We make love that grows bigger and bigger. Sometimes it
is like fighting. There is shaking and trembling and shouting. I
know when I am pleasing Beautiful Star. Her voice makes me
feel her pleasure."

Laughing One nodded. He had heard Beautiful Star's whimpering moan. So had most of the rest of the tribe. Sounds carried well in the village, and a woman's excited gasps did not
leave much space for imagining.

Trusted Friend looked at his brother confidingly. "If I am not
there, her hunger makes her go senseless. She cannot live without it. Perhaps she will sneak off with someone else. I am not
jealous. I cannot accuse her all the time when I am gone. Even
if I were to beat her, she would not stop. She would still be
doing these things. When the hunt is a long one and I am far
away, other men in our village often come looking for her. Summer Wind has seen them. But Beautiful Star does not call to
these men. They only follow her."

Laughing One did not want to hear more of this. He had
scratched his hands badly while trying to net the birds, and they
were hurting him. He said nothing, hoping that his brother
would soon tire of talking to himself. Instead, Trusted Friend
only changed topics.

"Now that White Bird's stomach has grown big, it is good
that you have Morning Land in your lodge," Trusted Friend

said. "There is still a woman to be bothering with at night. While White Bird squeezes the milk from her breasts and feeds her child, you will have another woman to go to. That second wife of yours is very beautiful. My own heart would want her if you were not my brother."

The expression on Laughing One's face forced Trusted Friend to laugh apologetically. "No, even if I liked her too much, I would never lie with your Morning Land," he assured Laughing One. "Beautiful Star would refuse me then. She would yell and scratch. My wife grinds her teeth each time Morning Land is near."

Trusted Friend paused expectantly, but when Laughing One said nothing, he hurried on. "But you, brother, you can touch Morning Land and make love to her whenever you choose. You can look at her beautiful face and feel her soft skin. All you need for lovemaking is the strength in your back."

"Morning Land does not sleep with me," Laughing One said. "She refuses."

The look of astonishment in Trusted Friend's face worried Laughing One. "Ehnn!" Trusted Friend exclaimed. "Why are you saying these things? She must have been refusing you for a long time."

"Morning Land is not willing," Laughing One said. "I want to sleep with her, but she is afraid. She is a good wife in many other ways. She gathers food, tends the hearth, and does all the other things that a wife is expected to do. But when it comes to lovemaking, she feels no desire."

"The two of you are never alone inside your lodge," Trusted Friend reminded him. "Perhaps it is only the nearness of her sister that makes Morning Land shy. If you were away from White Bird, if you were alone in the bush, then she might behave differently."

Laughing One shook his head. "We two have been alone in the bush many times," he said. "Even then she stays at a distance. We have never made love to each other."

"This is bad!" Trusted Friend exclaimed. "You are no longer the boy she met in the woods. You are a man now, and she is the woman our people have given to you. She is a grown woman, and she must know what a man does. Passing Shadow did not treat her as a sister."

"Morning Land ran away from Passing Shadow," Laughing One said quietly. "She shamed him before everyone. He could not beat her into coming back and he could not kill her."

Trusted Friend thought for a moment. Then he said, "She is a beautiful young woman who did not want to sleep with an ugly old man. Brother, you are not old and ugly. You are her young husband and the husband of her sister. She cried when you were hurt. She cured you. Each day she does things to keep your lodge happy. She cannot truly dislike you."

Laughing One shrugged. "Morning Land has done all of that," he admitted, "but she is still afraid to make love. I want her, but I do not want her to grow angry with me the way she became angry with the shaman."

"A wife's work is not finished with until she warms her husband at night," Trusted Friend insisted. "She must lie down with him and make love. That is the way it has always been. Lovemaking is pleasurable and good. It is not something that makes a woman angry."

"Perhaps it is the shaman's bad magic that keeps her from wanting men," Laughing One suggested.

Trusted Friend laughed. "You say this woman does not really want you, but a woman's heart often changes. Even if she does not want you at first, she may grow to like you. Do not let her coldness defeat you. Sleep with her at night. Lie down beside her and touch her. Kindness can heal a woman's hurts. Perhaps the love in her is only sick. You may be the one to cure her."

Laughing One was confused. Trusted Friend's words seemed convincing. "Morning Land's ways have made me weary," he admitted.

"I think Morning Land is only slightly sick," Trusted Friend advised. "She does not hurt too much. If you want to cure her, I will help you."

Trusted Friend went on to describe the methods of arousing women that he had learned from Beautiful Star. For a while Laughing One listened, but his mind was preoccupied by a new idea. He began to wonder if Morning land was really only waiting for him to approach her.

> "Waiting child, dear waiting child,
> Moving from dream to dream
> In a world I can touch but never see.
> Child who lies under my hands,
> Can you hear the song I sing to you?
> I sit on the ground by my hearth.
> I try to work, but my hands are impatient,
> Impatient with waiting.

I sleep, I eat, I follow the path of my husband
Again and again,
But always my thoughts are wandering
Far, far away;
Seeking the place where my child's spirit dwells.
Whatever path I follow,
Whatever footprints lead me,
I still wait for you.
Come near, my child.
Leave your dreaming, look on daylight.
Grow strong and gentle.
I am your mother.
I will give you milk and shelter.
In laughter may your life begin with me,
And may your days be great in number."

White Bird sat at the entrance of her lodge and sang to her unborn child. The song was like many of the lullabies of her people, but the words were new. White Bird had made them up especially for this one child, and since her song was in the Tideland tongue, Morning Land was the only other person who knew what the words meant.

Despite the joyfulness of her song, White Bird struggled to keep from crying. Pregnancy was difficult enough when Laughing One and her sister were at the lodge, but when she was alone she was often horrified by the changes in her body. Looking down, she saw two fat, sleek breasts, so full that they seemed ready to give milk at any moment, and so heavy that they flopped listlessly against the hard roundness of her great belly. Her stomach was not soft or sensual any longer. It had grown larger than she could ever have believed possible and intruded into every aspect of her life. It dragged at her when she walked, forced her to sleep in a special position, and was always in the way when she squatted down to tend the hearth fire or grind up food. As a young girl, White Bird had always laughed at the fat-bellied mothers who had sat down as often as they could and had seemed to be always giving suck. She had been contemptuous of the way they had sometimes squeezed at their nipples until the milk had spurted out or the way they had flipped a loosely sagging breast to one side so that a child could clutch at it without getting in their way. Now White Bird was becoming just like those women. It was a difficult change in so young a wife, and it hurt her.

Another thing that troubled White Bird was her growing bitterness toward Morning Land. There was no reason for it. Her sister collected most of the food and the firewood, treated the hides, and weaved most of the baskets. White Bird had little to do aside from tending her hearth, and sometimes Morning Land even did that. She was more caring and gentle than she had ever been before, but that did not stop the spitefulness from rising in White Bird whenever she saw Morning Land run uphill or glide quickly through deep water. Everything that was graceful in her seemed to mock White Bird's clumsiness.

White Bird heard someone calling her name and looked up to see Summer Wind approaching the lodge. The Tideland girl clenched her teeth. It was too much to expect her to endure this woman's incessant advice on top of everything else. White Bird looked around quickly for some excuse to leave, but all of the other women were out gathering. There was nothing left for her to do but stay and listen.

"*Yi-quay-is*, daughter, be happy," Summer Wind called. "The men have done well. They have found the roost of the Racciss. Already some of them have come back. Soon all of us will be cooking again." Summer Wind looked up at the position of the morning sun and added, "You must cook the Racciss as I showed you. Otherwise they will burn and the meat will be ruined."

"I will do this, Mother," White Bird said wearily.

"Cooking things properly is important," Summer Wind continued. "If you have a daughter, she will not just grow up by herself. She will remember what she learns while she lives in your lodge. You are the one who will have to teach her to become a woman."

"I will do this, Mother," White Bird repeated.

With barely a pause for breath, Summer Wind added, "We will give you many Racciss to roast. When your belly is so big, you must refuse to take food that others prepare for you. That will make your stomach feel very bad. As you are now, you must eat and sleep here in your own lodge. Only then will your child be strong."

"I will do this, Mother." White Bird's voice was becoming very weak, but Summer Wind did not seem to notice. She went on giving advice about what a woman should and should not do when she was pregnant. Much of what Summer Wind said made no sense at all to White Bird, but the young girl had learned that the easiest way out was to say yes to everything. Finally, as a way of stopping the older woman's talk, White Bird placed her hands over her swollen abdomen and said, "I do not like the way my big stomach keeps hurting me. It has grown too much. It stands too far out. The child inside it must be truly huge. How can I ever give birth to such a big child? I will be torn apart."

Summer Wind shook her head disapprovingly. "This is bad talk," she hissed. "When the pain comes, you must just sit quietly and feel it. Do not be afraid. Be clever. Do not weave baskets or tie your hair. This will twist the birth cord inside you. Sit quietly and sleep often. Let your strength build inside you."

"I grow tired now, Mother," White Bird said impatiently. "I wish to rest."

White Bird did not really want to sleep, but Summer Wind's continuous advice bored her. It was easier to be lying belly up in the lodge than to listen to Summer Wind.

Summer Wind accepted the hint reluctantly, and slowly moved on to finish her other chores, but not before she had watched White Bird crawl into the lodge. The Tideland girl was forced to live with her lie. Once inside, she stretched out on her back and stared up at the grass roof. Soon the baby inside her started to kick, and White Bird rolled onto her side to relieve the pressure. "I am still young," she grumbled. "My husband touched me only a little. Why did he make me grow so much? Now I sleep like an old woman."

In a short while she was truly asleep.

When Laughing One looked into his lodge at midday, he saw his wife lying on her side with her legs curled up protectively under her big belly. He could not see her face, but he could hear the soft, contented sound of her breathing. For a while he crouched in the lodge entranceway and just watched her. Her apron had lifted, leaving her almost naked in the orangish glow of filtered sunlight. Her stomach, buttocks, and breasts all looked very rounded and full, as if her body had suddenly ripened. She was familiar to him now. Her scent, her voice, and her ways were as much a part of his daily life as the hearth fire or the hunting brotherhood.

White Bird and everything else about his home seemed more desirable after the night in the glade. He was tempted to crawl in beside her, but the dust and dirt of the Racciss still clung to his skin. Instead of entering his lodge, he left his bundle of Racciss beside the hearth and walked down toward the lake.

Laughing One had barely passed the circle of lodges when he came upon Rainbow Pool. She was walking up the pathway from the lake and was carrying what looked like a basketful of gray mud. There were also patches of splattered mud on her arms and legs, as if she had been deliberately burrowing in the lake bottom. When she got closer, Laughing One realized that the basket was filled with Racciss that had been bundled in lake clay. Each bird had been completely coated, so that all of its feathers had become embedded in the clay. As soon as she returned to her own lodge, Rainbow Pool would place these gray bundles in the hot coals of her hearth fire and let the birds bake that way.

Rainbow Pool bowed her head courteously and asked, "Where are you going, young brother?"

"I am going to bathe," Laughing One replied, responding in the expected way.

Rainbow Pool smiled and shook her head. "The sun is not low in the morning sky any longer, young brother. The women have all left the village and gone to the lake before you. Each wife has gone out collecting bottom clay for her cooking. When they return home with what they have gathered, the water will be brown. This is no place for a man to bathe."

Rainbow Pool nodded again and hurried on, anxious to get her own feast ready.

Laughing One stood in the pathway, watching her, until she disappeared behind one of the lodges. He could hear the splashing and shouting of the women who were still down by the shore, and he guessed what it would be like there. He would find no pleasure in swimming beside those women. Sometimes light and playful, their joking could quickly turn to crude teasing if a lone man was about. A chief or hunting leader would be gently persuaded that he was interfering with their work, but an unimportant one like Laughing One would be shown no consideration whatsoever. Behind the broad smiles and sly glances was a kind of humor that often became cruel. As the loud, frantic teasing grew into high laughter and open mockery, no amount of blustering could hide the shame a man felt. The women's tormenting would persist until the hunter fled the area. Only a fool risked women's anger.

After a moment, Laughing One remembered the cove his wives often swam in. It lay to the north of the village, just beyond a group of trees that was barely visible from where he stood. At this time of day, its shore would be shaded by the shadows of surrounding trees. Convinced that no women would annoy him there, Laughing One stepped off the main path and began following a hunting trail that led north.

For a while, all he could hear as he walked were the shouts of the women behind him, but as he stepped down through the trees, those noises dropped away. The world seemed softer when he was surrounded by the cool rustle of summer leaves. Birds trilled at him from the branches overhead. Squirrels hopped across piles of dead leaves or scurried up the sides of tree trunks. When he came near the cove, a light lake breeze began to shift through the branches. There he heard a different sound, unlike the screaming laughter of the village women or the quiet bird trills of the forest. It was the soft-voiced chant of a Tidelander. Morning Land was already at the cove.

Laughing One hesitated at the edge of the trees, with the sun casting trembling leaf shadows around him. Out in the sunlight beyond those trees, where the water of the cove was a bright blue, Morning Land waded through the shallows. She was singing quietly to herself as she dipped her hands below the surface and splashed water across her chest. Laughing One did not call out to her immediately, for Trusted Friend's words had stayed with him. Instead, he walked silently to the place where Morning Land had left her apron and sat down.

He fingered the apron speculatively. It was no different from the type of hide worn by White Bird or any other woman of the tribe, but somehow the idea of its belonging to Morning Land excited him. A short while before, it had been near her skin, touching her in places he had never felt. Even now he could catch her scent on the hide as he brought his face close to it.

Somewhat guiltily, Laughing One let go of the apron and looked up. How the men would laugh to see him sitting there touching a woman's apron! Keeping still, he glanced quickly about, but there was no one near other than the beautifully formed Morning Land. Still unaware of him, she had bent down to soak her hair, and he could see the upper parts of her buttocks rising teasingly above the water. There was a swirl of small ripples where the tip of each long tress of her hair touched the surface. For a time, Morning Land stayed in this position, swinging her hair back and forth while she wet it with her hands. Partially hidden from view, Laughing One seemed to have found a favored watching place. He was content to remain motionless until a shift in the wind made him aware of his own

foul scent. The Racciss had covered enough of him with their
feathers and droppings to make him no more pleasant to be near
than the quilled porcupine. In any event, he had come to bathe,
not stalk his wife like a deer.

Resolved to forget Trusted Friend's talk, Laughing One got
up and walked loudly down to the edge of the water. The splash
of his feet startled Morning Land like a crack of thunder. She
immediately straightened and lifted her head high in sudden
alarm. When she saw who it was, the tension left her with a
loud sigh.

"*Shaa henaki!*" Morning Land whispered to herself. "You
make too little noise, husband. I taste fear inside my mouth!"

In a louder voice, she called, "*Tua-arikii!* I did not know you
were here."

"We killed many Racciss this day," Laughing One called
back, splashing water across his back and stomach. "We walked
hard to find them, and they dirtied our bodies with all their
droppings."

The stillness that had settled over the cove was broken by
vigorous splashing as Laughing One scraped and rubbed to rid
his arms and chest of bird droppings. It was difficult cleaning,
for the Racciss droppings had dried into a crackling film that
covered much of his skin. While he worked, he told Morning
Land about the hunters' encounter with the great flock. His
story was punctuated by heavy grunts as he scrubbed himself,
and the resulting talk sounded comical enough to bring a smile
to Morning Land's face.

Forgetting her momentary fear, she quietly waded closer. It
was obvious that Laughing One would never be able to chip all
of the droppings from his back by himself. She moved to help
him without hesitation. The hands that had once rubbed life into
Laughing One's back muscles raced over his shoulders, making
high squeaking sounds as they flicked and splashed the bird
dung away from his skin. For a while Laughing One continued
his story, and Morning Land became caught up in the wonder of
what the men had seen.

"*Atoshe!*" she exclaimed. "How can there be such birds?
They have hit you with their droppings many many times. Did
you kill them all? Did you leave only a few?"

"The Racciss have children without number," Laughing One
replied. "They are never finished having children. We could
have killed and killed and never stopped, there were so many.

What we took was unimportant to the Racciss. They just continue to live."

"Our husband hunts well," Morning Land said pleasantly. "We are happy to live in *Tua-arikii*'s lodge."

Laughing One peered up at Morning Land in round-eyed amazement. It was not often that she called him husband or used the name *Tua-arikii*. Her voice was soft and soothing, much like White Bird's but also excitingly different.

Unaware that Laughing One's mood had changed, Morning Land continued to compliment him.

"After our people died, White Bird and I just continued to live," she told Laughing One. "It was as if a great sickness had entered our hearts. We felt only pain. For many moons I felt little else. The shaman was very bad. I grew in strength many times when I lived with him, but he killed it all. Now I have left that bad one behind me. My heart has been happy in your lodge. As I am today, my sister and my husband have made me strong again."

While she spoke to him, Laughing One let his eyes explore the smooth, softly shaped form of this graceful second wife. At that moment, Trusted Friend's words seemed to carry great strength.

"I am still taking care of White Bird after all these seasons," Morning Land continued. "It seems almost as if I had given birth to her. She has been with me that long. Ehnn, I truly love this little sister."

Morning Land shifted her weight slightly and suddenly found Laughing One's arms embracing her.

"Shiiwe!" she exclaimed.

Deftly, Laughing One moved her close to him and began to fondle her. His touch was meant to be kindly, encouraging, but her body stiffened into hard muscles under his hands. When her breasts flattened against his chest, she stretched out her neck as if trying to lift her face away from him. After a pause, she turned her face aside and twisted her body in an effort to break free. Her every movement gave the impression of intense nervousness. Laughing One tightened his hold on her instinctively, not even aware that his fingers were digging into the flesh of her upper arms.

Feeling trapped, Morning Land straightened and pushed Laughing One with her hands, as if she could simply shove him out of her way. He was heavier and stronger. His tight grip gave her little room to move. For a moment, the two were frozen motionless, standing in a shallow part of the cove with the water dripping from them. Then Morning Land's nerves reached a breaking point. In one swift movement, she drove her right knee hard against Laughing One's groin. Before he became aware of what she was doing, he felt a sharp, splintering pain.

Morning Land should have evaded him easily after that, leaping nimbly aside and speeding away through the water, but Laughing One did not let go. Instead, he blundered forward awkwardly, tumbling head on into the water. Still caught in his grip, Morning Land splashed into the cove beside him.

Fear made her almost senseless. This all seemed too close to her nightmare struggle with the shaman. She had sense enough to lift her head high and keep her face above the surface, but there were tears filling her eyes. She lay rigidly on her back, her mouth hanging open. A sickening fear swept through her.

Laughing One felt her body become completely motionless under him and stopped moving as well. He had held on out of sheer pain, simply blundering in his resistence to her quick movements. Now he stared down numbly at the Tideland woman, shocked by the expression of fear in her blanched, tense face. Her mouth was open and gasping, as if each breath came with greater effort than the one before it. The thought that he might have hurt her made him quickly release his grip. He struggled to his feet, confused. When Morning Land remained as she was, he reached down to help her.

The Tideland woman wanted no part of him. She scrambled back with a wild sob, swirling about in the shallow water. When she reached a place where it was deep enough, she kicked out and sped away like a leaping seal. The smooth pull of her arm and leg muscles made Morning Land's escape an easy one. Soon the only sounds that reached her were her own strong breathing and the energetic beating of her heart. When she finally paused, she was so far distant from shore that the cove seemed like a small indentation in the green line of treetops.

Alone in deep water, an outraged Morning Land screamed angry curses at her husband. Terror had given way to fury. Laughing One had attacked her! After she had kept his lodge for him and healed his wounds and begun to trust her life again, he had ruined it all in one ugly moment. She hated him now. She wished that Passing Shadow had killed him. To calm her indignation, she swam back and forth in aimless circles.

On the shore of the cove, Laughing One heard his wife cursing him. He could barely see her in the distance and the language she spoke was still strange to him, but he guessed her meaning well enough. He walked about confusedly for a short time and ended up slumping onto the same rock that he had sat on awhile before. Morning Land's apron still lay beside him, but he no longer felt any curiosity about it. Everything had turned out wrong.

In truth, Laughing One was not entirely sure what had happened. He had tried to embrace and fondle Morning Land just as he had often fondled his other wife. White Bird had always giggled and snuggled against him when he had held her. Morning Land had kicked him and shoved him into the lake. Now she was swimming far away and shouting curses at him. None of it made sense. Though he had behaved as Trusted Friend had told him to, he had not cured Morning Land's fear. It had only grown worse.

Laughing One could not understand the guilt that he felt. Perhaps it was because Morning Land had been speaking gently to him for the first time; perhaps it was because White Bird was sleeping trustingly back at their lodge, already huge with their unborn child; or perhaps it was simply that Morning Land no longer trusted him. Whatever the reason, Laughing One knew that he had not behaved like the brave young hunter of his imaginings. For an instant in this cove he had felt the rage of Passing Shadow. After Morning Land had kicked him, he had wanted to hurt her. Only their tumble into the water had prevented him from striking her. It was bad medicine, and the young hunter did not like the way it tasted.

Morning Land was also beginning to doubt what had happened. Swimming in random circles soon tired her, and cold water was a poor place for anger. When the shock of being attacked left her, she stopped cursing long enough to consider.

Laughing One had not hit her. He had not held her down in the water after she had fallen. If his intention had been to attack her, it had been short-lived. But had he attacked her at all? The more she thought about it, the less certain she was. She had kicked him and they had both fallen into the water. She had not given him a chance to talk or tell her what he wanted.

The cold of the deep lake was beginning to force her to a decision. Already her arms and legs were starting to tremble between strokes. She would not be able to stay out much longer.

Without voicing the thought, Morning Land turned and began moving back toward the shore.

She swam slowly, trying to consider what she should do, and realizing that there was no other way. Her sister's lodge was the only home she had left, and Laughing One was White Bird's husband. He was also Morning Land's husband. That thought had not really troubled her until this moment. She knew that, by his people's customs, he could make love to her when and where he wished. He had never done so before, and she had hopefully assumed that he would continue to treat her as a sister. Now that hope was gone. She remembered enough of their brief struggle to know that he had wanted her.

Perhaps he would continue to bother her. At night in the lodge he might touch her again. How would she stop him then? White Bird would be too hurt and confused to help. The other villagers would either show no interest or else be glad that Morning Land was finally being forced to submit. There could be no running away this time.

When Morning Land was close enough to actually see Laughing One again, much of her fear left her. The young hunter was sitting high up on the bank, pushing stones with his feet and looking humiliated. He must have heard her approaching, but he kept his eyes lowered like a sulking boy. Morning Land was glad that he looked unhappy. She hoped she had hurt him when she had kicked him. She wanted him to feel as wretched as she did.

As Morning Land drew nearer to the shore, she began reaching down with her toes to feel for the bottom. Once she had found a spot shallow enough for her to stand comfortably, she stopped swimming and rested. Laughing One had still not looked up.

Morning Land no longer felt threatened. Everything around her was calm and smooth, and it was obvious that Laughing One was not going to attack her. She felt foolish standing in neck-deep water while he only sat there.

"*Shaa henaki!*" she exclaimed. "I am cold. I want to climb out of this water and sit in the sun." Her voice was much higher than she had intended it to be, but at least one of them had spoken.

She waited, and Laughing One slowly lifted his head to look at her. The hurt, worried expression on his face made her strangely pleased.

"I want to climb out to where it is warm," Morning Land repeated. "Do you hear what I am saying?" This time her voice was more demanding.

Laughing One nodded. He tried to speak, found that he could not, and coughed instead. With deliberate slowness, Morning Land moved closer into shore, still keeping her whole body submerged even though she had to crouch down to do so.

"Come out," Laughing One finally managed. "I am sitting alone. There is no one here who will hurt you."

Morning Land did not answer. Instead, she studied Laughing One coldly, enjoying his awkwardness. She was still upset enough to want to hurt him.

Laughing One was having difficulty meeting her stare. He muttered something that she could not understand. Morning Land edged in closer. She felt stronger than Laughing One now, and that made her bolder. When she was near the shore, she pointed imperiously at the hide apron that lay near Laughing One's feet.

"*Kai-tama* (waist skirt)," she said.

Though he had touched her apron eagerly enough before, the sense of expected behavior had come back to Laughing One with sudden force. A man did not willingly handle a woman's things. Instead of giving the apron to Morning Land, the young hunter backed away, allowing her to come out of the water to retrieve it.

Shivering, Morning Land stepped up onto the edge of the shore. She hurried forward, quickly grabbed her apron, and darted behind a screening bush, as if afraid that Laughing One would attack her again.

Until this moment, Laughing One's face had shown bewilderment, but when Morning Land snatched her apron from the sand and sprang away, his expression changed. He looked as if she had hit him. Suddenly Morning Land realized that he understood what she was trying to do. Forgetting her pretense, she stepped out into the open and pulled on her apron. The hide stuck to her wet skin in a way that was uncomfortable, but she ignored it.

"*Shiiwe*, this is a bad thing. You tried to hurt me," she accused. "Your heart rose up angrily."

"*Auuru* (No)!" Laughing One shook his head emphatically. "I did not grab your arm to hit you. I did not want to hurt you."

"My heart is miserable," Morning Land complained. "You followed me and waited for me here. You grabbed my arms and would have hurt me."

"You are too afraid," Laughing One retorted. "You kicked me and made me fall."

Morning Land considered this for a moment. She was still wary, but she was finding it hard to pretend anger. "I was afraid," she admitted.

"I am not Passing Shadow. I will not beat you to death. I do not hit you until your flesh swells. I would be kind to you, but you refuse me. You are not like *Yi-quay-is*." Laughing One spoke slowly. For the first time he realized just how great the difference between the sisters really was.

Morning Land studied his face, but her gaze was not hostile anymore. She was used to a world where what a man did to his wife was rarely questioned. "*Atoshe*, I am not like *Yi-quay-is*," she agreed.

Laughing One sat down again while she stepped cautiously across the shore sand. She could have escaped quite easily, for she knew that he would not try to stop her, but her body felt cold and tired and there was no purpose in running away. It was better to face Laughing One there in the cove rather than back at the lodge, where White Bird would be listening.

"A man is someone who has great strength," she said softly. "When he sees a woman and wants her, he does not just keep his thoughts in his own heart. He does what he wishes. For a woman it is different. If she feels hurt and angry, it does not matter. He will still be sleeping with her. He will still be wanting her."

Laughing One stared at her, his face flushed with embarrassment. "When you marry, a husband asks you for things," he said. "He asks you to help him gather food and make fires, and he asks you to sleep with him. A husband does not just leave a woman by herself."

Morning Land had expected this. For more than a moon she had dreaded such a moment and wondered what she would say. Now that it had come, she could not think of anything. She just stood there, shivering in her wet apron. The young man who was her husband wanted something from her she could not give, and there were no words that would take away his disappointment.

Laughing One looked up into Morning Land's calm, expressionless face and shook his head. "Why do you talk like this?" he asked. "Has sickness entered your chest? Does desire upset your mind? Are you afraid of having children?"

Morning Land bowed her head slightly, keeping her eyes focused on the ground. Her dark hair dangled in wet clumps on either side of her face. She reached up and stroked her hair tentatively, trying to smooth it with her fingers. The action reminded her of something.

"My heart has died," she said. "A bad man, a man full of sickness, slept with me all the time. His sickness hurt what was inside me. This is why I fear men. It is something in my heart."

Laughing One struggled with the idea. "You are not happy. You want to walk with the women and not sleep with a man. But you live in my lodge. When you are near, my leg is trembling. Your beauty makes my heart rise up."

Morning Land continued to stroke her hair with her fingers. "Am I the only wife you have?" she asked. "Am I the only woman you have left in your lodge?"

"*Yi-quay-is* will give birth very soon," Laughing One explained. "She spends each day doing the things she has to do to make her body ready. After the time of birth has passed, she will sleep alone. She will not need her husband to make love to her then. She will just live in my lodge, waiting for her child to grow strong. Even if she wants a man, she will only sit. That is the way of things when a child is born."

Morning Land slumped down onto the sand beside Laughing One. She was tired and the sun felt good on her skin. "Fear brought me to your lodge," she said. "My fear of the shaman chased me away from his village. That same fear grabs me now. It is a knife that cuts at me when I lie and try to sleep. It pushes against me when I dream. Only when this fear is gone will I want you to touch me. Only when it has been chased away will we start to live with each other truly."

"What use does this fear have?" Laughing One asked. "The things fear brings are not good. Fear makes your body feel sick. What can chase fear away?"

Morning Land shook her head. "I am afraid even of dreaming. My dreams often trick me, making me cry out in pain. If a person is cut, you put medicine on it and make the pain end. What medicine can you give to kill a dream? Sometimes I am so afraid that I will lie awake and not let myself sleep. Sometimes I shake and cry. I do not know what is making this fear so strong."

"You married an old man who was also a bad shaman," Laughing One said. "You have taken yourself from his village and now you are in my lodge. No man there will hold your legs and struggle against you. No man will hurt you now. You have stayed only a little while, and already you are stronger. If you continue to stay, you will get stronger and stronger."

Morning Land looked at him quizzically. "The fear that makes my mouth taste bad—the fear that makes me cry when men touch me—it may be many seasons before that has gone."

"I still stay beside you and watch you," Laughing One insisted. "I do not know how to cure people and make them strong, but I will wait with you. If you cry when men touch you, I will not rub my hands against you. I will only sit. I will not bother you again."

Morning Land crouched down closer to Laughing One. "Many days will pass," she warned him. "You will have two women in your lodge and neither will want you. It will make you angry. It will seem like you did not truly marry us."

Laughing One looked up at her in surprise, then shook his head. "I will do this thing. I will do what I have to do."

Morning Land was startled by this. She was beginning to think that her young hunter was not quite as ordinary as he seemed. "I will not leave you," she promised. "I will not have any lovers. One day this fear will leave me. Then when my husband wants to lie with me I will no longer refuse. We will sleep together, one night and then another. In the morning, I will get up and sit beside you."

"Until then, we will just continue to live," Laughing One concluded.

Late afternoon brought a feeling of peace to Wanderer's village. A cooling wind from out of the west pushed its way across the lake, rustling through the treetops and blowing the smoke of the cookfires away from the lodges. The smell of cooking birds was provokingly sweet in the air, making it difficult to think about anything other than eating. Women tried to ignore the growling in their bellies by talking excitedly to one another, but their children were less restrained. Most had stopped playing and were gathered hungrily around the hearths, eyeing the baking bundles and constantly interfering with their mothers' work. Soon the women would use sticks to pull the bundles out of the hot coals and crack open the burnt clay. The birds' feathers, which had been embedded in the clay, would be pulled away with it, leaving the Racciss cooked and plucked.

White Bird stirred her fire along with the other women. Like them, she had many carefully bundled Racciss cooking

amid the coals of her hearth, but she did not even pretend to
be happy about it. Her expression was tired, and every so often she would let out a heavy sigh, as if in protest against her
endless pregnancy. In earlier seasons she would have been
hunched over, with her arms resting across her knees, but her
big swollen belly made that impossible. Instead, she was often
forced to place her hands on the ground behind her as a brace
and lean back to take the pressure off her abdomen. She hated
being like this. In her mind, she was still a slender, long-
haired girl.

White Bird's mood had been made uglier by the prolonged
absence of her husband and her sister. She had awoken to find
the lodge empty. Before she had been able to look for the others, Summer Wind had arrived with a basketful of bundled
Racciss. Since the chief's wife had already done most of her
work for her, White Bird had had no choice but to stay and listen to the older woman's advice. Now it was getting late. Summer Wind had gone back to tend her own hearth, the sun was
nearing the trees, the birds were cooked, and there was still no
trace of her husband or her sister. White Bird was finding it difficult to pretend that she was not worried.

The smoke from the hearth kept away the biting insects, but
the breeze blew up sparks from the fire that could sting a woman's flesh just as well. One spark landed delicately on the brown
hide of White Bird's apron. Leaning close, she breathed on it
until the glow had died and the darkened ash rolled emptily
onto the ground. When White Bird looked up again, Morning
Land and Laughing One were approaching the lodge.

Though Morning Land stayed in place a few paces behind
Laughing One, White Bird could see immediately that something had changed between the two. Morning Land's nervous
ways had softened since the start of her stay in her sister's
lodge, but she had never seemed as confiding and calm as she
did on this night. She was watching the young hunter with an
interest she had never shown before. Without understanding
why, White Bird found herself becoming quietly furious.

Morning Land's walk was lithe and graceful as always, but
Laughing One moved stiffly. He seemed very self-conscious.
When he approached White Bird, the apologetic look on his
face did nothing to calm her mood.

"*Shaa henaki,*" White Bird grumbled. "Am I the only one
who will eat this food this day? Am I not to give any of it

away? My belly is too big already. I cannot just eat and eat and eat all by myself. I do not want to sit here eating alone."

"With my own eyes I see that you have meat," Morning Land said pleasantly. "We will soon put it inside our mouths. Already I seem to taste it."

Ignoring her sister, White Bird turned to Laughing One. "You have made me weary with waiting, husband. Have I taken something from you that you treat me this way?"

Laughing One had no desire for further quarrels. "All this cooking has finished the wood we have," he said quietly. "I must get up and find more."

Before White Bird could protest further, her husband had hurried away again. Frustrated and puzzled, the young wife stared balefully at Morning Land as the older sister crouched down lazily beside their hearth.

"You will let our husband just walk away without helping him?" White Bird demanded. "Does he not still live among us? Has he not been working hard with all this hunting?"

"A sickness has not entered his chest," Morning Land answered. "I have already helped him find the wood. It is only a small way off."

"*Shiiwe!* I see that I no longer have a sister to help me with these chores," White Bird said. "Now Summer Wind has started doing things for me. Perhaps I should have brought her into my lodge."

Surprised by this reply, Morning Land asked, "Do you smell rotten meat over here that you stare at me this way, sister? You sit angry by your hearth. Always you are angry. Day after day you cry until your tears drive away the rest of us. When will you be finished with this anger?"

White Bird grunted. It was meant to show contempt, but it seemed comical. Valley women like Summer Wind grunted from their bellies and could make a noise that was almost masculine in its deepness, but Tideland voices were too light for this. White Bird's grunt sounded more like a squeal, and Morning Land had to struggle to keep from laughing.

"The things I worry about are not important to you at all," White Bird said. "You have no trouble refusing them."

Morning Land responded to her sister's testiness by saying nothing. She was still cold from all the time she had spent in the lake, and the heat of the hearth fire felt good against her skin. For the moment she was content to just sit there, using her hands to wring out the water from her hair and apron.

"I have learned not to run away, but I am still afraid of what will happen to me," White Bird said. "I am afraid of this big belly. When I see how the children play and how their mothers play with them, I try to think what it will be like to be a mother. But I do not want this thing to happen. I want to just get up and leave. I want to run away from this big belly."

Morning Land started, surprised to hear White Bird using the Tideland tongue again.

"*Tua-arikii* has made me the fat one of his two wives," White Bird complained. "My stomach stands in one spot while my legs stand in another. My stomach will lie down before me. No one ever taught me about men and how they would make my stomach grow."

Morning Land sighed. She was becoming irritated with all of White Bird's complaints about her pregnancy. The girl was always talking on and on about it. "You are too easily angered," she grumbled. "Our mother went on working day after day when her stomach was big with you. She did not lie in her lodge and sleep. Not her! I went with her. When it was her time to give birth, I was the only one there. I saw how you were born. That was the kind of woman our mother was. She said that working gave her strength and helped the milk to grow in her breast. She slept only at night.

"All this resting is what makes your belly grow so big. You sit and sit and just grow fatter. To be strong enough, you must also work."

Surprised and bewildered by her sister's verbal attack, White Bird almost cried out. She flushed deeply and might have started crying if Laughing One had not suddenly returned with an armload of wood. Normally it was considered beneath a hunter to gather wood for his own hearth when there were women to do the work for him, but if a man's wife was heavily pregnant, such behavior would be grudgingly tolerated. Even so, White Bird saw no reason why Morning Land could not have carried in the wood instead of embarrassing Laughing One with it. She glared at her older sister, who stubbornly looked straight ahead into the fire.

The two sisters kept silent throughout the meal. Even when the birds were cooked and dripping grease crackled on the embers, the women ate quietly, each withdrawn into herself. While White Bird tasted the hot meat, her eyes were fixed on Laughing One. She wondered what he was thinking as he watched this quarrel between his two wives.

"Is this how it will be between us?" White Bird asked her sister. "My husband and I used to talk and talk together. Now we keep him at a distance."

"Why not just let the man eat?" Morning Land retorted. "Your anger and your fighting, that is what makes your husband so quiet. What do your thoughts tell you that you quarrel this way?"

The argument between the sisters would have gone on much longer had Laughing One not interrupted it. "You are my wives, and I know your tracks when I see them on the ground," he said, "but I do not know your words. This language you speak is filled with soft sounds. They fly back and forth like the cooing of the Racciss. All the time I have sat here, I have liked listening to you, only my mind does not understand. My tongue does not know how to talk like this."

White Bird blushed and looked away. She remembered how she had once scolded Morning Land for talking in the Tideland tongue when Laughing One was around.

"We were forgetful," Morning Land apologized. "We did not mean to leave you sitting by yourself."

"You are not a stranger to us," White Bird agreed. Her dark brown eyes were wet with the beginning of tears, but she no longer felt like crying. "You have given me this stomach. To sit here and talk without you would be a bad thing."

Laughing One smiled, and White Bird moved closer, pressing her back against his chest. The young hunter responded by resting his chin on the nape of her neck. In this position, White Bird began to sing, using her own musical language. Her voice was not wistful or shy any longer. It had a joyful, laughing quality to it, like a ripple of light reflecting across shaded water. With her body swaying back and forth in his arms, Laughing One felt each quick breath she took. He could smell the scent of pine needles and wood smoke in her hair.

After hesitating a moment, White Bird lifted her husband's hands and placed them over the rounded swell of her stomach, leaving his palms pressed flat against the soft skin of her abdomen. It was an intimate, impulsive act, but she did it without checking the flow of her song. Laughing One felt his heartbeat quicken almost as much as if she had been caressing him. White Bird had brought him inside the circle of her hands, making him part of her song. The soft pressure of her arms and the warm smoothness of her stomach soothed his senses.

While White Bird's song hummed in his ears, Laughing One glanced toward the older sister. Morning Land was watching them. Her mouth was curved in an uncertain smile and there was something in the look of her dark eyes that still made him uneasy. As she sat there, nearly motionless, she seemed to be much farther away than she really was.

CHAPTER SEVENTEEN

Sacred Dance

The Moon of Ripening Berries rose through the long twilights of late summer, marking days of drifting clouds and light breezes that blew mostly from the south. On such days, women went into the hills around the lake to harvest fruit, and children wandering through the beds of tall grass returned with mouthfuls of berries. Never quiet in this season, the children seemed to be always shouting, singing, telling crude stories, or laughing uncontrollably at some joke they had played. It was laughter that left their faces streaked with tears and berry juice, laughter that cut across the loneliness of the surrounding hills. Dirt-smeared and grinning, they would pause long enough to pick up yet another berry, hold it between thumb and forefinger, feel the glossy texture of its surface, and then pop it into a smiling mouth.

Up in the hill country, wives stopped to talk together beneath the trees. Young boys burrowed serpentine tunnels through the tall grass, their hidden movements shown only by the wavering tips of weeds, until they suddenly rose up in a swift rush and shouted victory. Dusted with seeds, burrs, and flower petals, they rolled about and wrestled in the brilliant sunshine.

Overlooking all of this were four village hunters who kept careful watch on the women. Spear Maker, Wanderer, Fighting Eagle, and Rock Breaker had stood for a long time at the craggy top of the highest hill, peering down across the rolling landscape. Below them, women and children were scattered amid the green hills, playing, nursing, or carefully filling their baskets.

The four hunters felt a certain sadness as they looked down through the sunshine at the activity far below. In a few more days the picking would be over and women would again carry heavy baskets along steep hunting trails. Each night the sun sank a little closer to the south. Soon the winged ants would rise from the ground, the leaves would become tinged with yellow and red, and the surface of the lake would ripple with long waves. Soon enough they would need to pile dry branches around the lodges. Autumn pools and foaming water were the signs of the Moon of Falling Leaves, when summer's ways were abandoned.

This day's watchfulness had another cause, however. During the season of berries, humans were not the only creatures that wandered the hills in search of fruit. Bears followed the grassy slopes as well. Sometimes the women gatherers did not see the bears' rump patches or black-masked faces in time to retrace their steps. In those densely overgrown places where even bears could hide their bodies, there was no chance to veer away wildly or run off shouting. Alertness was a woman's only defense. Those who reached into the reedy stretches of tall grass made plenty of noise and kept their necks stretched high as they peered warily over the plumed wildflowers.

Earlier that very morning, a woman had slipped on a pile of bear dung and stained her apron. She had shown the stains to Spear Maker before quietly going down to the lake to bathe. Guessing from the foul smell and reddish color of the dung that this was no wandering black bear, Spear Maker had searched the area where the woman had fallen. There he had found several massive footprints. The width of the pads and the long curved claw marks showed them to be the prints of one of the rare giant bears that roamed the savannah. Powerful enough to pull down a grown bison, these huge animals were more inclined to feed on flesh than berries. So the hunters waited, trying not to frighten anyone, but becoming increasingly nervous whenever one of the women wandered into heavy cover.

Some of the older women guessed that a bear must be near, and shouted loudly in the hope of warning the beast off. The rest seemed oblivious to any lurking danger. They sang and shouted simply because the noise made them happier. Eventually their own giggling and whistling began to seem more real than any threat from the forest. As midday settled in with its rising heat, the voices of even the more cautious wives echoed loudly across the hilltops.

When Summer Wind gagged on a berry she had been eating and spat it out with an unexpectedly rude-sounding bellow, everyone who heard her started laughing. After that, the women vied with each other to see who could be the crudest. Some stuffed berries into their mouths until their cheeks bulged, and then let the half-chewed mass dribble out in purple gore. Others whistled through their noses, belched deeply, or hurled berries at their neighbors. Seeing their parents behave this way, the children began wild tussles in the center of the grass that only ended when several of the youngest had run crying to their mothers. Still chuckling, the women hugged and comforted their children, checking to see that they were not truly hurt and wiping away tears with berry-stained aprons.

White Bird did not share in any of this laughter. Her big stomach was hurting her, and the pains came regularly, with only a long breathing space between them. As she walked across the open hillside, passing other women who were still cropping berries, the pains grew worse. White Bird scarcely noticed the soft grunts she was making while she walked or the fact that her basket was still almost empty. The sun seemed to be getting hotter, and the voices of the women echoed hollowly in her ears. The pain was now a harsh, swift-running ache that left her gasping for air. Suddenly there were sharp stabs that forced her breath out. Quite unexpectedly, she sat down.

"What is wrong with you?" a woman asked. "Does your stomach hurt you that much?"

White Bird grunted but shook her head. "No, I will just sit here quietly," she told the woman. "My sister walks quickly and I cannot. If I sit this way, the hurt will leave me."

Not entirely satisfied, the woman returned to her berry picking. White Bird remained as she was for a few moments, deliberately keeping her face passive. Though she knew that the pains would not leave her, she would not reveal her fear to anyone else except her sister. It was time to gather grass and make a bed for the child to be born onto. Morning Land had already started to prepare such a place, but in her dazed state White Bird had wandered off before it could be completed. Now White Bird did not even know where her sister was. Instead, she would have to find a place for herself and soon, before the pains grew so strong that she could no longer walk.

White Bird started moving again as soon as the birth spasms passed, but she did not get far. Every few steps she had to stop and crouch down as a new jolt of pain hit her. The pain worsened until tears formed in her eyes and slipped down her cheeks unnoticed.

"*Shiiwe*! This hurts!" she gasped.

Again the Tideland girl was forced to sit down. The same woman who had questioned her before returned.

"Your stomach is causing you a lot of pain," the woman accused. "The time of giving birth must be near."

White Bird tried to deny it, but a spasm of pain prevented her from replying. The other woman watched White Bird's body shiver and saw her face clench against the hurting.

"This is what birth is," the woman said. "You must not be afraid."

"Tell my sister I am here," White Bird gasped. "Tell her to come quickly."

As soon as the woman had run off, White Bird began mumbling to herself. "What is this baby doing?" she groaned. "Why should everything hurt this much?"

Near the opposite side of the field, Morning Land was surprised to suddenly find herself alone.

She had found a small clearing earlier that morning and had been quietly preparing a birthing place for White Bird ever since. Morning Land had seen enough births to know that White Bird's time was near simply by the cramped fashion in which the young girl walked.

Proud of her skills, Morning Land had prepared a bed of the softest grass, not simply making a mound of it, but creasing and shaping things so that the grass would cradle the child. She had fashioned a sharp stick to cut off the baby's birth cord and had a bark-cloth sling ready to slip around the infant. She had even found a nearby stream where White Bird would be able to wash away the stickiness from her own skin and that of her newborn baby. The only thing Morning Land had forgotten about was White Bird herself.

Morning Land had assumed that her sister would stay close by once the pains began to come. She glanced up now, expecting to see White Bird sitting in the shade. Instead, the clearing was empty. White Bird had gotten up without a word and had wandered off across the hills.

Wondering how this could have happened, Morning Land stepped out from behind the trees into a wild meadowland. Her eyes searched in every direction over the rolling, open hillside. Looking across the fields, she could see other women standing knee-deep in wildflowers and swaying grass. Whenever one of these women strayed too close to their feeding area, flocks of gray birds fluttered up out of the tall grass. Butterflies added flashes of color each time their flickering wings caught the sunlight. But there was no sign of White Bird. The more Morning

Land glanced up and down the slopes, the more exasperated she felt. When she and White Bird had started out to walk along the trail that day, Morning Land had imagined many troubles ahead of her. This had not been one of them.

Morning Land glanced away and looked back one more time, still searching for a familiar form in the midst of the surrounding, yellow-green fields. The stillness of a hot afternoon had settled over the land, and already families were finding resting spots beneath large trees. Half dozing in the heat, few would be aware of a round-eyed, frightened girl suffering through her first childbirth. Reluctantly, Morning Land walked away from the birthing place she had so carefully prepared. The longer she lingered there the less chance she would have of finding White Bird in time.

Staring intently in all directions, listening to every small woodland sound, following all the movements of familiar villagers, Morning Land continued walking across the open grass. She had paced some distance when a woman hurried up to her. The very fact that the woman was running on such a hot, still day immediately alerted Morning Land. The Tidelander was already tensed before the other woman began to speak.

"*Supai* (stop)!" the woman called. "Your sister, the shy one, her baby is coming. She feels much pain in her stomach. She will give birth in the field. Hurry. Come with me."

Morning Land stood motionless, momentarily unable to react.

"She will not sleep another night without this child," the woman insisted. "We must be quick or the child will be born without us."

"I will come with you now," Morning Land said. She did not go back for the sling or the carved stick or any of the other things she had prepared. Without pausing, the two women began a quick and silent trek across the hill slopes. Soft footsteps and the fluttering rustle of grass were the only sounds that marked their journey. Soon they came to the place where White Bird had been sitting in the grass. The Tideland girl had gotten up again and tried to go further, but Morning Land had no trouble following her sister's tracks. After a short walk, they saw White Bird lying uncomfortably in the shade of a small tree. Ignoring her companion, Morning Land rushed forward to be with her sister.

"*Shiiwe*! Why do you walk away from me?" Morning Land demanded. "You are a young woman, not a girl. You cannot run away from pain."

"Do not laugh at me," White Bird groaned. "I feel very wet. The pains come again and again, but the baby will not come out. It just wants to stay inside me. Help me to have it quickly."

From the pained expression on White Bird's face, it was obvious that the child had already begun to move inside her. As further proof, there were birth fluid stains along the lower part of White Bird's apron. The girl had done nothing to help herself. She had made no attempt to gather grass or pile it beside her. She simply lay belly up on the ground.

"You know how to walk well enough," Morning Land said soothingly. "You have already carried this big belly of yours all across the hills. Now stop shouting. You are a strong woman. Soon enough the child will come out."

"My older sister has learned how things are done." White Bird sighed. "I am glad I did not just sit in the village. I am glad I followed you here. My heart is not unhappy."

Morning Land got up quickly to gather what grass she could find. She never intended to slight the other woman. She had simply forgotten about everyone else the moment she had found her sister lying on the ground. The other woman had waited patiently, wondering if she would be needed further, but Morning Land darted past her without noticing. Hurt by the Tidelander's rudeness, the woman muttered to herself and walked over to where the rest of her friends were still gathering berries.

Morning Land began bundling up a mound of grass beside her sister.

"*Shiiwe*! This hurts!" White Bird complained again.

"Of course it hurts, senseless one," Morning Land grumbled. "Did you expect the baby to come out while you were sleeping? A woman has to be strong."

"What do I know about such things?" White Bird protested. "You are not the one giving birth to this child. A big belly like this. . . ." A spasm shortened White Bird's breath.

Morning Land squatted down beside White Bird and gently placed her hands over her sister's straining abdomen. "It is near," she whispered. "This pain is not for nothing. Your arms will not come back empty."

White Bird grunted as the pain left her. "Is this all a woman does?" she asked.

Without answering, Morning Land pulled off White Bird's stained apron. Then she gently massaged White Bird's belly. By coaxing her sister through the roughest jolts of pain and singing to her whenever there was a lull, Morning Land managed to convey a confidence that she never really felt. After a while, the young woman clutched Morning Land's arm and cried, "*Shiiwe!* This is much stronger now. I can feel the baby pulling at me."

"Do not lie here any longer," Morning Land said. "Your baby is already being born. Crawl to where the grass is. Crouch down above it."

"No," White Bird groaned. "This hurts me too much. I will just continue to lie here."

"*Shaa henaki,* worthless one," Morning Land grumbled. "This laziness is something I have no use for. Do not lie here useless when your child needs your strength. *Atoshe!*"

Morning Land dragged the bemused White Bird and pulled her to a kneeling position. Urged on in this rough manner, White Bird meekly crawled forward and knelt over the mound of grass.

"Ehnnn. Ehnnn. It hurts," the girl moaned. "Ehnnnn. It is moving."

"Bite your hand," Morning Land demanded. "Bite until the blood flows, but do not cry out anymore. You must not show your pain."

With clenched teeth, White Bird remained on her knees and managed to rock her hips back and forth while Morning Land massaged her swinging belly. Both girls' faces were very tense, but whereas White Bird grimaced each time the pain jolted her, Morning Land only frowned.

"Your baby will soon be lying on this grass," Morning Land urged. "Soon you and your child will see each other. Soon your talk will be shared."

White Bird let out a heavy grunt and squeezed. A moment later, glistening with birth fluid and its own protective coating, a newborn girl writhed uneasily on the grass.

Morning Land had not touched the child before this moment and did not do so now. Gifted though she was in herbal medicine, she knew that her help in this birthing was only a little thing. Her people believed that giving birth was something a woman should do alone. Sometimes, when a young girl like White Bird was bearing her first child, her mother or her sister might go with her, but even then the child was never pulled out by another woman's hands. To do so often meant the death of both the mother and her baby. Fingers that had spent their days grubbing in the soil after roots or peeling fruit and bark from trees were rarely clean enough to touch a woman's bleeding flesh. Exposed to sun and hearth fire smoke, even a young woman's hands were often rough-edged and hard. It was better to let the mother struggle on her own.

For this reason, Morning Land waited and watched until the afterbirth had come out as well. While the newborn girl lay there, moving her arms in random circles and unable to find even a finger to suck on, Morning Land bent close and examined it critically. Since the child looked healthy, she cut the umbilical cord with a freshly sharpened stick.

With the child out of her, White Bird felt lighter, but her head was dizzy. She seemed to have no energy left. Exhausted, she sat back on her haunches and stared down at the pale, wriggling form between her spread knees.

"The child is not dead," she gasped, "but it does not cry. What should a woman do?"

"Perhaps it cannot breathe enough," Morning Land suggested. "I will suck the water from its nostrils."

Morning Land did so, quickly spitting out the bad-tasting fluid. The child immediately seemed to breathe more strongly. After a few moments, she started to cry.

White Bird was scarcely able to believe that she had given birth to this child. The baby girl seemed unrelated to anything she and her sister had done. It was as if some strange little being had suddenly appeared on the grass beneath her. "I feel no more pains," she said. "The hurt is gone. Can this big child have truly been inside me?"

"Your heart was strong," Morning Land said. She lifted the afterbirth in her hands, saw that it was complete, and set it down on some clean grass. "This child must be carried to the lake and cleaned," she told her sister. "The child must be washed. Do not just leave her on the ground or the ants will come and bite her."

White Bird quickly picked up the child and held it to her breast. "My heart beats very hard inside me, and this sun does not make me feel warm," she said. "Will this child also be cold? Perhaps she will shiver and die."

"The child will not die this day," Morning Land assured her. "After she is washed, we will cover her with warm skins and you will sit together before the hearth fire."

While she spoke, Morning Land collected the stained grass and put it with the afterbirth, forming a bundle. She then covered the bundle with leaves and used a branch to mark the spot.

White Bird stood up slowly, cautiously, still clutching the

newborn next to her chest. "I can already walk well," she said, taking a few tentative steps down the hillside.

"Walk slowly," Morning Land cautioned. "You must not fall."

Caught in the brightness of summer sunlight, the two sisters descended together across the open slope. White Bird was smiling and pleased with herself. The baby's tiny pink-soled feet curled up against her stomach.

"See, my belly is already flatter," White Bird said.

A short while later, she seemed less certain. "What is left inside me to hurt?" she asked her sister. "There is still some pain."

"What has happened to you is strong," Morning Land told her. "This child is very big. That is why your insides still hurt. Soon the pain will be less."

Following the turnings of a familiar path, the sisters reached a secluded area of the shore.

"Sister, you have done much for this baby," White Bird said. "Hold her close to you now."

White Bird hesitated only long enough to ensure that Morning Land had a safe grip on the child. Then she waded into the shallows and started washing herself. The water felt cold, but White Bird splashed it vigorously against her thighs and groin in an effort to get the blood off.

"What will you call this child?" Morning Land asked.

"I will call her whatever *Tua-arikii* decides," White Bird answered. "That is the way of things with his people."

Morning Land scooped up handfuls of cold water with which she carefully washed the head and body of the newborn girl. The child cried and squirmed at the feel of the water. Each time it pulled its stomach in, droplets of blood formed at the end of the cut umbilical cord. Morning Land frowned when she saw this. Resting the unhappy baby on her knees, the Tideland woman opened a small pouch that hung from her neck and pulled out a fragment of puffball fungus. She took the part of the umbilical cord that was still attached to the infant and wrapped it around the puffball. Then she fastened them both to the child's navel with a loosely tied reed.

"Why should a man choose the name for a woman's child?" Morning Land demanded. "What do men have to do with these things?"

Having calmly washed the blood from her legs, White Bird

backed out of the water and sat down on a rock. "Be gentle, sister," she urged. "These people have many strange ways."

The young mother started to shiver, and the tremor sounded in her voice. "For three days Laughing One will not eat any meat," she continued. "Today he will not even drink water. He is a father now, and he cannot sleep with me again until this child crawls. All of these things are strong magic to his people."

"We were better off living in the bush," Morning Land snorted. She washed the baby a second time, rubbing small bits of puffball powder over its skin to prevent chafing. While she worked, she examined the infant yet again, checking to see that its limbs were strong and that the hands and feet were right. White Bird's child was bigger than most of the babies Morning Land had seen. Everything about it seemed plump and smooth, except for its face, which had the wizened pucker of an old Tidelander. Morning Land smiled as she watched the baby blink and squirm in her arms. Then, very reluctantly, she carried it over to White Bird.

"Let your husband go out hunting," she said. "We will eat meat even if he does not."

When White Bird reached out for her child, her black eyes were shining happily. "Laughing One is your husband also," she reminded Morning Land.

The baby had been cold, but as it pressed against White Bird's breast, it began to grow warm. The child's crying quieted, for White Bird's body was soft and comforting.

"See. She is quiet," White Bird whispered. "Lying still. Her little hand, it grabs at my chest. I am a mother now."

Morning Land said nothing. As she looked at the baby, her expression was a mixture of love and envy.

A short time later, Summer Wind crowded in on the sisters' solitude. She and Beautiful Star had been searching the hillsides for White Bird for much of the afternoon. Sweating from the heat, the chief's wife pressed forward angrily.

"What happened to you, daughter?" she scolded. "Why did you give birth to this baby all alone?" Seeing Morning Land, she added, "Why was this one the only woman to help?"

White Bird had put her left nipple in the child's mouth and was encouraging the baby to suck on it. The young mother smiled as she looked up at the chief's wife, but said nothing. Instead, she showed the two women her child.

"So it is finished," Summer Wind grunted. "I was frightened, for I have known how hard childbirth can be."

"I am not crying anymore," White Bird replied. "Nothing bad has happened. Morning Land stayed near me through it all."

Summer Wind grunted again and glanced quickly at Morning Land. "You should have made a fire to warm them," was all she said.

"The day is hot, Mother," White Bird insisted. "My sister did everything well. I did not even know how to give birth."

Unwilling to accept this, Summer Wind moved closer to study the child. "Ehnn. A little girl," the village matron crooned. "This little bird does no harm. She is different from many babies I have seen. She is very large. You are the mother of a strong girl."

Beautiful Star stood looking at the baby as well, but Trusted Friend's wife was more critical. "The child has only a little hair," she said. "When other babies are born, they have much more hair than this. Perhaps this child will grow cold and sickness will attack it."

"*Katto*! Stupid one!" Summer Wind growled. "Why do you say such senseless things? Whoever told you about children? Leave *Yi-quay-is* alone. Let the child grow up. Soon this girl will be a very beautiful woman and her long hair will fall all around her. You have looked at this child, but you have seen nothing."

Angry at being scolded in front of the two sisters, Beautiful Star started to walk away. After a few steps she thought better of it and turned to look at White Bird again. "I am glad you are strong," she said. "I did not mean to insult your child. I wish it only kindness."

White Bird nodded. "She will not always just lie here. When the milk fills my breasts and she grows strong, she will laugh like the other children. She will learn your people's ways."

Still annoyed, Summer Wind turned her attention to Morning Land. "Did you cut this child's cord?" she demanded. "Where are the things that came with this birth?"

"What are you asking of me?" Morning Land protested. "Am I not an adult? That which was born with this child is piled under leaves on the hill slope. A stick marks the place."

Summer Wind frowned. "Ehnn. There is strong magic in that. If a man finds it, his insides will become sore. He will be in great pain. It must be taken far away."

Squinting against the daylight, Summer Wind turned and walked up to Beautiful Star. She handed the younger woman an empty rawhide pouch.

"The things that were cut away at the birth must be picked up," she told Beautiful Star. "They must be placed in this pouch and carried far from the hill slopes. Fill this with all you find there. Take it into the woods and place it in a tree. Find a tree that stands away from the others. Tie the bundle to a high branch. This is strong medicine."

Beautiful Star took the pouch hesitantly. "What are you saying?" she asked. "I do not know how to work with medicines. Perhaps it will kill me."

"You are a woman," Summer Wind snorted. "No things of birth can hurt you. Do this quickly."

Disconcerted but willing to help, Beautiful Star accepted the task and walked away. While the others returned to the warmth of the village fires, Beautiful Star once again strode the hillsides.

The heat still lay heavy on the grass, though evening was now much closer. Because she was in no hurry to find the bundled afterbirth, Beautiful Star picked her way slowly up the slope, quietly looking around for the secluded spot. When she found the place marked by the stick and the tree, she slowed her pace even more. This was a silent test of her strength that she did not feel ready for. Moving alongside the tree, she circled the entire area once before actually approaching the leaf-covered bundle. When she drew near it, her worst suspicions proved true. Insects were already eating the sticky afterbirth.

Flies buzzed hungrily above the leaves, sometimes passing close to the bundle and sometimes zigzagging about in far-wandering flights. A few landed and pushed their bodies under the leaves. Foraging ants had also detected the bundle. A trail of them crossed the ground between food and hive. Under the layer of leaves, the soiled grass turned and twisted as a mass of small bodies moved through it.

The sight of the feeding insects almost drove Beautiful Star away. For a moment she actually considered tying the empty pouch to a tree and hiding the stick that marked the real bundle. Only her fear of bad medicine kept her there. She tried to take away the afterbirth by holding the pouch open with one hand while she used the marker stick to push the whole mass sideways. Flies eagerly buzzed about her and the ants continued to swarm, but Beautiful Star finally shoved the bundle inside the pouch. Then she grabbed up her prize in a sweeping rush, twisted tight the thong that sealed the pouch, and hurried away. It seemed that ants and flies were biting all along her legs. Any-

one seeing Beautiful Star at that instant would have quickly
jumped clear of her path, for she was carrying the pouch as if
it held some poisonous snake.

Still holding the pouch at arm's length and trying to ignore
the burning sensations in her legs, the slender woman hurried
along a northern hunting path until she reached a glade beside
a massive oak tree. The tree stood far enough apart to be well
out of the way of the hunters and was tall enough to satisfy
even Summer Wind. Beautiful Star certainly did not want to
search further. Any hunter foolish enough to come nosing about
under this huge tree deserved his stomach cramps. Taking a
deep breath, Beautiful Star hurried to the trunk of the tree and
started climbing.

The rough bark proved harder to cling to than she had expected. Twice, while she struggled to reach the upper limbs, the
pouch she was carrying swung back and slapped against her
belly. Both times Beautiful Star winced from the feel of it. By
the time she was high enough, her breath was coming in frightened gasps. She quickly tied the pouch onto a branch, said a
magical chant that she had learned as a girl, and fled to the bottom of the tree.

When she was standing on solid ground again, she started to
shiver. The task was done, but she did not feel safe. The magical pouch had touched her twice on the belly. She would bear
children now. She had to. Her stomach would swell until she
was as big as a buffalo cow. Her breasts would sag, and men
would no longer stare at her when she passed. Let Summer
Wind talk all she wanted about how a child made a woman's
marriage strong or how no girl could truly become an adult until
she had suckled her own baby. Beautiful Star did not want any
of that. She had seen the way hunters treated their fat-bellied
wives. Those women worked and nursed and were ignored
while Beautiful Star could have whatever she wished by simple
teasing. Her life had been easy before, but soon it would be different. Under that tree, with the leather pouch dangling above
her head, Beautiful Star sensed for the first time that she would
grow old.

Following a custom he had never thought of questioning,
Laughing One stayed apart, in his parents' lodge, on the night
after White Bird gave birth. His task was to find a name for the
child, and he would neither eat nor sleep until it was done.
Though he was only a young man, Laughing One understood

the importance of naming. The moment of birth was a powerful one over which a man had no control. A husband could not be with his wife then without losing his ability to hunt. He could not drive away her pain or keep sickness from her and her baby. All he could do was give the new child a name, one that would join the child with the world around her. This name would make her forever part of his people and his family. But though he understood its importance, the actual task of naming was something Laughing One had never done before. Names were like leaf shadows in the sunlight, always flickering and changing even as he tried to grasp them. Laughing One sat carefully watching his parents' hearth fire, as if the patterning of its flames might give him the name he sought.

Of the three people sitting in Wanderer's lodge that night, only Summer Wind was truly happy. She was glad to have her youngest son staying with her again, even if he came only as a visitor. Laughing One wanted to speak to his mother about the naming, but Summer Wind kept her silence. It was bad manners for a woman to interfere in these matters.

Wanderer was under no such restrictions. As chief, he felt a certain duty to help any new father. After a long pause, during which he just stared at his son, he finally spoke.

"You are a father now," Wanderer began. "You must find a name soon, before you hear this child's voice."

Laughing One nodded. He did not have to answer, for he knew that his father was just beginning.

"A name does not come only from your mouth," Wanderer continued. "It is a gift. Without it, everything is less important. Names are the only things that stay with us. They are the things we take with us wherever we go."

To prove what he said, Wanderer pulled out a stone knife that he wore during ceremonies and council meetings. It was a beautifully worked blade, fully as long as a man's outstretched hand and fastened to an ivory handle.

"This knife is a good thing," he told his son. "When I hold it, I remember how my own fingers made this point. But a knife is only very small in worth. Some day I will just give this one away and move on again and go on living without it. I will not cry because I have to leave a knife behind. It is not a thing of importance like my name.

"Each child has its own name, and these names are never the same. When a name has been used once, it is dead to the rest of the village. Only when a person truly dies, only then is the name free again."

Laughing One nodded and smiled politely. Wanderer's talk had been very moving, but it did not really tell him anything he had not already known. After a while, certain that he would find no answers at his parents' lodge, the young hunter got up and began wandering through the village.

Though the sun had already set and the world was growing dark, the sounds of village life were all around him. Women laughed and gossiped. Mothers scolded their daughters. Small boys chased girls around the darkened lodges until the girls grew tired of pretending to be frightened and finally turned on their pursuers. Near the center of the village, Spear Maker told stories to the hunters.

Laughing One circled well away from his own lodge and tried to avoid looking at the women who sat there. The seeming nearness of his family was the most difficult problem he faced. Laughing One could hear the Tideland sisters' distinctive voices only too clearly. He had to close his eyes as he passed in order to keep from speaking with them.

At Fighting Eagle's lodge, Laughing One found both of his brothers. Trusted Friend was vainly trying to impress the hunting leader by telling about some strange animals he had seen, but Fighting Eagle was obviously not interested. Grateful for any interruption, both men looked up pleasantly when they saw Laughing One.

"Father. It is Father," Trusted Friend said jokingly. "The little girl you married gave birth to a baby as big as herself. Never has any woman been so full with her baby. Your wife must have no strength left."

Turning to Fighting Eagle, Trusted Friend added, "She gave birth all alone in the field. Our mother was not even there."

"Her sister was with her," Laughing One said quietly.

"I thought your young wife was only a child and did not understand such things," Trusted Friend persisted. "She has been stronger than many older women. Now when you greet her, you can also say 'My daughter.'"

"I have no name for this daughter," Laughing One admitted. "I have sat alone, but the thoughts have not come. I am looking for someone to talk to."

"Naming is not so difficult a thing," Fighting Eagle said, speaking for the first time. "A man watches his child crawl and he smiles. He hears his baby laugh and his heart is strong. This baby is a thing of importance in his life. He should name the child for other things of importance. My son, Breaks a Tusk, was named for a hunt when we killed a great Ehina. The Ehina had fallen and broken its tusk. By giving him this name, I blessed my son with the luck of that hunt."

"My child is a girl," Laughing One said doubtfully.

"A girl can also have a strong name," Fighting Eagle assured him. "When my daughter was still inside her mother, I had a strong dream. In that dream, I saw a strange and beautiful pool of water. There were bubbles floating on that pool. When I awoke, I knew the name I would call my daughter. She is named Bubbles on the Water. You must do the same. Name this girl for something you have seen or done."

"What are you saying to us?" Trusted Friend scoffed. "Not all men are strong hunters like you. Would you have Laughing One call the child Sits by the Fire or Sleeps in the Lodge? These are the things our young brother does best. Or would you have him call his daughter Hides in a Tree after her mother?"

Indignant at this show of insolence, Fighting Eagle turned on Trusted Friend. "Has our brother come here to be insulted by you?" he demanded. "Your words rattle like a stick. A boy is taught by his brothers. I have taught both of you. The first piece of work," he said, pointing toward Trusted Friend, "that work was poor. The second"—here Fighting Eagle indicated Laughing One—"that work was better. He has done well from the beginning."

"You are not the only person who can talk," Trusted Friend retorted angrily. "The names you chose for your children, they were miserable things. Breaks a Tusk, Bubbles on the Water—my heart fell when I first heard you speak them. We live in the same village, but we do not see things the same way."

"*Katto*! Face of a wolf!" Fighting Eagle shouted. "Do you think my hearth is a good place to sit and be rude? You are still talking without care. You take my food, but you do not know how to share. You talk like someone I do not know. You make me weary with the bad things you say. What makes you so senseless that you insult me this way?"

Trusted Friend looked startled. Only at this moment did he realize how much he had hurt his brother. "My words were wrong," he apologized. "My talk was bad because my heart was angry. I have wanted a child many times, but my wife has never given me any. When others have children, I have seen how we are living alone in our lodge. All this time we have slept together, but Beautiful Star still eats alone. Her stomach is still small. Perhaps all the lovers she has taken have ruined her. She never refuses other men. She just lies with them. Perhaps I should tell her to go back and live in her own village, but my love for her has not died. Only I feel bad without a daughter. I want someone who will call me Father, someone I can take care of."

Somewhat appeased, Fighting Eagle said, "The men who have no children or the men whose children have grown up completely, these are the ones who think they know much. They have no child at their hearth who will cast away its food and make them angry. They never have to threaten with a stick, so they think they are gentle. Come, brother, your words are going to fall on us. Let them come down. Tell us about the naming of children that we may know how it is done."

Aware of his brother's mood, Trusted Friend spoke very quietly. "I would name a child for the things inside her," he said. "The words I choose would talk of her eyes or her hair or the loud voice of her heart. She would be named for the way she was."

"I have not seen this child," Laughing One said.

"See her spirit," Trusted Friend insisted. "Or name her for the woman who gave birth to her. The one who married you and sleeps with you when night sits—name her child for what she has done."

"Even a poor name is better than none," Fighting Eagle added.

The talk continued, with Laughing One considering all that his brothers said. Their words were sensible, but they were hunters, not shamans. Neither seemed skilled at naming.

Discouraged, Laughing One finally went back toward his parents' lodge. On the way, he once again heard the voices of his wives. A baby had begun crying, and Laughing One listened to it wail for a long moment before he realized that the child was his. Another voice accompanied the cries, a soothing, mother's voice. There was a pause in the crying and then silence as the baby tried to nurse. Soon afterward the mother started singing. Though her words were muffled, Laughing One recognized White Bird's song.

"Name the child for the woman who gave birth to her," Trusted Friend had said. Laughing One could not choose a living person's name, but he felt the truth of what Trusted Friend had told him. It was his days with these sisters, not hunting triumphs, that he wanted to remember. No hunter's tale could match the comfort of lying beside White Bird in a warm lodge while the wind's own voice rose through the dark outside. Where she laughed and talked, the menace of hidden things seemed to slide away.

As a boy, Laughing One had often heard the women speak about "the pathway of children." Before he had learned what childbirth was, he had imagined this to be a real pathway leading into dark forested areas where moss and leaves covered the ground. It had seemed like a place where children had had to step carefully to avoid slipping. That memory came back to him now, along with another of the sisters hiding in the huge tree beside the river. He remembered the sadness that had come into the women's faces when they had talked of the death of their village. Any name he chose would have to carry some part of all this.

Abruptly, almost as if White Bird had spoken to him herself, he knew what the child's name should be. He whispered it aloud, smiling as he did so. When he returned to his parents' lodge, Laughing One ate a heavy meal and slept easily.

White Bird held her newborn child on her knees and looked at it with wet, glistening eyes. "What is this soft noise you make?" she asked.

Since it was still early morning and she was largely unnoticed, White Bird spoke in her own Tideland tongue. The child simply blinked and sucked on its fists.

"I talk and talk but you do not listen to me," White Bird crooned in mock anger. "You only want to cry. Your voice is only great when your belly is empty."

On impulse, White Bird hugged the baby to her breasts, rubbed her nose against its nose, and snuggled the hollows of its neck and limbs. "You are all belly," she burbled. "Do not go away, little maker of noise. The milk in my breasts is growing stronger."

Morning Land, who patiently cooked their meal on the hearth fire, found all of this affection strangely irritating. Unable to direct her anger at her sister or the child, she grumbled about Laughing One instead.

"In this land a man makes much of himself," she told her sister. "Only he can give his daughter a name. We have done all the work, but we must sit here and take what he gives us."

"If a woman has had many lovers, her child might not even know who to look at when he said the word 'Father,' " White Bird replied. "A woman needs a man who will give her child a name. When he does this, he becomes that child's true father. He is the one both child and mother will listen to. Naming is an important thing. A man will do much for a child he has named."

White Bird placed her child on the ground but could not resist the urge to bend over and nuzzle it once more. She pretended to bite at its arms and legs, making a "*Burrrrit, burrrittt*," noise which sounded like the pulsating chirp of a small tree frog.

"Such black eyes," she muttered. "Such tiny fingers."

"We will soon learn what name to call this child of yours," Morning Land mumbled, pointing across the village to where Laughing One had just crawled through the entrance of his parents' lodge. "He no longer stays away from us."

"I have missed him," White Bird said as she picked up her child. Murmuring one last token of love in its ear, she raised the baby to her breast. "My heart is happy, *Tua-arikii*," she called.

Trying to act as if he had never been away, Laughing One crouched down on the man's side of the hearth. "I see you have a daughter who will call you 'Mother' now," he said awkwardly.

"What will we call her?" White Bird asked bluntly.

Laughing One let one of his fingers slide gently into the baby's right hand. The finger was firmly gripped and Laughing One grinned. "Sacred Dance," he said softly. "Her name is to be Sacred Dance."

Both sisters stared at him uneasily but said nothing.

Puzzled by this lack of response, Laughing One hesitated. He wondered if he had been wrong in naming the child after their mother. Though he had intended to honor the sisters, perhaps he had broken some secret taboo in doing so. Half expecting to be chided, he looked up questioningly at White Bird. The confusion he saw in her eyes convinced him that she had simply not understood. She had lived so long in his village that he had forgotten how strange his language was to her. Since he had chosen a name that was rare among his own people, White Bird could not guess at its meaning.

Kuva-irima," Laughing One said, translating the name into the Tideland tongue. "We will call her *Kuva-irima*."

"*Kuva-irima*," White Bird muttered.

There was a startled gasp, but White Bird could not tell

whether it came from her or her sister. Both Tideland women looked thoroughly flustered.

Tears blurred White Bird's eyes as she pressed her daughter against her breasts. "I have often cried for my mother," she said. "She gave me food and the thoughts that are still inside me. This name has strong magic."

Morning Land said nothing, but for a brief moment her face revealed the strength of the emotions she felt. There was a softness in her eyes that Laughing One had rarely seen before. Embarrassed by this unexpected openness, Morning Land quickly resumed her defensive aloofness.

Impulsively, White Bird handed Laughing One their child. The startled hunter let the baby rest in his lap while he tried to maneuver his hands around it.

"*Shiiwe*! This is not a piece of meat," Morning Land scolded. "She must continue to live. Put your arm further underneath or the child's pain will be great. Do not let her head fall back. Her neck is not strong. You must sit quietly. No. Do not move about so much."

Aware of his strangeness at such things, Laughing One accepted Morning Land's criticism meekly. White Bird smiled. Unlike Laughing One, she knew the love that lay behind Morning Land's scolding tone.

CHAPTER EIGHTEEN

The Changes of Autumn

During the autumn following the birth of Sacred Dance, Morning Land slowly began to realize that she wanted a child of her own.

At first, when Sacred Dance was barely strong enough to roll over by herself if she were placed on a length of bark cloth, Morning Land did not understand her own restlessness. She was too preoccupied with protecting the child to notice what was obvious to those around her. Each time she warned off careless children who had come too near the baby or scolded interfering relatives for handling the child too roughly, the villagers in nearby lodges would laugh and talk about her behind their hands. White Bird was grateful enough to leave Sacred Dance in Morning Land's arms while she checked the hearth or talked with neighbors, for anyone who saw how carefully Morning Land supported the child's head could not doubt the older sister's kind intentions, but sometimes Morning Land's overprotective ways worried the child's real mother. During the last days of summer, when the sun-heated ground was too hot for a baby's soft skin, Sacred Dance's chubby legs rested against Morning Land's right forearm at least as often as they kicked against White Bird's stomach. If the warmth of the sun set the baby crying or coughing, Morning Land rocked it gently in her arms and replaced the bark cloth under its body with materials of greater softness. Only when it was time for the child to nurse did the older sister yield her place. Even this was done with such reluctance that White Bird had reason to wish her sister would become a little less attentive.

Morning Land's mood changed each time she saw White Bird bring the baby to her breasts and start to nurse it. Raising her small lips to her mother's milky nipple, Sacred Dance would suckle happily, mumbling and curling her little feet at the same time. When she was satisfied, she gave her most attractive smile. Her gurgle of sheer joy burned at Morning Land's ears, for it reminded her of her own barrenness and of the want she felt. This one, only child was becoming a barrier between the sisters, and both of them sensed it.

When the Moon of the Hunter at last appeared, the autumn winds returned and Wanderer's people again traveled across the distance that separated them from the warmer lakes to the south. The women shouldered heavy baskets filled with hides and other domestic things. Older children ran at their mothers' sides as the villagers trekked through ever-shifting patterns of red and gold savannah grass. Little Sacred Dance rode in her sling, sometimes staring wide-eyed at the brightness of the open plains, but usually dropping into heavy sleep, rocked by the striding movements of her aunt or her mother. Southward into the slanting sunlight, under the high, clear skies of this slowly ebbing season, Wanderer's people moved as they had for countless generations.

Walking heavily, with her load secured by a strap around her forehead, Morning Land brooded. Her life would not become like this summer of old women, long and slowly weakening, with its withered leaves still clinging to the trees or lying useless along the pathway. She shared a very patient husband, and she would find a way to open her own belly to the pathway of children. In this she would need the help of her sister, for Laughing One still remembered the day at the river when she had refused him completely. He had waited all this time, hoping her heart would change, but she had taken too long. Now he had nearly forgotten he was married to her. He was so used to turning away from her in the lodge each night that she had become like an older sister to him. When she squatted down in front of him with little Sacred Dance in her arms, Laughing One stared only at the child. That would have to be changed.

The change did come many days later, when the southward journey was finished. After climbing into low-lying hills near the southern shore of a familiar lake, Wanderer's people finally camped on a tree-sheltered ridge. By the time the dust of the journey had been washed away and the first of the winter lodges had been built, the people were too tired to do more than sit. The end of their second day in their new home found them taking turns cooking old meat and dried berries on a series of small fires.

Perhaps it was Laughing One's tiredness that made him ignore the signals passing between his two wives. He was busy watching his daughter nursing at her mother's breast and did not see the sly smile on White Bird's lips or Morning Land's embarrassed flush. Little Sacred Dance seemed to know she was being watched, for she often stopped her suckling to play with White Bird's saber-toothed tusk as it dangled on the neck thong. Sometimes the child would use her tiny fists to bat at the dangling tusk, but most often she liked to grab it in both hands and jerk with all her strength. After a while, the tugging thong began to hurt White Bird's neck, so the young mother lifted the tooth out of reach.

"Your hands are strong, daughter," White Bird said, sighing. "You will break this necklace by cracking it against my belly. Your father has no reason to call you the shy one."

Since White Bird was getting tired, Laughing One expected her to hand the child to him, for he often tended the baby when her patience grew short. He enjoyed tickling his daughter until her plump little body squirmed with infant laughter. But as soon as the nursing was finished, White Bird began replacing the dry moss in Sacred Dance's winter carrying pouch, as if in a hurry to have the child asleep.

Sacred Dance was well protected against the growing chill of the autumn night. A softened deerskin was wrapped around the little girl's chest and stomach before she was placed inside the bag pouch that formed her winter home. When carefully laced up, this carrying pouch left only the child's face exposed to the air. The valley people always filled the lower part of the leather pouch with dry moss to cushion the baby's legs and absorb waste.

"Stay in there until your feet are hot," White Bird gently scolded. "This is the last time for you to play. Night sits beside the fire now."

"*Di dai minui,*" Sacred Dance babbled.

"Always you talk," White Bird chuckled. "You tell me things even when you are eating. Why should a baby just eat and eat without also talking? *Sujemou,* that is how you think."

Since the baby was fully covered, Laughing One realized that he would not play with her this night. To hide his disappointment, he glanced out across the village. The upper branches of the evergreen trees formed black patterns against the darkening blue of the sky. In front of the lodge next to his, Beautiful Star had lifted her apron and was using black paint to trace these tree-shadow patterns onto her bare legs. Laughing One had often wondered at the magic of Beautiful Star's painting. She seemed to do it whenever she wished to arouse a special passion in her husband, and no matter how tired or angry he was, Trusted Friend would always respond. Already Trusted Friend had edged closer to watch her. By the time Beautiful Star's agile fingers had traced the patterns to the base of her buttocks, her husband would be leaning against her. Then the painting would stop and the two would snuggle down inside their lodge to begin a loud, panting lovemaking that could be heard by most of the village.

Laughing One self-consciously shifted his gaze away from Beautiful Star. When he looked back at his own hearth, he saw that White Bird had handed the child to Morning Land. She stepped close to her husband and smiled down at him. Laughing One saw a look of amusement in her dark eyes, but could make nothing of it.

"*Atoshe*. Your hair has gathered visitors on this journey," she told him. "They must be made to leave."

Laughing One sighed as White Bird squatted down behind him to begin the delousing. The feel of her fingers searching through his hair made him uncomfortably aware of how seldom she had touched him since the birth of their child. He was a young man and he found this forced abstinence difficult.

"I have too many dreams these nights," he told her. "I cannot stop dreaming. It is a thing that troubles me."

"What does my husband dream of?" White Bird asked.

As she listened to his reply, she quickly crushed lice with her nails and tossed their bodies away into the dust.

"I dream of *Kairofa*," Laughing One said. "She brings many spirit women who have large fires burning where their eyes should be. They all dance and pull away their *kai-tamas* (waist skirts). When they touch me, their fingers burn."

Laughing One went on to describe the antics of these spirit women. He left out many of the things they did to him, but what he did say was enough to make White Bird laugh as she pulled his hair. She thoughtfully twisted his black locks back and forth to loosen any insect eggs that might be still clinging there.

"Go into the river," she advised. "It will wash this dust from you and kill those women's fires."

Laughing One grunted. After White Bird had finished with him, he stood up and went down to the lake to bathe. By the time he had returned, both White Bird and her child were already resting inside the lodge. Only Morning Land remained at the hearth.

Left alone with the older Tideland sister, Laughing One began to feel awkward. Morning Land was even more withdrawn than usual this night. Apart from the quiet working movements of her hands and an occasional flicker of her eyelids, she sat absolutely still. She was weaving shell decorations onto a dance apron, and Laughing One knew that after all the work was done the apron would end up being worn by someone else. Unlike Beautiful Star, Morning Land no longer bothered to decorate herself. Since her arrival in his lodge, she had made numerous aprons, bedecking them with juniper berries or shell tinklers or even dried pine nuts. Most of the women in the village wore some *kai-tama* that Morning Land had worked on, yet her own beautiful waist always remained covered by simple hides.

Laughing One's uneasiness increased as he watched her. She had lived with him for two full seasons, yet he could never guess the thoughts that passed through her mind. She must have known he was staring at her, but her black eyes never wavered from the apron she was working on. She could have been one of the village matrons, one of the tribe's grandmothers.

Full darkness had set in and the talk in the other lodges had become drowsy. As voices faded into sleep, the chirping of the crickets seemed to swell in volume, replacing most of the human noises. A sudden giggle from Trusted Friend's lodge reminded Laughing One that Beautiful Star was in a passionate mood. He did not want to stay out there beside the fire and listen to his brother making love. The silent woman beside him was no company. He might as well have been alone.

Laughing One got up suddenly and started to go inside. Then, just as he was about to enter the lodge, he turned back to look at the motionless figure beside the hearth. With a sigh, he walked over to her and touched her on the shoulder.

"*Supai* (stop)," he said. "You will not be giving away any *kai-tamas* this day. The other women already have all they need and do not want to share. You are the only one who gives."

Morning Land looked up at him for the first time. Her mouth seemed to tremble slightly as she spoke. "Ehnn. I am not going to give this one away."

"Do not just stay outside here in the circle of firelight," Laughing One urged. "Your eyes do not shine through the darkness. You cannot see where there is no light. Come into our lodge and be warm."

"It is almost ready," Morning Land said. "Go into the lodge ahead of me. I will follow soon."

Laughing One did not argue. Many of the things Morning Land did seemed stubborn and senseless to him, but her skills had saved his life more than once. He had given up trying to question her actions. With a parting shrug, he stooped down and entered the lodge.

Laughing One guessed from her heavy breathing that White Bird was already sleeping. There would be no chance to talk with anyone until morning. Grumbling to himself, he lay down on the hide beside his wife and pulled a fur robe across his chest.

Beautiful Star started her moaning almost as soon as he had closed his eyes. It was a high, eager sound that seemed to belong with the smell of leaves and flowers rather than the musky scent of the lodge. Though he did not want to listen, each new grunt or sigh excited Laughing One's imagination, making him remember the wild, erotic woman his brother had married. As Beautiful Star's love calls drifted in through the open lodge, he found himself longing for White Bird.

Laughing One rolled onto his side, trying to force the sweet sounds from his mind. How could he be sleeping now when the spirit of *Kairofa* herself was only a little distance away? With a quiver of shame, he remembered his dreams again and how often he had awoken in anger, with his waist cloth damp and only cold around him. He would soon lose his reason entirely. He could not just continue to sleep side by side with his wife this way. White Bird was not his sister. Her warm body disturbed him whenever he was near her. Things were not right if a man could find no rest in his own lodge.

Overcome by anger, Laughing One got up and went out into the night. He would not continue to dwell this way. Cursing aloud, he walked away from his hearth.

Behind him, unseen in the shadows, Morning Land pulled back in sudden shyness. Had Laughing One stayed silent only a short time longer, she would have lain with him. Instead, she remained as she was, no longer certain. When she did enter the lodge, she nearly bumped against White Bird, who had woken quickly only to find her husband rushing away into the darkness.

In muted whispers, the two sisters talked together long and earnestly. Nothing more could be done that night.

The next day, quite unexpectedly, the first of the winter storms began. Mist and rain met the villagers when they peered

out of their lodges that morning. They tried to keep warm by
bundling up in hides and settling down near their fires, but a
bitter northern wind sweeping south from the great ice sheet
blew straight through the village, lifting the ashes out of the
fires and drawing away their heat. Breath became small clouds
of steam that swirled away instantly in this wind, and even
squatting in the very path of the scattering smoke brought little
warmth. To walk about even for a short while was painful. The
hunters did not go out at all. There were no tracks to be seen in
a downpour, and even if the men had been willing to splash
through freezing puddles against a cold wind, the darkened sky
would have kept the game well hidden. Instead, the men stayed
with their family groups, huddled for warmth against the dripping air and staring out at the twilight world of the storm.

By midday, the lodges had begun leaking. Spears were used
to prop up shaggy, loose-fitting hides, but the wind-flung rain
smashed against them even harder, digging new holes through
the layers of leaf cover. As the cold rains grew stronger, the
hearths could not be kept burning. Wind shaking the treetops
brought down special drifts of rain that doused every hearth until all of them were smoldering. The circle of lodges seemed
like a drenched hollow in the dull gray light.

Later in the afternoon there was a change. The rain weakened
to a drizzle and then stopped entirely. For a while the wind remained cold, but it blew away the very clouds it had sent. Then
the sun appeared, and one dark cloud shadow after another slid
quickly across the land as milder air began to drift back in from
the southeast.

Laughing One left the rain-lashed village with its dripping
lodge fronts and walked down toward a lonely cove on the lake
shore. As he walked along the wet path, he could hear the
hoarse, hollow calls of migrating Racciss. From a distance, the
sounds resembled the hooting of an owl. Laughing One took little interest, for he knew that the birds would move away again
as quickly as they had arrived.

Pebbles scattered through the clay of the lakeshore kept his
feet from slipping when Laughing One reached the cove. He
found a level spot above the shore and paused, no longer sure
why he had walked this far. Jolted by the unevenness of the day,
he realized that the ways of the marriage lodge had troubled
him far too much. Lovers' songs and wives shamming sleep
were small worries when set against the suddenness of a winter

storm. This was a thing that could not be prevented. This was something a man might not survive.

Thoughts of death troubled Laughing One much more than they once had. There was too much uncertainty in his life now. Before meeting the sisters, he had walked a path that had been even and flat. Now it was all wet leaves and slipperiness. He seemed to be working his way upward all the time, circling backward and forward in a steep climb until he reached the edge of a place he would not be able to cross.

Because of his brooding, Laughing One had not been listening as well as he usually did when alone. He did not sense the nearly silent footfalls on the yielding forest path behind him.

Morning Land advanced among the trees very carefully, pausing at frequent intervals as she traced her husband's footsteps down to the water's edge. Draped over her head and shoulders she wore a lightly tanned hide as protection against the cold rainwater that was still dripping from the surrounding leaves. In her right arm, she cradled a small, soft-looking bundle.

"*Tua-arikii,*" she called softly.

Laughing One turned quickly at the sudden sound. He recognized the voice and the woman at once, but he could not understand why Morning Land had come creeping close this way. The hide she used to cover her head was less surprising to him. In such uncertain weather, any form of clothing would be right.

"I did not hear you," he admitted.

Morning Land's voice grew louder as she advanced. "White Bird wondered why you walked away from the village," she said.

Laughing One watched her coming slowly toward him. "As a man gets older, he starts to worry," he muttered.

Morning Land looked at him with her dark eyes and said, "A man should let the women he lives with share his worries."

Laughing One shrugged uneasily. "If I knew what it was I wished to say, then I would talk about it."

Once she had reached Laughing One, Morning Land stopped. "I have not followed you to this place just to stand here," she said. "I am a woman, and I live in your lodge. If you are unhappy there, then we have things to say to each other that are important."

Laughing One sensed a strangeness in Morning Land's manner and was a little afraid of it. He had trouble looking into her eyes. "I am not unhappy in my lodge," he stammered. "I have love for my daughter and my wife."

"You have two wives," Morning Land reminded him. "It is not your sister who stands here."

As she said this, Morning Land took off the robe she had been wearing over her head, folded it carefully, and set it aside on a nearby tree root. Except for a small beaded apron around her waist, she stood naked in front of him. The fading sunlight flickered in a reflected sheen across her body, emphasizing the warmth of her bare skin. Laughing One had caught his breath when she had first disrobed, and he let it out very slowly, as if afraid that any movement from him would startle her and make her dart away like some wild creature.

"You call White Bird the shy one, but I am the one who is truly shy," Morning Land told him. "Perhaps I have only been pretending sickness."

For the first time in many days, Laughing One allowed himself to really look at Morning Land. With her head lifted and her naked body quivering slightly in the growing coolness, she seemed as tall and beautiful as when he had first seen her. He noticed that her hair had been shortened in the fashion of his people. Its ends had the stiffness and jagged edge of hair that has been newly cut with a stone blade.

Morning Land looked away shyly and placed something in his hand. It was a bundle of soft hair, carefully tied up with leather thongs.

"I give you this little bundle of hair," she said quickly. "Now you are the husband and I am the wife."

"This is something I thought I would never hear," Laughing One admitted. The invitation in Morning Land's voice and manner seemed obvious. Had it been White Bird standing before him this way, he would have needed no further prodding, but Morning Land's moods were still mysterious to him.

"*Suyemou*," Morning Land whispered, bending closer until he could see the glisten of her soft, dark eyes. In Tideland fashion, she rubbed her nose against his nose, his cheeks, his ears. Her fingertips brushed across his body in swift but soft caresses. Laughing One's right hand tightened over the bundle of his wife's hair. A light breeze was stirring around them. It brought the scent of wet leaves and cold rain, and the soft smell of Morning Land standing very close to him.

In that instant, Laughing One understood how carefully this had been planned. Suddenly he knew why Morning Land had covered her head with a hide blanket and why White Bird had been so quiet and aloof the night before. The sisters were bringing still another change into his life.

Laughing One glanced around uneasily at the mossy slope, slippery shore clay, and dripping grass. The rain was over, but the ground was too wet and pebble-studded for lovemaking.

"The earth is very wet," he said uncertainly. "And the lake is too cold now even for a Tidelander."

For her answer, Morning Land nuzzled him a final time, stepped to where she had left the tanned hide, and began unfolding it. With considerable skill, she spread the hide across the flattest and most solid section of the slope. As he watched her, Laughing One smiled. Even in this, Morning Land was the caring older sister.

"Now it will be dry enough," she said quietly. While she spoke, she crouched down onto the hide. Though she tried to look comfortable, it was not easy to do so on the hard-packed ground. *"Atoshe!"* she exclaimed as her legs touched the cold wetness of some nearby grass. Then, remembering, she looked up at him and smiled.

Laughing One could hardly have refused her at that moment. What he felt was an intense rush of kindness rather than passion. For all her planning and improvising, the impression was inescapable that Morning Land was finding this very difficult. Laughing One came closer, repeating his own soft tones of endearment.

Morning Land had always been a mystery to him before, but the flesh he now felt was cool and shivery, not unearthly. His hands were shaking as they moved to hold her, and the trembling continued inside of him when her lips nuzzled him once more.

Morning Land rolled onto her back and pulled off the beaded apron. For a moment they were both silent. Then Morning Land smiled and whispered. *"Kai-tama.* I have made so many of these. I worked and worked, and the days kept passing. I had little shells and nuts that I tied to the edges. Always I thought that it was for myself I worked. I would put the finished apron on when I came to sleep with you. But when the apron was finished, I only sat. The fear was in me again. Other women would help me do some work and I would just give the aprons to them. Then I would go out and collect more shells or nuts. I have tried again and again and only given all the aprons away—until this time."

Laughing One wondered at the quiet sadness of this woman. "We are together here," he said slowly. "You should have no fear. Nothing bad is going to happen."

"I am a young woman, waiting," Morning Land answered. She sat up and nuzzled Laughing One again. Then she placed her hands behind his head and pulled him toward her so that they both rolled back onto the hide together. As Laughing One pressed his face against Morning Land's breasts, his confusion remained, but he could think of nothing else except holding and loving her. At that moment, Morning Land did not seem so very different from all the other women in the tribe.

Their first lovemaking was sudden and silent. As soon as Laughing One had responded to her coaxing, Morning Land's whispering ceased. The nuzzling and holding, the whirl of feeling that caught and held him, were all startlingly quick. As Laughing One listened to the deep notes of Morning Land's breathing, felt the hidden tangle of her hair under his fingers, and held her quivering body next to his own, all the shadows and sunlit places around him seemed as faint as floating vapor.

Later she lay on top of him, very still, with only a soft shuddering in her chest to show that she was not asleep. He felt wonderingly at the high, curved smoothness of her buttocks. Her flesh dimpled under her fingertips just as White Bird's would have, but she did not wriggle in response to his touch.

It took him awhile to realize that she was crying.

She did not sob or whimper. The only way he knew was from a slight shivering of her breasts against his chest and the wetness on her face.

"What is wrong with you?" he whispered. "Does your heart still refuse me?"

"I am only thinking of things that have died," Morning Land whispered. "They are things I cannot have any longer."

Once again Laughing One was reminded of how unlike her sister Morning Land really was. White Bird's voice sometimes became subdued and hushed after lovemaking, but she had never cried. She would sway her hips leisurely against him, and brush at his skin with her lips. There was never such sadness.

"Do not cry like this," Laughing One urged. "What we did is what men and women always do."

Morning Land touched his lips with her fingers. "As I am now, I will stay with you quietly." She sighed.

Laughing One did not know how to answer. He simply held her as she cried silently against his chest. After a while, she

SISTERS OF THE BLACK MOON

stopped. "I am not hurting because of you," she finally whispered.

Laughing One felt suddenly cool as Morning Land's warm body slid off him. "*Tua-arikii*," she said, standing up once more. "I have been happy living with you. You have taken care of White Bird and I and have never been unkind to us. I will not refuse to sleep beside you any longer. At night I will lie down next to you."

There was no more talk between them. Words could not help the feeling they shared.

Before getting up, Laughing One bent down beside a moss-covered stump and retrieved the soft bundle of Morning Land's hair. They had been lying in a lighted place, but now they were surrounded by darkness The short autumn twilight was already near. All along the western horizon the sky was filled with a fading orange glow. Gathering up the hide, Morning Land followed her husband back to their lodge.

CHAPTER NINETEEN

Clover Moon

Though the Tideland sisters would gladly have forgotten Passing Shadow, the bear shaman held a stronger memory of his disgrace. All through that rain-swept winter, while his two remaining wives huddled together for comfort and watched the old man with fearful uncertainty, Passing Shadow planned his revenge. Whenever a dark storm surged in over the mountains from the distant seacoast, the shaman would remain hunched near the back of his lodge, staring into the black shadows. Even as the rain grew heavier and drifted into the lodge with the wind, Passing Shadow did not move. The shaman studied the shadows. He looked out at the falling rain. He gazed up at the lowering sky. He said nothing. When all of his days seemed like nightmares, the wretchedness of a storm did not matter.

His memories were unforgettably clear: the betrayal, his struggle with Morning Land, his attempt to kill her and her sister. Mostly he remembered Morning Land as he had first known her, with her black hair long about her throat and her brown eyes staring at him in sick disbelief. He remembered walking around her, touching her, planning ways to make her his. Her skin had felt warm, but her eyes had always been cold. Sometimes he simply wanted her back, to make her part of his lodge once more, but more often the hate and anger stirred in him. He knew what he had to do. He could not leave her where she was, with her sister and her young lover, laughing at what she had done to him. He would pound her until her body lay shuddering. He would beat her until she was senseless. When his hands were covered in her blood, then it would be over.

While the shaman brooded, his wives worked around him, hurrying to stop each stream of water that forced its way through the lodge coverings, but Passing Shadow was as indifferent to their murmuring voices as he was to the sounds of the dripping runoff. Neither his wives nor the chill of that gloomy season could ever lessen the hatred he felt. Nothing mattered except that the woman who had so openly defied him was still alive.

He thought of Morning Land almost constantly, wondered what she was doing, imagined her lying down happily beside her young husband. At night the image of her would creep into his dreams. He would find himself looking up into her beautiful, hardened face and seeing the mocking hatred in her eyes. He had to destroy her. He had to force her beyond this side of darkness into a place where she would be forever alone, without sight or hearing or love. There must be no chance of her spirit finding him again. He would kill her husband and her sister along with her, and in a way so terrible that no one would ever want to remember what had happened to them or name a child after them.

By midwinter, in the Moon of Frosts, Passing Shadow had already begun his plan. Determined to learn the whereabouts of Wanderer's winter camp, the shaman started to spend the milder winter evenings sitting beside a fire with the young men from Black Snake's tribe. Resting his heels near the hearth, he sat down on a log that the other men kept clean for him and questioned them about the hunting trails they followed. In this way he grew to know the routes most often used by Wanderer's people. The men who sat beside him on those nights seldom guessed at the grim motives that lay behind his questioning. They listened to his talk because he was the most knowledgeable and powerful of shamans. He had killed many men with his bad medicine, had destroyed the circle of the Great Village, and had earned a reputation for evil deeds that had spread through all the tribes.

At first, Passing Shadow was treated respectfully. Shamans of lesser importance came to sit and listen to this person who had long ago ceased to be an ordinary man. Sometimes they would talk with him about the ways of calling forest spirits or about finding a pathway into the place of dreams. Mostly, though, Passing Shadow talked of blood and the need to avoid being stained by the touch of women. He spoke of women's habits with great disgust, describing their bodies in ritual tones that made his listeners shiver with nausea. Young men who were tempted by the nearness of their own pretty wives turned from their lodges with new resolve. Like the great bear shaman, they, too, would gain strength by sleeping alone.

Gradually though, some of the younger men grew tired of Passing Shadow's repeated warnings and began to mock him behind their hands. "Was it not true that this shaman had abused his power?" they asked each other. His soul was being eaten by the magic of a beautiful young girl. She had treated him so badly that he only wanted to avenge himself. Perhaps it would be safer to kill such a man rather than wait until he turned his evil magic against them.

These same men began to make up songs about a jealous old shaman whose beautiful wife refused him because of his bad smell. This young woman had gone to live with a man whose skin was clear. She laughed at the old shaman, despising him as a foul-smelling beast.

Ever watchful, Passing Shadow soon heard this refrain. He determined to punish the mocking young men, but only after he had killed Morning Land. His hatred for her was enough to quell his fury at these insults and to keep him outwardly calm.

Finally came the news that one of the Tideland sisters had given birth to a child. For a man who wanted only to think of his wife as dead, this was the greatest goad of all. Somewhere out there the woman who had hurt him so much was not only still alive but might even be bearing another man's children. He had been no more than a pause in her life, a mistake to be quickly forgotten. He had not killed her. His magic had not harmed anyone. That thought made him want to scream and claw at her face, at the face he saw in every dream.

The hunters who had laughed at him before thought even less of Passing Shadow now, for even young shamans were able to cause barrenness in their victims. Convinced that the hunters' mocking songs would continue to follow him wherever he went, Passing Shadow did not wait for the weather to clear before setting out to find the sisters. During the uncertain Moon of Storms, he made his first attempt.

One morning Passing Shadow's two remaining wives woke to find the shaman gone from their lodge. He had left at night, after painting his face black with ash paste. A few of Black Snake's hunters saw the shaman that sunrise. He was climbing a large hill beyond some distant trees. The men shouted, but the shaman was already too far away. Watching his hunched figure, the men saw him reach the highest point of ground, shake his war club violently at the clouding sky, and disappear down the opposite side of the hill. The men who witnessed this did not hunt long that morning, for the weather quickly worsened.

The western wind grew stronger as Passing Shadow neared the open savannah. He passed a tree filled with black crows that were already huddling close together. Another time he saw a flock of songbirds clustered densely under a low-standing bush. These signs were not good omens, but when Passing Shadow thought of the mocking faces of the hunters in the village behind him, he knew that he had to go on.

Following the directions he had learned from some of those hunters, Passing Shadow traveled westward into the wind, crossing over thorn hills until he reached the "river of birch trees" that the men had described. He walked upstream along the bank of that river, looking for further signs. In good seasons, the river's water flowed clear and blue over golden sand, but the clouds were more dense and closed than before, and the river reflected their darkness. Passing Shadow walked slowly, carefully scanning for signs of a trail or footpath. Keeping to the riverbank, he avoided the eroded places where the soil slipped out all too readily under a man's feet. Here at least, the trees provided some shelter and the wind had lessened. Old leaves, drifting in that wind, wavered through the air around him like falling snow. In places they piled up into brownish mounds.

He paused long enough to watch the leaves. In that miserable place, he decided that he did not want Morning Land to die quickly. It was important that she learn to suffer as he had. He wanted to know by her screams that he had brought her a sadness that would never go away. He wanted her winters to be as filled with horror and emptiness as his. Perhaps if he killed her child and her sister and her husband. If he tortured them in front of her, perhaps—Passing Shadow shook his head. She would only marry again and have more children. He must hurt her deeper than that. He must find the way that would hurt most of all.

Forcing his way onward, he noticed human tracks in the shore sand. The hunter's feet had left deep impressions and led to a furrowed trail. At a place where the bank of the river was quite high, the trail led away to the west and brought Passing Shadow under a high narrow ridge. Rain had begun to fall. The shaman sloshed through mud at the base of the ridge. Even this was better than what he would find on the open savannah. Staggering upward along a straggling pathway, he reached the top of the ridge and strained to see around him. The grasslands beyond were nearly lost in a blur of falling rain. The shaman could have holed up under the ridge, but he knew the rain might last for days. He decided to cross the savannah before the storm grew worse.

No longer sheltered by the ridge, Passing Shadow hurried down onto the open plains of the Great Valley. His path led through wet marshy hollows where spring wildflowers were just beginning to show themselves, and rose slowly over long, gently sloping hills. At times he was almost blinded by the rain. Ahead of him, the last traces of blue sky disappeared into a solid black mass of storm clouds. Somewhere farther on he would be caught in the full late-winter gale. Passing Shadow kept walking, slipping and sliding in places where the ground was suddenly no longer solid under his feet, until he found a rock outcropping to hide behind. There he settled for the night.

All through the long darkness he waited, sitting without a hearth fire while wind-swirled rain rushed by on either side. The entire world was now hidden behind the moving rain and black clouds.

Finally dawn light showed heavy and gray around him. Passing Shadow's head was hot and he knew that a fever was rising inside him. He walked to a rainwater stream and drank from it. He was weak, but not sick enough to be forced to return. Stumbling to his feet, he continued walking along the slopes and flatlands in the drizzling rain. He zigzagged around marshy hollows and stayed behind bushes wherever he could. Eventually he came out onto an open height overlooking the lake he had been searching for. Far off, outlined on a ridge by the lake itself, he saw the cluster of weathered lodges that formed Wanderer's village.

After this he began descending, and the trail grew smoother. Gusts of rain still swept through gaps in the trees to dig up bare patches of storm-scoured ground, but nothing the shaman met with there could slow him. He followed footpaths made by village women until, at the very edge of the village, he squatted down and waited.

There were no piles of winter debris around the village, and the banks of mud at the sides of the lodges seemed newly built. From this, Passing Shadow learned that the site had only recently been settled. Wanderer's people would probably continue to stay there for several moons. Everything seemed peaceful inside the camp. Children ran about from lodge to lodge in a game of ducking raindrops, women were chattering among themselves and stirring warm fires, some of the men had gathered in groups to repair weapons and talk of hunting.

So near his goal, Passing Shadow searched anxiously for some sign of the sisters. The lodges closest to him belonged to other families, so the shaman was forced to creep further forward and find a different position. As he walked, he avoided stepping in the middle of the path. Though none of the villagers expected an intruder, Passing Shadow was careful not to leave any identifiable footprints. He concealed himself again near the edge of a busy village trail.

At last he saw them—saw *her,* eating a meal and playing with a young child. The jolt of recognition made him almost cry out. She seemed happy, and her smile was like a poison in his heart. She had never smiled or sung in all her time with him. Unaccountably his eyes blurred over and he had to rub his face with his free hand before he could see again. Perhaps it was only the fever getting stronger.

She was close enough to be killed. He could hurl his war club across the short distance and strike her on the head. In his youth, he had killed many this way. If he hesitated now it was only because he no longer trusted his strength. The woman might not fall dead instantly. Then her outcry would bring many spears against him. Passing Shadow remembered Wanderer and Fighting Eagle's hatred for him. Neither man would hesitate to kill him instantly. There would be no warning spear thrown harmlessly over his head.

The more he looked at the setup of the village, the less convinced he was that he could succeed. The lodges were very close together, and bad weather had kept all of the hunters home. This was not the season for revenge killings. He would have to leave and return again during the time of the Clover Moon. On that night, when the hunters listened only to the voices of their lovers, he would be able to come and go as he wished.

Despite his decision to leave, Passing Shadow lingered for a long time, memorizing every detail of Laughing One's lodge. The happiness of the small family was painful to watch, but he would let them keep joy in their hearts for this day. Finally, after staring at Morning Land one last time, he fled from the village before anyone could guess that an enemy had been near.

Passing Shadow arrived home sick and remained feverish for many days. Then, to the great disappointment of his wives, he recovered. Ignoring the village hunters whom he had once met nightly with, the shaman began wandering the savannah for a different purpose. This time he sought the nesting sites of rattle-

snakes. After capturing four of the reptiles alive, he placed them
in a large sealed basket that he had forced his wives to make for
him. The creatures were not fed. After a time, the shaman
stalked and killed a doe. The deer's meat was tossed aside to
feed the scavengers. Only the doe's liver was kept.

One by one, Passing Shadow removed the captured snakes
and goaded them into striking at the piece of raw liver. When
a snake grew tired and appeared to lose interest, Passing
Shadow pinned its head with a forked stick. Holding the reptile
this way, he would strike its tail with his knife until it tried to
bite his hand. In its wounded fury, the snake again dug its fangs
into the piece of liver. At that moment, Passing Shadow chopped off the snake's head and let the reptile's reflex actions pump
the last of its poison into the meat. By the time he had finished
with all four snakes, the deer liver dripped with yellow venom.
To make sure of its strength, Passing Shadow licked the edge of
the liver with his tongue. The sweet tingling sensation that came
to his lips told him this venom would kill. Satisfied, he slipped
the poisoned liver inside a leather pouch and buried it in dry
sand.

A moon passed. Warm spring breezes moved across the land.
Birds flitted about in the branches, gathering food for their
ever-hungry young, whose hidden nests were surrounded by the
bright green of new leaves. In the clover-covered fields, bees
and wasps buzzed around the pink flowers, while grass-smeared
children hurled clumps of earth at one another in mock battles.
It was a time for chewing on clover and tasting its sweetness;
a time when men loitered around the village while their wives
collected spring bulbs and flowers; a time when young women
rubbed sweet-smelling leaves across their bodies and through
their hair, a time for "making children grow."

Passing Shadow had chosen this moment of turning seasons
to begin his final act of revenge. On the day that he left Black
Snake's village for the last time, he dug up the poison pouch.
Even this could not be done without a ritual. The shaman
walked to the place where the pouch had been buried, squatted
down on his heels, and spoke to the ground in a low voice. He
extolled the spirit and power of the snake god, whose poison
could settle in a man's body to inflict great pain and provoke
slow death. After explaining that he would need enough
strength to kill at least three people, he reverently dug into the
sandy earth and brought up the molded pouch with its shriveled,

slowly rotting bundle. This he immediately wrapped in a new carrying pouch.

"Let my enemies struggle before dying," he chanted. "Let this poison pass through them. Let their hearts break like rotten branches."

Passing Shadow's second journey to Wanderer's village was made when the spring grass was at its richest. Around him, in the fields and hollows of the savannah, grazing animals gave birth or lay in the grass and chewed dreamily. Passing Shadow moved among this, but was strangely untouched by it. His mind remained as intense as that of a hunting cat stalking a newborn fawn. While he did kill some small game along the way and built a fire at night to ward off predators, these were his only concessions to bodily needs. Through everything else, Passing Shadow remained preoccupied with the desperate, passionate killing that would mark the end of his journey.

It was late in the afternoon of the second day that he again came to the open ground overlooking Wanderer's lake. A glance at the distant village convinced him that it was still occupied. Hearth fires sent their pale smoke up into the blue sky. On a high bare part of that distant ridge, piles of gathered logs showed where the ritual fire and dance were to be held. This was the day of the full moon.

Passing Shadow descended to an isolated grove he had discovered during his first journey. There, hidden by a small stand of trees, he began the last part of his preparations.

The old shaman had taken as many of his weapons as he could safely carry. These consisted of his war club, a knife, a spear, and the likeness of a bear's paw that would fit snugly over his left hand. Wedged into this "paw" were four curved, ivory claws; each one as long as a man's thumb and carved to have a knifelike cutting edge. One slap from this paw could rip open a man's forehead, blinding him and making him an easy victim for the shaman's dagger.

The sun was moving toward the western horizon and already stood below the tops of the tallest trees. Passing Shadow had to move quickly, for the poison made its demands on those who used it. The shaman wished to be finished before darkness overtook him. After placing the pouch he had been carrying onto the ground, he tore it open and pulled out the dried and shriveled deer's liver that rested inside. He used his knife to cut scrapings from the ruined meat, then ground those scrapings to a powder.

This he poured out onto some wide maple leaves. Blended with the powder were the juices of two poisonous plants and a gummy resin that would make the mixture cling to a knife edge. The powder, juices, and resin had to be slowly stirred until they formed a thick fluid. While doing this, Passing Shadow chanted an invocation of curses.

The shaman prayed that his victims' hearts would stop, that their blood would spill easily, and that their muscles would grow rigid with pain. When the chanting was through, he used a reed brush to paint dabs of the poison onto his knife, his spear tip, and each of the four ivory claws. He worked carefully, trying to keep his fingers free of the fluid. Though the venom was harmless to unbroken skin, a simple cut could start it working, and Passing Shadow knew enough to keep himself safe from his own poison.

The freshly coated weapons had a slightly grayish tinge in the late afternoon light. Passing Shadow placed them against a shaded rock, where the cooler air would help to harden the poisonous gum, and sat down to consider the rest of his plan. The full moon would rise late, forcing him to cross most of the distance to the village in nearly total darkness. Even so, there was little chance of his being discovered. On this particular night, the men would be so involved with their women that they would leave the village unguarded. When all of the villagers were singing and chanting, no one would hear his footsteps even if he did stumble. The hunters would be watching the dancers, not the shadows. By the time the moon had finally risen, every strong young man would be making love out in the grass. This warm night, with its sensual darkness and murmuring lovers, could serve his needs very well.

As a final ritual, Passing Shadow opened his shaman's pouch and took out a yellowed saber-toothed tusk. It was the one he had stolen from Morning Land during the first season of their marriage. He used it now as a symbol of the victim he most wanted to kill. Laying the tusk at his feet, he spat on it several times and chanted.

"This night I shall be a hunter of women.
I shall kill many.
The one I seek will not flee like she did before.
Do not be friendly toward her, Yeane.
Do not let the scorched meat near her hearth drive you away.
Do not frighten her.

Let me fix my knife into her heart.
Let her feel fever.
Let her limbs grow heavy.
Let dizziness overcome her.
Make her ill with a sickness
from which she can never grow strong again.
Let her breasts be covered with her own blood."

In a field not far away, two of Passing Shadow's intended victims were busy preparing for the clover dance. Like the rest of the village women, they had spent the afternoon making grass skirts, and Morning Land crouched down patiently while White Bird rubbed her hair with scented grease. White Bird still wore her apron, for as a nursing mother she could not take part in the dance itself. She did not seem bothered by her exclusion. The fun of decorating her older sister was increased by Morning Land's obvious uneasiness. For the first time that White Bird could remember, Morning Land was behaving more like a shy girl than a woman.

As she smoothed Morning Land's hair with her fingers, White Bird giggled teasingly. "Eh. This hair will be shining out of the darkness. Many men will want to touch it. Your hair lives. Even after I cut it short to make a wife out of you, it still lives."

Morning Land glanced down at her bare, upturned breasts and sighed. "These breasts have not begun to droop, but my stomach already stands out."

"You carry the child well," White Bird insisted. "Your stomach stands out only a little way. The season of this child is still young."

"I am not an unmarried woman who has had only lovers," Morning Land said. "A woman who carries a child inside her should not dance. She should only sit there and watch the others."

"Listen. Only a few seasons ago, when Sacred Dance was very big inside my belly, I, too, danced. I did not cry out in fear. I had courage, and my stomach was much bigger than yours is this day."

White Bird stopped her finger-combing and began sprinkling grass flowers over Morning Land's black hair. "You have something so good that this child inside you does not matter," she said. "You will be the important one in this dance. All of the men, even those who are very old, all of them will want you."

"I do not want to be the important one," Morning Land grumbled. "When I give birth to this child, then I will be important. Now I only want to sit quietly with my sister and my husband. I do not want other men to chase after me." Touching White Bird's soft belly, Morning Land added, "When you danced inside the circle, other women did not hate you. I have watched Beautiful Star stare at me. If she could, she would throw me down onto this sand and stab me again and again with her bone needle."

White Bird laughed. "She is afraid of the things you will do. Always before when she danced, you were not there. Everyone spoke of how well she had done. Her heart was happy that men desired her. That is what she wanted. Now things rush ahead of her. Any one of these other women could not dance the way you will dance. Beautiful Star knows this, and makes angry faces." With barely a pause, White Bird added, "Stand up, my sister."

Morning Land obeyed and White Bird moved in a slow circle around her, tugging at the edges of the grass skirt until it rested easily over Morning Land's hips. When White Bird was satisfied, the younger sister stepped back and stared at Morning Land with obvious admiration.

"The child that is now inside you will have a beautiful mother," White Bird exclaimed.

Morning Land lowered her eyes and did not reply. The very fact that she was submitting to this ritual showed how much the winter season had changed her. Laughing One's lovemaking and White Bird's kindness had made Morning Land feel safe in this village. With a young child growing inside her, it seemed that she would at last find her place as a woman of the tribe.

White Bird glanced at the rest of the village women. Without any spoken commands, they had already formed into two groups. It was more than dress that distinguished these groups. The dancers had a special bearing, a way of holding their young bodies erect that showed both self-pride and expectation. Most were as strong and graceful now as they would ever be.

"*Atoshe*, we must hurry," White Bird told her sister. "The other women are ready to move away."

Morning Land was suddenly frightened. "What will I do when the men begin to chase after me?" she asked.

With a gesture that was rapidly becoming habit, White Bird twisted her head to stare at her child. Sacred Dance rested in a bag pouch slung across White Bird's back and was sleeping with her face turned to one side.

"You are not a baby girl," White Bird told Morning Land. "You are a grown woman. You know how to run. Only do not run too far away. You do not wish to sleep alone in the bush. *Tua-arikii* will follow your footsteps and find you."

"What if others are looking for me?" Morning Land persisted. "How can I know that it is Laughing One who follows me?"

White Bird sighed. "Tell me where you will be hidden," she suggested, "and I will whisper this to our husband. He will find his own wife even if it is dark."

Morning Land whispered some quick words into her sister's ear. Then, only slightly reassured, she prepared to join the others.

"You should not be worried," White Bird told her. "My memories of this dance are good ones."

Morning Land remained doubtful. She stood last in the line of dancers and was taller and less experienced than the others. Even when the girls crouched in the high grass to conceal themselves, Morning Land had to crouch lower than anyone else. To be the oldest of the dancers and the one who knew nothing about the ritual was unpleasant. To have the uneven-tempered, glowering Beautiful Star as the dance leader was even more unpleasant.

Once they were hunched down and moving forward through the tall grass in a mock stalking of the village, the other girls seemed to forget about Morning Land. From their excited whispers, Morning Land soon realized that each of these girls was able to recognize her lover by the sound of his footsteps. Despite all her training in the ways of the forest, Morning Land doubted if she could do the same. There was a great deal of joking about the less attractive hunters.

"I will run faster if that one sees me. He just lies with a woman and does not know what to do."

"He gets tired too soon. It would take more than I have to make his back alive again."

"He is kind but he always smells bad. Being with him is like lying beside a dead buffalo calf."

The girls' talk led to an irrepressible giggling that grew so loud that one of the village matrons threatened to slap the girls' ears if they would not be quiet. After that, the whispering became softer, but the joking continued until a warning hiss from Beautiful Star finally silenced it.

By this time they had reached their hiding place at the bottom of the ridge. The girls crouched even lower amid some bushes, keeping their heads turned to one side as they listened for Spear Maker's signal. There was a long moment when the women's repressed breathing blended with the sounds of the field. Then Spear Maker's prayer began. Though she strained to listen, Morning Land could not make sense of the old man's words. Along with his voice there was a loud clattering that gradually became a recognizable drumbeat. Each time the other men shouted, the dancers tensed. Morning Land could feel their excitement. They seemed ready to run up onto the open ridge at any moment.

Unaccountably, Beautiful Star and Summer Wind suddenly began shouting as well.

"We are near, Father," they cried.

"We come up out of the ground.

"We have heard your song.

"We have heard your singing."

Then the dancers were all moving again. The girls hurried up the ridge, anxious to get near the dancing circle at its peak. The caution they had shown when approaching the village was forgotten. Bushes shivered as the young women brushed past. One branch slapped back unexpectedly at Morning Land's face.

Beautiful Star screamed something else and Spear Maker muttered a reply. Abruptly both lines of women stood up. As Morning Land walked to the top of the ridge, she saw a circle of men waiting for them and felt an impulse to run. She wanted to hide in the safety of her lodge. Instead, she strode forward with a grimly determined expression on her face. She had one final glimpse of White Bird as the lines of women separated. Then the dancers stood alone.

The girls had grown suddenly shy, although a few of them did manage to glance around quickly to see if their men were watching. Of the group, only Beautiful Star seemed aware of what came next. She answered each of Spear Maker's mumbled chants and was the first to begin moving sideways in a ritualized shuffle step. As the other girls started walking sideways as well, the dance leader's stride became more bouncing, and she swayed her buttocks rhythmically, producing a pleasing swish of the grass skirt. Morning Land tried to mimic all of this. At first the movements seemed awkward to her, but the clapping hands and aggressive chanting of the leader were like a goad to her pride. She would not simply stumble about.

What happened then was unexpected. The clover dance,

which was supposed to be a pleasantly sensual ritual, soon became the setting for a contest between two proud women. From the very first moments of the dance, Beautiful Star sensed a rival in the orange firelight. Morning Land stood sleek and tall before the men, but more startling than her physical beauty was the suppleness of her movements. The stiffened posture that the Tidelander usually assumed when she was being watched had entirely vanished. Instead, her body followed the drum rhythm with surprising ease. Each time Beautiful Star swung her leg sideways, Morning Land matched the action precisely, so that both women's feet touched ground at the same instant. And though the dancers were constantly shifting weight as they swung around the fire, the Tidelander never seemed to be caught off balance.

The fast rhythm of the drumbeat could not match Beautiful Star's own inner fury. With an impatient gesture, she pushed away the girls on either side of her and let her arms drop. Then she swung in toward the fire to begin dancing on her own. While the other girls held back, chanting and swaying their hips gently, Beautiful Star forced her body to move to a more demanding rhythm. The dance leader made her hips shake until the trembling rustle of the grass skirt was as loud in her ears as the drumbeat. She swung her buttocks in a rapid tempo that kept time with her own pounding heart. During other dances, these actions had excited those who watched her, but now there was something too frantic about her movements. Beautiful Star's expression was intense and angry, not sensual. She seemed to have lost the joy in what she did.

On the opposite side of the fire, Morning Land had moved in close and was again imitating the leader's actions. Her own rounded buttocks swung easily from side to side as she spun around near the flames. There was nothing tense about her dancing. It was simply a gifted mimicking, so nearly perfect that Beautiful Star could have been dancing before her own reflection—only this time the reflected image was more beautiful than its model.

Through flowing hip motions and quick, unexpected turns, Beautiful Star tried to regain the attention of the watching hunters. She made short sideways lunges, raised her arms above her head like a woman overwhelmed by passion, and twisted her waist until her hips vibrated and tingled with the effort. Even though her breath was coming in gasps like that of an exhausted runner, Beautiful Star felt a frustrating sense of failure. Her rival was just as quick as she was, and bold gesturing could not hide the fact that Morning Land was more beautiful.

Beautiful Star wanted to go on dancing before the fire until the Tidelander began to falter, but tiredness finally made the dance leader slow her pace. Her legs spread wide in an effort to retain balance. There was a ringing sensation in her head and her chest felt raging hot, as if something inside had burst. With tears flowing down the sides of her face, she stopped moving about. The watchers seemed to accept this signal, for their singing abruptly ended.

The sudden change in tempo left Morning Land off balance. She spread her legs in imitation øf Beautiful Star and stared at the dance leader expectantly, but she was to get no direction this time. Beautiful Star suddenly ran off into the darkness. The rest of the dancers abruptly spun around and burst out toward the open field as well. Then the whole village seemed to awaken.

The delightful sensation of having danced well, the pleasant tingling in her arms and legs from hard-worked muscles, lulled Morning Land. Slippery with sweat, she remained still for a long moment after the others had begun to run. Her peaceful feeling ended in a jolt of fear when a strange man hurriedly grabbed at her from inside the ring of firelight. Morning Land's short scream had barely left her lips as she ducked out ahead of the hunter into the cool night air.

This sudden scare made her forget about Laughing One and the words she had whispered to White Bird. She only heard the thudding of other footsteps behind her, as if the entire tribe were closing in. Terrified at having so many men rush toward her, Morning Land fled from them as she would have fled from an enemy. She ran for the cover of the woods. Swinging branches whipped around her as she plunged deeper and deeper into the brush.

It took a long while for her to grow calm again. The hunters had been seeking pleasure, not scratches and nettles. They followed for only a short distance before abandoning the chase and veering back into the open field. Left alone but unaware of it, Morning Land continued to dart through the scrub like a fly-angered buck. The tangle of low shrubs scratched her legs. Twisted roots caught at her feet. Only after she had nearly fallen did she slow her pace and begin to walk carefully, in a flat-footed fashion.

Shivering and cursing by turns, Morning Land worked her way forward through the darkness. Now that she had stopped running, she felt the long thorn cuts on her legs, the sweat clinging to her skin, and the coolness of the night air. Worse than the cold or her sore muscles was the embarrassment she felt at having panicked. The murmuring of the villagers had sunk away behind her and all she could smell through the darkness were the ancient scents of forest mold and decaying leaves. There was no need to hide now. How White Bird would enjoy teasing her about this.

The deep spring night had been very dark before, but now the full moon finally lifted above the horizon. Morning Land stood in the middle of the shadows and stared out into the moonlight. She was near the edge of a low stretch of marshland. To her left loomed the black bulk of the ridge, with the lake shimmering behind it.

Having found a pathway close at hand, Morning Land stepped clear of the woods and worked her way back toward the village. With the moonlight pushing away the shadows, she was able to avoid most of the weeds and nettles that nuzzled at her legs on either side. She moved quickly along the path under the black trees, suddenly anxious to be beside her own lodge again. The night of dancers and running hunters had slipped away behind her, leaving her strangely cold and lonely. She almost began singing to herself for comfort, but some warning sense kept her quiet. Then, from somewhere ahead near the empty lodges, she heard a faint scream.

It was White Bird's voice.

Morning Land felt her heartbeat growing loud in her chest once more. Her skin suddenly felt snow-cold under the white moonlight. Something was very wrong.

Laughing One had looked on bemusedly as Morning Land had performed her writhing dance before the circle of men. Unlike many of the other watchers, he had not been completely surprised by the cleverness of her mimickry. His married life with the Tidelanders had taught him that the sisters were never fully predictable. Like the words of White Bird's songs, the dances of the Tidelanders were always changing. Even so, Morning Land's dancing that night had held a special fascination. The shivering of her hips at each step, the sweep of her grass skirt against her thighs, the shine of the firelight on her swaying body, her pausing and yielding to the flow of music— all had made her movements seem so much easier than those of the dance leader.

Since White Bird had already told him about Morning Land's nervousness, Laughing One knew that the Tidelander expected him to meet with her in a special place behind the fire. Determined to act properly, he did not run forward too quickly when the dance ended. Laughing One wanted to give his wife time to overcome her timid feelings.

The young hunter's plans ended almost as abruptly as the dance itself. He was starting toward Morning Land when he felt a sudden shove that knocked him off balance. In the moment it took him to recover, three other men had rushed ahead of him. Morning Land was to be properly chased that night.

While the Tideland woman ran for the protection of the forest and hurled herself through sharp bushes, Laughing One searched hopefully for her in the place where he had been told to look. Already other couples were settling down in the field. They would play at lovemaking until morning, but for Laughing One everything had gone wrong. He had been left to himself like those ugly men the woman always laughed at. Perhaps White Bird's sister was hidden in one of the dark and shadowy places around the edge of the field, or perhaps she was among the couples already lying in the grass. Some bolder hunter might have taken her while Laughing One had been politely waiting. This last thought infuriated Laughing One so much that he continued to pace around in the dark long after he had given up any hope of finding his wife.

Unable to see well in the blackness, Laughing One came quite close to a pair of lovers before he realized that they were there. The girl giggled loudly at his approach, but the hunter did not bother to look up as Laughing One passed. From the heaviness of the girl's breathing, Laughing One knew that her lover was lying on top of her. The other heaving grunts and noises the couple made had an obvious cause. Laughing One continued walking, feeling more and more foolish. Ignored by the lovers on all sides, he was still tormented by their sounds. The moans of some girls were low and soft, like a shallow wind, but others gasped and squealed as if they were being burned. Though none of the voices resembled Morning Land's, he found himself listening for her in spite of this. When he had made his way all across the field, he finally became convinced she was not there. After that, there was no point in continuing.

At the lodge, White Bird sat quietly nursing her child. She shifted position from time to time so the baby's mouth could take hold of her nipples more easily, and she began a rhythmic rocking each time the child started to squirm, but her dark eyes seemed utterly indifferent. As she stared at the hearth fire, she imagined her husband and sister making love out in the field among the other couples. It was not a cheering thought. Later, while Morning Land tried to find her way back through the darkened forest and a dejected Laughing One turned toward his own hearth, White Bird replaced the moss in her baby's carrying pouch. For a few moments Sacred Dance kicked the soft tufts of clean moss as she stretched her arms and legs. Then White Bird laced up the front of the bag to keep the infant from getting cold.

Laughing One arrived home in time to watch her doing this. He could not understand why White Bird seemed so different from the girl he had chased into the fields at the last clover dance. She was heavier. Her stomach jiggled slightly when she moved, and her breasts sagged a little from the weight of the milk they carried, but the changes he felt were greater than this. She had somehow joined with the other mothers of the tribe, becoming so much like them that when he saw the village women gathering food on a distant slope it was often difficult to distinguish White Bird from the rest.

She looked up at him balefully as he stepped toward the hearth. "Are you the only one who comes here?" she asked. "Where is my sister?"

"Let me be the first to tell you," Laughing One grumbled. "Your sister ran far away from the fire. She hid herself in the forest like a deer. I have walked and walked, all by myself. I never found her."

"*Shiiwe!* My sister is truly senseless," White Bird exclaimed.

Trying hard not to show how pleased she was by this turn of events, White Bird took her sleeping child inside the lodge and placed Sacred Dance near the family's bark-cloth mats. The baby would remain inside the bag pouch all night. Over the winter season, little Sacred Dance had become so used to being laced up snugly that she refused to sleep any other way.

When White Bird crawled out of the lodge again, there was no trace of her earlier annoyance. She smiled at Laughing One as she said, "My sister is a strange one. At times she is very clever and at other times she just has no sense. There are days when she will not take food when it is offered. No, not her. She agrees to let her husband find her and then she just is not there."

"She must still be hiding somewhere in the bush," Laughing

One said regretfully. "I could not find her anywhere out in the field."

"There is no reason to keep on looking for her," White Bird assured him. "She will return to the lodge when she is ready. You have done all that any woman could ask of a husband."

Laughing One grunted doubtfully and edged closer. After the frustration of searching, he found White Bird's smile very comforting. As he sat down next to her, White Bird added, "You have another wife who has learned not to run away."

They began to caress each other, with White Bird's fingers moving in soothing circles across Laughing One's back while his hands stroked the smoothness of her legs. "I am the woman you have already made your own," White Bird told him.

Feeling wanted again, Laughing One pressed his face against her neck. "My wife," he whispered. "When you lie down with me . . ."

Suddenly White Bird's hands grew tense. "I hear someone," she hissed.

Laughing One looked up resentfully. "It must be Morning Land," he muttered. "She is the only one who would come near our lodge on this night."

"Perhaps," White Bird whispered uncertainly.

"Call out to her," Laughing One suggested.

"*Atoshe!* Morning Land! *Atoshe!*" White Bird called. "Why are you so quiet? There is no one here to hurt you."

"She would answer you if she were near," Laughing One grumbled. More annoyed than interested, he lifted his head and searched the shadows. All he could see beyond the range of firelight was blackness.

As soon as Laughing One had moved his head away, White Bird crossed her arms defensively over her bare breasts. She listened intently, trying to detect some warning clue that would give a reason for her uneasiness. There was nothing.

Laughing one stretched and stood up.

"The moon has risen," White Bird told him. "The moon stands in the sky and you can see beyond our fire."

Laughing One stared away from the fire for a long moment, allowing his eyes to grow used to the darkness. Though he had heard and seen nothing, he was becoming uneasy. White Bird was not a woman who started at shadows. The young hunter felt around by the lodge entrance until he had found his best spear. After picking it up and testing its weight, he glanced at White Bird. "Stay near the lodge," he told her.

His tone said more than his words. White Bird understood at once that Laughing One did not expect to find her sister out there in the darkness. It was the fear of something else, of something far less friendly, which had made him pick up his spear. Not pausing to reply, she slipped back inside the lodge. Left alone, Laughing One carried his spear with him as he moved very slowly toward the darkened side of their home. He was still unsure of what he should be looking for.

Like all hunters, he studied the ground in his search for signs. Even in the dimness of moonlight, the prints of human feet were distinctive enough for him to tell who had been near his lodge that night. Now he saw that the only visible tracks were the ones his wives had left on their way to and from the bushes. If there was a man nearby, it was one who stepped carefully, hiding his footmarks. That could only mean an enemy.

White Bird came out of the lodge to stand behind him. She had brought his hunting knife and her own woman's knife. Laughing One took the hunting knife from her and slipped it through a loop in his loincloth. "What did you hear?" he asked.

"A person walking," White Bird told him. "Someone stepping inside the bushes. There is no wind, and still the leaves rustled." In a harsh whisper, she added, "I think it is the bad one. I think it is Passing Shadow. No one else would trouble us this way."

Laughing One shook his head. He had begun to doubt if anyone was out there in the darkness.

"It is Passing Shadow," White Bird hissed. "I know his smell."

Laughing One sniffed at the air curiously. There was a faintly stale smell, but he had assumed it was from bad meat left by someone's hearth.

White Bird tugged at his arm insistently. "It is not safe to stay here alone," she pleaded. "He will kill us."

"Everyone else is still by the great fire," Laughing One said slowly. "Either there or out in the fields. All of these lodges are empty."

"Then no one will hear me when I scream," White Bird whispered.

The idea startled Laughing One, giving him a new sense of danger. He stared harder at the surrounding woods. The moonlight shimmered off the surface leaves of nearby bushes, but revealed nothing of the shadows deeper in. As he stood there, trying to see some half-imagined enemy, a sick feeling began to rise in Laughing One's stomach. He was losing confidence in himself.

"Do not say anything more," he whispered. "Go into the lodge and take Sacred Dance. Walk slowly. When you have your baby, sit near the lodge entrance and build up the fire. Do not try to run. If there is a man hiding out there, he would be waiting for that."

From his place amid the shadows and tree roots, Passing Shadow had watched all of this. He was less concerned with what the woman did than he was with the actions of the young hunter, for he had already decided to kill Laughing One first. Though White Bird's young husband was strong, Passing Shadow did not fear him. An inexperienced hunter was no match for a bear shaman. Before he could understand what was happening to him, Laughing One would have a poisoned spear shoved through his knees. With her husband crippled, it would be an easy thing to kill the wife. She would be too worried about her child to resist him.

The only thing that had kept the family safe thus far was the absence of Morning Land. Passing Shadow had expected to kill all of the family together, in one quick stroke, and then flee into the forest before any other villagers could guess at the damage he had done. By not being near the lodge, Morning Land had confused things. If she had found another lover, then killing her sister's family might not be enough.

Passing Shadow was about to withdraw and seek out the older Tideland sister when Laughing One grabbed up his spear. With the hunter alerted, Passing Shadow knew he could not afford to wait. He would have to attack soon.

For an instant, Laughing One thought he saw a face against the blackness of the trees. Two eyes seemed to be watching him. Then, as he stepped forward, the face was gone again, without a single leaf turning. There were only bushes in front of him.

Still searching for what he thought he had seen, Laughing One raised his spear to a striking position.

Laughing One did not see the shaman's spear. He only heard the flat twanging sound it made as its poisoned tip cut into his leg. He gasped and tried to jump back, but his entire body jerked uncontrollably from the blow. Passing Shadow's weapon had missed the knees and cut into Laughing One's right thigh instead. The wound was dangerous, but not crippling.

"Yi-quay-is!" Laughing One cried out. "Make the fire high! They have hit me with a spear!"

White Bird screamed and grabbed up her child. With her free hand, she used a short branch to jab frantically at the hearth coals in an effort to stir up the flames. All the while she worked, she cried out her fear in a loud resounding wail.

Hunched down from the wound in his leg, Laughing One sensed his enemy coming toward him. He did not hear the soft sound of brushing leaves or the thump of moccasined feet speeding across the ground. All of this was blocked out by White Bird's screaming. Deprived of these direction-finding clues, he could only hurl his spear at the dim shadow he saw hurrying toward him. The weapon sailed past uselessly over the shaman's head and clattered against the ground farther on.

Caution forgotten, Laughing One tried to pull out his knife. Before he could free the blade from his loincloth, four poisoned claws slashed down across his forehead, ripping open his scalp in a series of jagged ruptures. While blood spurted down into the young man's eyes, the shaman's knife blade sunk into the soft flesh of Laughing One's upper arm. The young hunter cried out in pain and rolled sideways. He let out a second cry as the shaman's knife jerked free of his flesh.

White Bird was on her feet, screaming in wild, piercing shrieks that echoed across the empty village. With her crying child in one hand and a burning stick in the other, she stared at the two shadowy figures struggling near the bushes. Each time her breath came back to her, she screamed again, even louder than before.

"Atoshe! They have hit him! They have hit my husband," she screamed. "They will kill us! They will kill all of us!"

These were the sounds that hurried Morning Land up the pathway. Unseen by the others, she moved quickly but cautiously, keeping to the shadows. It did not take long for her to understand what was happening. White Bird screamed for all to hear.

"Shiiwe! It is the shaman who is killing us! He is killing my husband! He has come from far away. He has come all this way only to kill us!"

In the fields, the villagers stirred from their lovemaking. No one hearing those screams could doubt the terror that lay behind them.

"What is happening?" White Bird howled. "Why will no one help us? Have you all run away?"

Convinced that he had already crippled Laughing One, Passing Shadow did not stay to kill the young hunter. Nearly blinded from the blood pouring out of his forehead, Laughing One was allowed to stumble away into the scrub. Passing Shadow would finish the young one later. He wanted to kill the loud-voiced woman before her screams brought all of the villagers against him. Slipping the knife he had used back into its pouch, he pulled his war club free of the thong that held it to his waist. Then he turned and raced toward White Bird. As he ran, he swung the club above his head and yelled a war cry.

White Bird screamed right back at him. All the while she had been shouting, she had been moving about hesitantly, taking several quick steps in one direction and then quickly retreating again, but always staying well within the circle of firelight. She would not loosen her grip on either the burning stick or Sacred Dance. As Passing Shadow hurried toward her like an enraged bear, she stepped back, numbly aware of her own helplessness. In the last moment before he struck her, White Bird tried to shove the burning brand into Passing Shadow's face. The shaman's swinging club quickly knocked it from her hand. His next blow caught White Bird on her left shoulder and sent her and her child tumbling into the darkness.

Passing Shadow had forgotten the demands that age made on a warrior's strength. In his mind, he was still the dread killer who came at night and slashed men to pieces with quick, frightening blows. For his body, it was otherwise. Passing Shadow thought that he had crippled Laughing One by a spear through the knee, but the spear had swung too high and cut thigh muscles instead. Passing Shadow believed that his knife had punctured one of the hunter's lungs, but the blade had been deflected and had only hit the upper arm. Not hopelessly crippled at all, the young hunter was enraged and deadly. It was true that Laughing One could no longer see well, but he had already pulled the spear free of his leg. He would use that spear to defend his wife and child.

While Passing Shadow stared through the darkness to find his victim, Laughing One ran across the circle of firelight and jabbed the shaman with his own poisoned spear. Passing Shadow's first wound of the night was a bad one. The sharpened stone blade cut a deep slice up the old man's back, from his waist to his shoulder. It was the shaman's turn to feel great pain.

Even when the spear slashed him and cut a quivering trail of blood up his back, Passing Shadow did not cry out. With only a deep grunt to acknowledge the hurt, he spun about and used his club to knock at the spear's handle. Laughing One's grip was stronger than White Bird's had been. The spear did not just fly away like a burning stick. Instead, the two weapons cracked hard against each other. Club and spear knocked together several times while Passing Shadow attempted to drive his enemy's weapon to the ground. Using his left foot, Passing Shadow kicked Laughing One's stomach. Laughing One in turn kicked Passing Shadow's legs to trip him, and both men tumbled to the earth together. Meanwhile club and spear had caught against each other and were knocked sideways to sweep away uselessly into the night.

This was the moment when Morning Land reached the area behind the lodge. She had already discarded the sensual but noisy grass skirt of the clover dance, preferring to move in silence. No one noticed her as she stepped out from the sheltering trees and crossed the flat, open area of ground. Naked and unarmed, her first thought was to find a weapon. In this, chance favored her. She was watching the two men struggling when one of her bare feet kicked the handle of Laughing One's discarded spear. Morning Land bent down and gripped it eagerly with both hands. Then slowly, very slowly, she stood up again.

Ahead of her, Laughing One rolled to his knees and leapt free into the shadows. His legs pushed him away just in time to avoid a slashing blow from the shaman's bear claws. Before the shaman could strike again, Laughing One was moving quickly through the black pathway beneath the trees. One thing favored him. Though hurt and partially blinded, he knew the ground far better than the shaman. After many days of camping in the area, he could guess the location and shape of every tree or bush. His mind drew on that knowledge as he darted through regions of nearly total darkness with only his outstretched fingers to guide him. There was no time to think of strategy, but he was instinctively following a circular route that would soon bring him back toward the fire.

Blood fury had made the shaman forget his earlier cleverness. A wiser hunter would have recognized the folly of trying to kill a prey that was fully alerted. It was time to pull back and work out a path of retreat, but the frenzied thoughts that howled in Passing Shadow's brain were no longer rational. He did not run in pursuit of Laughing One. The wounded youth was allowed to move freely under the trees. Instead, Passing Shadow got up again and walked to where White Bird crouched with her child.

Too upset to even look at the struggling men, White Bird hugged both arms around the crying Sacred Dance. White Bird's left arm was red with blood from where the shaman's club had struck her. Since she could not move it easily, she had chosen to stay where she was, vainly hoping that the darkness would hide her. Though she herself was motionless and silent, her crying baby drew the shaman to her.

Passing Shadow smiled when he saw them. He had guessed that the woman would not leave her child. Her attempt to protect the infant kept her pinned in one place. Enjoying his power, he advanced slowly toward the frightened mother. As his eyes focused on her, his knife twitched in his eager hand. This at least would be easy.

It was Laughing One who stopped him.

The young hunter had already circled back and was crouching just beyond the range of firelight when Passing Shadow closed in on White Bird. Clutching his knife in his right hand, Laughing One began a desperate run at the shaman.

Passing Shadow heard his approach and swung around to meet him. The shaman's knife made a soft whistling sound as it sliced through the air with deadly speed. It landed high, for Laughing One had ducked his head at the last moment. Instead of ripping open the young hunter's throat, the blade tore off most of one ear. Laughing One's head swirled with a new agony, but his own knife sank in.

The young hunter had stabbed upward, plunging his blade into the muscles just below the shaman's ribs. The knife cut so deeply that part of the blade broke off against the inside of the old man's chest as Laughing One yanked it out again. The hole it left was quickly filled with a rush of spouting blood. Passing Shadow staggered, and Laughing One was spared another slashing blow from the shaman's claw hand.

Both men were badly hurt. The poison from Passing Shadow's weapons was already affecting Laughing One's senses. His pain was making it harder and harder for him to concentrate on his enemy. Each step the young hunter took seemed strangely muffled. Each time he tried to shake the blood from his face, everything began to cloud in front of him. He was close to collapsing.

Then the shaman gave a bearlike growl, lurched erect, and leapt forward at the hunter.

Laughing One rolled out of the way as the shaman's knife slashed down on him. He avoided the slicing blade, but he landed badly, jarring his head against the earth. For an instant he was knocked senseless.

Passing Shadow's move to finish his enemy was never completed. Even as the shaman came forward, Morning Land jumped out of the darkness and plunged Laughing One's spear into Passing Shadow's belly. It was a deep, clean thrust that passed through from one side to the other. When she pulled out the blade, there was a great wound in Passing Shadow's stomach and yellow fat protruding. The shaman fell sideways, with both arms clutching his abdomen, but Morning Land was not finished with him.

The Tidelander closed in fast and continued to strike him. She speared his face, his stomach, his neck, and his legs. Passing Shadow tried to stand, fell back, and squirmed about. He grabbed for the spear in a vain effort to pull it from her hands. Morning Land was relentless. She kicked his hands away and struck still deeper, chopping his stomach until it was bleeding mush. The shaman's flesh shivered numbly under the thumping blows. His knife was lost. His empty hands fluttered in useless spasms. All red with blood but not yet dead, he did not even scream. His body was almost split open before he finally lost all his senses. Morning Land's spear thrusts were soon the only force that continued to shake him.

Morning Land never knew when Passing Shadow died. She just struck down again and again, mindless to everything but her need to kill this enemy. Later she would have grim dreams about the repulsive body that squirmed and clawed beneath her. Later she would remember the splattering blood and weep. But that night she was not bothered by the blood smell or the soft crunching of the carcass. What she felt was exhilaration, a kind of wild, dark joy.

Laughing One was closest to her. He opened his eyes and rolled onto his back, still groggy. With his face swollen and a trembling pain cutting through his head, he could do nothing more. The ground everywhere around him was soiled with blood. He could hear the sounds the spear made as its stone blade cut down through the shaman's body again and again and again until its tip struck earth. As he looked up into Morning Land's face, he began to understand how strong her hatred was. She would not be done with the shaman until he had been crushed entirely.

CHAPTER TWENTY

Moon of Falling Leaves

When the moons of summer had given way to the Moon of Falling Leaves, Trusted Friend and Laughing One found themselves once more amid the reeds and shadows of a predawn marsh. The purple of dawn had begun to show in the east, and the surface of the water, seen against the green silhouettes of cattails and water weeds, was flashing pink sparks of reflected light. Dancing swarms of flying gnats rose up above the weeds and spun away on either side as the two hunters reached the water. The night's cold was still in the air, making the water feel almost warm when the brothers waded into it. Their feet plunged down through the drifting light sheen of the surface, trailing long silver ripples which sank lower and lower before fading into the dark shadows of the shoreline.

They were stalking a pair of great, whistling swans that Trusted Friend had been watching for days. Trusted Friend knew exactly where the birds would roost and was moving directly to them. There was no hesitation, no searching, and no uncertainty on his part. He could have wounded one of the great birds easily with a single throw of his hunting spear, but Trusted Friend would make no effort to kill anything this day. Once more it was Laughing One whose skills were being tested.

Wanderer's youngest son had not slain anything since the night of Passing Shadow's death many moons before. The wounds he had gotten during that struggle had nearly crippled him. Even now, though he could flex the fingers of his left hand and hold a spear, his left arm lacked the strength to throw a weapon. To compensate, his right arm had grown more muscular until he had developed a slightly lopsided appearance when seen from the front. Fighting Eagle had taught him how to hold and throw a spear with his one good arm. Trusted Friend had shown him how to use the curious floating blades known as *iikiri*. It was time to see how much Laughing One had learned.

The men waded ever deeper, their bodies still shaded by the

branches of willow trees that grew tall on the slope behind
them. Dark with shadow on one side, lighted by the rising sun
on the other, the willow branches cast a strange, skeletal pattern
across the marsh. Somewhere at the edge of one of these shadows, the white swans rested.

As he moved, Laughing One fingered the two *iikiri* he held.
The blade of each weapon was formed in the shape of a waning
moon, and was attached to a thick wooden handle that would
keep it floating after it had landed on the water. Since anyone
with a single strong arm could hurl the *iikiri* across the lake's
surface like a skipping stone, it seemed well suited for Laughing One.

The swans were awake when the men reached the area of
their nest. The male had already begun to swim about amid the
reeds. Laughing One hunched motionless in shadow and waited
for it to come closer. He knew that he would have to cripple it
with his first throw. There was a moment's hesitation as one of
his feet caught in a tangle of roots. Then he kicked free, lurched
forward and hurled his weapon. The *iikiri* flashed out across the
sparkling water just as the alerted bird raised its white wings.
There was a sharp cracking sound as the right wing broke under
the impact of the blade. Fluttering and beating at the water, the
swan plunged back amid a flood of spray and feathers. Its struggles ended an instant later when Laughing One's second blade
snapped its neck. Then the two men who had wielded these curious moon-shaped weapons waded over to fetch their kill.

Grateful to have proved himself a hunter again, Laughing
One started talking immediately. "This is a hunter's way," he
said excitedly. "This is how to do things. I am no longer like
Ehina walking in the bush. My wives' teeth will not have to be
worn down from chewing the skins of last season's kill."

Trusted Friend did not reply. He was busy gathering the floating *iikiri* from off the top of the water and watching to see what
the swan's mate would do. Fortunately, the big female bird had
moved off in a flutter of wings and outraged honking.

"Those men who say that I can no longer hunt, who say that
I just walk while other men kill food, how will they laugh at
this?" Laughing One demanded, grabbing the neck of the swan
and holding the bird up for his brother to see. "Will they complain that I found this bird lying dead on the path and am giving
my wives something that a cat or wolf has already eaten? They
have made jokes like that before. One told me that the vultures
had all left this lake because there was nothing dead for them to

eat. He said I had already found all the dead things and had brought them home to my wives."

Trusted Friend shook his head and smiled sadly. "No, brother, they will not say that anymore. This bird came out of the morning mist to greet us. Your blade kept it from flying away again."

Laughing One continued as if Trusted Friend had not spoken. "They tell me that the kills I speak of only happened in my dreams. They say that my wives have learned to feed themselves because they could not wait for their husband to bring home meat."

"No, brother," Trusted Friend said quietly. He was worried by the strained tone of his brother's voice. Until that moment, Trusted Friend had not known how much the mocking jokes of the others had hurt Laughing One. "We tracked this bird and killed it openly," Trusted Friend assured him. "The blood on it is fresh. Everyone will see where your blade broke its wing and where its neck was cut."

"All summer you and Fighting Eagle came to my lodge bringing my wives big pieces of meat," Laughing One muttered as he dragged the dead swan in toward the shore. "Everything else, my wives found and gave to me. I only sat and ate. No one could get fat from eating the meat I had killed."

While Trusted Friend waded in silently beside his brother, he noticed how the dawn's rays highlighted the scars on Laughing One's body. It seemed as if there were wounds everywhere: claw scratches and knife cuts on Laughing One's thighs, a great knife wound in his left upper arm, one ear missing, and deep scratches across his face. His long hair allowed him to cover the area where his ear had been torn away, but the puckered slash marks across his forehead were as prominent as a burn.

In the days following the shaman's attack, these wounds had been much worse. Laughing One's face had been gray and his eyes had been swollen tight shut. The skin around his scalp had blackened frighteningly. In some places it had seemed to shine with reflected light. Along his arm there had been great blisters that had broken unexpectedly to drip wet ooze over his skin.

"He will not live very long," Rock Breaker had told Trusted Friend. "The shaman left him nearly dead. The poison has dug too deep. At each move, he bleeds."

"Even if he lives, he will never grow strong again," Bear Killer had added. "His face is ruined and his arm is crippled. He will never hunt. It would be better if he just died."

"They should cut the places where it is swollen and let out the blood," Trusted Friend had protested. "The scars they make will not show against his other wounds."

"What does that matter?" Rock Breaker had demanded. "Let him die quickly. He fought like a warrior. Give him a man's death."

"His wives are both young women," Bear Killer had pointed out. "They should leave him now. This wounded one cannot raise children. Let them find someone strong enough to hunt."

"The tall one will not stay," Rock Breaker had predicted. "She never stays with her husbands. Now that the shaman no longer hunts her, she will do as she wishes. She will leave this man with his ruined face and find someone stronger."

Trusted Friend had quarreled with both men, and in the end both men had been proven wrong. Instead of leaving, Morning Land had nursed Laughing One through one night and then another until the swelling had grown less and strength had come back to him. His scars had not upset her. Like him, she also bore the marks of the shaman they had killed. It seemed a blood bond between them. Though many men had wanted Morning Land in the days since then, she had refused all lovers. Laughing One was the only man in her heart. For White Bird, too, there had never been any question.

"Never trouble yourself about what other men say," Trusted Friend told Laughing One as the two dragged the dead swan up onto the shore. "Many are only jealous of your wives. You have killed the shaman who destroyed so many others. Nothing said in anger can change that."

Laughing One nodded and hoisted the body of the big swan onto his back, letting its great wings fall down on either side of him to drag against the ground. "I do not remember those things very well," he said.

This was true. Everything about that time was clouded in his mind. It had all been pain and fever, with his eyes feeling as if smoke had stung them. He remembered waking once to feel the warm dawn wind blowing around his lodge and to hear the voices of his wives whispering soothing words through his pain. Morning Land had placed red powder over his blisters until the wet seeping had dried. Her great calmness had healed him just as much as the bits of herbs she had used. Each evening, while he had groaned toward sleep, the sisters' voices singing to him had reminded him that he was still alive.

"That shaman was nearly crushed," Trusted Friend told his

brother. "He was hacked to pieces in the dirt. It was as if the bear spirit had come and torn his flesh. His back was cut deep and his stomach was open. I saw all the places where he had bled." Trusted Friend did not add that he had also seen Fighting Eagle take the bloodied spear from Morning Land's hands.

"We left the shaman's body where we found it," Trusted Friend continued as the brothers crossed out of the marsh. "I was one of the hunters who piled the rocks around him. The stone mound is still in that place. Even now, no hunter will cross too close to the ridge. It is said that they will sicken if they camp near its shadow."

Laughing One pulled the swan higher up across his back and nodded.

"We thought there would be great trouble with Black Snake's village," Trusted Friend confided, "but Black Snake had been troubled enough by his brother when the shaman was alive. There were no further quarrels because of the old man's death. Black Snake did not even bother to come and see the mound for himself. Everyone just wanted to forget."

"What happened to the shaman's other wives?" Laughing One asked.

Trusted Friend shrugged. "They cut off their hair and rubbed ashes across their faces like any other widows," he said doubtfully. "They were better to have no husband at all than to be living with that shaman."

The two brothers grew quiet and continued following the lakeshore back toward the village. Laughing One, who had needed no urging to carry the body of the swan at first, was beginning to wonder when his brother would offer to help, but Trusted Friend seemed content just to walk behind him. Laughing One was about to complain when he heard soft, high voices coming from a cove ahead of them. Both men recognized the voices, and even if they had not, there were only two women in the village who could have sung such songs.

Though Laughing One did not notice, Trusted Friend stopped walking. He stood on the trail and watched as his younger brother moved ahead on his own. "This kill is yours, brother," he murmured. Then he turned and started on a different route toward the village.

Laughing One walked to the front of the cove and saw his wives. Morning Land lay on a flat boulder at the edge of the shore. Droplets of water on her skin showed that she had just come up out of the lake. She was wearing her decorated dance apron, and above it her stomach swelled with the firmly rounded contours of a woman who has been pregnant for several moons. While she sunned herself, Morning Land kept her head tilted to one side so that she could watch the actions of her sister's child. Little Sacred Dance had already discovered Morning Land's collecting pouch. The child's agile hands were pulling clam shells out of the pouch and setting them down on the rock beside her.

White Bird was in the water searching for clams with her feet. She tested the bottom mud with her toes until she found an object with the right shape and feel. Then she held it between her toes and reached down with her fingers to pull it up. Utterly unconscious of being watched, she moved in a quick, energetic fashion. The shaking movements of her legs made her wide buttocks jiggle back and forth sensuously, and each time she bent forward her hanging breasts brushed against the water's surface.

Though the swan was heavy on his back and his left arm was already hurting, Laughing One stood and watched the sisters. He wanted to keep all of what he saw: the frail stillness of this morning, the sustained quiet in Morning Land's eyes as she lay beside Sacred Dance in the sunlight, the way White Bird half waded and half danced in the shallows, sinking lower each time one of her feet felt out for the shape of a clam. Young as he was, Laughing One already understood that life was rarely this gentle.

It was Morning Land who first saw him. She was watching White Bird splash about when she noticed a brown form standing under a willow tree on the opposite side of the cove. For a moment she simply stared, for the dead swan draped across his back gave Laughing One a curious appearance.

"What man is hiding over there?" she called out. "The way he is dressed seems very strange."

White Bird turned about quickly in the water, saw where her sister was pointing to, and squinted against the sunlight. A moment later she recognized Laughing One and grinned widely. "Do not start to run again, sister." She laughed. "It is your own husband who stands over there. He has killed something big." Returning her attention to Laughing One, she shouted, "Why are you so quiet? You should be shouting for us to come and help you with that. When a kill that big is made, the women are the ones who bring it back to camp."

Laughing One smiled back, for White Bird was already wading in toward him. Her body glowed in the sunlight as she moved through the long rushes, and he could see the rippling tremors her legs made in her hurry to reach him. On the shore, Morning Land picked up little Sacred Dance and began gathering their things.

"This bird is heavy," Laughing One cautioned when White Bird stepped up onto the shore beside him.

"Not for two," White Bird said, nodding toward her sister.

Morning Land handed him Sacred Dance and picked up the swan's dangling neck. At the same time, White Bird lifted the lower part of the carcass.

As Laughing One placed Sacred Dance on his shoulders, the child squirmed and giggled. Her chubby legs dangled across her father's chest while she clung to his head with both arms. In this position, the two started back toward their lodge.

Behind them, the sisters juggled the weight of the bird. "This root you have given me," White Bird whispered, "will it truly keep my stomach small?"

"It has strength," Morning Land assured her. "When a woman chews on it, no babies grow inside her."

"I have never heard of such a root," White Bird said.

"Our people did not use it," Morning Land told her. "This is a thing I learned from the shaman's wives."

The sisters began following the path their husband had taken. As they stepped through the cove's green shadows and patches of gleaming sunlight, White Bird thought about this. Finally she said, "*Shiiwe.* All that time they lived in his lodge they would not grow any babies."

"Passing Shadow made war on his wives," Morning Land replied. "Such men never have children who will call them 'Father.'"

"You will not need this root now," White Bird said. "You have already decided to let your stomach grow."

Morning Land did not answer. Instead, she began to sing a Tideland love song, her voice straining slightly from the effort of carrying the swan. White Bird soon joined her, singing just as loudly. Their high musical voices told the people in the village that a hunter had made a kill and his wives were carrying it home.